Praise for *New York Times* bestselling author Heather Graham

"An incredible storyteller."
—*Los Angeles Daily News*

"Graham is the Queen of romantic suspense."
—*RT Book Reviews*

"Intricate, fast-paced, and intense, this riveting thriller blends romance and suspense in perfect combination and keeps readers guessing and the tension taut until the very end."
—*Library Journal* on *Flawless*

Praise for *New York Times* bestselling author Carla Cassidy

"Small towns, dangerous secrets and painful pasts are expertly conveyed in Cassidy's clever hands, speeding readers toward surprising revelations."
—*RT Book Reviews* on *Scene of the Crime: Widow Creek*

"Cassidy crafts sympathetic characters...along with a strong, well-developed plot. A charmingly sweet and ruggedly strong hero is the icing on the cake."
—*RT Book Reviews* on *Cowboy with a Cause*

"With flawed but heartwarming characters, and a flair for storytelling, Carla Cassidy shines."
—*RT Book Reviews* on *To Wed and Protect*

NEW YORK TIMES BESTSELLING AUTHOR

HEATHER GRAHAM

SUSPICIOUS

HARLEQUIN®

ISBN-13: 978-1-335-40996-6

Suspicious
First published in 2005.
This edition published in 2021.
Copyright © 2005 by Heather Graham Pozzessere

A Hero of Her Own
First published in 2009.
This edition published in 2021.
Copyright © 2009 by Harlequin Books S.A.

Special thanks and acknowledgment are given to Carla Cassidy
for her contribution to The Coltons: Family First miniseries.

This edition published by arrangement with Harlequin Books S.A.

For questions and comments about the quality of this book,
please contact us at CustomerService@Harlequin.com.

Harlequin Enterprises ULC
22 Adelaide St. West, 40th Floor
Toronto, Ontario M5H 4E3, Canada
www.Harlequin.com

Printed in U.S.A.

Recycling programs
for this product may
not exist in your area.

CONTENTS

SUSPICIOUS   7
Heather Graham

A HERO OF HER OWN   269
Carla Cassidy

New York Times and *USA TODAY* bestselling author **Heather Graham** has written more than a hundred novels. She's a winner of the Romance Writers of America's Lifetime Achievement Award, a Thriller Writers' Silver Bullet and, in 2016, the Thriller Master Award from ITS. She is an active member of International Thriller Writers and Mystery Writers of America, and is the founder of The Slush Pile Players, an author band and theatrical group. An avid scuba diver, ballroom dancer and mother of five, she still enjoys her South Florida home, but also loves to travel.

For more information, check out her website, theoriginalheathergraham.com, or find Heather on Facebook.

Books by Heather Graham

Harlequin Intrigue

Undercover Connection
Out of the Darkness
Shadows in the Night
Law and Disorder
Tangled Threat

MIRA

New York Confidential

Flawless
A Perfect Obsession
A Dangerous Game
A Lethal Legacy
The Final Deception

Visit the Author Profile page
at Harlequin.com for more titles.

SUSPICIOUS

Heather Graham

To the Miccosukee tribe of Florida.

Prologue

The eyes stared across the water.

They were soulless eyes, the eyes of a cold-blooded predator, an animal equipped throughout millions of years of existence to hunt and kill.

Just visible over the water's surface, the eyes appeared as innately evil as a pair of black pits in hell.

The prehistoric monster watched. It waited.

From the center seat of his beat-to-shit motorboat, Billy Ray Hare lifted his beer can to the creature. He squinted as he tried to make out the size of the beast, an estimation at best, since the bulk of the body was hidden by the water. Big boy, he thought. Didn't see too many of the really big boys down here anymore. He'd even read some article about the Everglades alligators being kind of thin and scrawny these days, since they were surviving on insects and small prey. But every once in a while now, he'd still see a big beast sunning along the banks of the canals in the deep swamp.

He heard a slithering sound from the canal bank and turned. A smaller gator, maybe five feet long, was moving. Despite the ugly and awkward appearance of the creature, it was swift, fluid and graceful. Uncannily fast. The smaller crocodilian eased down the damp embankment and into the water. Billy watched. He knew the canals, and he knew gators, and he knew that the long-legged, hapless crane fishing for shiners near the shore was a goner.

"Hey, birdie, birdie," Billy Ray crooned. "Ain't you seen the sun? It's dinnertime, baby, dinnertime."

The gator slid into the water, only its eyes visible as the body swiftly disappeared.

A split second later, the beast burst from the water with a spray of power and gaping jaws. The bird let out a screech; its white wings frantically, pathetically, beat the water. But the huge jaws were clamped. The gator slung its head back and forth, shaking its prey near death, then slid back into the water to issue the coup de grâce, drowning its victim.

"It's a damned dog-eat-dog world, ain't it?" Billy murmured dryly aloud. He finished his beer, groped for another, and realized that he'd finished the last of his twelve-pack. Swearing, he noticed that the big gator across the canal hadn't moved. Black reptilian eyes, evil as Satan's own, continued to survey him. He threw his beer can in the direction of the creature. "Eat that, ugly whoreson!" he croaked, and began to laugh. Then he sobered, looking around, thinking for a minute that Jesse Crane might be behind him, ready to haul him

in for desecrating his precious muck hole. But Billy
Ray was alone in the swamp. Alone with the bugs and
birds and reptiles, with no more beer and no fish biting.
"Bang-bang, you're dead! I'm hungry, and it's dinnertime. Damned environmentalists." Once upon a time,
he could have shot the gator. Now the damn things were
protected. You had to wait for gator season to kill the
suckers, and then you had to play by all kinds of rules.
You could only kill the wretched things according to
certain regulations. Too bad. Once upon a time, a big
gator like that could have meant some big money....

Big money. What the heck.

They made big money out at that gator farm. Old
Harry and his scientist fellow, Dr. Michael, the stinking
Australian who thought he was Crocodile Dundee, and
Jack Pine, the Seminole, and hell, that whole lot. They
made money on alligators. Damn Jesse and his reeking
white man's law. Now he was the frigging tribal police.

Billy Ray shook his head. The hell with Jesse Crane
and his whole bleeding-heart crowd. What did Jesse
know? Tall and dark and too damned good-looking,
and all powerful, one foot in the swamp, the other foot
firmly planted in the white world. College education,
plenty of money now—his late *wife's* money, at that.
The hell with him, the hell with all the environmentalists, the hell with the whites all the way. They'd been the
ones who screwed up the swamp to begin with. While
the whole country was running around screaming about
rights—equal pay for women, real justice for blacks,
food stamps for refugees—Jesse Crane didn't see that
the Indians—the *Native Americans*—were still rotting
in the swamps. Jesse had a habit of just leaning back,

shrugging, and staring at him with those cool green—
white-blooded—eyes of his and saying that no white
man was making old Billy Ray be a mean, dirty alcoholic who liked to beat up on his wife. Jesse wanted
him in jail. But Ginny, bless her fat, ugly butt, Ginny
wouldn't file charges against him. Ginny knew where
a wife's place was supposed to be.

Alcoholic, hell. He wasn't no alcoholic. God, he
wanted another beer. Screw Jesse Crane.

"And screw you," he said aloud, staring at the gator.
Those black eyes hadn't moved; the creature was still
staring at him like some prehistoric sentinel. Maybe
it was already dead. He squinted, staring hard. Tough
now to see, because it was growing late. Dinnertime.

Sunset. It was almost night. He didn't know what
he wanted more, something to eat or another beer. He
had neither. No fish, and he'd used up his government
money.

The sky was orange and red, the beautiful shades that
came right before the sun pitched into the horizon. But
now the dying orb was creating a beautiful but eerie
mantle of color on the water, the trees that draped their
branches over it, and the seemingly endless "river of
grass" that made up the Everglades. With sunset, everything took on a different hue; white birds were cast
in pink and gold, and even the killer heat took a brief
holiday. Jesse would sit out here like a lump on a log
himself, just thinking that the place—with its thick car-
pet of mosquitoes and frequent smell of rot—was only
a small step from heaven. Their land. Hell, he had news
for Jesse. They hadn't been the first Indians—Native
Americans—here. The first ones who'd been here had

been wiped out far worse than animals ever had. But Jesse seemed to think that being half Indian made him Lord Protector of the realm or something.

Billy smiled. Screw Jesse. It gave him great pleasure just to think nasty thoughts about the man.

A crane called overhead, swooped and soared low, making a sudden catch in the shimmering water, flying away with a fish dangling from its beak. Smart bird— caught his fish, flew away, didn't wait around to become bait himself. In fact, it was a darned great scene, Billy thought sourly. Right out of *National Geographic*. It was all just one rosy-hued, beautiful picture. The damn crane had captured his dinner, the five-foot gator had captured *his* dinner, and all Billy Ray had caught himself was a deeper burn and a beer headache.

And that other gator. The big one. Big enough to gulp up the five-footer. Hell, it was big enough, maybe, to be well over ten feet long. Maybe it was way more than that, even. Son of a bitch, he didn't know. He couldn't tell its size; it was just one big mother, that was all. It was still staring at him. Eyes like glittering onyx as the sun set. Not looking, not moving. The creature didn't seem to blink.

Maybe the big ole gator staring at him was dead. Maybe he could haul the monster in, skin and eat it before any of the sappy-eyed ecologists got wind of the situation.

Ginny always knew what to do with gator meat. She'd "gourmeted" it long before fashionable restaurants had started putting it on their menus. Hell, with that gator, they could eat for weeks....

"Hey, there, you butt-ugly thing!" Billy Ray called.

He stood up; the boat rocked. Better sit down. The beer had gotten to him more than he'd realized. He picked up an oar and started slowly toward the big gator. It still didn't move. He lifted his oar from the water. Damn, but he was one asshole himself, he realized. Gator had to be alive, the way it was just sitting there in the water, eyes above the surface.

Watching him.

Watching him, just like the smaller gator had watched the crane.

"Oh, no, you big ugly asshole!" Billy Ray called out. "Don't you get any ideas. It's *my* dinnertime."

As if duly challenged, the gator suddenly began to move. Billy Ray saw more of its length. More and more…ten feet, twelve, fifteen…hell more, maybe…it was the biggest damned gator he'd seen in his whole life. Maybe it was a stray croc—no, he knew a croc, and he knew a gator. This fellow had a broad snout and clearly separated nostrils, it was just one big mother…cruising. Cruising smoothly toward him, massive body just gliding through the water. Coming fast, fast, faster…

He frowned, shaking his head, realizing he really was in something of a beer fog. Gators didn't come after boats and ram them. They might swim along and take a bite at a hand trailing in the water, but he'd only seen a gator make a run at a boat once, and that was a mother protecting her nest, and she only charged the boat, she didn't ram it.

This one was just warning him away. Hell, where was his gun? He had his shotgun in the boat somewhere….

Unable to tear his eyes from the creature's menacing

black orbs, he groped in the boat for his shotgun. His hand gripped the weapon; the creature was still coming. He half stood again, taking aim.

He fired.

He hit the sucker; he knew he hit it.

But the gator kept coming with a sudden ferocious speed.

The animal rammed the boat.

Billy Ray pitched over.

Sunset.

The water had grown dark. He couldn't see a damned thing. He began to kick madly, aiming for the bank. He swam. He had hit the gator with a shotgun. Surely he had pierced the creature's tough hide; it had just taken the stupid monster a long time to die. He'd been an idiot. His rifle was at the bottom of the muck now; his boat was wrecked, and the water was cool and sobering.

Sober...yeah, dammit, all of a sudden he was just too damned sober.

He twisted around and was just in time to see the monster. Like the others of its kind, it stalked him smoothly. Gracefully. He saw the eyes again, briefly. Cold, brutal, merciless, the eyes of a hell-spawned predator. He saw the head, the long jaws. Biggest damn head he'd ever seen. Couldn't be real.

The eyes slipped beneath the surface.

Billy Ray started to scream. He felt more sober than he had ever felt in his life. Felt everything perfectly clearly.

Felt the movement in the water, the rush beneath him...

He screamed and screamed and screamed. Until the

giant jaws snapped shut on him. He felt the excruciating, piercing pain. Then he ceased to scream as the razor-sharp teeth pierced his rib cage, lungs and windpipe.

The creature began to toss its massive head, literally shaking its prey into more easily digestible pieces.

The giant gator sank beneath the surface.

And more of Billy Ray's bones began to crunch....

Billy Ray had been right all along.

It was dinnertime.

Chapter 1

At first it seemed that the sound of the siren wasn't even penetrating the driver's mind.

Either that, or the Lexus intended to race him all the way across the lower portion of the state to the city of Naples, Jesse Crane thought irritably.

It was natural to speed out here—it felt like one of the world's longest, strangest drives, with mile after mile of grass and muck and canal, interspersed by a gas station or tackle shop here or there, the airboat rides, and the Miccosukee camps.

But after you passed the casino, heading west, traces of civilization became few and far between. Despite that, the road was a treacherous one. Impatient drivers trying to pass had caused many a traffic fatality.

He overlooked it when someone seemed competent and was going a rational number of miles over the limit.

But this Lexus…

At last the driver seemed to become aware that he was trailing, the siren blazing. The Lexus pulled over on the embankment.

As Jesse pulled his cruiser off on the shoulder, he saw a blond head dipping—the occupant was obviously searching for the registration. *Or a gun?* There were plenty of toughs who made it out to this section of the world, because there was enough godforsaken space out here for all manner of things to go on. He trod carefully. He was a man who always trod carefully.

As he approached the car, the window came down and a blond head appeared. He was startled, faltering for a fraction of a second.

The woman was stunning. Not just attractive. Stunning. She had the kind of golden beauty that was almost spellbinding. Blond hair that caught the daylight. Delicate features. Huge eyes that reflected a multitude of colors: green, brown, rimmed with gray. Sweeping lashes. Full lips, colored in shell-pink gloss. Perfect for her light complexion and hair.

"Was I speeding?" She sounded as if he were merely a distraction in her important life.

Yeah, the kind of beauty that was almost *spellbinding. But there was also something about her that was irritating as hell!*

The soft sound of a splash drew his attention. Her head jerked around, and she shuddered as they both looked toward the canal. A small alligator had left its sunning spot on the high mud and slipped into the water.

Then she turned back to him and gave him her full

attention. She studied him for a moment. "Is this…a joke?"

"No, ma'am. No joke," he said curtly. "License and registration, please."

"Was I speeding?" she asked again, and her seriousness was well done, especially after her earlier remark.

"Speeding? Oh, yeah," he said. "License and registration, please."

"Surely I wasn't going that fast," she said. She was staring at him, not distracted anymore, and frowning. "Are you really a cop?" she demanded suddenly.

"Yes."

She twisted around. "That's not a Metro-Dade car."

"No, I'm not Metro-Dade."

"Then—"

"Miccosukee. Indian police," he said curtly.

"Indian police?" she said, and looked back to him. His temper rose. He felt as if he might as well have said *play* police, or *pretend* police.

"This is my jurisdiction," he said curtly. "One more time. License and registration."

She gritted her teeth, staring at him, antagonism replacing the curiosity in her eyes. Then, every movement irate, she dug into the glove compartment. "Registration," she snapped, handing him the document.

"And license," he said politely.

"Yes, of course. I need to get it."

"Do you know how fast you were going?"

"Um…not that far over the speed limit, surely?"

"Way over," he told her. "See that sign? It says fifty-five. You were topping that by thirty miles an hour."

"I'm sorry," she said. "It didn't feel like I was going that fast."

She dug in her handbag, which was tightly packed and jumbled, in contrast to the businesslike appearance of the pale blue jacket she wore over a tailored shirt. He began writing the ticket. She produced her license. He kept writing. Her fingers, long, elegant, curled tightly around the steering wheel. "I don't know what's waiting for you in Naples, Miss Fortier, but it's not worth dying for. And if you're not worried about killing yourself, try to remember that you could kill someone else. Slow down on this road."

"I still don't believe I was going that fast," she murmured.

"Trust me, you were," he assured her curtly. He didn't know why she was getting beneath his skin to such a degree. She was passing through. Lots of people tried to speed their way through, east to west, west to east, completely careless of their surroundings, immune to the fact that the populations of Seminoles and Miccosukees in the area might be small, but they existed.

And their lives were as important as any others.

"Fine, then," she murmured, as if barely aware of him, just anxious to be on her way.

"Hey!" He demanded her attention.

She blinked, staring at him. She definitely seemed distracted. And yet, when she stared at him, it was with a strange interest. As if she wanted to listen but somehow couldn't.

"Slow down," he repeated softly and firmly.

She nodded curtly and reached out, accepting her

license and registration back, along with the ticket he had written.

Then she shook her head slightly, trying to control her temper. "Thanks," she muttered.

"I'm a real cop, and it's a real ticket, Ms. Fortier."

"Yes, thank you. I'll pay it, with real money," she said sweetly.

He forced a grim smile in return. *Spoiled little rich girl, heading from the playgrounds of Miami Beach to the playgrounds of the western coast of the state.*

He tipped his hat, grateful that she couldn't know what he was thinking. His sunglasses were darkly tinted, well able to hide his thoughts. "Good day, Miss Fortier."

He turned to leave.

"Jerk!" he heard her mutter.

He stiffened, straightened, turned back.

"Pardon? Did you say something?" he asked politely.

She forced a smile. "I said good day to you, too, Officer."

"That's what I thought you said," he told her, turning to go. "Bitch," he murmured beneath his breath.

Or, at least, he thought he'd murmured beneath his breath.

"What did you say?" she demanded sharply.

He turned back. "I said we should both have a lovely day. One big old wonderful, lovely day. Take care, Ms. Fortier."

He proceeded back to his car.

The Lexus slid back onto the road.

He followed it for a good twenty miles. And she knew it. She drove the speed limit.

Not a mile under.

Not a mile over.

The dash phone buzzed softly. He hit the answer button. "Hey, Chief. What's up? Some good ol' boy beating up on his wife again?" He spoke evenly, hoping that was all it was. Too often, out here, it was something else. Something that seldom had to do with his people, his work. The Everglades was a beautiful place for those who loved nature, but pure temptation for those who chose to commit certain crimes.

Over the distance, Emmy sighed. "Nope, just a call from Lars. He wants you to have lunch with him at the new fish place just east of the casino next Friday."

"Tell him sure," Jesse said. "See you soon. Time for me to call it a day."

Clayton Harrison's place was just up ahead. The driveway wasn't easily discernible from the trail, but Jesse knew right where it was. He took a sharp left, turned around and headed back.

He was certain that, as he did so, the Lexus once again picked up speed.

Lorena Fortier set down her pen, sighed, stood and stretched. She left her desk and walked to the door that led out to the hallway in the staff quarters of Harry's Alligator Farm and Museum. She hesitated, looked both ways, then walked down the shadowy hallway. Dim night-lights showed the signs on the various doors she passed.

Her second full day on the job. And her second day of living a deception. She thought about Naples and

Marco Island. If only one of those lovely beach communities had been her destination.

She felt herself bristling again as she remembered being stopped the day before by the Miccosukee officer. She had been speeding, and she should have slowed down. It was just that her mind had been racing, and her foot had apparently gone along with it.

And the man who had stopped her…

She felt an odd little tremor shoot through her. He'd just been so startling, and then even a little frightening. For the good or bad, she couldn't remember anyone who had made such an impression on her in a long time. His appearance had been so striking, not at all what she expected from a police officer.

She had apparently made an impression on him, as well. *Rich bitch, no care for anything local…*

She gave herself a shake. Forget it! Move on. Concentrate on the matter at hand!

Large letters on the third door down read Dr. Michael Preston, Research.

She hesitated, then tried the knob. The door, as she had expected, was locked. She slipped her hand into the pocket of her lab coat, curling her fingers around the small lock pick she carried. She was about to work the door open when she heard voices coming from the far end of the hallway.

"So how are the tours going, Michael?" It was her new boss, Harry Rogers, speaking. He was a huge man, with a smile as wide as his belly.

Dr. Michael Preston replied with forced enthusiasm. "Great!"

"I know that you're a researcher, Michael, but part of my dream here is to educate people about reptiles."

"I don't mind the tours. I think I'm pretty good at conveying what we're doing."

Okay, so what did she do now? Lorena wondered. She was new at this whole secret-investigation thing. Should she run back down the hall and into her own office? Or should she bluff it out, walk on down the hall to meet the two of them and ask some kind of lame question?

Running would be insane. They might see her. She would have to bluff.

"Harry, Dr. Preston!" she called, smiling and starting toward them.

"You're the boss, but she calls you 'Harry,' while I'm 'Dr. Preston,'" Michael said to Harry with a groan.

"She knows she can trust me," Harry said, grinning. "She's the new girl on the block—she can't tell yet if you're a dangerously handsome devil, or simply an innocent charmer, a true bookworm."

Lorena laughed softly. "Which is it, Dr. Preston? Are you a devil in disguise? Or a man who is totally trustworthy?" she asked. He was a striking man, not bookish in appearance in the least, considering his reputation as a dedicated researcher, completely passionate about his work. The man was actually the epitome of "tall, dark and handsome," with a wicked grin that could easily seduce a woman into trusting him.

She didn't like the sound of her own laugh, or her question. She tended to be forthright; she wasn't a flirt or a tease, and acting like a coquette felt ridiculous.

But, as she was learning, Dr. Preston was aware of

his looks, and more than willing to make use of his natural charm.

He turned it on her now, smiling in her direction, even though he directed his questions to their boss. "What about the lovely Ms. Fortier? Our mystery woman, a glorious golden-haired beauty suddenly landing in this small oasis in the middle of a swamp. Can she be totally trustworthy?" he asked Harry. "Or has she come to seduce our secrets out of us?"

"Well, whatever secrets I have aren't too fascinating, son," Harry said apologetically.

"And I'm afraid my mystery life is rather dull, as well," Lorena said sweetly.

"Were you looking for me?" Harry asked.

"Um…yes. You told me that you had a small gym for the employees. I thought I would take a look at it. If you could just direct me…"

"The gym is just past the holding pens. Be careful in the dark. The pens are walled, but you don't want to go getting curious, try to bend over the walls and fall in, you know. My gators are well fed, but they're wild animals, after all. And even though I've got security out there, the guards patrol, and with gators, help can never come fast enough."

"I know to be careful, Harry. Thanks." She flashed them both a smile and turned away, feeling frustrated. Did Preston sleep in his lab?

She returned to her room and changed into bike shorts and a tank top. When she left her room again, she could still hear Harry and Michael talking. They were in Preston's lab.

Maybe the gym wasn't such a bad idea, after all.

She left the staff area and started across the huge compound. There were hundreds of gators here, in various stages of growth. Then there was the special pen with Old Elijah. He was huge, a good fifteen feet. He was never part of any show; he was just there for visitors to look at. Next to him were Pat and Darien, both of them adolescents, five feet in length, the gators that were wrestled for the amusement of the crowds.

Jack Pine, a tall, well-muscled Seminole, was standing by the pens with Hugh Humphrey, a wiry blond handler from Australia. Hugh had experience with Outback crocs, and Harry valued having him. When she walked over, the two men were talking quietly with a tall, white-haired man and a veritable giant.

The white-haired man said goodbye, starting away before Lorena got close enough to be introduced to him.

The big man followed. He seemed to grunt, kind of like the alligators, but she assumed that was his way of saying goodbye.

"Ms. Fortier!" Hugh called to her, seeing her as he turned away from the pair who were leaving.

"Hi there!" she called back as she crossed over to the western arc of the building complex. "Who was that?" she asked.

"Who was who?" Hugh asked.

"The men who just left. Do they work here?"

"No, no. They do work for Harry now and then, but they're totally independent. The old guy is Dr. Thiessen, a local vet, and the Neanderthal is the doc's assistant, John Smith. I should have had Doc stay to meet you, but I didn't see you, and he's always busy. He just checks in with us now and then. Doc Thiessen is a hero among the local kids—he's the only guy out there who can really treat a sick turtle or a ball python. You'll meet him soon enough, I wager. He's something. Also knows cattle, gators—and dogs and cats."

"Ah," she murmured. "The big guy is kind of…big."

"Creepy, is that what you mean?" Hugh asked with a laugh.

"No, just…big."

"And dumb. But he's a good worker. Thiessen needs someone like that. He works with some big animals."

"That's certainly understandable. You guys work with some big animals, too," she reminded them.

Hugh offered a grin. "But we're fit and muscled— perfect specimens of manhood. You're supposed to notice that."

She laughed. "You're both in great shape."

"Thanks," Jack Pine offered. "You're welcome to go on about us if you want, but…how are you enjoying the work so far?"

"So far, things have been quite easy. I know you need a nurse on staff, but I haven't even had to deal with a skinned knee yet."

"But you like the place all right?" Hugh asked.

"Yes, just fine."

"A lot of women would find it incredibly weird," Jack told her, inclining his head in a way that made her feel special. Like Preston, he was an intriguing man. Unlike Preston, there didn't seem to be anything cerebral about the attraction. His hair was dark and slick, his eyes nearly as black as his hair; he was bronzed and built—just as he had said. She had liked him instantly— but warily, as well.

He had proudly shown her when they'd met that he'd lost the pinkie finger on his left hand to a gator when he'd learned to wrestle the big reptiles as a boy growing up at Big Cypress Reservation. He seemed to be fearless.

"I like animals," she said.

"These guys are hardly cute and cuddly," Hugh remarked. As if they'd heard him, a number of the alligators set up a racket. They made the strangest noise, as if they were pigs grunting. The cacophony was eerie. She shivered, then thought about the animal's deadly jaws.

She thought about her reasons for being here. Whether she liked the guys who worked here or not, she had to remember to be wary.

She shivered again, suddenly uneasy about being with either man around the prehistoric predators.

Come to think of it, she thought, *she didn't want to be here at all, not at all.*

But she had to be. It was that simple. She had to be.

"You both seem to like gators a lot," she said.

Hugh shrugged. "Well, I made a good living off crocs, so I figure I can make a good living off their cousins, too."

"Like 'em? Hell, no. Respect 'em? Hell, yes," Jack said with a shrug. "But if you're going to work with them, you need to know them. And I can definitely say I know them. I was born and bred in the swamp, so I knew about gators long before I knew about lions, tigers and bears." He grinned and shrugged. "But you, young lady, need to remember a few things that will be important if you ever get in trouble down here. Never get closer than fifteen feet to one of these suckers. And if he's hissing, back away slowly and get the hell away."

"And if you can't get away, make sure you get your weight on its back and push down hard on the nose. It's the top jaw that exerts the pressure. The lower jaw is pretty much worthless," Hugh said.

"I don't intend to get that close to any of them," she assured the men. "You're right—alligators definitely aren't cuddly, but so far, I like this place a lot. I seem to be working with great people," she said, forcing herself to sound nonchalant. They were giving her friendly warnings, nothing more. Despite the grunts from the creatures, which seemed more eerie and foreboding by the moment, she couldn't scream and run away.

"Why, shucks, thanks, ma'am," Hugh teased.

"Thank you both, and good night. See you guys in the morning."

She walked away. She could have sworn she heard the man whisper in her wake. Her skin crawled as she wondered what they were saying.

She entered the gym feeling winded, gasping for breath, though she hadn't walked far at all. She didn't want to work out; she wanted to lock herself into her room. Still, in case she was being followed or watched, she had to act normal. She'd come here to work out, so that was what she would do. She walked to a stationary bike, crawled on and pedaled away.

Fifteen minutes was enough for the night.

She exited the employee gym, more tired from feeling nervous than from her workout. She opened the door a crack, then paused, looking out.

There was a man in the compound. He was standing between two of the alligator pens, hands on hips. At first he was very still, nothing but a dark silhouette in the moonlight. He was tall, broad-shouldered, yet lithe-looking, somehow exuding energy, even in his stillness. He stood in plain view; then he walked around one of the pens, and she noticed that he moved with a sure, fluid stride that was both graceful and, somehow, menacing. Dangerous.

And oddly familiar.

It was her mind tonight, she thought. Everyone she saw seemed furtive, dangerous.

He might just be the security guard. There were several of them, she knew. And, she had been assured, their backgrounds had been checked out by the same careful procedures that casinos used.

No. This man wasn't a security guard. Somehow she knew it.

As he moved and her eyes became more accustomed to the shadows, she could see him more clearly.

He was in black jeans and a black T-shirt. The short sleeves were rolled, and in the moonlight, she could see the bulge of his arm muscles beneath the rolled cotton. His hair was on the long side, sleek, touching his shoulders. Very dark.

The cop! It was the jerk who had given her the ticket!

He turned toward the gym suddenly, as if he knew he was being watched. He couldn't, of course. The light was out. He had no way to know the door was open even a crack.

She continued to study him from her safe distance, trying to determine just what made him so imposing and unique.

His features were compelling. Hardened, fascinating. He was a combination of Native, white and God knew what else. His skin was bronzed, his cheekbones broad, his chin square, like that of a man who knew where he was going—and where he had been. His nose was slightly crooked, as if it might have been broken at some time. She couldn't make out the color of his eyes against the darkness of his hair and the bronze of his flesh. He couldn't possibly see her; still, she felt as if he was staring right through her. She almost stepped back, feeling as if she had been physically touched, as if a rush of smoke and fire had swept through her.

"Jesse," a soft feminine voice said from behind her.

She gasped, then spun around. Sally Dickerson, the head cashier and bookkeeper, was standing behind her. In her early thirties, she was an attractive redhead. Harry said she had a temper, a way with men, and one heck of a way with numbers that had dollar signs attached to them.

"Sorry, you startled me," Lorena said.

Sally glanced at her, and she realized the woman hadn't even heard her gasp. Her attention had been on the man in the moonlight.

"No, *I'm* sorry—I came in the back way, and I didn't realize you hadn't heard me." She was still staring at the man and didn't offer anything more.

"Jesse?" Lorena pressed lightly.

Sally's eyes flicked her way, and the woman smiled broadly. "Yeah, Jesse. He's a cop. A local cop. On the Miccosukee force. He hasn't been back long."

"Oh, I realize that he's a cop," Lorena murmured,

wondering if Sally could hear the slight note of bitterness in her tone. "But…he's back from where?"

"Oh…the city. He's something, huh?"

Lorena turned back to study the man in question. Sally didn't need an answer.

Yes, something. He seemed to be both pure grace and pure menace. Powerful, smooth. Sensual, she thought, with some embarrassment. In a thousand years, she never would have admitted that she understood exactly what Sally meant.

No, no, no, no. He was definitely a man with an attitude, and that attitude definitely contained an element of disdain for her. She shook her head slightly, mentally emitting an oath. It now seemed likely that she would meet him again.

Apparently, he hung out around here. And that made him…suspicious.

Cops had been known to be dirty, dirtier even than other men. Sometimes they needed money. Sometimes even good men went bad, seeing how the rich could buy good lawyers and get away with all kinds of things. They had more chance to abuse power, to sneak around, to bribe…

To threaten.

To kill?

"Interesting. We have security guards. Why is he here?" Lorena asked, looking at Sally once again.

"He checks in now and then, makes sure everything is running smoothly."

"Why did he come back?" she asked.

"Oh," Sally said slowly, "his wife was murdered. He was devastated."

"How horrible."

"I know. Damn, I have a busy night ahead of me... but still... Jesse. Excuse me, will you, honey? I want to talk to the man."

"Sure...friends help when you're devastated," Lorena said pleasantly.

Sally shot her a quick glance. "Honey, I said he was devastated, not dead. Take another look at the man, will you?" She opened the door fully and exited the gym. With a sway of her hips, she approached him, calling his name. He turned to her, arching a brow, acknowledging her presence. Sally went straight to him, placing her hands on his chest. She said something softly. He lowered his head, grinning, and the two turned to walk toward the staff quarters.

When they were gone, Lorena left the gym and hurried back across the compound. The alligators began to grunt in a wild, staccato song.

She let herself into her own room, closed and locked the door. She was breathing too heavily once again.

Maybe she was the wrong woman for this job.

No, there was no maybe about it, but that didn't matter. She had to become the right woman, and she would.

She showered, slipped into a nightgown, and assured herself once again that her door was securely locked. Even then, she also checked once more on the small Smith & Wesson she carried. It was loaded, safety on, but close at hand in the top drawer of the nightstand next to the bed. She took one last look at it before she lay down to sleep.

Despite that, she dreamed.

She didn't want to have nightmares; she didn't want

to toss and turn. She dreamed far too often of horrible things. She knew that dreams were often extensions of the day's worries, and she *was* constantly worried.

But that night, she didn't dream horrible things. She dreamed about him. The cop. The world was all foggy, and people were screaming all around her, but he was walking toward her, and she was waiting, heedless of whatever danger might be threatening her because he was watching her, coming for her....

She awoke, drenched with sweat, shaking.

She was definitely the wrong woman for this job. She was losing her mind.

No, she had to toughen up. What the hell was wrong with her? She had to be here.

Had to.

Because she, of all people, had to know the truth.

East of the deep swamp, Maria Hernandez plucked the last of her wash from the clothesline. The darkness had come; night dampness had set it. She pressed her clean sheets to her nose, deciding that they still smelled of the sunshine, even if she had cleaned up dinner late and gotten the clothes down even later. Sometimes it seemed that darkness came slowly. Sometimes it descended like a curtain, swift and complete.

But tonight...

Tonight was different.

There were lights. Strange lights appearing erratically down by the canal.

"Hector! Come see!" she called to her husband. He'd been picking all day. He picked their own crops, then rented his labor out like a migrant worker. This was the land of opportunity; and indeed, she had her nice little house, even if it was on the verge of the swamps, but one had to work very hard for opportunity.

"Maria, let me be!" Hector shouted back to her.

"But you must see."

"What is it?"

"Lights."

Hector appeared at the back of the house, a beer in his hand. He was a good man. One beer. Just one beer when he came in at night. He loved his children. They had grown quickly in this land of opportunity, and they had their own homes now. He was a hardworking and very good man. He had provided them with a dream.

But now he was tired.

"Lights?" He had spoken in English. Now he swore in Spanish, waving a hand in the air. "Maria, it's a plane. It's boys out in an airboat. It's poachers. What do I care? Come inside."

But the lights were so strange that Maria found herself walking toward them. The farther she got from the house, the stranger it seemed that there should be lights. What would children be doing out here? Or poachers? Yes, she was on the edge of the swamp, land just grasped from it, but...

Then she heard the noises.

Strange noises...

There was a big lump on the earth. She walked toward it, then paused. Instinctively, she knew she should go back. There were stories about things that needed to be watched out for—things that came from the swamp. Snakes...bad snakes. And there were reports of alligators snatching foolish dogs from the banks of the canal.

She started to back away from the lump on the ground, but then, just as she had instinctively felt that she was facing danger, she suddenly knew that the lump was a dead thing. She kept walking to it.

Clouds drifted against the dark sky, freeing the moon for a brief moment.

It was an alligator, but a dead one.

She didn't know much about alligators. Oh, yes, she lived out here; she had driven along the Trail, seen them basking in the sun. They came in close—the canals were theirs, really, this close to the Glades. But she didn't do foolish things. She didn't try to feed them, heaven forbid! She knew enough to stay away, and little else. But this one was dead, harmless, so she moved closer. And closer.

Because this one seemed very strange.

It had been big, very big. It lay on its back, and it looked almost as if it had been stuffed, and as if all the stuffing had been pulled out of it. There was a strange hole in the center of its chest, as if a fire had burned a perfect circle in the center of the white underbelly. Toes were missing. The jaw gaped open in death.

The lights started flickering again. Maria lifted a hand to her eyes so that they would not blind her.

Her heart quickened.

UFOs! Aliens, spacemen. She was proud of her English; she read all the papers in line at the grocery store. They came down to study earth creatures; they abducted men and women.

She'd seen lights before. Strange lights, late at night. In fact, she'd told her daughter, Julie, about them not so long ago, laughing at her own silliness, because of course Maria had never believed in aliens until now, and Hector scoffed at such silliness. But the lights…

And the alligator…

If they were UFOs, then her initial instinct to run had been right. She had to get back to the house and ask Hector to call the police. Maybe the tall Indian policeman was close by and could help them quickly, far more quickly than the white policemen from the city would make it.

She started to back away. At first it had seemed that the lights were coming from the sky. But now…

They were coming from the brush. From the foliage where the swampland that had not been reclaimed started, just feet from where her lawn began.

Suddenly she was very afraid. She looked at the alligator. A hole in its underbelly. Toes cut off. Eyes…

Eyes cut out.

She turned and started to run.

"Hector!"

A single bullet killed her. A rifle shot straight through her back, tearing through the anterior region of her heart.

Hector heard his wife's scream. He came running out.

The shot that killed him was square between his eyes. He dropped dead still wondering why his wife had called him.

Chapter 2

It had already been one hell of a bad morning.

It had started out with Ginny Hare calling first thing, before it had even begun to be light outside. Jesse was an early riser, but hell, Ginny's hysterical voice before coffee was not a good way to start off the morning.

Billy Ray hadn't come home.

He'd tried to calm Ginny. Lots of times Billy Ray would crash out wherever he'd been and find his way home the next morning.

This was different—Ginny was insistent. He'd gone out fishing with a twelve-pack of beer. And he hadn't come in the morning, the afternoon or the night, and now it was morning again and Billy Ray still wasn't back.

Jesse had tried to soothe her.

"Ginny, I'll get out there looking for him, but you

quit worrying. A twelve-pack of beer, Ginny, think about it."

"But, Jesse, he's stayed out two nights!"

"Ginny, I'll look for him, I promise. But he probably got himself as drunk as a skunk and he's sleeping it off somewhere—or, he woke up and knew he'd be in major trouble, and he's trying to figure out how to come home."

When he'd hung up, he'd wondered about the power of love. Billy Ray Hare was the worst loser he'd ever met—white, Native, Hispanic or black. He hit Ginny all the time, though he denied it, as Ginny did herself. He was her man, and in Ginny's eyes, whatever he did, he was hers, and she was going to stand up for him.

Jesse knew that Billy Ray hated him. That was all right. He had no use whatsoever for Billy Ray. Billy Ray liked to call him "white boy," which was all right, because yes, his father had been white. But his mother could trace her lineage back to Billy, Old King Micanopy, back before the start of the Seminole Wars, back before the government had even recognized the Miccosukee as an independent tribe, speaking a different language from the Seminoles with whom they had intermarried and fought throughout the years. Billy Ray never understood that Jesse was proud of being Native American—and furious when men like Billy Ray fell into stereotypes and became lazy-ass alcoholics.

So Billy Ray was useless. But despite the fact that she loved Billy Ray, there was something very special about Ginny. And for her, Jesse would spend half his day in the sweltering heat of summer looking for her no-good husband.

But he hadn't had a chance to look for Billy Ray yet.

Before he'd gotten out of the house, he'd gotten the call about Hector and Maria Hernandez.

Their property was on the county line, so the Metro Police were already on the scene. The homicide detective in charge of the case was Lars Garcia, a man with whom Jesse had gone to college up at the University of Florida. His Cuban refugee father had married a Danish model, thus his ink-dark hair, slim, athletic build and bright powder-blue eyes. The media liked to make it sound as if the Indian—or Native American cops— were half-wits who were given only a small measure of authority and who hated their ever-present big brothers, the Metro cops. Jesse resented the media for that, because it simply wasn't true. The Metro-Dade force had suffered through some rough years, with rogue cops and accusations of corruption and drug abuse. But they'd cleaned house, and they weren't out to make fools of the Miccosukee policing their own.

Besides which, he'd been a Metro homicide cop himself before making the decision to join the Miccosukee police force.

He felt lucky wherever he got to work with Lars when a body was discovered. Unfortunately, that wasn't a rare happening.

A swamp was a good place to dump a body. There had been the bizarre—body pieces dredged up in suitcases—and there had been the historical: bodies discovered that had lain in the muck and mud for more than a century. Man's inhumanity to man was not a new thing. Sad as it might be, he was accustomed to the cruel and vicious.

Homicides happened.

But the unfairness of homicide happening to good people never ceased to upset him.

Jesse had known Hector and Maria. Known and liked them. They were as homespun as cotton jeans, without guile or cunning. She always wanted to bring him in and feed him; Hector always wanted him to taste a fresh strawberry or tomato. They had loved their small home, loved their land more. It was theirs. He'd never seen two people appreciate the simple things in life with such pure and humble gratitude and pleasure.

Uniformed cops were cordoning off the crime scene as he arrived; Lars had been talking with the fingerprint expert but excused himself and walked over to Jesse as soon as he saw him. "Terrible thing, huh? It's technically outside your jurisdiction, but the killers must have come from somewhere. Maybe they were hiding in the swamp, maybe…" His voice trailed off.

"The bodies?" Jesse said.

"You don't have to see them."

"Yeah, I do."

Hector's body was covered when they walked to it; Lars hunkered down and pulled back the blanket. Hector looked oddly at peace. His eyes were closed; he just lay there—normal-looking except for the bullet hole in his forehead. Nothing had been done to the body; the killer probably hadn't even come near him.

"Tracks?" Jesse asked.

Lars shook his head. "None so far. The lawn is all grassy…then there's foliage, and the canal. No tracks yet."

Jimmy Page from the medical examiner's office was

still bending over Maria when they reached her. She lay facedown, her head twisted. Her eyes were still open.

She had seen something terrible.

There was a hole through her back.

"Hi, Jesse," Jimmy said, making notes. "I'm sorry as hell, I heard you knew them."

"Yeah. Nice couple. Really good people. Have the children been notified?"

"The son is in the navy, on active duty—they're trying to reach him. The daughter will be here this afternoon."

He winced. Julie was going to come home alone to see her murdered parents. He would have to make a point of being available later.

"Know when she's coming in?"

"American Airlines, two-thirty flight from LaGuardia. Want to meet her with me?" Lars asked.

"Yeah."

"Thanks. I wasn't looking forward to talking to her on my own."

"Have you got anything, Jimmy?" Jesse asked. "I mean…" He looked down into Maria's eyes, thinking he would remember the way she looked for a very long time to come. "This is no drug hit. These people were as clean as they came."

Jimmy shook his head. "Jesse… I've got to admit, about all we're going to know is the caliber of bullet that hit them, maybe the weapon that fired it, an approximate time of death and maybe a trajectory. They were shot," he said, sounding angry. "As to why they were shot… Jesus, you're right. Who can tell?"

"Mind if I take a look around?" Jesse asked Lars.

"Be my guest. We think the killers must have been to the southwest, from the way Maria fell. She was running. Hector was coming to help her."

Jesse nodded, surveying the expanse of lawn. The neat yard the couple had tended so lovingly reached a point where it became long, thick grasses. Back in the grass, the water table began to rise and mangroves grew. Beyond that lay the canal.

He walked carefully to where the thick grass began to grow, studying the lawn. Although his relations with the Metro police were good, he wondered if any of the beat cops were cracking jokes about an Indian being better at finding footprints than they were.

Hell. He was going to look for them, anyway. He was going to look for anything.

He turned, calling back to Lars, "I think an airboat came through here. See the flattening?"

"Yeah."

"And…" Jesse began, then trailed off. He walked a little further, seeing something in the grass. He moved closer. Bent over. Frowned.

"What is it?" Lars asked.

"Got a glove and an evidence bag?"

"Yeah."

Lars came over to him, slipping his hand into a glove. Jesse pointed to the grass. Lars reached for what appeared to be a branch.

"That?" he inquired. "Jesse, it's just a tree limb."

"No, it isn't."

"Then, what the hell…?"

"It's a gator arm," Jesse said. "From one damn big gator."

"A gator arm? What the hell do I want with a gator arm?"

"I don't know, but where's the rest of the body?"

"It looks like it was sliced off."

"I think the rest of the body was moved, and then this arm tore off."

"But…" Lars began.

"But why? And just where the hell is the rest of the body?"

Lars shook his head. "Maybe…"

"Maybe a dead gator and the murder have nothing to do with each other," Jesse said. "And maybe they do."

"Well, they shouldn't have anything to do with each other," Lars said. "Hell. I can't believe that someone out alligator-poaching would murder two people in cold blood just because he was seen. I mean, it's not as if we execute people for killing gators out of season without a license."

"No, it's not," Jesse agreed. He looked at Lars and shrugged. "But what else is there? Like Jimmy said, there are bullets, there's a time of death…but where the hell is a motive? You're not going to get prints, no fluids for DNA…that's all you've got—an alligator arm."

"I've got nothing," Lars said hollowly.

"Maybe. Maybe not. Send the gator limb to Dr. Thiessen. See what you can get, if anything."

"Of course we'll get it to the vet," Lars said impatiently. "Because you're right. I haven't got anything else. And I'm damned sorry that I may have to tell a young woman who loved her parents that I can't begin to explain why they're dead, except that maybe her mother saw an alligator poacher in the backyard!"

"Lars, you tell me. What else is there?" Jesse said. "This kind of killing looks like an execution, as if it were connected to drugs. But it wasn't. I'd bet my life on that. I'm telling you, Lars, I knew these people. They were bone clean."

"They must have seen something, then. They must have known something, but…you're sure? I mean, sometimes we think we know people, but they're living double lives."

"No. I knew them, Lars."

"All right. Maybe the daughter can help us."

"I doubt it. But I'll go with you. I'll talk to her with you. But, Lars, after today…you'll keep me informed on this one all the way, right?"

"Yes."

"No matter what goes on in Homicide?"

"Yes!"

"Swear it?"

Lars looked at him, arching a brow. "We're already blood brothers," he reminded him with a rueful grimace.

Jesse stared at him, shaking his head. Yeah. Forever ago, when they had been young and going to college.

Strangely, or so it seemed now, their college mascot had been an alligator.

They had both pledged the same fraternity. It had been during that period that they'd been out drinking together and Lars had gotten into the blood brother thing, having seen one too many John Wayne movies, Jesse decided.

"Yeah, blood brothers," Jesse returned, surprised that he could almost smile, even if that smile was grim.

"Jesse, the only thing—"

"I won't go off half cocked to shoot to kill if I find out who did it. I'm a cop. I'll bring them in."

Lars watched him for a moment. Jesse locked his jaw, staring back at his friend. Maybe Lars had the right to doubt him. When Connie had died…

Fate had kept him from killing the man who had murdered her. But there had been no question in his mind that, given the chance, he might well have committed murder himself in turn, so great had been his rage.

"I'm telling you, I'll be a by-the-book lawman." He shook his head, sobering. "They didn't deserve this, Lars."

"I swear, I will keep you up on what's happening. I'll have to—the killer or killers probably came from the swamp and maybe ran back that way. We'll have lots of our guys in your territory."

"I'll brief my men, as well."

"Get a warning out to them right away."

"Will do."

"You want to take this piece of gator over to Doc Thiessen?" Lars asked him. "You're more familiar with the damn things than I am." He didn't add, Jesse noticed, that he was probably also far more convinced than Lars was that the alligator remains might have something to do with the case.

They started back toward the house. Jesse found himself pausing by Maria's body. The forensic photographers were still at work. He looked into her eyes. In Metro Homicide, he'd seen a lot. A bullet was a fairly quick, clean way to die. He'd seen mutilations that had turned even his strong stomach.

But this…

He'd seen her face alight and beautiful when she'd smiled.

"Jesse, quit looking at her," Lars said.

"Yeah. Well, I'll inform the office, then get out there looking for Billy Ray Hare."

"Billy Ray? You don't think—"

"That Billy Ray killed these two? Not on your life. Billy Ray may be a drunk, and he may not be a prime husband, but he keeps to himself and wouldn't step outside the area he's accustomed to. And he'd also be too damned drunk to make it this far by that time of night. I've got work to do, and so do you. I'll meet you at two so we can get to the airport. Where?"

"The restaurant at the turnpike entrance."

"I'll be there," Jesse said.

When he left, his first stop was the vet's. Dr. Thorne Thiessen was a rare man, pleased to live deep in the Everglades, and fascinated more by birds and reptiles than the more cuddly creatures customarily kept as pets. He was such an expert with snakes that people traveled down from Palm Beach County, a good hour or so away, to bring him their pythons and boas, king snakes, rat snakes and more.

He was in his early fifties, both blond and bronzed, almost as weathered as some of the creatures he tended with such keen interest. He was just finishing with a little boy and his turtle when Jesse arrived, bearing the alligator limb.

He looked at Jesse with surprise. "People usually call on me with living creatures, you know."

"Yeah, but Metro-Dade and I both think you can help on this one. You *are* the reptile expert. You can make some preliminary findings, then pass some samples upstate. Hopefully, someone will figure something out."

Thiessen had been smiling; now he frowned. "What have you got?"

"What do you think?"

"I think it's a piece of an alligator."

"Great."

"No, no, I can do tissue and blood samples, do a profile…and get samples upstate, just like you suggested, but why?"

Jesse explained. Thiessen stared at him for long moments. "And you found this at the scene?"

"Yes."

"Jesse…"

Jesse sighed. "They weren't into drugs."

"Still, they might have witnessed an exchange in the Everglades, or, hell, God forbid, another murder."

"They might have. But this is what we've got for now."

Thiessen shrugged. "Big sucker," he said.

"Yep," Jesse agreed.

"I'll do what I can," Thiessen promised.

Jesse thanked him. In the waiting room, he looked for Jim Hidalgo, who worked for the vet, but then he remembered that Jim worked nights.

The man at the desk was a big guy, John Smith. He was so big, in fact, that he was almost apelike. Jesse didn't remember when he hadn't been with the vet.

Good man to have on, Jesse thought. Big enough to cope with any animal out there.

At least, almost any animal out there.

He grunted to Jesse in a combination of hello and goodbye.

Come to think of it, a grunt was the only conversation Jesse had ever shared with the man.

He waved and went out.

"Look into the eyes of death! Stare into the burning pits of monster hell. See what it would have been like to face the hunger and rage of a carnivore older than the mighty *Tyrannosaurus rex!* Ah, but, believe it or not, once upon a Triassic age, this was an even more ferocious and terrifying creature, in fact, one that made minced meat of the mighty dinosaurs themselves." Michael Preston paused for effect as he talked to the small, wriggling creature he held in his right hand.

The week-old hatchling let out a strange little squeaking sound, its jaws opening, then snapping shut. The eyes were yellow with central stripes of black. It was small, almost cute in a weird sort of way, but the mouth shut with a pressure that was chilling, despite its size.

The hatchling began squealing and wriggling again.

"Loudmouth," Michael said, shrugging. He liked the fact that the American alligator made noise. Noise was good. Noise was warning. "But you *are* being awfully dramatic here," he told the hatchling. "Okay, so I'm a little dramatic myself. Because I *hate* tour groups," he grumbled.

Even as he slipped the hatchling back into its tank, the door to his lab opened and Lorena entered.

"Watch out—the monsters are coming," she warned.

Michael arched a brow. "Monsters," she whispered, emphasizing the warning. Then she turned, a beautiful smile plastered on her face as she allowed room for the tour group to enter. Ten in all, a full tour: two young couples, perhaps on their way to register for college, maybe on honeymoon. They looked like ecology-minded types, surveying the wonder of the Everglades. There was an attractive, elderly woman, probably a widow, seeing the Sunshine State now that old Harvey or whoever had finally bitten the dust. Then there was a harried-looking couple with three boys who looked to be about twelve. The woman had once been pretty. The man had a good smile and looked like a decent father. The boys seemed to be the monsters. They walked right up to his lab table, barged against it, then leaned on it, peering into his tanks and petri dishes.

"Uh, uh, uh—back now," Michael said, frowning at Lorena as if she might have forgotten to warn her group that the tour was hands-off. She shrugged innocently and grinned back with a combination of mischief and amusement. No doubt the boys had been a handful since they'd started their tour. Actually, Lorena wasn't responsible for leading tours. She was a trouper, though. She seemed to like to be in the middle of things; when there were no injuries or sniffles to attend to, her work was probably boring. And it wasn't as if there were a dozen malls or movie theaters in the area to keep her busy.

"Back, boys," he repeated. "Even hatchlings can be dangerous."

"Those little things? What can they do?" demanded

the biggest boy as he stuck his hand into the tank with the week-old hatchlings.

Michael grabbed his hand with a no-nonsense grip that seemed to surprise the boy.

"They can bite," Michael said firmly.

"Mark Henson, stand back and behave, now," the boy's obviously stressed mother said, stepping forward to set a hand on Mark's shoulders. "We're guests here. The doctor has asked you—"

"He ain't no doctor—are you?" the boy demanded.

The woman shot Michael an apologetic look. "I'm so sorry. Mark is my son Ben's cousin, and I don't think he gets out very often."

"It's all right," Michael said. He was lying. Mark was a brat. "Mark seems to be very curious. Yes, Mark, I *am* a doctor. I have a doctorate in marine science. Salt- and freshwater reptiles are my specialty. I also studied biochemistry, animal behavior and psychology, so trust me, hatchlings can give you a nasty bite. Especially these hatchlings."

"Why *those* hatchlings?" Mark demanded immediately.

Because we breed them especially to chew up nasty little rugrats like you! he was tempted to say. But Lorena was already answering for him.

"Because they're tough little critters, survivors," Lorena said flatly. "Ladies and gentlemen, Dr. Preston is in charge of our selective-breeding department. He knows a tremendous amount about crocodilians, past and present. He'll tell you all about his work now—for those interested in hearing," she finished with just the slightest edge of warning in her voice for the boys. They stared at her as she spoke, surveying her intently. No wonder she was glad to let the group heckle *him* now. Lorena was an exceptionally attractive woman with lush hair, brilliant eyes, and a build that not even a lab coat could hide.

The two older boys were at that age when they were just going into adolescence, a state when squeaky sopranos erupted every ten minutes, and sexual fantasies began. And they were obviously having a few of those over Lorena. She made a face at Michael, surprised him by slipping quickly from his lab. Well, she didn't have to be here, he told himself. It wasn't her job. But she'd seemed fascinated by everything here ever since she'd arrived.

Even him.

Not that he minded.

Except that…

She was bright. And really beautiful. So what was she doing out here?

She was good with people, he would definitely give her that. The complete opposite of the way he felt. He hated having to deal with people.

He gave the boys a sudden, ever-so-slightly malicious smile. "Well, gentlemen, let me introduce you more fully to these hatchlings. Alligators, as you might have heard already, date back to prehistoric times. They didn't descend from the dinosaurs. They were actually cousins to them. They shared common ancestors known as thecodonts. And way back in the late Cretaceous period, there was a creature called Deinosuchus—a distant relative of these guys—with a head that was six feet in length. Imagine that fellow opening his jaws on you. True crocodilians have been around for about two million years. They're fantastic survivors. They have no natural enemies—"

"That's not true!" Mark announced. "I saw a program on alligators and crocs. An anaconda can eat an alligator, I saw it. You could see the shape of the alligator in the snake. Man, it was cool—"

"We don't have anacondas in the Everglades," Michael said, gritting his teeth hard before he could continue. "Birds, snakes and small mammals eat alligator eggs, and it's easy for hatchlings to be picked off, but once it's reached a certain size, an alligator really only has one enemy here. And that's…?"

He let the question trail off, arching a brow toward Mark. He looked like a jock. Probably played football or basketball, at the very least. He liked to talk, but he didn't seem to have the answer to this one.

"Man," said one of the boys. He was thinner than his companion, with enormous dark eyes and long hair that fell over his forehead. Nice-looking kid. Shy, maybe, more of a bookish type than Mark. "Man is the only enemy of a grown alligator in the Everglades."

"That's right," Michael said, an honest smile curving his lips. He could tell that this kid had a real interest in learning. "You're Ben?" Michael asked.

The boy nodded. He pulled the third kid up beside him. "This is my other cousin, Josh."

"Josh, Ben and Mark."

"Do we get to see the alligators eat a deer or something?" Mark asked.

"Sorry, you don't get to see them eat any living creatures here, kid. The juveniles and adults out in the pools and pens are fed chicken."

"They're so cool," Ben said, his brown eyes wide on Michael.

Michael nodded. "Yep, they're incredible. Alligators were near extinction here when I was young, but then they became protected. The alligator has made one of the most incredible comebacks in the world, mainly because of farms like this, but also in the wild. They look ugly, and they certainly can be fearsome creatures, but they have their place in the scheme of life, as well, keeping down the populations of other animals, often weeding out the sick and injured because they're easy prey."

"I think they're horrible creatures," Ben's mother said with a shudder.

"Some people hate spiders—but spiders keep down insect populations. And lots of people hate snakes, but snakes are largely responsible for controlling rodent populations," Michael said.

"What's that mean?" Mark asked.

"It means we'd be overrun by rats if it weren't for snakes," Ben answered, then flushed, staring at Michael.

"That's exactly what it means," Michael said.

"What do you do here, Dr. Preston?" the third kid, cousin Josh, asked.

"That's easy. He's a baby doctor for the alligators," Mark insisted.

"I study the growth patterns of alligators," Michael said. "We raise alligators here, but this is far from a petting zoo. We farm alligators just like some people farm beef cattle. We bring tourists in—and other scientists, by the way, to learn from the work we do here—but the owners are in this for the same reason other farmers work with animals. For the money. Alligators are valuable for their skins, and, more and more, for their meat."

"Tastes like chicken," Mark said.

"That's what some people say," Michael agreed, bristling inside at the boy's know-it-all attitude. "They're a good food source. The meat is nutritious, and little of the animal goes to waste. We're always working on methods to make the skin more resilient, the meat tastier and even more nutritious. By selective breeding and using the scientific method, we can create skins that improve upon what nature made nearly perfect to begin with."

"Perfect?" Ben's mother said with a shudder. Her husband slipped an arm around her.

"They make great boots," he said cheerfully.

"Belts, purses and other stuff, too," Ben supplied.

"You'll see more of that as your tour progresses," Michael said. "I'll tell you a bit more about what goes on in here, then you can watch them eat, Mark, and at the end, guess what?"

"We can all buy boots, belts and purses made out of alligator skin?" one of the young women inquired with a pleasant smile.

"That's right," Michael agreed.

"And we really get to see them chomp on chickens?" Mark demanded, as if that were the only possible reason for coming on the tour.

"Yeah, you can see them chomp on chickens," Michael agreed. He pointed at Ben. "Come back here, Ben, and you can help me." Michael looked up at the adults in the crowd. He never brought a kid back behind his workstation, but for some reason, it seemed important to let Ben lord it over Mark. He was sure that life usually went the other way around. "One of the most incredible things we're able to do in working with crocodilians is studying the growth of the embryo in the egg. Ben, lift that tray, so they can see what I mean."

"Wow!" Mark gasped, stepping forward again. Even he was impressed.

"It's possible to crack and remove the top of the alligators' eggs to study the growth of the embryos without killing them. It's also possible to cause changes and mutations in the growing embryos by introducing different drugs, genetic materials or even stimuli such as heat or cold. Here…in this egg, you'll see a naturally occurring mutation. This creature cannot survive even if it does reach the stage of hatching. You see, it's missing a lower jaw. Can you imagine an alligator incapable of using its jaws? Everywhere in nature, there are mishaps and imperfections. Over here, in this egg, you have an albino alligator. They have tremendous difficulty surviving because—"

"Because they sunburn!" Mark interrupted, laughing as if he'd made a joke.

"Actually, that's true. They have trouble coping with the intense sun that their relatives need to survive. They also lack the element of surprise in their attacks—they're easily seen in greenish or muddy waters where their relatives are camouflaged by their surroundings."

"He's a goner," Mark said.

"Well, not here," Michael told him. "He'll hatch and

grow, and he'll have a nice home at the farm, and we'll feed him and take care of him—you know why?"

"Why?"

"Because he's unusual, and our visitors will like looking at him, that's why," Michael said, pleased with himself because he seemed to be growing a little more tolerant of Mark.

"So that's what you do—you try to make white alligators?" Mark asked.

Michael shook his head. "Selective breeding...well, it's what makes collies furry or Siamese cats Siamese. We find the alligators with the best skins and we breed them, and then we breed their offspring until we create a line of animals with incredibly hardy skins that make the very best boots and bags and purses. We also find the alligators that give the most meat with the most nutritional value—"

"Because it's a farm, and it's out to make money," Ben's mother said, and she shuddered again. "Thank God!"

"She thinks you should kill them all," Ben's father said.

Michael shrugged. "Like I said—"

"They should all be killed," the attractive older woman said, speaking out at last. She had keen blue eyes, and she stared at Michael, somehow giving him the creeps. "They eat people."

"They *do* eat people, right?" Mark demanded with a morbid determination.

"There have been instances, yes."

"A friend of mine was eaten!" the elderly woman

said, and she kept staring at Michael, as if it was all his fault.

"Anytime man cohabits with nature, there can be a certain danger," he said gently. He looked at the others. "It's dangerous to feed alligators. The alligators are repopulating Florida, and they do get into residential canals, especially during mating season. I know of one incident in particular when a woman was feeding the alligators…and, well, to the alligator, there is no distinction between food and a hand offering food."

"And children," the woman said, growing shrill. "Children! It's happened. It's horrible, and they should all be destroyed. Little children, just walking by lakes, looking at flowers—these monsters need to be killed! All of them! How can you people do this, how can you!" Her voice had risen; she was shouting.

There was a buzzer beneath his workstation; all Michael had to do was hit it and the security people would come. Sign of the times. But Michael didn't touch the button; the older woman had stunned him by suddenly going so ballistic, and he just stared at her.

She pointed a finger at him. "Tell them. Tell them the truth. Tell them about the attacks."

"Yes, there have been attacks, and of course that's horrible. But we need to live sensibly with nature. In Africa, along the river, the Nile crocodiles are far more ferocious, but they're a part of the environment. We can't just eliminate animal populations because the animals are predators. We're predators ourselves, ma'am."

She shook her finger at him, and her voice grew more strident. "They're going to eat you. They're going to eat you all. Rise up and tear you to pieces, rip you to shreds—that's how they do it, you know, little boy!" she said, suddenly gripping Mark by the shoulders. She stared at him with her wild eyes. "They clamp down on your body, and they shake you, and they break you and rip you, and your bones crunch and your veins burst. Your blood streams into the water, and you're dying already while they drown you."

"Oh, my God, please!" Ben's mother cried, trying to pull Mark from the woman's grip.

"Hey now!" Michael said, and he came around his station, setting an arm around the woman's shoulders to hold her while Ben's mother, pale as a shadow, pulled Mark to her.

"You!" the elderly woman said, turning on him again. "You! They'll eat *you*. You made them, and they'll eat you. They'll tear you to bits, and your own mother won't be able to find enough bloody pieces to bury you!"

"Now, really, I didn't invent alligators, ma'am—"

"You'll die!" she screeched.

He reached for her again, aware that he had to take control of the situation before it became a monumental disaster. He could see her going completely insane and destroying his lab. Then the cops would be called in, and soon reporters would be crawling everywhere, and then…

"Please, now—" he began.

The door suddenly opened. Security hadn't come; Lorena had, presumably drawn by the noise. She stared reproachfully at Michael.

"What happened?"

"That lady is telling Dr. Preston that the alligators should eat him!" Mark said excitedly.

"We have a problem," Michael agreed. "I think I should call Security—" he began.

"No, no, we're all right." Lorena—who, he had been told, had a degree in psychology and another in public relations, as well as being an RN—assessed the situation quickly and took charge. "Mrs. Manning, right? Come along and tell me about it. We'll get you something cold to drink. It can be so hot here, even with the air-conditioning on the heat can get to you and—"

"Young woman, I am not suffering from the heat!" the elderly woman proclaimed. But her shoulders sank, and she suddenly seemed to deflate. "I'm sorry, I'm sorry. I'm not a lunatic, I don't usually behave this way.... I shouldn't have come. Yes, young woman, you may get me something cold to drink."

Lorena led her quickly toward the door, but once there, the woman stopped and turned back, staring at Michael. She pointed at him again. "I hope they don't eat you, young man," she said. Then she smiled, but it wasn't a pleasant expression, and despite himself, he felt the strangest chill snake along his spine.

Then she was gone, as Lorena whisked her out the door.

Michael, with the nine remaining members of the tour group, was dead silent as seconds ticked by.

He suddenly felt a small hand slipping into his. He looked down. Ben was staring up at him. "Don't worry. She was just crazy. She probably had a friend who got eaten, and she probably misses her. I'm sure you're not going to get eaten, Dr. Preston."

Michael smiled; the chill dissipated.

"All right, everyone. I have a question for you. What animal is most dangerous to Americans?"

There was silence for a moment, then Mark cried out, "I know, I know! Bees!"

"Bees are up there in the top ten, but they're not in the number-one slot."

"I know what it is." A young man, one of the two who looked like a newlywed, was speaking for the first time. He held his wife tightly against him, and seemed pale himself, probably shaken by the older woman's display. "The deer."

"The deer?" Ben protested.

"That's right," Michael said.

"The deer? You mean like Bambi?" Josh asked.

"More Americans are killed each year due to accidents involving deer than are killed by any rattler, spider, shark or reptile out there. So we have to remember to always be careful in any animal's environment," Michael said.

His door opened again; Peggy Martin, one of the guides, stepped in. "Well, ladies and gentlemen, it's time to move on to the pens, or straight into either the gift or coffee shop, if you'd rather," she said cheerfully.

"Mark, you get to see the gators eat chickens," Josh said.

Mark looked at Ben's parents. "I'm really hungry. Maybe we could just get a hamburger. Please?" he said politely.

"Sure, sure," Ben's father said. He looked at Michael. "Thank you for the information, Dr. Preston."

"Yeah, it was great," one of the pretty young women Michael had pegged as a newlywed agreed.

"Thanks," Michael said. "Thanks very much, you were, er, a great group."

He leaned back against his workstation, strangely exhausted. The old woman had given him the creeps. He kept a false smile plastered to his face as the group filed out, the boys in the rear.

Mark was the last. Before he exited, he turned back, looking uneasy.

"Dr. Preston?"

"Yes?"

The boy seemed about to say something, but then he shook his head. "Thanks. You were all right."

Michael nodded.

"Come back sometime," he told Mark, wondering if he meant it or not.

"Yeah."

The door closed behind Mark.

The hatchlings began to squeak.

Chapter 3

In the gift shop, Josh began to play with a two-foot-long plastic alligator. "I've got five dollars," he told Ben. "Think this looks real?"

"Yeah, it's cool," Ben told him.

Mark walked up to the pair in the corner of the shop. He still looked a little pale—they had all been kind of spooked, the old lady had been *really, really* creepy, scarier than the alligators—but he was kind of swaggering again, which Ben was sure meant that Mark was all right.

"That don't look real, Josh. Not compared to this!"

Reaching into the pocket of his baggy, oversize jeans, he pulled out one of the hatchlings. The little creature's mouth was opened wide. Tiny teeth were already chillingly visible.

"Mark! You stole one of the hatchlings—" Josh began.

"Shh," Mark protested.

"Oh, man, you've got to give that back," Ben said.

"No way," Mark said. "Look at him!"

The jaw opened, snapped.

Mark shoved the hatchling toward Josh, who jumped back. "Don't do that, Mark."

"He's going to eat you all up," Mark said, laughing as he started to stuff the creature back into his pocket.

But suddenly he cried out, his hand still in his pocket.

"Oh, shut up," Ben commanded. His cousin was big stuff around school; he had looked up to Mark, and he'd wanted to be like him. But Ben had never been on an outing like this with Mark before. Mark was always on, like maybe there were always girls watching or something. Now the way people were staring was just embarrassing. "Come on, Mark, stop it. People are looking—"

Mark jerked his hand from his pocket. "Get it off! Get it off!" he screamed. The hatchling had his forefinger in its mouth. To Ben's amazement, there was a trail of blood dripping down his cousin's finger.

Instinctively, he reached for the hatchling. But Mark started screaming again. "No, no, don't pull. You'll tear my whole finger off!"

People were beginning to stare. Ben pushed Mark toward a rear door. It read No Admittance: Staff Only, but Ben ignored that; the way the buildings were set up, he could tell that the door led back into the hallway where the labs were housed.

"What are we doing? Where are we going?" Mark cried frantically. "Oh, my God, it hurts! He's eating me!"

"Shut up, shut up, we're taking him back!" Ben said. He moved Mark faster and faster down the hall, pushing back into Dr. Preston's lab without knocking at the door.

Dr. Preston was there, thankfully, standing almost where they had left him. He started when they entered, standing taller in his lab coat. He wasn't very old for a doctor; he was tall and nice-looking, with sandy hair and green eyes, and if Mark hadn't been such a jerk—and if the old lady hadn't freaked out—he might have spent more time with them and told them a lot more neat stuff.

"What the—" Dr. Preston began.

"Mark took one of the babies, but it bit him and we can't get it off and we're real sorry, honest to God, we're real sorry, but can you help—"

Preston helped. Right away, he knew where to pinch the hatchling so that it let go rather than ripping. He dropped the hatchling back into a tank. By then there were tears in Mark's eyes, ready to spill down his face.

"Come over here," Preston said to Mark, taking him back behind his workstation, washing the wound at a sterile-looking sink, then covering it with some slimy cream. "We'll have to take you to the nurse and tell your folks—"

"No, please, no!" Mark protested. "I'm here with Ben's parents. If my parents ever found out I—that I tried to steal from this place, they'd…"

Preston stared at Mark, then at Ben, and then at Josh, who had followed them, silent and so white that his freckles stood out on his face.

"Mark, you were bitten—"

"It's a tiny hole. Look, you can barely see it."

"Yes, but—"

"I've had a tetanus shot, honest."

"Mark, there's always a rare chance that reptiles can carry disease—"

"Not alligator-farm reptiles!" Mark said. "Please, please, please don't say anything. You don't know my dad."

Preston hesitated.

"Please," Mark whispered. "Please."

Ben held his breath. Preston was staring at Mark, studying his face.

The door behind them quietly opened and closed. Ben jumped, turning around. It was their first guide, the really pretty lady with the dark hair and bright blue eyes.

She didn't say anything, just leaned against the door, watching the situation. Dr. Preston looked at her. He lifted Mark's fingers. "They were trying to leave with a souvenir."

"Ah…" she murmured to the boys. "What were you going to do? Drop him in your hotel swimming pool?" She turned to Dr. Preston. "I need to look at that, and then we need to file a report."

Mark went pale.

"I was thinking about letting him go. I think he already paid enough of a price," Dr. Preston said.

Ben was surprised to see that the beautiful nurse was the one who seemed to think they needed the authorities. She was staring at Dr. Preston. "We really shouldn't take the chance. Just in case there are consequences, an infection…"

Dr. Preston stared back at her. "This is one of the

cleanest labs you're ever going to find." He sounded indignant.

The nurse, however, wasn't backing down. "I don't know...."

"Please," Mark begged.

"Hey, I'd never let anything happen to a kid," Dr. Preston swore. "Though this one...all right. Call in the authorities."

"No, please," Mark begged.

The woman stared at Dr. Preston for a moment longer.

Then she looked at the boys. They were staring at her with downright prayers glittering in their eyes.

She nodded, a smile twitching at her lips; then she walked over to look at Mark's finger. Her glance at Michael assured him that it was a minor injury. "We have some antibacterial medicine to put on that."

Preston stared at Mark. "You know, Ms. Fortier has a point. This is against my better judgment. I could lose my job. I could be sued. Who knows, maybe I could go to jail. Lorena, could I go to jail for this?"

"I don't know, but there's a cop outside. Jesse Crane." She made a tsking sound. "I've heard that he feels passionately about people messing with things like this. The Everglades, well, this place is his passion. So I've heard."

"I'll never say a word, never, even if my finger drops off—even if my whole hand explodes!" Mark swore.

Lorena pulled a tube of cream from her pocket and dabbed some of the contents on the injured finger.

She took a bandage from another pocket and covered the bite. When she was finished, though, she was in a real hurry. "I've got to get back to the office. I just came by to make sure everyone was okay. That poor woman is still…well, in bad shape."

"This is just a tiny bite," Mark said apologetically. He gulped. "Thank you, Nurse," he murmured.

She took off. Preston watched her go.

Ben was surprised and pleased to see that Dr. Preston was actually smiling when he said, "Mark, you take this as a lesson. And if your hand swells up, don't keep it a secret. Tell the doctor you stuck your hand in the tank and got bitten by a hatchling, and then you have them call me right away, got it?"

"Yes, sir," Mark swore.

He turned, flying for the door. Ben ran after him. At the door, Mark stopped. Ben crashed into him. Josh, always close, crashed into Ben.

Mark didn't notice the pileup. He was staring back at Dr. Preston. "Thanks, Doc. Honest. I'll make it up to you one day."

Preston nodded at him.

"Okay. I'll hold you to your word."

The boys hurried back out to the gift shop. Ben plowed right into his mother.

"There you are! Thank God. If you're buying anything, do it now. I can't wait to leave this place. Honestly, Howard," she said to his father, "couldn't we have taken them on an overnighter to Disney World? I can't believe we're going from here to an airboat ride and a night in one of those open-air chickee things!"

"It will be fine, dear," Ben's father said. He winked at Ben.

"I knew I should have gone with Sally and the Girl Scouts," she said.

Ben flashed a quick smile to Mark. Mark smiled back. It was going to be all right.

No one was in trouble. The alligator farm wasn't going to call the police or Mark's parents; Ben's folks weren't even any the wiser.

The day was saved.

The airboat ride was next.

Jesse had pulled into the parking lot at the alligator farm already tired. He hadn't found Billy Ray. Where the hell the man had crawled off to, he didn't know. He would need lots more time to comb the swamp to find Billy Ray.

Just what he needed to be doing when two friends had been shot down in their own yard for no apparent reason.

And now this.

A call because a woman had gone into a fit while visiting the alligator farm.

Lots of tourists, he noticed. That was good. Along the Tamiami Trail, a lot of the Miccosukee Indians depended on the tourist trade for a living. Along Alligator Alley, stretching from Broward westward across the state in a slightly more northerly route, a lot of the state's Seminole families depended on the tourist trade, as well. The big alligator farms pulled people in, and then they stayed and paid good tourist dollars for airboat rides, canoe treks along the endless canals at sunset, and even camping in traditional chickees. The locals made money, which was good, because they needed it.

Of course, the biggest earner in the area was the casino. Still, there were a lot of other good ways to make a living from tourists. Either way, it was money honestly earned, and to Jesse, the setting alone was worth the price of admission. The Everglades was a unique environment, and though civilization was steadily encroaching on the rare, semitropical wilderness, it was still just that: a wilderness. Deep in the "river of grass," a man could be so entirely alone with God and nature that civilization itself might not exist. There were miles and miles, acres and acres, where no one had as yet managed to lay a single cable or wire; there were places where even cell phones were no use. There were dangerous snakes and at times the insects were thick in the air. But it was also a place of peace unlike anything else he'd ever experienced. Every once in a while he thought of himself as a rare individual indeed—a man finally at peace with himself, satisfied with his job, and certain, most of the time, that he was the best man for it.

At least, he usually felt at peace with himself and as if he could make a difference in his work.

Today…

Today the world didn't make sense. That a couple as fine and hardworking as Maria and her husband could meet such a fate…hell, what good were the police then? Even if they solved the crime, his friends were still dead.

But thanks to his work, he wasn't powerless. He would find the killers and see justice done. That was his job, and it was one worth doing.

He wasn't making a fortune or knocking the world dead, but he didn't need money. He needed solitude, and the opportunity to be alone when he chose. And he needed to feel that he had some control over his own life and destiny, and this job certainly gave him that. Sometimes, he was very much alone, but that was a choice he had made, consciously or perhaps subconsciously, when he had lost Connie.

"Jesse!"

Harry Rogers, major stockholder and acting president and supervisor of Harry's Alligator Farm and Museum, hurried toward Jesse, who got out of his car. Harry was a big man, six foot two by what sometimes appeared to be six foot two of girth. He'd been born in a Deep South section of northern Florida, and he was proud of being a "Cracker," even if he'd gone on to acquire a degree in business administration from none other than such a prestigious Yankee institution as Harvard.

"Thank God!" Harry exclaimed, clapping him on the back. "We got a lady went berserk in the middle of Michael's speech, started screaming that he was going to get eaten up, and going on and on about how dangerous the gators were. I didn't want the Metro cops coming in here with their sirens blazing and all…and God knows, we don't need the community up in arms about the gators any worse than they already are, but…"

"Where is she?"

"My office, and is she a loose cannon or what? I'm telling you, she's downright scary. I've got Lorena, the new nurse, with her. We made her some tea, Lorena's talking to her, but she's still going off every few minutes or so."

Harry stopped talking and looked at Jesse closely. "Hey, what's the matter? You look grim."

"I am. An old Cuban couple in that new development east of here was murdered."

"How?"

"Shot."

"That your jurisdiction?" Harry asked, scratching his head.

"No, but they were friends."

"I'm sorry. Real sorry. Were they into drugs?"

That was the usual question, especially in a shooting. "No, it had nothing to do with drugs."

"You sure?" Harry asked skeptically.

Jesse gritted his teeth. "Yes, I'm sure."

"Well, if I can help...but at the moment, you've got to be a cop here for me, since this is your jurisdiction."

"All right. I'll see what I can do, but if this lady has really lost her mind, we may need some professionals out here, and we may have to call in the county boys."

"I hate the county boys."

"Hell, I like to settle our own problems, too, Harry. You know that."

"Sure do," Harry said. "'Course, you're the only man among us I've seen put those boys down."

"There are good county cops, Harry. We're a small community out here."

"We're an Indian community," Harry said dryly.

"Doesn't matter. We're small. You have to have the big boys around when you need real help. Hopefully, we don't need it now. Do you know where this woman is from? Has she said?"

Harry shook his head. "Every time we ask her, she

goes on about her friend who was eaten. She's got to
live near a lake somewhere, but that could be half the
state. Don't that just beat all? The old broad has a friend
eaten by a gator—so she comes to visit a gator farm.
Folks are weird as hell, huh?"

"Folks are weird," Jesse agreed without elaborating.
The whole thing was weird, he thought. The woman
here had a friend who'd been eaten by an alligator.

A piece of an alligator had been found where two
innocent people had been murdered.

He followed Harry in through a side entrance to the
administrative buildings and down a long hallway.

The place might be an alligator farm out in the
swamp, but Harry knew how to furnish an office. It
was at the end of a long hallway. A single door opened
onto a room with a massive oak desk surrounded by the
best in leather sofas and chairs. To the rear were more
seats, a large-screen TV, and state-of-the-art speakers
for his elaborate sound system. Harry loved the Everglades; he even loved reptiles. He was part Creek, not
Seminole or Miccosukee, but he'd worked his way up
from cotton picking at the age of three to millionaire
businessman, and he liked his creature comforts. His
office might have been on Park Avenue.

Jesse could hear the woman as he followed Harry in.
She was speaking in a shrill voice, talking about how
nothing had been found of "Matty" other than a hand
with a little flesh left on the fingers. Jesse glanced at
Harry, then walked over to the woman, who was standing in a corner, flattened against the wall. Her hair was
silver, her eyes a soft powder blue. She was trim and
very attractive, except that now the flesh around her

eyes was puffy from crying, and she gazed around with a hunted, trapped look of panic on her face.

In front of her, trying to calm her, was a young woman in a nurse's standard white uniform. Jesse couldn't see her face because a fall of sleek, honey-colored hair hid her features, but before she turned, he knew that he'd already met her.

And she was certainly the last person he'd expected to see at Harry's.

A woman who looked like that and drove a car like that, pedal to the metal...

To get *here?*

She stared back at him for a fleeting moment, instantly hostile—or defensive?

"You're going to get eaten!" the woman was shrieking, pointing at the nurse. "You've got to get out of here. Don't help these people breed monsters. They'll kill you, too. Crush you, drown you... Oh my God, a hand, a hand was all that was left...some flesh, just bits and pieces of flesh...."

"Hey, now, ma'am," Jesse said, stepping forward, trying to remember what he had learned in Psychology 101. "It's going to be all right, honest. Calm down. The alligators here are being raised as food. They're no danger to anyone on the outside—"

"They'll get loose!" the woman protested. But she had given Jesse her attention. He had kept his voice low, deep and calm—Psychology 101—and his firm tone seemed to be working with her. He stepped closer to her, reaching out a hand.

"They're not going to get loose. No one's going to let them get loose." He smiled. "Besides, Harry here is a charter member of the National Rifle Association. He and his staff wouldn't hesitate to shoot any gator that moved in the wrong direction. He's not out to save the gators, ma'am, he's out to make money off them."

She took his hand, staring into his eyes.

Next to him, Jesse heard a deep sigh of relief. He glanced at the woman standing by him, Harry's new nurse. Despite himself, he felt a little electric tremor.

Nature, simple biology, kicking in.

She was probably one of the most beautiful women he had ever seen.

Harry had a habit of finding pretty girls. Strange that a fat old man who owned an alligator farm could convince any young woman to come work in the middle of a swamp. Not that Harry was a lecher; he was as faithful as could be to Mathilda, his equally round and cheerful wife of thirty-odd years. But he did like attractive young people, and he had managed to fill the place with them, so this new nurse shouldn't have been too much of a surprise. Still, Jesse felt himself pause, as he hadn't in a very long time, staring at her.

Maybe it was just the day he'd had so far.

She looked back at him gravely, studying him with the same intensity as he had studied her. Then she looked down, biting her lower lip, embarrassed. In a moment she looked up again, straightening her shoulders and inclining her head, an acknowledgment that he had defused an uncomfortable situation. Her eyes were a dark-rimmed light hazel, startling against the classical, pure cream perfection of her face. Her hair was like a halo of crowning glory; she looked almost fragile in her blond beauty, yet he sensed that there was a lot of substance to her, as well.

He felt the warmth of the older woman's hand and, with a start, looked back to the gray-haired visitor—his current objective. He gave himself a little shake, surprised that Harry's new nurse had so impressed him, and continued to talk to the older woman. "It's okay. We're going to get you home. Except you're going to have to give us a bit of a hand to do that," he continued. "I'm Jesse Crane, a police officer out here. I'd like—"

"Oh!" the woman cried. "So now you're going to arrest me for telling the truth about these monsters and the horrible people purposely breeding them."

"No, ma'am, I just want to get you home and make sure you're going to be all right."

"Oh, like hell. You're just trying to shut me up!"

Jesse smiled at her. He couldn't help it. She was a tough old broad. She might be going over the edge, but she was going with passion and style.

"What's your name?"

"Theresa Manning."

"How do you do, Mrs. Manning? You're free to call the newspapers, or buy a banner ad and have a plane drag it through the sky. We guarantee freedom of speech in this country. But you're hot and miserable, and if you lost a friend to an alligator, this is not a good place for you to be. Let me take you home."

Theresa Manning hesitated, then sighed deeply.

"Where is your home?" he prodded.

"The Redlands."

"All right." He glanced at his watch. It was important

to him that he meet Lars to go to the airport and pick up Julie Hernandez. "Let's go. Let me take you home now."

She nodded, looking at him. But as she rose, she suddenly gripped the nurse's hand.

"You, too. Please."

"But, Mrs. Manning—" the nurse protested.

"Please," Theresa Manning insisted.

"Go with her," Harry said softly to the nurse.

"Harry, I won't be able to bring her back for a while," Jesse said.

"Oh, please," Theresa Manning said, starting to grow hysterical again.

"Lorena, just go with him. When you get back, you get back!" Harry said impatiently.

Lorena's startling eyes fixed on Jesse's, and she said, "All right. If Mrs. Manning wants me with her, I'll be with her, and whatever you have to do, Officer, I'll wait until you're able to get me back. Shall we go?"

Jesse lifted his hands in surrender. He almost smiled. Maybe she felt this was her way of getting back at him for what had happened yesterday.

Fine. If she wanted to wind up involved in a murder investigation and not get back until the wee hours of the morning, so be it.

"Yeah. Sure. Let's go," he said flatly. "Mrs. Manning?" He smiled, taking the older woman's arm. She actually smiled back.

He let Lorena follow behind as he escorted Theresa Manning from the office to his car.

Damn, this was one hell of a day.

Chapter 4

Lorena sat in the back of the car, while Theresa Manning sat in the front with Jesse Crane.

She felt somewhat useless being there, but the woman had been insistent. And though Lorena felt a twinge of guilt, aware that she had been eager to come not so much to help out—which she certainly was willing to do—but because she wanted the time with Jesse Crane.

As Sally had pointed out, the man was something special. But that wasn't why she was interested in him.

Despite the heavy traffic, he drove smoothly and adeptly. They left the Trail and headed south. He kept up a casual stream of conversation with Mrs. Manning, pointing out birds, asking about her home and family. By the time they neared her neighborhood, she seemed relaxed, even apologetic. Jesse told her not to be sorry, then suggested that she not take any more tours in the Everglades for a while.

At her house, she asked them in. Jesse very respectfully declined, but he gave her a card, telling her to call him if she needed him.

When they got back in the car, Lorena told him, "That was impressive."

He shrugged. "The woman isn't a maniac, just really upset. And maybe feeling that kind of rage we all do when something horrible has happened and we're powerless to change it." He glanced at his watch, then at her. "Sorry, I have to get to the airport, and it's not going to be pleasant."

"I told you...whatever you need to do...do it. I'll hang in the background," Lorena said.

He nodded, and after a few minutes she realized that he was heading for the turnpike. He glanced over at her, a curious smile tugging at his lips. "What brought you to our neck of the woods?" he asked her.

She shrugged, looking out the window. Then she looked at him sharply. "Well, I thought you'd already figured that out. I was racing out to one of the resorts. A spa. To be pampered."

"I'm sure you'll find time to slip out and hit some of the prime places," he said dryly.

"Really?" she murmured.

He couldn't resist a taunting smile. "You do your own hair and nails?" he asked.

"As a matter of fact, I do," she told him.

He shook his head. "You don't look the type," he said.

"You have to look a type to work out here?"

"You'll burn like a tomato in a matter of minutes," he warned her.

"They do make sunscreen," she returned.

"So… I repeat, what are you doing out here?"

"The job at Harry's," she said simply.

"There are nursing jobs all over the state. And most of them not in the Everglades."

She gazed over at him, surprised to realize that she was telling the truth when she said, "I like it out here."

"You're fond of mosquitoes the size of hippos and reptiles that grunt through the night?"

"I think the sunsets out here are some of the most beautiful I've ever seen. As to the alligators…well, they're just part of the environment, really. The birds are glorious. And the pay's exceptional."

"I see. Well, it's still a lonely existence."

It was her turn to smile. "Okay, so it may take an hour to get anywhere, but…it's a straight shot east to Miami and a straight shot west to Naples. Not so bad."

"I guess not. But in bad weather, you can be stuck out here and feel as if you're living in the Twilight Zone."

"You came back out here to work," she said softly.

There was silence for a minute. "This is home for me," he said.

"It's not so far off from home for me," she said.

"It's pretty far."

She glanced at him sharply.

"Jacksonville. I took your license, remember? And now that I know you were flying like a bat out of hell to reach Harry's, I'm more stunned than ever."

"I was starting a new job," she said defensively. "And

however far it might be, I *am* from this state." Great. Now he was curious. What if *he* decided to investigate *her*?

She noticed that they had left the turnpike and were following the signs for the airport. He glanced at her again. "I'm meeting with a Metro-Dade detective. We're meeting a detective named Lars Garcia and picking up an old friend of mine." He hesitated just slightly. "That's why I didn't want you along. It's not going to be pleasant. Julie's parents were murdered last night."

"Oh, my God! I'm so sorry."

"I warned you."

"What happened?"

"They were shot," he said flatly.

She decided not to ask any questions for the next few minutes. He'd obviously been deeply affected by the murders.

They parked at the airport. Jesse knew where he was going and walked quickly. Lorena followed him. Outside the North Terminal, he walked over to a man in a plain suit, a man with light brown hair and green eyes, but dark brows and lashes. Even before she was introduced, Lorena knew that this was Lars Garcia.

She felt the keen assessment he gave her. Part of his job, she imagined. Summing people up quickly.

"So you're working out at Harry's?" he murmured.

She didn't have time to answer.

"There she is," Jesse said softly, spotting his old friend, Julie.

"I'll go," Lars Garcia offered.

But Jesse shook his head.

He left Lars and Lorena, and walked toward the dark-haired, exotic-looking Latin beauty who was coming their way. She was wearing glasses, apparently to hide the redness in her eyes, which was apparent when she saw Jesse and took them off. Then she dropped the overnight bag she'd been carrying and went into his arms, sobbing.

Lorena looked down, feeling like an intruder. "It's all right," Lars Garcia said softly.

She looked up at him.

"They're just good friends."

Lorena felt her cheeks flush hotly. "No, no, don't get the wrong impression. I'm just here…by accident, really. I barely know Officer Crane."

Lars Garcia continued to assess her as Jesse, an arm around Julie, led her to where Lorena and Lars stood waiting.

"Julie, this is Detective Lars Garcia. He's in charge of the case," Jesse said. "And this is… Lorena. Lars, Lorena, Julie Hernandez."

Julie offered Lorena a teary, distraught but somehow still warm smile.

"Julie, I'm so sorry," Lorena murmured, feeling totally inadequate and wrenched by the girl's pain. She could all too easily remember the feelings of agony, frustration and fury, and always the question of why?

And after that, the *who?*

And now?

And now the gut-deep fury and determination that the truth would be known.

"Thank you." Julie looked at her for a long moment, as if sensing Lorena's sincerity. Then she turned to Garcia. "Whoever did this…why? My parents never hurt a soul in their entire lives."

"We're going to find out why," Lars vowed softly. "We need your help, though. We need anything you can give us."

Julie visibly toughened then, summoning her anger and determination from deep within, her inner reserves rising over the natural agony she was feeling. "I was just telling Jesse… I have no idea. They had no enemies. But I promise you, I'll help you in any way I can."

"Are you up to coming to the station with me now?" Lars asked. "It can wait, if you'd rather."

"No. No, I'll go now," Julie said, and swallowed. She looked at Jesse. "Jesse…?"

"Call me when you're done."

She nodded, trying to smile.

Lars took Julie's arm and cast a grateful glance over her dark head at Jesse.

The two walked off.

"I'm so sorry," Lorena said. She had never met the couple, but the sense of loss had seemed to envelop her. Impossible to see Julie and not feel it. She felt horrible, like an intruder, again. "I…wish there were something I could say, do."

Jesse nodded, then said only, "I can get you back now."

The silence, growing awkward between them, lasted as they left the airport, taking the expressway to the Trail, then heading straight down the road that stretched the width of the southern tip of the peninsula.

They passed homes and developments, and then the

casino. After that, houses and businesses became few and far between.

She was startled when Jesse suddenly said, "Can you give me another half hour?" He turned and looked at her with those startling eyes of his. She wondered if he had decided he didn't feel quite so much contempt for her, or if he was merely so distracted he'd barely even been aware till then that she was there with him.

"I...of course. Of course. Harry said it was no problem," she murmured.

They pulled off onto something she wasn't sure she would have categorized as a road. As they proceeded along a winding trail, she realized that they were on farmland.

A minute later, she saw the crime tape. Jesse Crane pulled off the road.

"Excuse me. Stay here—I'll be just a minute," he said.

He exited the car, leaving her in the passenger's seat. Lorena hesitated for the briefest fraction of a second, then followed him.

She wasn't about to stay.

Jesse wasn't in the area enclosed by the tape. He was standing just outside of it, talking to a uniformed officer and a man in street clothes who had an ease in being there that suggested he was also a cop.

As she walked up, she could hear the man in street clothes talking. "Yeah, Doc Thiessen has the gator arm...the leg, whatever, that you discovered. I really don't see how it's going to help us. The Hernandezes were killed by bullets, not wildlife run amok!" He saw

Lorena approaching before Jesse did, and he watched her, curiously and appreciatively, as she walked up to the scene.

Jesse turned to look at her with annoyance, a serious frown furrowing his brow.

"I told you to wait in the car," he said coldly.

"Hello, ma'am," the young uniformed officer said.

"Yes, hello," the man in plainclothes said. "How do you do? I'm Abe Hershall."

"Officer Gene Valley, ma'am," the uniform said.

"How do you do?" She shook hands with the tall, slender, dark-eyed man who was obviously a detective, and the uniformed officer. Jesse stood by silently, waiting, not apologizing for his rudeness, and certainly not offering any information about her.

"I'm working at Harry's," she said herself.

"The new nurse," Gene Valley said. "Well, welcome to the area."

"Thanks," she said softly.

"Working for old Harry, huh?" Abe Hershall said, shaking his head ruefully. "Well, good for Harry."

"This is a crime scene," Jesse reminded them all. "Ms. Fortier, now that you've met everyone, I believe it's time for me to get you back."

Taking Lorena by an elbow, he steered her forcefully back to the car.

"I can walk on my own," she said.

"I told you to stay in the car."

"It's a million degrees in there." She looked him in the eye. "Who was that?" she asked. "Abe…is he Lars's partner?"

"Yes."

He forced her determinedly back into the car. The door slammed. She gritted her teeth.

"You found a piece of a gator out there?" she asked when he was in the driver's seat.

"This is the Everglades. There are lots of alligators, and naturally, some die." He put the car in gear and started driving, his eyes straight ahead.

"But you found a *piece* of one."

Jesse slammed on the brakes, turned and stared at her, angry. Whether with her, or with himself, she wasn't sure. "Look, we found a piece of an alligator, yes. And I'd appreciate it if you would just shut up about it. I'm trying to keep that bit of information out of the press. You see, I'd really like to know if there's a connection between that and a murder. Damn! This is all my fault. I shouldn't have brought you out here, and I sure as hell shouldn't have counted on you staying in the car just because *I told you to!*"

Lorena looked straight ahead. "I have no intention of leaking any information," she said.

He stared at her. "Really? And should I ask for that as a guarantee, written in stone? After all, I don't know anything about you."

She grated her teeth. "Do I look like someone who would shoot an innocent couple?"

"No. But you don't look like someone who'd be working at Harry's, either," he said sharply.

She let out an explosion of exasperation. "I don't suppose you'd believe I actually like it out here?"

"Right. Nothing like being a nurse at an alligator farm," he murmured.

"Maybe it's just an easy gig," she said.

He didn't reply. Her heart sank. She had a feeling that he was going to know everything there was to know about her within the next forty-eight hours.

Maybe she should just tell him.

Maybe not. He obviously thought of her as some kind of fragile cream puff. Maybe a rich brat playing games. She shouldn't have brought her own car, she thought, hindsight bringing sudden brilliance.

If he found out anything about what she was doing, he might well find a way to get her out of Harry's—fast. Even that evening.

Could he do such a thing? Was he good friends with Harry—or whoever was involved?

She kept silent.

A few minutes later, they drove back into the complex that comprised Harry's Alligator Farm and Museum.

"Thanks," Lorena murmured, getting ready to hop out of the car as quickly as possible.

He caught her hand lightly. She held still, not meeting his eyes, but careful not to make any attempt to jerk free. She realized that he frightened her. Not because she thought he would hurt her, but because he aroused something in her, something emotional. She found herself waiting to tell him everything, wanting just to be with him.

"Be careful," he warned softly.

"Of…?" she murmured.

"Well, an elderly couple was just shot," he said impatiently.

"I'll be all right," she said. Then she pulled free.

There was something far too unnerving about his touch. She didn't like the fact that though she barely knew him, she respected him already. Admired him. Even *liked* him. "Thanks."

"I'll be seeing you," he said pleasantly.

"Of course," she said, and then, at last, she managed to flee.

There wasn't much daylight left, but since Ginny had called in to the station several times saying that Billy Ray hadn't yet come home, Jesse decided it was time to check out his fishing spots.

Billy Ray was lazy, a creature of habit, and Jesse wasn't surprised when he found the man's beat-up old boat at his first stop in the vast grounds off the Trail.

The boat had been floating in the middle of the canal—already suspicious—and there was no sign of Billy Ray.

Jesse began walking along the embankment. At first he let his mind wander, mentally reminding himself that he had a record of Lorena Fortier's driver's license, enough to find out something about the woman. Frankly, he admitted to himself, he was worried about her. He could hardly say that he knew her from their two encounters, but there was something about her eyes, about the very real compassion she had shown the elderly woman, that made him feel she was—despite his original assessment—a decent human being.

There was something about her that made him feel a lot more, as well. Now that he'd gotten closer to her, it was far more than the simple fact that she was stunning, though that was good for a swift, hot rise of the libido. She was quick to show empathy, and in the right way. She seemed to sense pain and use her warmth to heal it. Her energy was electric.

Sensual.

He swore out loud, reminding himself that he was here trying to determine what had happened to Billy Ray Hare.

Still…

She had roused not just his senses, but thoughts that he had kept at bay for a long time. There was nothing casual about her. She evoked real interest—and very real desire. But, he realized, not the kind that could be easily sated, then forgotten.

What was it about her?

Her eyes? Her behavior? Or the way she looked? Like a blond goddess, tempting in the extreme.

He mentally shook his head, reminding himself again that this wasn't the time to discover that there was life not just in his limbs, but in his soul. Two good people had been murdered, and Billy Ray was missing. This definitely wasn't the time to be feeling a stab of desire just because a woman had walked into his neck of the woods.

Still, even as he concentrated his attention on the wet ground, the endless saw grass and the canal, he felt a strange sense of tension regarding *her*.

She was involved. Somehow, she was involved.

Just as that thought came to his mind, he found Billy Ray.

What was left of him.

* * *

Sally finished up with the day's entrance receipts, locked her strongbox and papers in the safe, and smoothed back her hair. Quite a day. All the commotion.

So much going on. Admittedly, most of the time so little went on here. That was why she had to make things happen. With that in mind, she started humming.

She was done for the day.

She walked determinedly down the hallway. News, any little bit of it, spread like wildfire around here. She loved to be the first to know any little tidbit.

She headed across the center of the complex.

"Hey, Sally!"

She smiled at the man leaning against one of the support poles.

"Hey, yourself," she said softly. Teasingly. It got boring out here, after all.

"Got anything for me?" he asked softly, since there were still both tourists and co-workers around.

She walked up to him, smiled, placed a hand lightly on his chest. "Maybe," she murmured seductively.

"Maybe?"

"Well, it depends."

"On what?"

"On what *you've* got for *me*," she whispered.

She let her hand linger for a moment. A promise, just like her whisper. Then she walked away.

She could be warm; she could give.

But she fully intended to receive in return. After all, there was pleasure.

And then there was business.

* * *

The gates had closed; the last of the tourists were flooding out as Lorena returned. She headed straight for her room, a quick shower and a change of clothes.

Though she wasn't accustomed to choosing her wardrobe for the purpose of seduction, she did so that night. A soft, pale blue halter dress seemed the right thing—cool enough for the summer heat, a garment that molded over the human form. She brushed her hair until it shone, then played with different ways to part it. She found a few of the effects amusing, but decided to go back to a simple side part and a sleek look. A touch of makeup, and she was off.

She found Dr. Michael Preston in the company cafeteria. The kitchen was centrally located between the employee dining area/lounge and the massive buffet area where visitors were welcome. During the day, a head chef worked with two assistants and three buffet hostesses. By night, only the offerings of the day and two cafeteria workers remained.

Alligator—sautéed, fried and even barbecued—was always on the menu. Lorena had dined on it in the past, but tonight she didn't want it, not in any form.

As she'd expected, she saw Michael Preston—who hadn't ordered gator, either—sitting with the keepers, the blond Australian, Hugh Humphrey, and the tall, striking Seminole, Jack Pine.

The three men rose as she approached. Jack whistled softly. "Wow! And welcome. Are you joining us?"

"If you don't mind."

"Are you kidding?" Hugh demanded pleasantly.

"You're definitely a breath of beautiful fresh air around this place," Jack assured her.

"Please," Michael Preston said, pulling out a chair.

She smiled, thanked him and sat down.

"I heard we had a bit of a freak-out today, and that you went with Jesse to take the woman home," Jack said. "Bizarre, huh?"

"Her friend was…eaten," Lorena said softly. "Why she was out here after that, I don't know."

Michael made an impatient sound. "Do you know what happens most of the time when gators kill? Some idiot thinks you can feed them like you feed the ducks at a pond." He shook his head. "First we destroy their natural habitat. Every year, development spreads farther west, into the Everglades. Naturally there are waterways. Then people wonder what the alligators are doing in their canals."

"Well, trust me," Jack said ruefully, his tone light and teasing, "you're not going to stop progress."

Hugh looked at Lorena seriously. "You're not afraid of being eaten, are you?"

She shook her head. "Trust me, I have no intention of feeding the gators. I'll leave that to you guys."

"Man is not the alligator's natural prey," Michael said. "Go out to Shark Valley. You can walk those trails, and, trust me, there are hundreds of gators around, but they don't bother anyone."

"It really is unusual, and there's always a reason, when a human is attacked," Jack explained. "Most of the time Hugh and I get called because a gator has strayed into a heavily populated area. We catch it and bring it back out to the wilds. The end."

"Do you ever keep the ones you 'rescue'?" Lorena asked.

"No. We breed our own alligators here," Michael said. "Harry's been here a long time now. He started up with a small place when they were still really endangered, so a couple were captured. But now all our gators are farm raised, because they do make good eating. And their hides make spectacular leather. Farms like this one are an important part of the state's economy. They're much more than just tourist attractions."

Lorena smiled. "They really are fascinating creatures," she told Michael. "I'm absolutely intrigued by your work."

"Cool," Jack said, folding his arms over his chest and leaning back. "We get a nurse who not only patches up our scrapes, she's into the entire operation. I hear that you don't mind working with the tour groups, either."

She shrugged. "I'd die of boredom here if I weren't interested."

"Hey, did you want something to eat?" Jack asked her.

She turned slightly to see that one of the remaining kitchen workers was standing by her side.

"Mary, have you met Lorena yet?" Jack continued, speaking to the heavyset woman at his side.

Mary shook her head, then pointed across the room to where Harry was sitting, engaged in conversation with Sally.

"The boss said to check on you," Mary said, looking at Lorena. "Usually people come up to the buffet. So are you hungry? You'd better eat now. We break down in half an hour, then there's nothing except the vending machines until morning—unless you want to drive for an hour to find something open." She shrugged. "You go into Miami, you got some places open twenty-four hours a day. But you want to drive back here in the middle of the night?" Mary shuddered. She'd been looking grim, but then she smiled. "You want some alligator?"

"Um, actually, no, thank you," Lorena said. "Is there another choice?"

"There's always chicken," Michael offered, grinning at last.

"How about a salad?" Lorena asked. She wasn't a vegetarian; she just didn't think that at the moment she wanted meat of any sort. Especially crocodilian.

"Caesar?" Mary suggested.

"Lovely."

"Of course, we do offer the caesar with a choice of chicken, sirloin or alligator," Mary said.

"A plain caesar would be perfect," Lorena said.

Mary shrugged, as if a plain caesar was probably the least appetizing thing in the world. "Something to drink?"

Lorena ordered iced tea and thanked Mary, assuring her that she would know to go to the buffet herself from then on.

When Mary was gone, Jack Pine nudged Lorena, his dark eyes dancing with amusement. "She's all right, really. Just a bit grim."

"She doesn't like alligators at all," Michael said.

"Why does she work out here?" Lorena asked.

"Harry pays well," Michael said. He leaned forward suddenly. "The guys and I were going to head to the casino for a few hours. Want to come?"

"We'd love to have you," Jack said.

"You look far too lovely to hang around here," Hugh said, grinning.

If they were all leaving, this might well be her best chance to get into Michael's laboratory. She yawned. "Actually, I'd love to take you guys up on that, but at a later date? I'm just getting accustomed to my new surroundings, and I'm feeling pretty tired."

"You really should come," Michael said, placing a hand over hers.

She smiled at him, as if enjoying the contact. "I will. Next time," she said sweetly.

Mary arrived with her salad. The men remained politely waiting for her to eat, then rose together when she was done. Lorena said that she would walk them out to the parking lot, then head for her room.

The three men climbed into Jack Pine's Range Rover, and she waved.

As soon as they were gone, she headed for the inner workings of the museum.

And Dr. Michael Preston's lab.

Lars and Abe stood by Jesse on the embankment, watching as the M.E. bagged the remnants of Billy Ray.

At the moment, Jesse felt the weight of the world on his shoulders.

There was no one else who could go to see Ginny. This was going to be his responsibility, and with the Metro-Dade force on the scene, that meant he could go to her now.

But he hesitated, seeing the floodlights illuminate

the immediate darkness and feeling the oppressive heat of the ebony beyond.

"I don't believe it," Lars said, staring in the direction of the M.E., shaking his head.

"I'm not quite sure I do, either," Jesse said. He pointed. "The best I can figure it, Billy Ray was in his boat. His shotgun was still in it, and it had been fired. It looks as if an alligator actually rammed the boat, Billy fell out, and…well, you know how they kill, shaking their prey, then drowning it."

"Alligators don't ram boats," Lars said.

"Looks like this one did," Jesse said.

Abe frowned, staring at Jesse. "Alligators may follow a boat, looking for a hand out—literally." He smiled grimly. "But they don't ram boats. I'd say maybe someone was out here with Billy Ray. Maybe they fought. Maybe Billy Ray even shot at him. Then the fight sent him overboard, and a hungry old male might have been around. A really hungry old male, since we all know gators don't choose humans."

"Gentlemen, this is my neck of the woods, and God knows, I want tourists out here as much as anyone, but I'd say it was time we get some kind of warning out," Jesse said.

"Warning?" Abe protested. "Like what? Don't head into the Everglades? Killer alligators on the loose?"

"Yeah, something like that," Jesse said flatly.

Abe shook his head. "Jesse, you're nuts. What do you want to do, destroy the entire economy out here?"

"I'll tell you this, I intend to issue a warning," Jesse said.

"Hey, you do what you want," Abe said.

"What the hell are you saying?" Jesse demanded, his temper rising. "We all know that Billy Ray was killed by a gator."

"How do we know that?" Abe demanded. "Seriously. You do an autopsy I don't know about?"

Jesse stared at him, incredulous. "What?"

"We have a ripped-up body. You said yourself that Billy Ray's gun had been shot. Maybe someone shot back at him, he wound up in the water, bleeding, and then the gator attacked him. That's a far more likely scenario."

"Stop it," Lars protested. "Both of you. We've got a bad situation here."

"Yeah, we do. A couple shot to death—with the remains of an alligator found nearby. Now a fellow who knew this place better than any living human being, killed by an alligator. If that isn't enough—" Jesse said.

"That couple were killed because they saw something going on in the swamp—I'd lay odds on it. And alligators don't shoot people," Lars argued. "These incidents are totally unrelated."

Jesse just stared at him, so irritated he longed to take a jab at Abe's out-thrust, obstinate jaw. Instead, he turned and walked away. "You do what you want. So will I."

"Hey!" Lars called after him.

Jesse turned back.

"Jesse…you may want to be on the lookout for a… well, I don't know. A rogue alligator. A big one," Lars suggested.

"Yeah. Are you going to contact the rangers, or should I?" Jesse asked.

"I'll see that they're notified," Lars assured him grimly.

Abe snorted. "Yeah. We'll handle this one by the book. This is your neck of the woods, Jesse. Billy Ray was one of yours. Homicide only comes in when we've got a murder. We'll see that the site is investigated, and then we'll sign off on it. This is your ball game."

"And I'll get warnings out on Indian land. And I also intend to arrange a hunt."

"It ain't season, Jesse," Abe said.

Jesse crossed his arms over his chest. "Maybe not, but it *is* tribal land. Like you said, it's my call. At the least, we're talking about a nuisance animal. I'll be taking steps."

Abe threw up his hands.

"This one is your call, Jesse," Lars told him.

"Fine. And you know the call I've made. You put out the warnings in your territory."

"Because of one alligator?"

"How do we know it's just one?" Jesse demanded.

"And how do we know Billy Ray didn't just drink himself silly, then irritate the creature—a normal, everyday predator that happens to live out here—and make the mistake of going in right where a big boy was hungry?"

"What was an alligator limb doing out where Hector and Maria were killed?" Jesse demanded.

Abe shook his head. "People murdered with big guns—and a natural predator attack. There's no damned connection!"

"Hey," Lars said. "The matter will be under investigation."

"Abe, I'm warning you, there could be a lot more trouble," Jesse said.

"Great. I'm warned," Abe said.

"Jesse, no one is going at this with a closed mind," Lars assured him. "Hell, I'm a cop, not a kindergarten teacher. We're professionals. We'll complete our investigation of the scene and sign this one over to you. Abe, dammit—you know as well as I do that anything is possible. All right, children?"

"Sure," Abe said.

"Yeah," Jesse said. "You're right. And now I have to go talk to a woman about the fact that her husband is dead."

Abe snorted. "She should be relieved."

Lars exploded, swearing.

Jesse turned away.

He couldn't put it off any longer. He had to go to see Ginny.

And then...

Then he would have to talk to Julie.

The night ahead seemed bleak indeed.

Chapter 5

Since she was carrying a lock pick in her purse, Lorena had no problem waving with a smile as the car drove away, then heading straight back inside and down the hall to Dr. Michael Preston's lab.

She stood for several seconds in the hallway, but the place was entirely empty.

There were guards on duty, of course. But they were outside, protecting the alligator farm. She had made a point in the beginning of seeing whether there were cameras in the hallways, but there weren't—not unless they were exceptionally well hidden.

She headed for the door, reaching into her purse.

"Lorena!"

Stunned, she spun around. Michael was there in the hallway, right behind her.

"Hey!" she said cheerfully, approaching him quickly.

"I thought you were going to get some rest tonight?" he said, frowning.

"I changed my mind. I was hoping to find you."

"In the hallway? You just waved goodbye to us."

"I don't know—sixth sense, maybe. You're back, and I'm so glad. I can still go with you. If you're still going."

He nodded. "I forgot my cell phone, so I came back to get it."

"Great. I'll wait for you."

He nodded, still appearing puzzled, but she kept her smile in place, following him into the lab.

The hatchlings squeaked from their terrariums.

Lorena stood politely by the door, waiting. As she had before, she inventoried what she could see of the lab.

The file cabinets. Michael's desk. The pharmaceutical shelves. The computer.

He took his cell phone from the desktop, then joined her. She linked arms with him, and felt the tension in him ease.

"Are you a poker player?" he asked her.

"Not really," she admitted.

"There's not too much else," he warned.

"I love slot machines," she assured him.

He smiled back at her. Apparently her attempt at flirtation was working. He slipped an arm around her shoulders. He was a good-looking man, with a sense of humor, and though it seemed he sometimes wondered if he were too much of an egghead in comparison with the rugged handlers, he apparently also had faith in his own charisma. "Let's head out, then, shall we?" he asked, and there was a husky note in his voice. If she was happy in his company, it apparently wasn't too big a surprise to him.

Then again, she'd been trying to keep the right balance. Flirt just the right amount with the bunch of them.

"Let's head out," she agreed, and she fell into step with him, aware of his arm around her shoulder—and also aware that the lab was where she really needed to be.

Jesse had a feeling that Ms. Lorena Fortier from Jacksonville would be quite surprised when she learned that the Miccosukee police department currently consisted of a staff of twenty-seven, nine of them civilian employees, the other eighteen officers deployed throughout the community in three main areas: north of the Everglades in Broward County; the Krome Avenue area, encompassing the casino and environs; and the largest center of tribal operations, on the Tamiami Trail. The pay was good, and the Miccosukee cops were a respected group. The department had been created in '76, because most of the tribal areas were so remote that a specific force was necessary to protect the community, and to work with both the state and federal agencies in tracking down crime.

Jesse wondered if Lorena was under the impression that he was working as the Lone Ranger.

Before he made his dreaded trip to Ginny's place, he returned to the station. His crews were up on everything that happened in the jurisdiction, but he hadn't been back in himself yet, and he disliked being in a situation where communication wasn't tight as a drum.

The night crew was coming on, but he was in time to

catch the nine-to-fivers and give everyone his personal briefing on both the double homicide and the death of Billy Ray.

He liked being at the office; he wasn't a one-man show, but the department was still small enough that every officer and civilian employee knew that they mattered, and that their opinions were respected. He got the different departments researching activities in the area, possible drug connections, the backgrounds of Hector and Maria, and anything that might strike their minds as unusual, or any kind of connection.

Barry Silverstein, one of the night patrolmen, was especially interested in the alligator limb that had been brought to the veterinarian for examination. "Strange that you found only a piece," he said. "Think maybe we're looking for a poacher?" he asked.

"Could be," Jesse said. "But it's not likely. We have an alligator season, and a license is easy enough to obtain. Besides, the alligator farms have pretty much taken the profit out of poaching."

"Kids?" Brenda Hardy, the one woman on night duty, inquired. "You know, teenagers, maybe. Or college students. Say that the piece of the alligator has nothing to do with the murders. Maybe some kids pledging a fraternity or just making ridiculous dares to one another."

"I sure hope it's not a trend," Barry said. "They may have gotten that gator, but you start playing around with some of the big boys out there...well, hell, we know what they're capable of."

"Poor Billy Ray," Brenda said sadly, shaking her head. She was a pretty woman, tall and slim, and all business. She was light-skinned and light-haired, probably of Germanic or Nordic descent. You didn't have to be Native American to be on the force. Barry, who was Jewish and had had ancestors in the States so long he didn't know where they'd originally come from, always liked to tease her that she was an Indian wannabe. Brenda had once gravely shut him up by assuring him that she had been a Native American in her previous life.

"I'll tell you frankly that this situation scares the hell out of me. These people are brutal and ruthless. Everyone has to be alert," Jesse warned.

George Osceola, one of the Native officers on the force, a tall man with huge shoulders and a calm, controlled way of speaking that made him even more imposing, had been watching the entire time. He spoke then. "Jesse, you think these incidents are related, don't you. How?"

"That's what I can't figure. Murders that cold-blooded are usually drug related. And we're not ruling that out," Jesse said.

"Could we be dealing with some kind of cult?" George asked.

"I don't know. What I do believe is that we've got to get to the bottom of it fast. George, ask questions, see if anyone has seen anything out of the ordinary. People coming through who aren't out to enjoy nature or a day at the village. Strangers who hang around. Anything out of the ordinary. *Anything.* Metro-Dade homicide is working the murders. I'm afraid we may find the killers closer to home."

"We'll all be on it," Brenda said.

Jesse nodded. "Brenda, do me a favor. Get background investigations busy for me, will you?"

"On the Hernandez family?" Brenda asked, sounding puzzled.

"No. On a woman named Lorena Fortier. I just wrote her a ticket, so we'll have her driver's license information. Find out more about where she comes from, what she's been doing."

"Lorena Fortier?"

"She just started working at Harry's."

"All right," Brenda said, still puzzled, but asking no more questions.

"You going out to Ginny's now?" Barry asked.

"Yeah," Jesse said. "And then to see Julie."

No one replied. No one offered to take on the responsibility. He didn't want them to, and they knew it. These were things he had to do.

He left to see Ginny, and it was rough. As rough as he had expected.

Eventually he left Ginny with her sister and niece, both of whom apparently thought that Billy Ray had come by accident to an end that he deserved. Thankfully, they weren't saying that to Ginny, though; they were just holding her and soothing her. Anne, Ginny's niece, had told him that as soon as possible, she was going to take her aunt away for a while. For the moment, they had called the doctor, who had prescribed a sedative for her.

Before he left, Ginny had gripped his hand. Her large dark eyes had touched his.

"Help me, Jesse—please. Find out…find out what happened."

"Ginny, he met with a mean gator," her sister said.

But Ginny shook her head. "Billy Ray knew gators. Jesse, you have to help. I have to know...*why*. Oh, God, oh, God... Jesse I need to know, and you're the only one who can help."

With her words ringing in his ears, he had gone on to meet Julie.

Hell of a night.

So now he sat with his old friend in the upstairs bar of the casino hotel where she had chosen to stay. Julie had told him that she appreciated his offer to let her stay at his place, but she had wanted to be closer to the city and couldn't quite bring herself to stay in her parents' house.

He agreed that she shouldn't stay at her folks' house—certainly not alone. Neither he nor the Metro-Dade police had any idea what had happened, and the houses in that area were way too few and far between for him to feel safe with her there.

"I'm telling you, Jesse, there's no way my folks were connected to anything criminal," Julie said, at a loss. "I'd give my eyeteeth to help. In fact... I think I could kill with my own bare hands, if I knew who did this. But they were as honest as the day is long."

"I know that, Julie."

She sighed, running a finger around the glass of wine she had ordered. "I'm glad you're on this, Jesse. The other guys...they didn't know my folks."

"Lars is a good man. So is Abe. A bit of an ass, but a good detective."

That brought a hint of a smile to her lips. "Still, no matter what you tell people...everybody seems certain that my dad had turned a blind eye to some drug deal, at the very least. The thing is, you and I both know that there was no such thing going on."

"Of course." He patted her hand. "Did your mom or dad ever say anything to you about anything strange going on out there?"

Julie shook her head. "No." She hesitated, frowning. "Actually, once…" She fell silent, shrugging.

"Once what?"

"Oh, something silly. It can't have anything to do with what happened," Julie said.

Jesse touched her hand. "Julie, I don't care how silly you may think something sounds. Tell me what it is."

"Um, well, I lose track of time, but a few days ago, maybe a week, when I was talking to my mom, she was getting into talking about ETs. You know, extra-terrestrials."

"Oh?"

"She said there were weird lights. I'm sure it was just someone out in an airboat, but…"

"But?"

"Well, my mom was getting on in years, but her vision was good. She thought the lights were coming from the sky. That's why she got it into her head that aliens were searching the Everglades."

"A lot of planes come in that way," Jesse pointed out.

"The lights from planes don't stay still."

"Helicopters," Jesse said.

Julie shrugged. Then her face crumpled and she began to cry. Jesse didn't try to tell her that it would be okay. He just came around the table and held her.

Helicopters. If anything big had been going on—the

police searching for someone, for instance—he would have known about it.

Maria had had fine eyesight, no more fanciful than the next person. And she had seen lights.

Jesse knew that there had been an airboat behind the house the night Julie's parents had been killed. That wasn't surprising. Airboats abounded. But helicopters...

They were uncommon, especially in that area. Not unless someone was looking for something.

But in the middle of the night?

"Jesse, what could it have been?" Julie whispered, as if she had been reading his thoughts.

"I don't know. But I swear, Julie, I will find out."

The casino didn't compare with a place in Las Vegas or Atlantic City—there were no roulette tables and no craps—but it was nice, and it was apparently quite convenient for people in Miami with a free night but not the time to really get away.

It was thriving when they arrived.

The three men tried to encourage Lorena to try her hand at one of the poker tables, but she managed to convince them that she preferred slots and would be happy wandering around, just getting to know the place. There were several restaurants, and though there were tables offering free coffee, she opted for café con leche at the twenty-four-hour deli. She noted the numerous security officers and stopped to chat with one young man. His name was Bob Walker, and he had bright blue eyes, thanks to a dad who had come to the States from the Canary Islands, and superb bone structure, thanks to a Seminole mom. He told her that casino security departments and the Miccosukee Police were two separate entities, but of course they worked together, just as Security would work with the Metro-Dade police or any other law enforcement agency. He'd sounded a little touchy at first, but as they spoke, he explained with a grin, "Too many gamblers drink, lose and get belligerent. And they think we can't take care of them. We do. We have the authority."

She grinned. "I don't intend to get rowdy," she assured him.

He flushed, and she thanked him and went on.

The place was big, and she wandered a while before finding a slot machine that looked like fun. It had a little mouse, and a round where you got points for picking the right cheese. She liked the game—it might be stealing her money, but it was entertaining.

Out twenty bucks, she left to walk around some more.

It was fascinating, she thought. The crowd was truly representative of the area, running the entire ethnic gamut. Miccosukee, Hispanic, Afro-American, and whatever the blend was that ended up as Caucasian on a census form.

She could see the poker tables and was aware that, from their separate poker games, the guys were also keeping an eye on her.

She was frustrated, throwing away quarters when she should have thought of a better lie when she had run into Michael in the hallway. This would have been the perfect time to have gotten into the lab. Still, since the mouse game was diverting, she went back to it. She was just choosing her cheese bonus when she was startled by an already familiar voice.

"What are you doing here?"

She looked up to see Jesse Crane, leaning casually against her machine. It made her uneasy to realize that his scent was provocative, and that he looked even better in his tailored shirt, khakis and sport jacket. When she glanced up, the bright green of his eyes against the bronze of his face was intense. She wouldn't want to face him at an inquiry, that was certain.

She wondered what it was about certain people that made them instantly attractive. About certain *men,* she corrected herself, and the thought was even more disturbing. Michael Preston was definitely good-looking; Hugh was charming; Jack Pine exuded a quiet strength. But Jesse Crane…just the sound of his voice seemed like a sexual stimulant. The least brush of his fingers spoke erotically to her innermost recesses. She was tempted to touch him, because just the feel of crisp fabric over muscled flesh would be arousing.

A blush was rising to her cheeks. She looked away from his eyes, but her gaze fell on his chest. And then below.

She closed her eyes.

"Hello?" he said softly.

What *was* she doing here? She forced herself to focus. To shake off the ridiculous sensation of instant seduction and sensuality.

Nothing, frankly, accomplishing nothing. "Um… gambling," she murmured.

She arched a brow, shrugging as she looked at him

and hit the button on the machine again. "Losing money. What about you?"

He shrugged. "I live in the area."

"So do I, remember?"

"Who did you come with?"

"A group from Harry's."

"And who would that group be?"

"Michael, Jack and Hugh." She stared at the machine, trying not to let him see her mind working. "Are you out for a night on the town? Or just passing through?" Her machine did some binging and banging—three cheeses in a row. She had a return of ten dollars. Not bad.

"Why?" he asked.

"Just curious. Well, actually, if you're heading out…" She yawned, moving away from the machine. "I'm not much of a gambler. I was thinking of going back, but I came with the guys."

"I'll give you a ride," he told her. "Who should we tell you're leaving? Michael?"

"Um…any of them, I guess," she murmured. *Not Michael. He might get suspicious.* "Hugh is right there—we'll just tell him."

She slid off the stool, ready to head for Hugh's poker table.

"Aren't you forgetting something?" Jesse asked.

"What?"

"Your money."

"Oh. I didn't lose it all?"

"No. There's more than a hundred dollars there."

"Oh. Of course I want it," she said.

His eyes seemed to drill right through her. "Do you?"

he inquired lightly. "I didn't think money means a thing to you."

She ignored him and gave her attention to the machine, hitting the "cash out" button.

"You have to wait for an attendant," he told her. "I'll let Hugh know you're leaving."

"Sure. Thanks."

The place was busy, the wait for an attendant long. She was ready to leave her winnings for some lucky stranger, she was so antsy, but she didn't know whether she was being watched. By the time they actually left, she fumed silently, the men might well be right behind them.

Finally, money stuffed into her bag, Lorena hurried past the slots and found Jesse waiting for her at the end of the row.

She quickly checked to make sure that the three men from the alligator farm were still at their tables.

They were.

"Sure you want to go?" Jesse inquired.

"Yes, thank you."

As they turned to leave, he set his palm against the small of her back, nothing more than a polite gesture. Even so, she felt that touch as if she had connected with a live electric current.

Outside, Jesse didn't speak as he politely seated her on the passenger side and slid behind the wheel.

She felt the silence.

"Thanks for taking me back," she said nervously.

"Not a problem."

Again there was silence. Uncomfortable silence. It

should have been a casual drive. It wasn't. It felt as if the air between them was combustible.

"Is our casino a little too tame for you?" he asked at last.

"No. Honestly, I liked it a lot. All I ever play is slots, anyway. I don't understand craps, so it doesn't matter to me if there's a table or not. I guess I'm just not that much of a gambler."

"I'd say you were."

"Pardon?"

He glanced at her sharply. "Oh, you take chances. Racing out here like the wind. Working at Harry's. Going out with three men you've barely met. Especially when there have just been two truly gruesome murders in the area." His tone was amazingly matter-of-fact.

"I hardly think I'm in danger with my co-workers."

He didn't say any more until they had taken the turn into Harry's. She was digging in her purse for the pass that would open the door after hours when he startled her by leaning over and gripping her shoulder. The force was electric, and when she looked at him, she was certain she had guilt written all over her features.

"I really don't understand why you're lying to me. Or what makes you think I'm such a fool that I believe you. What are you doing here?" he demanded roughly.

"Working!"

"You know I'll have you checked out by morning," he said.

She prayed that he couldn't feel the trembling that was suddenly racing through her.

"Go right ahead. Check me out. I'm an RN. You'll find that to be a fact." She reached for the door handle.

"You're playing with fire."

"I'm working. Earning a living."

"Two people, shot. I'd bet everything I have that the killer or killers didn't even know them. It was cold-blooded murder, as cold as it gets."

"Look, I know you're going to check me out. Believe me, you won't find a criminal record. I'm out here to work."

"Right." The green of his eyes was sharp, even in the dim light. "You've come down here to start over, start a new life, that's all."

"May I get out of the car now?"

He released her. The sudden loss of his touch created a chill.

Tell him the truth!

But she couldn't. She had nothing to go on. And he couldn't help, not if she couldn't offer him some kind of proof. And, anyway, could she be certain, absolutely certain, that he wasn't in any way involved?

Actually, yes. Somewhere deep inside, based on instinct, she simply knew the man was completely ethical.

But she didn't dare speak. He would send her packing.

"I'll tell you what you're not," he said softly.

"Oh?"

"A very good liar. So whatever you're up to, God help you."

She stared straight at him. "I am a registered nurse."

"And what else?"

"I dabbled in psychology, but a lot of those classes went toward the nursing degree."

"So you came down here to bandage knees and psychoanalyze the great American alligator?" he inquired dryly. "What else should I know about you?"

"There's this—I'm really tired," she told him.

"And stubborn as hell. You've barely arrived and everything has gone insane. So I'm going to hope that you're not dangerously stupid—or carelessly reckless."

She wondered how he could simply look at her and be able to read everything about her. Or was she that transparent to everyone?

It's just him, she thought with annoyance. Even when he wasn't touching her, it somehow felt as if he was. And even when he grilled her, she was tempted to lean closer to him, to do anything just to touch him, feel a sense of warmth. Even with so much at stake, no matter how she tried to control her mind, it kept running to thoughts of what it would be like just to lie beside him....

"May I get out of the car now?" she asked again, once more feeling drawn to tell him that she actually wanted to stay. Put her head on his shoulders. Tell him the whole truth. But she didn't dare.

"Well, I can't arrest you. At the moment." He turned away from her, shaking his dark head. "Good night, Ms. Fortier. And lock your door," he said.

"I intend to," she assured him, then exited the car as quickly as she could. Her fingers slipped on the little plastic ID entry card. She had to work it three times.

At last the door opened.

Jesse waited until she was inside, then drove away.

When he was gone, she didn't bother heading toward her own room. She walked straight to Michael Preston's lab. With no one around, she surprised herself with her ability to quickly pick the lock.

She knew it was dangerously stupid as she checked the big wall clock over the door, but she didn't stop. The hatchlings began to squeal the minute she entered the room.

Almost as if they sensed prey.

She ignored the sound and started with the desk drawers, then the computer. She knew that she would need a password to access his important files, but she hoped to study his general entries and discover whether he was involved or not.

The clock ticked as she worked. She read and read, keeping an eye on the clock.

Almost an hour since she had left the casino.

Regretfully, she turned off the computer and made a last survey to assure herself she'd left nothing out of order.

Then she left the room, quietly closing the door behind her. She listened for the lock to automatically slip into place.

Just in time. As she hurried down the hall, she heard voices. She quickly turned the corner, out of sight.

"If you're not bright enough to ask that woman out on a real date, I will."

Lorena recognized the voice. It was Hugh.

Michael answered, laughing dryly, "Yeah, well, I kind of thought that she was interested. But she lit out like a bat out of hell once Jesse arrived."

"She's not a poker player. One of us should have stayed with her."

"Is that it?" Michael said dryly. "Women *have* been known to find Jesse appealing."

"Yeah, and then they find out that they're lusting after the unobtainable."

"He won't be grieving forever," Michael said. "And either she went with him because she wanted to, or…"

"Or what?" Hugh demanded sharply.

"Or she wanted to get back here without the three of us."

She heard the rattle of the lab doorknob then. "Locked," he murmured.

"I'm asking her out," Hugh said. "For an airboat ride. That's innocent enough."

"Hey, every man for himself, huh?" Michael said.

Hugh laughed. "Yep, every man for himself."

She heard the lab door open and shut. Not knowing if Hugh had joined Michael or would be heading on down the hallway, Lorena fled.

As soon as she reached her own room, she thought of Jesse's warning and made sure her own door was locked.

Then she dragged a chair in front of it, wedging it tightly beneath the knob.

Still, it was a long time before she slept.

Jesse sat outside the alligator farm complex, watching.

He'd left, parked on the embankment, and waited.

Once he'd seen Preston's car return, he'd counted the seconds carefully, then slipped his car back into gear to follow.

Just in the shadows, off the drive near the main entrance, he parked.

He spent the night in the car, his senses on alert.

The grunts of the gators, loud in the night, sounded now and then, sometimes just one or two, sometimes a cacophony.

Strange creatures. He'd been around them all his life. They were an amazing species, having survived longer than almost any other creature to have walked the earth.

Their calls and cries could be eerie, though.

He stayed until daybreak, waiting, though for what, he wasn't certain. Something. Some sign of danger.

Dawn broke. Light came softly, filling the horizon with pastels. There was a breeze. Birds cried and soared overhead.

He began to feel like a fool.

Then he heard the scream.

Chapter 6

Lorena bolted out of the bed, stunned and disoriented. The first sharp, staccato shriek that had awakened her had been followed by other screams and cries.

She threw on a robe and went flying out of her room, down the hall, and then burst out back to the ponds, the area from which the sounds of distress were still coming.

Then she heard the distant sound of sirens.

It was far too early for the gates to have opened to tourists, and she couldn't imagine what had happened. Her heart was thundering as she saw that most of the employees had gathered around the deep trench pond where Old Elijah was kept.

The biggest, meanest alligator in the place.

At first she stood on the periphery of the crowd, trying to ascertain what had happened, listening to the shouts that rose around her.

"How in hell did *he* fall in?" one of the waitresses asked, incredulous.

"Roger has been a guard here from the beginning… what would make him lean far enough over to fall in?" asked one of the ticket-takers.

"Jesse's in there now. He'll get him out," a feminine voice said.

Lorena swung around to see that Sally Dickerson was there, threading her fingers through her long red hair. She turned to stare at Lorena. Where everyone else seemed to have eyes filled with concern, Sally's had a gleam. She was enjoying the excitement.

"What?" Lorena said.

"Jesse's gone in. He'll get Roger out."

Lorena wasn't sure who she pushed out of the way then, but she rushed to the concrete rim of the great dipped pond and natural habitat that held Old Elijah.

There was a man on the ground, next to the concrete wall. Jack Pine and Hugh Humphrey were there at the side of the wall, maneuvering some kind of rope-rigged gurney down to the fallen guard, who was apparently unconscious.

There was Jesse.

And there was Old Elijah.

The way the habitat was set up, there was the concrete wall and rim, a pond area, and then a re-creation of a wetland hummock.

The great alligator had so far remained on the other side of the water. He watched with ancient black eyes as Jesse Crane moved with care to manipulate the body of the fallen guard with the greatest care possible onto the gurney.

Jesse was no fool. He kept his eye on the alligator the whole time.

"Where the hell is Harry with that tranq gun?" Jack demanded hoarsely.

"Got him!" Jesse shouted. "Haul him up, haul him up!"

Tense, giving directions to one another as they brought up the gurney, the men were careful to raise it without unbalancing the unconscious figure held in place by buckled straps. Jesse helped guide the gurney until it was over his head.

And all the time, Old Elijah watched.

Motionless, still as death, only the eyes alive.

Others jumped in to help as the gurney rose. Jesse reached for the rope ladder that he'd come down and started up.

And then Old Elijah moved.

He was like a bullet, a streak of lightning. Someone screamed.

The massive jaws opened.

They snapped shut.

They caught the tail end of the rope ladder, and the great head of the beast began to thrash back and forth.

Jesse, nearing the top, teetered dangerously. A collective cry rose; then he caught the rim of the concrete barrier and hauled himself over.

At the same time, they heard the whistle of a shot.

Harry had arrived, holding a huge tranquilizer gun on his shoulder.

The dart struck Old Elijah on the shoulder.

At first, it was as if a fly had landed on his back, nothing more.

The gator backed away, drawing the remnants of the rope ladder with him. Then, as if he were some type of blow-up toy with the air seeping from him, Old Elijah fell. The eyes that had blazed with such an ancient predatory fervor went blank.

The crowd was cheering Jesse; med techs were racing up, and more officers had arrived to control the space and let the emergency techs work.

Jack slammed a hand on Jesse's shoulder. Hugh shook his head and fell back against the barrier, relieved.

Jesse looked down into the enclosure, shaking his head as he stared at Old Elijah. Then his gaze rose, almost instinctively, and met Lorena's.

She stared back, oddly frightened to see the way his eyes narrowed as he regarded her, filled with suspicion. His mouth was hard. She flushed; he didn't look away.

Someone caught his attention, and he turned.

"Damn, Harry, it took you long enough to get that gun," Jack called, shaking his head.

"Jack Pine, you're the damned handler, so get a handle on what happened here," Harry shouted back.

"Calm down. We're going to have an inquiry," Jesse said.

"Inquiry?" Harry snorted. "Roger was out here by himself. What the fool was doing leaning over the concrete, I don't know. We'll just have to wait until he's regained consciousness to find out."

"Yeah, *if* he regains consciousness," Jack snorted.

He was tense, and his features were hard as he stared at Harry.

"Hell of a thing—" Harry began, and then realized that he had an audience, more than a dozen employees hanging around. He stopped speaking and shook his head again. "This show's over, folks. Back to work, everybody back to work." Then he turned to Jesse. "Hell, Jesse, what kind of questions could anybody have?"

"That will come later. I'm getting in the ambulance copter with Roger," Jesse said, brushing past Harry.

He stared at Lorena again then. His features remained taut and grim, and his eyes now held...

A warning?

He hesitated, speaking to a couple of officers who had arrived along with the med techs, then hurried after the stretcher.

A man in one of the Miccosukee force uniforms spoke up, his voice calm and reassuring, yet filled with authority. "Go ahead, folks, get going. We'll be speaking with you all one by one."

The crowd slowly began to disperse. Harry was complaining to the officer. "I don't get it. What could your questions be? For some fool reason, Roger got stupid and leaned too far over the barrier. No one else was out here. Security was his job."

"Harry, we have to ask questions," the officer said. "Hey, if there were an outsider in here, giving Roger or anyone a problem, you'd want to know, right?"

"Well, yeah," Harry said, as if the idea had just occurred to him. "You boys go right ahead. Question everyone. Damned right, I'd want to know."

He turned to walk away, then saw that several of his employees hadn't left.

"Get going, folks. It's a workday, and this isn't a charity. So get to work. And everyone, give these officers your fullest cooperation." Then he walked away himself, followed by one of the officers.

Lorena nearly jumped a mile when she felt a hand on her shoulder. She swung around. Michael was there, looking sleepy, concerned but foggy, also clad in a robe.

"What the hell happened?"

She explained.

He shook his head. "Well, that's about as weird as it gets. Roger has been here forever. He should have known better."

"Would that alligator… Old Elijah…would he have eaten the man, do you think?" Lorena queried softly.

"He's really well fed, so…who knows," Michael said. "Eaten him? Maybe. More likely he just would have gotten angry, taken a bite, tossed him around, drowned him. Who knows. I don't question Old Elijah. There's only one thing I can say with certainty about alligators."

"And that is?"

Michael's eyes met hers directly. "That you'll never really know anything about them," he said flatly. "You'll never know what goes on behind the evil in those eyes."

Jesse sat in the back of the emergency helicopter, doing his best to keep out of the way of the men desperately working to save Roger's life. He didn't need to ask questions, not that they would be heard above the roar of the blades, not from where he sat. A glance at the med tech who had taken the man's vitals and affixed his IV line told him that Roger had not regained consciousness.

As soon as they reached the hospital, Jesse paced the emergency room waiting lounge. Hell of a place. He knew the hospital was good; one of the best in the nation for trauma. But it was also the place where those without insurance came for help, and the place was thick with the ill, the injured and those who had brought them.

He wasn't the only law enforcement officer there. As he waited, two drug overdoses and a man with a knife in his back were rushed in, escorted by cops. Strange place, he thought. Stranger here, in the heart of the city, than out in the Glades. The wealth to be found in the area was astounding; movie stars, rock stars and celebrities of all kinds had multimillion-dollar mansions out on the islands, in the Gables and scattered throughout the county. At the same time, refugees from Central and South America abounded, many who slept under bridges, or lived in the crack houses that could be found not so far from the million-dollar mansions.

At length, one of the doctors came out. "Well, we've got him stabilized. But he's in a coma. He's not going to be talking."

"Will he come out of it?" Jesse asked.

"I don't know," the doctor told him honestly.

Jesse nodded, and handed the doctor his business card.

"I'll call you first thing, and I mean first thing, if there's any change at all," the doctor promised.

Jesse thanked him. There was a Florida Highway Patrol officer in the waiting room who had just finished with an accident victim. He offered to drive Jesse back. It was a long way, and Jesse thanked him for the offer.

"Heard you've been having some bad business around here," the officer, Tom Hennesy, said as they drove. "Anything new on those shootings?"

"No. Metro-Dade Homicide is handling that case, though."

Hennesy nodded. "You had a fatal gator attack, too."

Jesse nodded.

"Strange, huh?" Hennesy said. "Usually that kind of thing only happens when someone wanders into the wrong place." He shrugged. "Of course, the 'wrong' place is getting harder to avoid these days, what with developers eating up the Everglades. Still, it's usually only the big gators that will attack an adult. It's usually toddlers. Or pets." He cast a sideways glance at Jesse and flushed slightly. "I was reading up after the attack the other day. Since 1948, there have been fewer than 350 attacks on humans in this state, and the number of fatal attacks is only in the teens." He laughed. "I remember when the creatures were endangered, and when the first alligator farm opened in 1985. My uncle used to come out to the Glades, sit in a cabin and drink beer, and go out and hunt gators—till they made the endangered list. And now…my wife wanted to move close to the water. Now, after the latest incident, she wants to move out of state and up into the mountains somewhere."

Jesse smiled at the man, offering what he hoped was polite empathy.

"Hell, you're down here all the time," Hennesy said. "Think about it. How many attacks have you seen?"

Jesse looked at him. "Well, my uncle Pete lost a

thumb, but he was one of the best wrestlers the village down there ever had. He was proud of it, actually. I don't think you can call that an attack, though."

When they at last reached the alligator farm, Jesse was disturbed to realize that more than half the day was gone.

The place was full of tourists, as if nothing had happened. A discreet inquiry assured him that Lorena was busy, helping out with Michael Preston's hatchling speeches.

He took a glance into the lab and saw that there were at least twenty people on the current tour. Lorena didn't see him. He watched her, watched the way she smiled, seemingly at ease. But in reality she was moving around the lab looking for something, he realized. She was subtle, leaning against a cabinet, a desk, casually assessing the contents, but she was definitely searching for something.

He was tempted to shout at her. *Stupid!*

Was she stupid, or dangerously reckless? Why? What was driving her?

A little while later, when he drove away from the farm, he realized that he'd been afraid to leave, afraid to head home for a shower. He was tired as hell, but the shower was necessary. Sleep would have to wait.

Lorena heard that Jesse had returned to Harry's. That he had spoken with a number of people.

Just not her.

The next morning she met Thorne Thiessen, the veterinarian. He had come to take a look at Old Elijah.

He was a distinguished-looking man, weather-worn,

with a pleasant disposition, very tall, very fit. He had his assistant with him, a huge guy named John Smith. They both looked like extremely powerful men, in exceptional shape.

Maybe that was a requirement for survival in the swamp. Or else something in the genetics of the men in the area.

Watching Thiessen examine Old Elijah had been a real education. They had pulled out a lot of equipment—Elijah was one big beast—and they had snared him, something that had taken Jack Pine, Hugh, John Smith and two part-time wranglers to manage. The gator had thrashed, even when caught, and sent several of the handlers flying. Between them, however, they got the creature still, with Jack making the leap to the animal's back, shutting the great jaw and taping it closed.

Only then did Thiessen go into the pit. He took blood samples, checked the crocodilian's eyes, did some kind of a temperature reading and checked out his hide.

Despite the time she'd spent in school, Lorena really didn't know how the vet was determining if the ancient creature was in good health or not. Personally, she thought that the way he had been able to toss grown men around as if they were weightless seemed to prove that he was doing okay.

Jesse showed up right when Thiessen was leaving. Lorena, who had been watching from the pit area, did her best to eavesdrop. The men greeted each other cordially enough, but then Jesse pressed the vet, who in turn became defensive.

"I'm working on it, Jesse. But come on, Homicide doesn't see any connection between the alligator limb and the murders. Something ate the rest of the thing, that's all. Poachers don't kill people with high-powered rifles."

Jesse shrugged. "I can see where this may not be at the top of your priority list, but it *is* high on mine. If you don't want to deal with the responsibility, I can just take it to the FBI lab."

Thorne frowned, even more indignant. "No one knows reptiles the way that I do!"

"That's why I brought the specimen to you. Another day or so, Thorne, then I'm going to have to go for second best."

As he finished speaking, Lorena realized that he'd noticed she was there. She had forgotten to eavesdrop discreetly.

But there were others around, too. Jack and Hugh were speaking together, just a few feet away. Sally was standing politely to the rear, obviously waiting for a chance to have a word with Jesse.

Even Harry was still by the pit, calling out orders to the two wary part-time handlers, who had been left to free Old Elijah from the tape on his snout.

Michael Preston was there, too, sipping coffee with a thoughtful frown as he watched all the activity.

Jesse, however, was gazing thoughtfully at *her*.

"Ms. Fortier," he murmured. "I need to see you later," he said.

He turned to leave. Sally tapped him on the arm, asking a question that Lorena couldn't hear. As Jesse walked away, Sally was still at his side.

"Hey!" Harry called. "Doors are opening."

Lorena realized that although she was always distracted when she brought visitors through Michael's lab, she actually enjoyed his talks. He had a nice flair for the dramatic. That morning, though, she felt the frustration of not being able to find anything out of the ordinary. Except for the eggs with the cracked shells. That was where changes—or *enhancements*—might take place. But they were out in the open. Part of the show.

In the afternoon, she watched as Jack and Hugh both put on their own demonstrations. Jack wrestled a six-foot gator to the amusement of the crowd. Hugh brought out gators in various stages of growth, thrilling the children, who were allowed to touch the animals. After the last show, Hugh approached her.

"How about an airboat ride? See some of the scenery up close and personal?" he suggested, his grin charming and hopeful.

She agreed, and soon, they were out in the Glades. She had been afraid, at first, when it had looked as if they were trying to take off over solid ground. But it wasn't ground at all.

The river of grass. That was what it was and exactly the way it looked. As they traveled, Hugh educated her about their environs, shouting to be heard over the motor. The Everglades really wasn't a swamp but a constantly moving river; it was simply that the rate at which the water moved was so slow that it wasn't discernible to the naked eye.

Hugh obviously loved the area. Before they started out, he had explained that he was an Aussie, would always be an Aussie at heart, but that he had come to love this place as home.

Trees on hummocks seemed to rush by with tremendous speed. Ahead of them, brilliantly colored birds, large and small, burst out of the water and into the sky. At last Hugh cut the motor, and the airboat came to rest in the middle of what seemed like a strange and forgotten expanse of endless water, space and humid heat.

"So how do you like the airboat?" Hugh asked. He had a cooler in the rear of the boat and edged around carefully to open it. He produced two bottles of beer.

She accepted one.

"The feel of the wind is great," she told him.

He took a seat again, grinning as he looked at her. "You like it out here?"

"It's strange. A bit to get used to. But yes. I don't think I've ever seen more magnificent birds. Not even in a zoo."

"Around the early 1900s, some of them were hunted into extinction. Their feathers were needed for every stylish hat," Hugh said, leaning back. "But they *are* fabulous, aren't they?"

She nodded. "So, Hugh, were you a croc hunter back home in the Outback?"

He laughed. "Actually, I was born and raised in Sydney, but I always wanted to find out about the wilds. We've got some beautiful country at home, but there's just something here…the loneliness, the trees, the birds, the… I don't know. Some people simply fall in love with the land. Despite the SST-size mosquitoes, the venomous snakes and the alligators."

"Have you been a handler ever since you got here?" she asked. "I mean, did you ever help with the research side of things?"

He laughed. "Research?" He shook his head. "I know enough about gators without that. I know when they mate, know that a mother gator is one of the fiercest creatures known to man. And I know about the jaws, and that's what counts."

He sat back easily, adjusting his hat. He was attentive and clearly glad to be with her. In fact, he really seemed like a nice guy.

And he knew nothing about research.

Or so he claimed.

But here they were, in the middle of nowhere, and if he had wanted to cause her any harm…

"Damn!" he said suddenly.

"What?" she asked.

He lifted his beer, indicating something west of them. She peered in that direction, squinting, trying to see what he was seeing.

She realized that there was an embankment, and that they were in a canal. Trees grew at the water's edge, and it seemed that there was a small hummock in the direction he was pointing.

Limbs were down here and there, no doubt a result of the early summer rainstorms she had heard came frequently here.

"There… They really are amazing creatures. They blend perfectly with their environment," Hugh said, his voice a whisper touched with awe. "See him?"

Suddenly she did. Just the eyes and a hint of the nose were visible above the water. And then, way behind the head, she could see the slight rise of the back.

"He's huge!" Hugh continued softly. "I've never seen one that big. I've never even seen a croc that big."

"How can you tell his size?" she asked, whispering, too, though she didn't know why. Actually, she did, she realized. She didn't want to attract the creature's attention.

"Well," Hugh said, "if you look at the water—"

"The water looks black," she protested.

He laughed softly. "It's not the water, it's the vegetation. But look closely. You can see the length of the body. We're talking huge. Maybe twenty-something feet."

"They don't get that big here!" she heard herself protest.

As they watched, the alligator suddenly submerged. Lorena felt a sharp stab of fear, sudden and primitive. She was certain that the creature was coming for them.

The airboat was small and built for two, with both seats at the rear. The nose of the vehicle offered only a small bit of space for supplies. The boat was fairly flat-bottomed, and it would be hard to knock over, but...

How much could a creature like that weigh?

"Man, I would have liked to see him up close," Hugh marveled.

Lorena couldn't speak. She was certain that Hugh was going to get his wish, that the gator would be there, beneath them, in a matter of seconds.

Frowning, Hugh rose. Despite the rocking of the airboat, he moved easily and confidently. She was about to scream to him to sit down, that he needed his gun, that...

She heard it then. The motor of another airboat.

Just then something brushed by their boat. Just touching it. Nosing it.

Testing it?

Then the other airboat came into the picture, whipping over the water. It was a much larger vehicle, with the motor and giant fan far in the rear, and with more storage space and six seats in front of the helm. She noticed that it bore a tribal insignia.

Then she saw Jesse.

She released a long breath, aware that she wasn't afraid anymore, that even his airboat seemed to shout of authority.

The creature had disappeared; it was no longer touching their airboat.

"Hey!" Jesse shouted, cutting his motor as his vehicle drew next to theirs.

"Hey, Jesse," Hugh said dryly. It was apparent that his romantic plans had just been shattered.

"What are you two doing out here?" Jesse asked with a frown.

Hugh cocked his head, his hands on his hips. "I asked the lady out, and she agreed."

Jesse looked impatient. "Hugh, I don't know how you missed my notice. We've got a man-eater out here. We're going to get a group of hunting guides out here and go after it. The medical examiner says that Billy Ray was bushwhacked by one big son of a bitch. We're going after it. It's not safe out here right now."

Hugh snorted. "Jesse, I've been dealing with gators for half my life. I'm armed, and I can take care of Lorena. I carry more than one big gun."

Jesse shook his head. "Hugh, you're one of the best. But Billy Ray knew alligators, too. Take your airboat on back. Lorena, step over here."

"Now, wait a minute!" Hugh protested. "Lorena is with me."

"She's coming in for questioning," Jesse said.

"What?" she and Hugh asked simultaneously.

Those startling green eyes leveled upon her hard. "Lorena needs to answer some questions about an incident at the alligator farm the other day."

"Jesse, you are crazy—" Lorena began.

"I can put the cuffs on you," he assured her.

"What the hell are you talking about?" Hugh demanded.

Jesse leveled his eyes on Lorena as he answered Hugh's question. "Something to do with a little kid getting a bite. I'm sure Harry wants it kept quiet. Therefore, I need a few answers."

Hugh frowned, staring at Lorena. "You don't have to go with him. What are you trying to pull here, Jesse Crane?" Hugh demanded.

"I think that Lorena wants to come with me," Jesse said, staring at her meaningfully.

Her skin prickled. It wasn't with the kind of panic she had felt when she believed that a monster gator was stalking her, but with an overwhelming sense of unease. *He knew.*

And maybe he was giving her a chance to talk to him before he blew the whistle on her.

She sighed, rising. The boat rocked.

"There was a bit of a problem with one of the children the other morning, Hugh. Easily taken care of. I'll just go with Jesse now," she said smoothly.

Panic seized her once again when she was ready to step from boat to boat. Where had the gator gone?

Whatever ruffled male feathers had begun to fly, the situation was suddenly eased as Hugh, holding her arm as she moved to join Jesse, said, "I think we just saw your alligator."

"Here?" Jesse asked.

There was about a foot and a half of empty space between the boats as they rocked gently in the water. Lorena looked down.

Her heart slammed into her throat.

There it was. Submerged, and moving in fluid silence, just beneath the surface.

She nearly threw herself into Jesse's arms.

"There!" she said. "Underneath us."

He frowned at her, dark brows drawn, eyes narrowed. He forced her into a seat and strode back to the edge of the airboat. "Where? Hugh, you see it?"

Hugh was also searching the water. He had a shotgun in the back of the airboat. He reached for it and stood still, watching.

Time passed.

It felt like an eternity to Lorena, who heard the drone of a mosquito but was afraid to move, too frozen even to swat at the creature.

At last Jesse sighed.

"It might have been here, but I don't see it now," he said. "But this might well be its territory, so we'll start here tomorrow."

"Sunset?" Hugh asked.

"Right before. You gonna join us?"

"Yeah," Hugh said. "I travel around here all the time, though. I haven't seen that gator before."

"What was left of Billy Ray's body was tangled in

the trees not too far from here. You know, right around the bend, where he had his favorite fishing spot. Yes, this is its territory. I'll pick you up at Harry's, six o'clock sharp tomorrow evening."

Jesse started up his motor.

The sound was like the sudden whirr of a thousand birds, rising from the swamp.

She gripped her chair, still feeling cold. Hugh waved.

She couldn't wave back.

The wind lashed around her, whipping her hair around her face. She closed her eyes.

She was startled when the motor died, along with the forward motion of the boat.

She opened her eyes. They still seemed to be in the middle of nowhere.

There was a hummock where they had come to rest, land that wasn't covered in the deceptive saw grass that grew where the water ran, making a person believe that there was terra firma beneath.

And yet in all directions, she still saw only wilderness.

There was no sound, except for the cries of birds, the rustle of foliage.

She swallowed, frowned, and stared at Jesse uneasily.

"Where are we?"

"My place," he said. "And you can talk to me here, tell me the truth, or we'll just head downtown, to the FBI office. Here's your chance, Lorena. Truth or dare. What do you know, and what the hell are you really doing here?"

Chapter 7

Despite the fact that there was a well-maintained dock, Jesse could see that Lorena was more than a bit concerned about where they were going when he helped her out of the airboat.

His house had been built on a hummock and, he thought, combined the best of tradition and the modern world. There were still members of his tribe who made their homes in chickees, but for the most part, beyond the village and the other tourist stops, tribal members lived in normal houses, concrete block and stucco, sturdy structures that offered the same comforts as those enjoyed by everyone else.

He was lucky to own the land, which had been his father's. And it was a good stretch of hummock, rich with trees and foliage, and high enough to keep it from flooding during hurricanes or the rainy season. As they came in from the rear, winding along the path from the canal, the first sight was a chickee. Chickees had first come into being when various tribes—once grouped together under the term "Seminoles"—had moved deep into the Everglades to escape persecution and the white determination to export every last Native American to the western reservations. High above the ground, the chickee offered protection from snakes and gators. The open sides allowed the breezes to pass through continually, keeping the inhabitants cool year round.

Lorena gave the chickee a nervous glance, and he saw the relief on her face when they rounded a bend and she saw the house.

There was a screened-in patio with a pool, and sliding glass doors that led from it into the house. He owned a fairly typical ranch-style dwelling, with the large rear, "Florida room" extending the width of the back. He had a good entertainment center and comfortable sofas and chairs, which often led to him being the one to host Sunday football get-togethers. His home probably differed from some in that it was filled with Indian artifacts: Miccosukee, Seminole and others, including South American and Inuit. He had totem poles, lances, spears, shields and buffalo skulls, all artistically—at least in his mind—arranged, and he had come to love the feeling that he was surrounded by both past and present, tradition and the need for all Americans to be aware of the modern world. He considered education the most necessary tool for any Native American, and finding the path between prosperity and ethnicity was not an easy one.

"Thank God for bingo," he murmured aloud.

"What?"

Her eyes were wide; he could tell that she was decidedly uncomfortable, yet apparently relieved at the same time.

"Coffee? Tea? Soda? Beer or wine?" he asked. "Sorry, that's all I keep around." He left her standing in the Florida room and walked through the hall, hanging a quick left into the kitchen, where a bypass over the counter opened to allow him to keep an eye on her.

She shook her head uneasily. "I'm fine."

"Then I'll have coffee."

He reached into the cupboards for the paraphernalia he needed, watching her as he did so.

Some of the trepidation in her face had eased. She was walking around, studying the various pieces on the walls. She turned suddenly, as if feeling him watching her.

"Have you always lived here?" she asked, trying to sound casual.

"In the general area, yes. This house is new, though."

"Ah."

"And, let's see…you were raised in Jacksonville. Attended the University of Florida. Where you did indeed earn a nursing degree."

"Yes," she murmured, looking away.

"And a law degree."

Her eyes flew to his again. Belligerent, defensive.

"All right, so I've spent the last few years with a law firm. My nursing credentials are still good. You seem to know everything, so you must know that, too."

"I do," he assured her grimly. "Sure you don't want a cup of coffee?"

"All right," she murmured.

She walked around to join him in the kitchen. He wondered how she could have spent the late afternoon in an airboat in the swamp and still manage to retain such an alluring scent.

"Sugar...cream," he said, indicating the containers.

She added a touch of cream to her cup, not looking at him. Her fingers were shaking as she stirred, but she quickly returned to the Florida room, taking a seat on one of the sofas that looked out over the pool.

"All right," he said, taking a seat next to her. "We need to start communicating here. This is serious. Shall I continue, or do you just want to talk to me?"

"You're going to try to get me out of here," she said, not looking at him. Then her eyes shot to his. "And I'm not inept. Actually, I'm a crack shot."

"Your life seems filled with accomplishments," he said with obvious irony.

She blushed, looking away. "I thought I wanted to go into nursing...but then I wound up taking some legal courses related to medical ethics and I found out that I liked the law. I was able to work part-time in a hospital while I went back to college. I was lucky. My dad was associated with a firm that was known for going to bat for the underdog. They hired me right out of law school."

"Which has nothing to do with why you're here," he said softly.

"Actually, in a way it does," she murmured, staring down again. Then she looked up at him. "One thing about studying the law is that you learn you need proof to go to court."

He shook his head, looking at her, then taking the cup from her and setting it on the coffee table. He took both her hands. "All right, here's the rest of what I know. You're going under the name Fortier because that was your mother's maiden name. Your father was Dr. Eugene Duval, working for Eco-smart, a company that, among other facilities, ran an alligator farm. He died last year after a fall down a stairway. So why does that bring you here?"

She shook her head. "He didn't fall."

"Lorena, I've read the police reports. He was alone in the building at the time."

"No. He did *not* just fall."

Jesse sighed, squeezing her hands. "Lorena, I know what it's like to desperately seek something behind the obvious. Your father fell down a stairway. He broke his neck."

"No," she said stubbornly.

"Why are you so convinced it wasn't an accident?"

"Because he had something. Something that his killer wanted."

"And that was?" Jesse persisted.

She hesitated, realizing that he didn't know everything.

He squeezed her hands more tightly. The lingering scent of her cologne wafted around him, seemed to permeate his system. He realized that his own heart was pounding, that the blood was rushing in a hot wave through his system. He was torn between the desire to gently touch her face and the equally strong desire to draw her into his arms, shake her, tell her none of this was worth her life.

He desperately wanted to hold her. And more. The texture of her skin was suddenly so fascinating that he longed to explore it with the tips of his fingers. Her features were so delicate, elegant and determined that he was tempted to test them with the palm of his hand.

He fought the desire that had begun to build in his system the first time he had seen her. She was angry, lost, determined...and trusting. He knew he should pull his hands away. He didn't. He couldn't. He had to get answers from her—now.

"Lorena, what did your father have?" he demanded.

She stared back at him, clenching her teeth; then she shook her head. "You mean you don't know? It's obvious. He had a formula."

"A formula for what?"

"Well, basically, steroids," she said flatly. "There were other ingredients, but the formula was based on steroids." She inhaled, exhaled, looking away but not drawing away. "My father was a great man. He wanted to feed the world. He worked with all kinds of animals, trying to find a way to improve the amount and quality of their meat without creating the chemical dangers you so often find in farmed meats. He saw alligators as the wave of the future. A creature that had been endangered—nearly wiped off the face of the earth—then raised in captivity to return with a vengeance. In his mind, we were going to be looking to a number of basically new food sources, new to the American public, at least. Emu. Beefalo. Different fish. Eels. And alligators. He thought they were magnificent creatures, with hides that could be used for all kinds of things and meat that could be improved in taste, quality and quantity.

So he began working on a formula. Now he's dead and someone else has it—and I think Harry's place may be involved."

Jesse stared at her blankly, wondering why something like this hadn't occurred to him. *Because it was right out of a science fiction novel, that was why.*

"Lots of people work with alligators," he said, his tone sharper than he had intended. "Lots of scientists work with formulas to improve breeding and supply."

"Maybe, but my father had found one that improved the creatures' size to such an extent that…that he destroyed his own specimens."

Jesse felt frozen for a moment. It was all beginning to make sense. Too much sense. He was accustomed to drug-related crimes in the Everglades, or illegal immigrants, and the big money and guns that came with both. He knew the tragedy of greed, gangs, and the jealousy and fury behind domestic violence, and the tribulations brought on by the abuse of alcohol. And now industrial espionage might well be exactly what they were looking for. *A formula that was dangerous, but that could take a business to the top of the heap?* It made way too much sense. A couple killed for what appeared to be nothing had probably seen something they shouldn't see. A man who knew the Glades like the back of his hand, dead, killed by an alligator. But what kind of an alligator? Perhaps one scientifically induced to grow bigger—and more dangerous?

"All right, your father was working on a formula, but he's been dead for more than a year. There are all kinds of establishments working with alligators, all through

Florida, Georgia, Texas and more. What brought you here?" he asked.

She hesitated. "I finally cleaned out all my dad's business communications. An old e-mail I found from Harry's Alligator Farm and Museum seemed to point in this direction."

"Was Harry Rogers ever in Jacksonville? Did he know your father?"

She shook her head. "Not that I know of."

"I assume your father communicated with a lot of other institutions."

"Yes, but…none of the others were…well, located in such a wilderness. A place where it's possible to hide so much."

"Exactly what did the e-mail say, and who was it from?"

"I don't know. It wasn't signed. It was just a query, but there was something off about it. Something greedy. My father wrote back that he couldn't help."

"Then…?"

"It came right after there had been an article about my dad that mentioned the kind of research he was doing. So I came here, and…that couple got killed, and you found a piece of an alligator there, and then that poor man was…eaten."

"Still…"

"Jesse, I'm telling you, there was nothing else to go on, nothing."

"What about the other employees where your dad worked? What did they say?"

She shook her head in disgust. "According to every-one, my father had destroyed his research, the formula and his specimens. He worked for a very aboveboard corporation. When he said his research had taken a dangerous turn, they gave him the freedom to start over. So now they're all sorry, and they all understand that I'm upset. But as far as they're concerned, it was an accident."

She stared at him, then grasped his hands. "But it *wasn't* an accident. I know it. Harry—or someone here—got my father's formula, and they killed him to do it. You have to believe me! And now they've lost a few of their specimens, and those gators are running around the Glades killing people. They're trying to track them down, but they don't want to get caught, and I think that's why your friends were killed. Whoever was out there picking up the specimen decided that Hector and Maria had seen too much. But what really scares me is that I think they're still trying to use the formula. Jesse, please, think about it. You said that Hector and Maria were wonderful people, that they couldn't have been drug-running. So you have to go to the next conclusion—that they were killed for something they saw, for what they might know. Come on! Why else would anyone kill your friends? They were shot because they saw the alligator. And the killers dared to murder them because they knew everyone would just assume it had something to do with drugs. Jesse, I'm right, and you know it."

He drew away from her at last, then stood and walked to the glass doors, looking out at the pool and the deep, rich green of the hummock beyond, not seeing. "Lorena, your dad has been dead more than a year, right?" he said softly.

"Right."

"And his research went back several years. But alligators, even pampered hatchlings, only grow about a foot a year. To get a creature big enough to kill a man would take well over a decade."

"Jesse, you don't understand just what can be done once man starts messing with nature. My father began his studies about five years ago, and with the alterations he could create, a gator could grow as much as four feet in a year. You figure it out. Do the math. See where we'd be right now," she said softly.

"I don't believe it," he said, but he wondered, *Was it possible?*

"You've got to get out of here," he said flatly. "This is about the wildest theory I've heard in my entire life, but if there's any truth in it whatsoever, someone is going to find out who you are. You've got to get away." He spun on her. "And another thing. Why the hell didn't you tell me about this when you arrived down here?"

"Hey! The second time I ever saw you, you were *at* Harry's. Sally told me you come there all the time. How could I know for certain that you weren't involved somehow?"

He sighed, looking down. "I'm a cop, Lorena. And just like I said at the beginning—a real one."

She rose, staring back at him. "And you're going to tell me that there haven't been dirty cops?"

He lifted his hands; then his eyes narrowed, and he strode over to her, taking her by the shoulders, ready to shake her for real. His fingers tensed where he held her, his teeth locked. He fought both his temper and his fears for her. At last he said, "You couldn't tell? You couldn't tell by *getting to know me* that I wasn't crooked?"

She inhaled, staring at him, eyes wide. She parted her lips, ready to speak, but words didn't come. She moistened her lips, ready to speak again, then just shook her head and, to his surprise, leaned it against him.

He wrapped his arms around her. Time ticked away as they stood there and he felt the soft force of her body against his, his own emotions washing through him with the force of a tidal wave. Heat began to fill him. He was torn, ready to rush out and pound his fist into anyone who would so coldly kill and let loose such a danger. But he was a police officer, sworn to uphold the law. He'd been a detective, trained to find out the truth before ripping into something like a maniac.

But he was also simply a man.

And here *she* was, in his arms. She had elicited emotion and longing in him from the first time he had seen the green-and-gold magic in her eyes, heard the tone of her voice. He'd been irritated, angered, enchanted. He'd seen the empathy in her eyes for others, the spark of fire when she was angry.

This wasn't the time.

He had taken her away from Hugh, and Hugh would be angry now, telling the tale to everyone.

And at Harry's, they might be suspicious....

"You can't go back there," he said, and he lifted her chin, his thumb playing over the flesh of her cheek.

Her eyes met his. Her fingers moved down his back, dancing lightly along the length of his spine. "I *have* to go back," she whispered.

"No," he said. And he brought his lips to hers. She

didn't protest or hesitate for a second. It was as if they had both been simmering, awaiting the boiling point, and when they touched at last...

She melted into his arms, breasts and hips fitting neatly into his form. Her fingers threaded into his hair; her mouth tasted of mint and fire.

They broke apart. "I have to..." she said, and her meaning was unclear, because they fused together again, and her hands worked down to his hips, then below, cupping his buttocks, drawing him closer.

At last he caressed her face as he had longed to, exploring texture and shape. Then his fingers fell to the buttons of her shirt, and the fabric obediently parted. His fingers slid along the flesh of her throat, stroked, then careered down the length of her neck. Beneath the cotton of her shirt, he found her bra strap, slipped it away, and his lips dropped to her shoulder, while his fingers continued to disrobe her, baring more flesh for the eager whisper of his tongue. He felt her hands at his belt, then realized his gun was there. He released her long enough to discard his gun belt, then drew her back quickly, fevered, heedless of anything then but the wanting and the heady knowledge that she was just as hungry as he was.

Her skirt and delicate lace bra fell to the floor, and the sleek length of her back was available to be savored by the touch of his fingers, while his lips found the hollows at her collarbone, then moved steadily down, finding her breasts. He felt the quickening of her breath, and that, too, was an aphrodisiac. She was smooth and soft, erotic, hot, vibrant. Her lips and teeth on his shoulders, bathing, biting, aroused him. Her hands, deft and seductive, were at the waistband of his trousers. It was then he realized that, remote as his house might be, the glass panes opened to the glory of the Everglades—and the eyes of anyone who might wander by. He caught her up into his arms, heedless of the clothing they left scattered behind, and strode down the hallway to his bedroom. As he did so, her eyes met his, dazed and mercurial, fascinating, poignant pools. And then her fingers swept back a dark lock of his hair, touching his face as he had so tenderly touched hers.

Night was coming to the Everglades. Coming in hues of crimson and purple, red and gold. The light shone dimly into the room, illuminating them as they fell onto the bed and came together again in a fury of naked flesh. Every little nuance of her seemed to touch and awaken and arouse him. Whispers and soft moans escaped her lips, a siren's song, as he reveled in the discovery of her, the tautness of her abdomen, the length of her legs, the firm fullness of her breasts. And in return…her hands were on him, touching without restraint, fingers no more than a whisper, and then a tease that brought the blood thundering through his veins again, his own breath a drumbeat, the tension in him unbearable.

And yet the anguish was sweet. As if the moment would not come again and had to be cherished, savored. He felt he died a thousand little deaths, not willing to allow it to end, hands upon her everywhere, lips tasting, teasing, giving homage, demanding response. He held himself above her, found her mouth, his tongue thrusting within, gentle at first, then almost angry. Finally he allowed his body to slide slowly against hers as he eased himself lower, again finding the fullness of her breasts, the rose-tipped peaks of her nipples, and below, his tongue stroking a rib, delving into her naval, the lean, low skin of her midriff, then…a kneecap, outer thigh, inner thigh, and the crux of her sex.

He heard the anxious, heady sound of her whispers and moans, protest, encouragement. She writhed against him and into him, and he felt the pulse of her body, until at last he rose above her again and thrust into her, his eyes locked with hers, his soul needing to encompass the length and breadth and being of her with the same searing need that ruled his body. The world rocked in the colors of the sunset, soaring, shooting reds, golds that burned into heart and mind. He moved, and she moved with him, a fit as sweet as it was erotic. Fever seized him, and the rhythm of their union became staccato and desperate. The sounds of their breathing rose to storm pitch, hearts attuned in physical cacophony. Searing lava seemed to rip through his veins, and he fought it, until he felt her surge against him, and then his own climax seized him with violence and majesty.

He moved to her side, and felt the thundering in his chest decrease to a steady beat, the pulse slow, the air move. The colors of sunset faded. Mauve darkness settled over them as she curled against him. He touched her hair in wonder, but his voice rang harsh again when he spoke. "You can't go back there."

The wrong words. She pushed away from him.

"I have to."

"No."

"Jesse…"

"Shh."

"I have to go back. And I have to go back soon."

"Not now."

"They'll know I'm with you."

"It's early."

"But…"

"Shh."

"Jesse, you can work with me or against me," she whispered.

He didn't reply. He was fascinated by the color of her hair against his sheets in the dying light. She went rigid beside him, so he smoothed her hair, then her brow. Then he kissed her forehead, her lips.

And then it began all over again, and this time, when the final thunder came, the black of night had descended fully.

They didn't speak, just held each other for the longest time, her head on his chest, their legs entwined. At last she pushed away from him, rose and found the shower.

He found her there. And in the spray of heat and steam, he found himself exploring anew, touching, tasting, licking tiny water drops from her flesh….

Feeling them licked from his own skin, feeling himself touched, taken, stroked.

Soap upon flesh, flesh upon flesh, a night in which he found he could not be sated, in which he soared, in which he was afraid. And he didn't want it to end, because, when it did…

Eventually they managed an actual shower. The lights on, they moved in silence, finding all the scattered pieces of their clothing. And then, a new cup of coffee in his hand, Jesse told her firmly, "You can't go back."

She was rigid and determined; he could see that immediately. She regally smoothed back a piece of wet hair and said, "I told you, you can work with me and keep me safe, if that's what you feel you have to do. But I *am* going back."

"I can stop you," he told her.

She lifted her chin. "You'd really arrest me?" she demanded. "For what?"

His teeth grated.

"I can tell Harry that you're acting suspiciously. That I think you're dangerous." He lifted his hands in frustration. "Lorena, your being there is pure insanity. You've told me that someone killed your father. An innocent couple was shot down in cold blood. A man was eaten by a gator. If someone at Harry's is involved, that someone is ruthless."

She set her hands on her hips, indignant, eyes narrowing dangerously. "What? I'm a woman, and that means I have to be incompetent?"

"I didn't say that. But I'm not letting you go back there."

"Then you'll never find the killers you're after!" she told him.

He stared back at her, feeling anger rise in him again.

"I need to go back. And I need to go back now. I'm already going to have to think of something to say when everyone wants to know why you detained me."

"I told both you and Hugh that I was going to talk to you about the incident at the farm," he said flatly. He shook his head in disgust. "You're playing a dangerous game. You haven't just entered a pit of vipers, you're asking them to bite."

"What?"

"Oh, come on. You're flirting with the pack of them."

"I went for a ride in an airboat," she said. "So what?" But there was no conviction in her tone.

He stared at her, torn, impotent, and furious because he knew that, on the one hand, she was right.

He had no proof of anything. So…what? Wait until something else terrible happened and hope he was there to save her? Find some reason for a search warrant, a legal way to get into Harry's, and rip the place apart?

"No one was suspicious of me except you," she reminded him. "Honestly, Jesse, I told you I'm a crack shot. I carry a gun, and I'm licensed."

"Great. And do you walk around armed all day?"

She let out a sigh. "Do you really think anyone is going to hurt me in front of dozens of witnesses?"

"Two days," he said.

"What?" she asked him, frowning.

"Two more days. That's what I'll give you. And you have to swear to me that you'll go nowhere alone with any of those men. When it's night, you lock yourself in. When it's morning, you get where you need to be—fast."

"I need to get back into the lab," she said.

"You can do that when I'm there."

She cocked her head to the side, wary. "And we'll manage that how?"

"Easy. I'm around enough."

She hesitated. "Jesse—"

"That's the deal. Take it or leave it." He shook his head angrily. "You toe the line, and I mean it. It's going to be busy as hell right now, too, because I have to arrange hunting parties to find your scientifically mutated alligators—assuming they even exist. Every one of them has to be caught and killed. God knows how many people could die if some super race of huge, aggressive gators starts breeding out there."

"Two days, then," she said softly. "But, Jesse…that's my point, don't you see? I have to find the truth. I have to find out what they know and just how they've altered the alligators, not to mention just how many of them are out there."

"I need enough evidence to get a search warrant, nothing more," he said.

She nodded, then said softly, "I really have to go back now."

"I need a minute to get a few things," he told her.

"For what?"

"For the morning."

"You can't stay out there," she protested.

"Yes, I can."

"They'll know! Someone will definitely get suspicious if you start staying out there."

"No one is going to know."

"And how can that be?"

He smiled grimly. "Because you're going to sneak me into your room at night."

Her breath seemed to catch in her throat as she stared at him.

"Jesse, I've told you, I'm a crack shot."

"So was my wife," he informed her softly.

Then he turned away.

Chapter 8

Harry was beside the canal, looking both anxious and edgy, when they returned in the airboat.

Lorena cast Jesse a quick frown to warn him that they had clearly made the man suspicious.

"What are you two doing out this late at night?" he demanded.

Jesse managed to look a little sheepish as he tied up the airboat and helped Lorena to the embankment. She was surprised that he bothered, and that he could sound so casual as he said, "Just trying to avoid a problem."

"Maybe you want to let me in on it?" Harry said.

"We had a complaint, Harry," Jesse said. "But don't worry, it's all been nipped in the bud."

"What do you mean, don't worry? I thought I owned this place!"

"Just some kid said he'd been bitten by a hatchling.

Turns out, it was the kid's fault. He was trying to steal it," Jesse explained.

"Steal one of my hatchlings?" Harry looked enraged.

"Yep, and that's why the parents have dropped the whole thing. I just needed Lorena's account of the problem. There's nothing to worry about, Harry. I thought it would be a minor thing, and it was. If there had been anything to worry about, naturally I would have spoken with you immediately."

"This could mean a lawsuit," Harry protested.

"It might have, but it isn't going to," Jesse said.

Harry was still glowering. "It's my place. I need to be apprised of everything that happens here."

"Harry, chill. The complaint has been dropped. Lorena told me everything I needed to know. There was no reason to upset you."

Harry stared hard at Lorena. She tried to decide if he looked worried or not. Mostly he just seemed concerned about his place. And angry with Jesse. "You're not doing your job right, Jesse Crane," Harry said angrily. "Cutting corners, kidnapping my nurse."

Lorena was instantly aware that Harry had said the wrong thing. Jesse stiffened, and the look in his eyes turned chilling. "Harry, two good people have been shot to death, a tribal member has been killed by an alligator, and you've got a security guard in the hospital, hovering between life and death. Drop it," he said icily.

Harry backed down, instantly. "I, uh, I just checked on Roger. He's still in a coma," he said gruffly. "You found out anything else on the murders?" he asked.

"No," Jesse said simply. "Nor can I tell you anything else about Billy Ray. But we're going out gator-hunting from here tomorrow evening around six. The office will set things up with the guys who run the licensed hunts. I'll be needing Jack Pine and Hugh. We know we've got a man-eater out there, and it's got to be put down."

"Now you're going to take my handlers?" Harry said incredulously. "Like hell! This is a business."

"And you can do business tomorrow. You'll just be minus a couple of handlers come six o'clock."

"Dammit, Jesse—"

"How many tourists do you think you're going to have if this rogue gator attacks more people?" Jesse demanded.

Harry waved a dismissive hand. "Are you going to need my nurse again, too?" he demanded.

"Hopefully not," Jesse said calmly, not raising his own voice to meet Harry's indignant tone.

"You coming in for dinner?" Harry asked Jesse, clearly changing the subject to avoid an argument.

Jesse glanced at Lorena. "If there's still dinner, might as well," he murmured.

Harry made an unhappy snorting sound, and they walked together toward the main building. As they went, they could hear the bellowing of the alligators in their ponds.

Soon they reached the cafeteria. "I've eaten," Harry said curtly. "You two go on."

Lorena murmured, "Thank you," and stepped in ahead of Jesse.

Sally was seated at one of the tables, with Jack Pine and Hugh.

Hugh rose when he saw them enter.

"Well, that took a while," he said dryly.

"We got to talking, that's all," Jesse said.

Sally set a hand on his arm. "Jesse, how are you doing?" she asked, real concern in her voice.

Jesse frowned at her. "I'm worried," he said flatly.

Jack Pine waved a hand in the air. "Jesse, there may be one big gator out there, but face it, Billy Ray was a drunk. Do we really want to cause a panic out there when for all we know he passed out, fell in the water and drowned, and *then* got eaten by that gator?"

"No panic. Just a hunt," Jesse said.

"Let me get you all some food," Sally said sweetly, flashing a smile at Jesse, then Lorena. "It's late, they're closing down, so I'll just make sure you two get to eat."

"Thanks, Sally," Jesse said, smiling back at her.

Lorena found herself remembering how Sally had talked about Jesse earlier. *Devastated, but not dead!* She felt at a loss for a moment, realizing that she knew so little about him. The night had been strange. Intimacy had been sudden and yet…she felt as if it had been something that, unbeknownst to herself, she had actually been awaiting. But she didn't know anything about whatever might have gone on with him—and Sally?— before she got here. She did know that he'd had a wife, and that she was dead.…

And that she'd been a crack shot.

"Harry teed off about the hunt?" Hugh asked.

Jesse shrugged.

"Harry's all about the bottom line," Jack said. "He doesn't even give a damn about Michael's research. He just wants to please the tourists, grow the gators, harvest the meat and hides."

"Yeah, but if we catch the rogue that killed Billy Ray,

he'll want it on display, don't you think?" Sally said, returning to the table. One of the waiters was behind her, carrying two plates piled with something Lorena couldn't identify.

"Jesse won't be letting Harry have that old gator, will you, Jess?" Jack said.

"Why not?" Harry asked.

"It should go to the village, to the Miccosukee," Jack said flatly.

"Let's catch the thing first," Jesse said.

"Hey...you're not going soft, are you? Thinking it's just a good ol' predator doing what comes naturally, and planning to transplant it somewhere deeper in the Glades?" Hugh asked.

Jesse shook his head. "No. It's dangerous. We have to put it down. There's one thing I'm really hoping, though."

"What's that?" Sally asked.

"That it *is* an 'it.' That we're not searching for more than one really dangerous alligator."

"There's one thing *I'm* wondering," Jack said.

"And what's that?" Lorena asked.

He stared at her. "Where the hell did a bugger that big and vicious come from?"

There was silence at the table. Lorena found herself intensely interested in her meal.

The conversation never really recovered after that.

Jack left the table first, a few minutes later. Then Hugh. Sally didn't seem to want to leave, though.

But finally Jesse stood. "Ladies, I've still got some work to do, so I'll bid you good night."

Sally watched him go, obviously appreciating the view.

Lorena cleared her throat. Sally glanced at her, her eyes sparkling with amusement. "Well, I see that you're coming to enjoy our local…wildlife, shall I say?"

Lorena ignored the other woman's teasing tone. "What happened to his wife?" she asked.

Sally didn't seem to mind dispensing information. "She was a cop, too. Some coked-up prostitute she was trying to help walked up to the back of her car one night and—on the order of her pimp—put a bullet into the back of her head."

Lorena let out a long breath. There was really nothing to say except "Oh."

"She was something, I'll tell you. An heiress determined to make the world better through law enforcement." Sally assessed Lorena carefully. "Don't go getting any ideas. He'll never marry again."

Lorena forced a smile. "Sally, I barely know the man."

"But you know enough, don't you?"

Lorena rose. "Like I said, I barely know the man. Thank you for making sure we could eat."

"He's interested in one thing, and one thing only. So you'd better play like a big girl, if you intend to play."

"Thanks for the advice," Lorena said lightly. "Good night."

As Lorena started walking away, Sally called softly after her, "Be careful."

Lorena spun back around. "Why?"

"Well, hell!" Sally laughed. "Old Billy Ray—eaten.

And Roger... Just goes to show, you can never trust a gator. Believe me, I'm going to be very careful myself."

"Are you suggesting that Roger was helped into that pit?"

"Good God, no! He must have thought he heard something. Then leaned too far over the edge."

"So you think he fell in?" Lorena asked.

"Of course. Who would have pushed him?" Sally demanded.

"Hey, you're the one who warned *me*," Lorena said lightly, then smiled and left.

On her way to her room, she paused at the door to Michael Preston's lab and started to test the knob. Then she heard his voice from inside and stopped, listening. She thought maybe he was on the phone. His voice was low but intense.

She tried desperately to eavesdrop, but she couldn't make out his words. Nothing other than *giant* and *hunt*. There was nothing suspicious about that. By now everyone knew that Billy Ray had been killed by an alligator, a big one, and that it had to be hunted down and destroyed.

Still, she lingered, listening, until the sound of footsteps down the hallway warned her that she'd better get going. Worried that he might eventually have said something useful and now she was going to miss it, she gave up and hurried on to her own room.

Jesse took the airboat back to headquarters and checked in with his staff.

Brenda Hardy was there, doing paperwork. She perched on the edge of Jesse's desk. "I don't care what anyone says. There's more going on here than just some big gator. Billy Ray had a shotgun with him, he could shoot dead drunk. I'd bet cash money you're thinking what I'm thinking. All this happening at one time is too much to be coincidence."

Jesse nodded to her, then excused himself as his cell phone rang. It was Julie.

"Jesse."

"Julie. You all right?"

"Yeah…yeah. You know what I've been doing? Playing bingo out at the casino. I bought about a million cards. You can't think when you're trying to put little dots on a zillion numbers at once."

"Good, Julie. I'm glad. Anything that works for you is what you need to be doing."

"Right, I know. I had to tell you, Jesse. I drove out by the house before, and…and I drove back here as quickly as I could. I didn't go in. I didn't even get out of my car. But I saw the lights. I saw lights…like my mother said. I know why she thought aliens were landing. It was creepy…the way they seemed to come out of the swamp and the sky at the same time."

"Julie, don't go back there. Stay at the casino, stay in the bingo hall, at the machines, or locked in your room, all right? And don't tell anyone you drove by the house."

"All right, Jesse. I just thought you should know."

"I should, and I'm glad you called me. But you have to keep yourself safe. You understand?"

"I will, Jesse. I guess I thought I needed to go back to believe it. But I'll stay away."

"Promise?"

"I swear."

Jesse hung up. As he did, George Osceola walked over to his desk. Jesse looked up.

"You're not going to like this," George warned.

"What?"

"Dr. Thiessen, the vet, just called," George said.

"And?"

"He went back into his office tonight to get some notes. He'd decided to send the specimen and his samples to the FBI lab."

"And?"

When he got there, his night security man slash animal sitter was out cold in the kennel area."

"And let me guess. The alligator specimen and all the tissue and blood samples were gone?" Jesse said.

George nodded. "I'm meeting some of the fellows from the county out there now."

"I've got a drive to make," Jesse said. "Then I'll meet you there."

He got in his car and started speeding along the Trail, only slowing as he neared Julie's parents' house. He turned off his lights before he entered the drive, knowing that, even for him, that was foolhardy, considering the terrain.

He parked on the embankment that bordered the property. The crime tape still hung limply around the house itself and the place where Maria had died. The whole area seemed forlorn, desolate.

Whatever Julie had seen, Jesse realized after about twenty minutes of watching from the front seat, it was gone now. Tomorrow night, if Lars couldn't send a man to keep watch, he would send one of his own men, or even keep watch himself.

He got out of the car, carrying his large flashlight, and walked toward the water. As he reached the wet saw grass area that fell away from the hummock toward the water, he saw that the long razor-edged blades were pushed down. Once again, someone had been through with an airboat. He looked around but didn't see anything else suspicious.

When he got back to his car, he put a call through to Lars Garcia, despite the time. Lars already knew about the break-in at the vet's and was on his way out there.

When Jesse arrived at Doc Thiessen's, he found that the CSI team were already working, dusting for fingerprints, looking for footprints, searching for tire tracks, seeking any small piece of evidence.

Doc Thiessen had been born into a family of fruit-and-vegetable farmers in Homestead. He'd earned his veterinary degree at Florida State University and determined to come back to his own area to work. Now he had a head full of snow-white hair and a gentle, lined face. He worked with domestic as well as farm animals, and was known in several counties for his abilities to help with pet turtles, snakes, lizards, birds and commercial reptiles.

He was standing with Lars and the uniforms who had apparently been first on the scene when Jesse arrived. He shook his head as Jesse approached. "Jesse, I'm damned sorry. I was trying to prepare my samples properly, study them myself… I should have sent them straight out."

Jesse placed a hand on his shoulder. "It's not your fault. You couldn't have known this was going to happen. What about your night man? Jim? Did he see any-thing?"

"He's over there," Lars said, pointing. "Go on. I've already spoken with him."

Doc's night guard was a man named Jim Hidalgo, half Peruvian, half Miccosukee. He and Jesse were distantly related. They shook hands, and Jim looked at him, wincing. "Jesse, I didn't even see it coming. We've got a few dogs in the kennels, you know, belonging to folks on vacation. I heard something, went to check on the pups. One little beagle was going wild, and I walked over to it and…that's the last thing I remember until Doc was standing over me, taking my pulse."

"Thanks, Jim." The man had a bump the size of Kansas on the back of his head. Jesse stared at it and whistled softly. "You're lucky you're alive."

"They're insisting I go to the hospital," Jim said.

"Yeah, well…that's quite a bump. Let them keep an eye on you, at least overnight."

Jim sighed. "All right. If you say so."

Jesse walked back to Lars, who was waiting for him. He told him about Julie's call and his trip out to the house.

"I had officers out there last night," Lars said with a sigh. "It's just that the department only stretches so far. But I'll send some men out again, twenty-four-hour watch. Anything else? You find your rogue gator?"

"Not yet. We're doing an organized hunt tomorrow night." He hesitated. "We may be on to something, though."

"What?"

"I need someone else to explain it to you."

Lars's partner, Abe, walked up then. "You know something, Jesse? If so—"

"Know something? Let's see. A couple is murdered, and there's an alligator limb at the scene. A man is attacked and killed by an alligator. A guard falls or is pushed into an alligator pit, and now the vet's guard has been attacked and specimens have been stolen. Gee. Think anything might be related here? Does the word 'gator' mean anything to you?"

"Go to hell, Jesse," Abe snapped. "I want to know what you've got to go on. I'm Homicide. I look for human killers. You're the alligator wrestler."

"An alligator is a natural predator, Abe."

"My point. I can hardly arrest one."

"If an animal is trained to kill, that makes the trainer a murderer, doesn't it?" Jesse asked dryly.

"I just said that if you've got something—"

Jesse ignored Abe and turned to Lars. "How about lunch tomorrow? The Miccosukee restaurant? On me."

"Yeah, we can make it," Abe answered for Lars.

Jesse shook his head. "I have someone who may know something. But she won't talk if we make this too big a party. Abe, just let Lars handle it."

"Who is she?" Abe said angrily. "We can just bring her in."

"And do what? Issue a lot of threats and get nothing back?" Jesse asked angrily.

Lars set a hand on Abe's shoulder. "Partner, whatever I get, you know we share. So…"

Abe glared at Jesse. Jesse glared back. "Dammit, Abe, I'm not asking Lars to hide anything from you, and I'm not trying to hide anything myself. Hell, I'd invite anyone who could bring justice for Hector and Maria. But, Abe, you're not a guy with a gentle touch. Let Lars take this one. He can call you the minute he leaves."

"Fine," Abe grated.

With the crime-scene people busy at the vet's, Jesse knew there was nothing he could do there for the night. "I'm going to have a last word with Jim," Jesse said. "Lars, see you tomorrow."

They were almost ready to take Jim to the hospital for observation. He was being laid out on a stretcher.

"Jim?"

"Yeah, Jess?"

"You walked back to the beagle. You were hit on the head. Then nothing, nothing at all until Doc was there?"

"Nothing, Jesse. I'm sorry."

"That's all right."

"Does Doc usually come in at night?"

"No, but he'd been worrying about finishing up the work you wanted, 'cuz he hasn't been able to get to it during the day. We've been really busy lately. It's a bitch, huh?"

"Yeah, it's a bitch."

Then the med tech gave Jesse a thumbs-up and rolled Jim into the vehicle.

Jesse waved and headed out.

Lorena should have been dog-tired, but she was nervous. Television couldn't hold her attention. She found herself prowling the room as the hour grew later.

He had said he would be here.

Irritated with herself, she sat down and tried staring at the television again. She thought she was just blanking on the screen, since she didn't understand a word that was being said.

Then she realized she was on a Spanish-language channel.

Insane.

She should work, she told herself.

Work, and not wonder if Jesse was really coming.

Work, and not feel on fire with such breathless anxiety, both physical and emotional....

What she'd told Sally was true: she barely knew the man.

It was also true that she needed to work. She hadn't managed much of her "real job" since she had come here. But then she had happened to arrive just when there had been terrible murders, and when a Native American who knew the canals better than his own features had met with his fate in those waters. There should have been time. Time to become trusted. Time to flirt, if necessary.

She needed to get into that lab.

She was convinced there were answers to be found there. She was usually so organized and analytical. But she was afraid to make notes, afraid that her room might be searched and her real purpose discovered.

She showered more to hear the sound of the water and feel the pounding of it against her flesh than anything else. Then she slipped into a cotton nightshirt and lay on her bed, but she still felt ridiculously keyed up.

Had he been serious? Was Jesse really coming back here?

Forget Jesse, she told herself.

She tried to fathom the truth from what she had been

able to glean from Michael's files. As yet, nothing that was proof positive. He was experimenting with gator eggs, of course. The temperature at which they were hatched determined the sex of an alligator; that kind of manipulation was easy. Breeding was basic biology. And here, at an alligator farm, it made sense to weed out characteristics one didn't like and fine-tune those features that were favorable to farming. Sex, size, the quality of the meat and hide.

But selective breeding hadn't created the monster she had seen today. Steroids and a formula—one that her father had known was too dangerous to exist—were behind what she had seen. Still, even if she got back into Preston's lab and found out what he was working on, how could she prove he had stolen her father's work?

Two days. Jesse had given her two days.

Just as she thought of the man, she heard a soft rapping at her door. She glanced at her glow-in-the-dark Mickey Mouse watch. It was after 1:00 a.m. She leapt from the bed, her heart thundering, and angry because of it.

The tapping sounded again. Then, softly, "Lorena, will you open the door?"

She hurried over, threw it open. "It's after one in the morning," she informed him.

He closed the door. "Shh."

"I actually do sleep at night. I have a job to do here. I wake up and start early. I—"

He drew her into his arms. "Shh."

"Jesse, I have to tell you—"

"Shh."

There was warmth in the depth of his eyes as well

as amusement. There was something possessive in his hold, and she felt him slipping into her heart even as he inflamed her desires.

He's devastated, not dead. He'll never marry again. He's interested in one thing, and one thing only, so you'd better play like a big girl, if you intend to play.

He started to frown, staring into her eyes. "What's wrong? Has something happened?"

Lorena placed her fingers against his lips. "Shh," she said, and moved closer to him. His flesh was rich and warm, burnt copper, vibrant, vital.

He groaned softly, pulling her to him, and his lips found hers, pure fire. When they broke, she heard his whisper against her forehead, felt the power of his touch against her. "Lorena."

Fumbling, she found the light switch. And once again she said very softly, "Shh…"

Then she was in his arms. And the hour of the day or night didn't matter in the least.

When the alarm rang, rudely indicating that morning had come and it was time for the workday to begin, he was gone.

Chapter 9

It seemed to be business as usual at the alligator farm.

Lorena went through greeting the tourists and taking them to their first stop: Michael Preston's lab.

While working with a group of children, she tried to get a good look at the hatchlings and at the cracked eggs.

They appeared normal, as far as she could tell. She wished she had been more interested in her father's work at the time he'd been doing it, but she had simply never liked alligators.

It was the eyes, she was certain.

Two more groups of tourists came through. Michael was his usual self, valiantly trying to give a good speech, but obviously uncomfortable. Or maybe he only seemed so to Lorena because she knew he loved research and hated tourists. He did seem happy, however, to have her come through with the groups.

Happy to have her stay.

At eleven, her cell phone rang. It was Jesse. "I'm coming to get you for lunch," he told her.

"I'm not sure I'm supposed to leave during the day," she said.

"Everyone gets lunch. You won't even be ten miles away," he assured her.

At noon, he picked her up in front of the farm. He was in uniform. "Where are we going?" she asked.

He grinned. "A restaurant."

"Okay."

She had passed the place on her way out to Harry's she realized when they got there. It was directly across from the Miccosukee village.

Jesse glanced her way dryly. "Don't worry. You won't have to eat grilled gator or anything."

"I never thought I would," she responded. "You have a chip on your shoulder."

"I do not," he said indignantly, and she had to smile.

She balked when they reached the place and she saw that Lars Garcia was standing out front.

"What is this?" she demanded heatedly.

"You have to tell him what you think is going on."

"You gave me two days!" she said.

"There's been a complication. The vet's office was broken into. Another man was attacked. Thankfully, we have hard heads out here. He survived."

Jesse was grim, but she was still furious. She had nothing, no evidence at all, really, and he had brought her here to tell her story to another policeman. She was stiff and still angry when they went in.

Lars was as polite and decent as ever. He chatted about the weather while they waited for their food, and he and Jesse talked about an upcoming musical festival put on by the Miccosukee tribe in the Glades. "People come by the hundreds. It's great," Lars said.

When their food came—she'd ordered a very boring meal: hamburger, fries and an iced tea—Lars lowered his voice and said, "Jesse says I need to know why you're here."

She'd thought she was tense already, but now her muscles constricted to an even greater degree, and she shot Jesse a furious glance.

"Lorena, it's important I know."

"Then I'm surprised Jesse didn't tell you," she said.

"I need to hear it from you."

She clenched her teeth, set her hamburger down, shot Jesse one last filthy stare, and explained what she knew and feared to Lars. He listened without mocking or doubting her, though he glanced at Jesse several times, as if Jesse might have put him in the middle of a science fiction tale, but when she finished, he sighed and asked, "Your father's death was ruled an accident?"

"Yes. But I know it wasn't."

"That's going to be very difficult to prove."

"Maybe not now, when other people are dying," she said.

That caused a glance between Lars and Jesse.

"What was in the e-mail from the alligator farm?" Lars asked.

She shrugged. "It was vague. They were interested,

of course, in learning about any developments to increase quality and efficiency. They suggested that they could pay well."

"What was your father's reply?" Lars asked.

"That he had nothing ready as of yet. And he explained that research was difficult, that all genetic scientists had to take the greatest care when playing with the makeup of any life form."

"Did other alligator farms contact your father?" Lars asked.

She shrugged. "Yes."

"So why are you concentrating on this one?"

"Every other e-mail was signed by a specific person. At Harry's, the same e-mail account can be used by almost anyone who works there."

"We can trace the computer," Lars said.

"If so, what will that prove?" Lorena asked.

"Whether it was in the office, in the lab or somewhere else," Lars said.

"Preston would have to be involved, wouldn't he?" Jesse asked.

"There are no 'have-tos,' Jesse. We both know that," Lars said. He looked at Lorena. "You need to get out of that place."

She tensed again, staring at Jesse. "I can't see how I can be in any personal danger. I had nothing to do with my father's work."

"Anyone can be in danger," Lars said softly.

Lars sat back, wiped his mouth and stared at Lorena. "I'll have to talk to the D.A.'s office about a search warrant. In the meantime, you shouldn't go back."

Lorena leaned forward, speaking heatedly. "My father is dead. A local couple have been killed. You don't know how many enhanced alligators you might have running around the Everglades. You need me, and you need my help."

"There's something I don't understand here," Lars said, and he glanced at Jesse, frowning. "This research has to be fairly new. Alligators take time to mature and grow. How could this one have gotten so big so fast?"

Lorena shook her head. "The formula causes an increase in the growth rate. Take people. Better diets, rich in protein, make for taller, stronger teens. Body builders bulk up with steroids. You'd be amazed at what chemicals can do to the body. That's why it's so important not only that we find out who was doing what but to just how many specimens."

"We need a search warrant," Lars said simply.

"Do you think you can get one?" Lorena asked anxiously.

He shrugged. "If I can argue well enough. And prove just cause. Well, I should get moving." He lifted a hand to ask for the check. Jesse caught his arm.

"I told you yesterday. This one is on the tribe."

"Thanks." He rose. Lorena and Jesse did the same.

When Lars had walked out, Lorena turned on Jesse. "You told me that I had two days."

"Lorena, what do you think you're going to find in two days?" Jesse demanded.

"More than anyone else?"

"Is biochemistry another of your degrees?"

She gritted her teeth, staring at him. "No. But I know what might have been stolen from my father."

"Lorena, face it, you're not going to be able to do anything if you're dead!"

She turned away from him and headed toward the door, clearly indicating that lunch was over for her, as well.

He followed. As soon as he came out, she got into the car. There was no possibility that she was going to walk back to work.

He didn't pull straight back onto the road but instead drove almost directly across the street. She gazed at him with hostility. "You have a few minutes left. I thought you might want to see the village."

She didn't have a chance to refuse. He had already gotten out of the car.

They entered the gift shop first. It offered Indian goods from around the country. There were a number of the exquisite colorful shirts, skirts and jackets for which both the Seminoles and Miccosukees had become famous, along with dream catchers, posters, T-shirts, postcards, drums, hand-carved "totem" recorders and jewelry. Some of the unique beadwork designs on the jewelry might well have attracted Lorena's attention, but Jesse was already headed straight out the back. There was an entry fee, but Jesse just smiled at the girl, and he, with Lorena trailing behind him, walked on through. She offered the girl an awkward smile, as well.

Out back, there were a number of chickees, along with more items for sale. Women were there working on intricate basketry, sewing the beautiful colored clothing and designing jewelry.

Lorena, fascinated, would have paused, but Jesse

was again moving on to one of the huge pits where alligators lived with a colony of turtles.

Looking into the pit, Lorena noted that a number of the gators were large, very large. But not one of them was more than ten feet.

"Jesse, what's up?"

A man with ink-dark hair and Native American features, wearing a T-shirt that advertised a popular rock band, walked up to them.

Jesse nodded to him. "Mike. This is Lorena Fortier. She's working at Harry's."

The man studied her with a smile. "Welcome."

"I thought she might want to see the village."

Mike smiled and shrugged. "Well, there's the museum, the pits, we do some wrestling, give a few history lessons."

"She's on lunch break. I just thought she should come look around. And I wanted to make sure you'd seen the notice."

"About the hunt tonight? I'll be there," Mike said grimly. He shook his head. "Billy Ray...well, he wasn't the kind of man that gave us a lot of pride, but hell, I wouldn't have wanted my worst enemy to go that way."

"Right. Make sure everyone knows we're hunting something big, really big. Close to twenty feet, maybe even more."

Mike whistled softly. "We do know what we're doing, Jesse," he said. "But it's good to be warned."

"See you later, then. And extend my thanks to everyone showing up from the tribe."

Mike nodded. "See you then."

Jesse turned and headed toward the exit without a

word to Lorena. She had been angry, but now he was the one who seemed irritated. They reached the car, where, despite his apparent anger, he opened her door.

"You're the one who betrayed me," she reminded him.

He shot her a scowling glance. "I'm trying to get you out of what might be a dangerous situation. But you know what? I don't usually have a chip on my shoulder, but today, I do. Chemists, biochemists, biologists! They're playing with life. Interesting, sure. Let's see how we can improve what God made. But, the thing is, people play God, and things can happen. Billy Ray was no prize specimen of humanity. But you heard it in Mike's voice. He was one of ours. We're a small tribe. We were forced down to this land, and we learned how to live on it. Billy Ray had every right in the world to be fishing. Hell, if he wanted to drink himself silly, that was his choice, too. He shouldn't have been attacked by an animal that was only there because someone decided to play God."

Lorena gasped. "My father wanted to help people," she insisted angrily. "And when he was afraid he might be on to something dangerous, he was willing to destroy years of research!"

"Too bad you couldn't have explained that to Billy Ray while he was being eaten," Jesse said.

Lorena stared at him incredulously. "Evil people come in all colors and nationalities, you know!"

The drive from the village to the alligator farm was short. Jesse pulled in just as Lorena finished her tirade, and she was out the door before the engine could die. She walked around to his window. "Thank you for your concern for my safety, but since you've turned things over to Metro-Dade now, I'm sure I'll be just fine. You can feel secure in the fact that I'll be safe without your assistance."

She spun around, her feet crunching on the gravel path, heedless as to whether he called her back or not.

Lunch was over. It was time to get back to work.

She did so, energetically, talking to the tourists, helping Michael, even going with the tours to the pits and watching while Jack wrestled one of the six-foot alligators.

It didn't matter what she did, as long as she did something. With Michael in his lab, she certainly wasn't going to get anywhere there, so she put her heart into the business of people. Anything at all to keep busy.

To keep from thinking.

She shouldn't have gotten so close so fast. Getting intimate with someone so unique, so unusual, so very much…everything she might have wanted in life…had been more than foolhardy. She had let herself become far too emotionally involved, and then…

She'd felt that wretched knife in her back. His bitterness against her father had been unexpected and deeply painful.

That afternoon, she actually put her nursing skills to the test. A little girl fell on one of the paths.

Nothing like a registered nurse to apply disinfectant and a bandage.

As she tended the child, Lorena suddenly wondered why Harry had decided that he needed a nurse on the premises. It had made sense at first. The alligator farm was in an isolated location. But she had seen the local services in action. Help had arrived almost instantly when Roger had been found in the pit. Helicopters provided a swift transport to the emergency room.

Of course, nothing so drastic was necessary for little scrapes and bruises, but still…

Still, the question gave her pause. She forced herself to concentrate on it. It was good—no, it was *necessary*—to think about something—anything—other than Jesse Crane and the startling color of his eyes, the sleek bronze warmth of his flesh, the sound of his voice, the way he touched her, the structure of his face and the way she just wanted to be with him…

No! She had to think of something else.

He would be back at the end of the day, there to organize the hunt. As it veered toward five o'clock and closing, she determined to spend some quality time with Dr. Michael Preston.

By the time Lorena stalked off, Jesse had already cooled down and realized that he'd been a fool, taking his frustration over what had happened out on her.

What was it about the woman? She made him forget everything the moment he was with her, even though she wasn't his type at all.

And why not?

Because she was blond?

Elegant, feminine…a powder puff, or so he had assumed at first.

But she wasn't. She was determined. Reckless, maybe, but determined and fierce, and she had told him that she was a crack shot. Not a powder puff at all.

But also not the kind to spend a lifetime in the wilds.

Then he reminded himself ruefully that his "wilds" were just a forty-five-minute drive from an urban Mecca with clubs, malls, theaters and more.

What was he doing, arguing with himself, convincing himself that his lifestyle was a good one? Because…?

Because he hadn't felt the way he felt about her in a very long time. In fact, he'd thought he'd buried those feelings along with Connie, that as long as he threw himself back into his passion for the land and the tribe, he could learn to live without all they had shared, the tenderness and sense of being one, loving, laughing, waking together, sleeping each night entwined. There was the chemistry that brought people together, and, if you were lucky, the chemistry, excitement and hunger that remained. And more. The longing to see someone's eyes opening to the new day, the times when no words were necessary, the nights when life was good just because the world could be shared.

He lowered his head, wincing, feeling as if the scars that had covered his wounds were ripping open. As if they were raw and bleeding, all because of the promise of something, some*one,* else. But that promise brought with it the one emotion he dreaded more than anything. Fear. No wonder he'd pushed her away.

He clenched and unclenched his fists. This wasn't the right time. In fact, it was idiotic. And, anyway, she was furious with him, probably regretting the very fact that they'd touched.

He forced his mind onto the case.

He felt that they were closing in, that Lars would be able to get the search warrant after what he had learned from Lorena. There were, however, other alligator farms in the area. It might be tough for him to convince the D.A.'s office, without concrete proof, not only that there really were "enhanced" alligators in the Everglades, but that Harry's Alligator Farm and Museum was responsible, and that whoever had gone to the extremes of biochemical manipulation was also willing to kill for it.

He hesitated, then decided to take another drive out to Dr. Thiessen's place to see if the Metro-Dade cops had missed anything, though he doubted it. They were good.

Then again, this was a world he knew far better than anyone else, a world that could not be taught in any lab or classroom.

In her room, Lorena found herself amazed to be carefully considering her wardrobe for the evening.

She hadn't been asked on the hunt, which made sense. Only experienced alligator trappers were going, and that definitely did not include her.

Nor, she suspected, did it include Michael Preston.

Which was good, because she wanted to spend some time with Michael. She didn't want to appear as if she had dressed to seduce, but she *did* want to look attractive.

Not in an aggressive way. Just enough to be compelling, so she could conduct her own hunt this evening.

She opted for casual slacks and a soft silk halter top. When she was dressed, she headed for his lab, listened, and heard movement. She tapped on the door.

"Yes?"

Lorena slipped in. "Hey. Are you going on that hunt this evening?" she asked him.

He arched a brow, grimaced and shook his head. "I'm a scientist. The brains, not the brawn."

"Ah."

"I guess you're into brawn."

"I am?"

"Well…" He perched on the edge of his desk, still in his lab coat. "You've been spending a lot of time with our bronzed-and-buff policeman, Ms. Fortier."

She shrugged casually. "Not really. I wound up driving with him when that poor woman freaked out over her friend having been killed. And I probably shouldn't have headed out to the casino to begin with, the night I left with him. Too tired. And then someone told him about the incident with the hatchlings, so he wanted to talk to me."

"Not me."

"Did you tell anyone here?" Lorena asked.

He lifted his shoulders. "I don't think so. Maybe the kid complained in the end, I don't know. Maybe we shouldn't have let the little brat off the hook."

"Maybe not," she agreed. She walked closer, then sat on the other corner of his desk. She frowned. "Michael, did you ever believe any of those stories about kids buying baby alligators and then their parents flushing them down the toilet, so they wound up in the sewers of New York, that kind of thing?"

He waved a hand in the air. "Science fiction," he assured her. "Alligators, even in a sewer, wouldn't last long in New York. They need the sun, the heat. You know that."

"Right," she mused. "But...down here, I wonder how many alligators wind up free after they've been lifted from a place like this one by a kid like that brat. I mean it's possible. We both know that."

He slipped from his position on the desk and approached her, a smile on his face. She was a bit unnerved when he came very close, leaning toward her, resting his hands on the desktop on either side of her. "Possible," he said softly, his face just a whisper away. "But no kid is going to steal a hatchling from here, then let it loose in the New York sewers to grow into a monster."

"But there's at least one monster alligator out in the canals right now," she said. "That's what they're hunting tonight."

She saw a pulse ticking in his cheek. He didn't move. "Just what are you suggesting, Ms. Fortier?" he asked very softly.

"What else could it be?" she asked innocently. "I think that alligator escaped or was stolen from a lab," she said, and shrugged.

"From here?" he asked.

"From somewhere," she breathed. He was close. So close. And he might be the brains and not the brawn, but he still had quite an impressive build, and she just might have taken things too far.

"If I could create a super-gator, I'd be rich," he said, sounding surprisingly disgusted.

But she could see the tension in his face, feel it in his muscles. Her recklessness could prove dangerous. This, however, had been the time to take chances. Dozens of men from around the area would be arriving shortly. If he came any closer…

If she felt a deeper surge of unease…

All she had to do was scream.

He was staring at her intently. Searching her eyes.

He started to raise a hand toward her face, smiling.

"Michael?"

The call and a fierce knocking were followed by the door simply opening.

Lorena slipped from the edge of the desk as Michael turned.

Harry was there.

"Michael, can you get out here and help with the equipment? This is insane, if you ask me. Half the guys have no supplies. Damn Jesse. Leave it to him to get the full cooperation of the Florida Wildlife and Game Commission for a wild-goose chase."

If Harry had noticed that he had interrupted something, he gave no sign. But maybe he hadn't noticed, she thought. He seemed much more upset about the hunt than that a man had been killed by a gator.

Lorena grimaced as she caught Michael's eye, then escaped in Harry's wake.

Hurrying out back to the canal, she saw an unbelievable lineup of airboats and canoes. Jesse was up on some kind of a huge tackle box, giving instructions. "Remember, folks, we're looking for something really large—not indiscriminately killing off a population for trophies."

"How big, Jesse?" a man shouted from one of the canoes.

"Bigger than the norm," Michael Preston answered

for him, hurrying forward. "The biggest gator ever recorded in Florida was seventeen feet, five inches long. The biggest gator recorded in Louisiana was nineteen feet, two inches. So if you find anything smaller than that—wrong gator."

"Ah, hell!" the same fellow snorted. "We have to have something real to go by."

"You heard the man. We're looking for fifteen feet or over. All right?" Jesse asked.

"We get to harvest what we get?"

She saw Jesse defer to a man who looked like he was about to go on safari, in khakis and a straw hat. He was tall and lean.

Jesse reached a hand down and helped the man up on the box. "This is Steven Bear, Florida Wildlife and Game Commission."

"We can harvest the fellas, huh?" another man called.

"Gentlemen, the important thing is this—we're not out on a regular hunt. Make sure your quarry is over fifteen feet. Then the meat is yours. Nothing small is to be taken. Understood?"

She saw both Steven Bear and Jesse jump down from the box. Someone asked Jesse a question, and he answered, then headed for an airboat with a number of men already aboard.

Michael came up behind her. "Half those guys see this as a free-for-all," he murmured.

She turned to him, frowning herself. "I don't get it. I mean, there are so many boats. Are they going to try to sneak up on it with all those lights, all that noise?"

"You'll see," Michael said.

And she did. It had seemed like chaos, but when the

airboats took off, they headed in all different directions. Once again, she had forgotten that what appeared like solid ground in this area most often wasn't.

River of grass.

They were taking off over that river in a dozen different directions.

"Well, they'll be gone awhile," Michael said. "Why don't we have some dinner?"

"Sure."

They ambled to the cafeteria together, chose pork chops for their meals, and sat together.

The place was almost eerily empty. "Did Sally go on the hunt?" Lorena asked, curious that the outspoken, sexy redhead was nowhere to be seen.

"I didn't see her," Michael said.

"Does she help with the research here at all?" Lorena asked.

Michael laughed. "There's only one green thing that Sally would research—money," he told her.

"Oh?"

"Um."

Lorena smiled, smoothing back a lock of hair. "I don't get it then. Why is she working out here?"

"I think she's trying to be so indispensable to Harry that he makes her a partner. He owns land all over the place. And we're doing well here...but I think he'd like to open another facility, closer down by the Keys. He's already opened a few shops in Key Largo."

She frowned again. "Michael, this is a totally dumb question. But Harry raises gators for their meat and hides, right? So where does he—"

"Lorena!" Michael said, grinning. "You don't 'harvest' animals where you show them off to the tourists! I told you—Harry owns a lot of land closer to the Keys, down in the Florida City–Homestead area."

"Ah."

"You really are interested, aren't you?" When she nodded, he said, "I can show you a few things, then. Are you done?"

"Um, yes," she murmured.

He wiggled his eyebrows in a manner suggestive of a hunched Igor in a horror movie. "Come, my dear, I'll show you my lab," he growled jokingly.

Lorena froze for a moment. She'd been doing every-thing in her power to sneak into the lab, and now he was making this offer.

While anyone who might have come to her rescue was off hunting for a rogue alligator.

No. There were more live-ins around the compound. And Harry hadn't gone on the hunt; he was around somewhere.

Besides, she had waited far too long for this oppor-tunity. She could take care of herself.

And she was going in.

"Let's see what you've got to show me," she said with a smile.

He flashed her a smile in return, showing very white teeth. They rose and walked across the compound. She noted that there was another guard on duty.

She noted as well that he was spooked. When he heard their footsteps, his hand flew to the hilt of his gun, buckled at his hip.

"Just Ms. Fortier and me," Michael said.

"Evenin'," the guard replied.

When they reached the door to the lab, Michael drew out his keys and opened it, pressing the small of Lorena's back lightly to get her to proceed inside.

He followed, closed the door, then locked it.

Then he turned and stared at her. "I don't know why I bother. Someone picked it open the other day."

"Oh?"

He shook his head, approaching her. She cocked her head, looking at him. The guard had just seen the two of them together. He couldn't possibly be planning anything...evil.

Not unless he meant to go back out and kill the guard as well!

He was still smiling, as if his intent was to seduce, but she knew it wasn't. She found herself backed against the desk.

He was the brain, he had said, not the brawn. But he was a liar. She could feel the heat and strength of his muscles.

And his anger.

His menace...

"You picked the lock, Lorena, didn't you?" he asked softly.

"What?"

"Ah, the innocence. Like hell, Ms. Fortier. You're flirting madly with me, while it's more than obvious that it's Jesse Crane who's really stirred your senses. And yet you're charming as hell to Jack and Hugh, too. Are you just a little vamp, Ms. Fortier? I don't think so. I think you're up to something. You want something in this lab. Tell me what it is. Here we are, you and me, alone, finally. So...it's time. You want to see what's going on in here? You might as well. I think you should see exactly what you've been wanting to see. Now. *Right now.*"

Chapter 10

Nighttime in the Everglades, and it was eerie.

No matter how well a man knew the place, the near-total darkness hid the predators haunting the swamp and made this a dangerous place.

When light touched the gators' eyes, they glowed, as if they were demons from hell, not of this world at all.

Jesse was accustomed to the glowing eyes, and yet even he found them chilling in the dark of the night.

Despite his familiarity with the creatures, it was difficult for him to determine the size of one with only the eyes to go on. Sometimes, he knew instantly when he was looking at an animal of no more than five to eight feet, but with just the eyes above the water to go by, more often than not it was a crap shoot.

Twice they snared a creature only to realize that the

specimen they had in their loops was no more than nine feet, ten tops.

Each time they released their catch. Enraged, the alligators made swift departures from the area once they had been freed.

The rest of the group on the airboat, Jack, Leo and Sam Tiger, were soaked and exasperated, but no one suggested giving up as they moved closer to the location where Billy Ray had been attacked and killed.

They had been out a few hours and had just cut the motor, and only the noises of the night were echoing in the air around them, when Jack Pine said softly, "There," and pointed.

Jesse looked in the direction Jack was indicating.

The alligator wasn't completely submerged. The length of the head was incredible. He focused hard and saw the length of the animal as it floated just beneath the surface.

And he knew they had found the beast they were searching for.

Sam whistled softly. "I have never seen anything remotely near that size before," he said.

"Let's bait it," Jesse murmured.

Their bait was chicken. He tied several pieces on the line.

The alligator watched them as they approached. It didn't move; it showed no fear.

When the line was cast in the water, the animal moved at last.

It went for the bait. They were ready with their snares.

A massive snap of the mighty jaws severed the lines

as well as securing the meat, but Jack managed to get a noose around the neck.

The alligator made one swing of that massive head. Jack went flying off the airboat, a shout of surprise escaping his lips. The animal instantly began to close in on him.

Sam quickly started the engine and headed in for a rescue. Jesse went for one of the high-powered revolvers. He aimed and fired, aimed and fired, as they neared Jack.

Sam swore, shouting to Jack.

In a frenzy, Jack moved toward the airboat.

Jesse, taking care to miss the man, fired again and again.

Ten bullets into the gator.

It kept coming, heedless of the men, heedless of the bullets that had pierced its hide.

They reached Jack. Sam and Leo instantly reached for him, and he reached back, grabbing their hands, the muscles bulging in his forearms and a look of dread in his eyes.

They were just dragging Jack over the edge of the airboat platform when the gator's head emerged, mammoth jaws wide with their shocking power.

Jesse aimed again, dead into one of the eyes.

The explosion ripped through the night.

The eye and part of the head evaporated.

And at last, with Jack's feet just clearing the water, the creature began to fall back.

Jesse fired again and again, aiming at what was left of the disappearing head.

He felt a hand on his arm. Sam's. "You got it," Sam said softly.

And from where he lay on the floor of the airboat, Jack said softly, "Dear God."

In the silence that followed his statement, they heard the whir of motors, saw approaching lights and heard the shouts of others.

More airboats and canoes arrived, and the area was suddenly aglow with floodlights.

"You got it?" Hugh called from another vessel.

Jesse realized that he was shaking. He nodded, turned, lowered his gun and found a seat.

The others began to haul the creature in.

"Well, Lorena?" Michael asked huskily.

Great, she thought.

She had a gun, and she was a crack shot. But she had let her eagerness to find the truth lead to stupidity, so here she was, boxed in by her main suspect, and he was challenging her....

She slid her hands backward on his desk. In all the old movies, there was a letter opener on a desk, ready to be used by a desperate victim as a weapon.

There was nothing on Michael Preston's desk but his computer and a few papers.

Not even a paperweight.

"Well..." she murmured, as he came closer. Closer.

There was nothing of use on the desk.

She told herself to scream!

It was all she had left.

"How could you?" Michael said suddenly, turning abruptly away from her.

She gulped down her scream.

"What?"

"How in the world could you suspect me of anything? Although what you think I've been doing, I still don't know. You've been on my computer. You've been searching this lab. What do you think that I've done? Or are *you* out to steal something from *me?*" he demanded.

She stared at him, a frown furrowing her brow. He seemed to be genuinely upset, and he also seemed to be as much at a loss as she was herself right now.

But if not Michael Preston…who? He was the scientist here.

The brains, not the brawn.

"What?" she repeated, stalling for time, rapidly trying to determine just what to say.

"Are you a thief?" he queried.

"Of course not!" she protested.

"Then what have you been doing?"

She sighed, looking downward. "Trying to understand," she murmured.

"Understand what?" he demanded.

"Well, you know, more of what's going on around here."

"Really. Didn't the concept of simply asking occur to you?"

Again she sighed. "Well…no. It's all so strange. This place, the people here."

"Except for Jesse Crane."

She stared at him, then shrugged. "He seems to be a decent guy. I like him," she murmured.

"In a way you don't like me?"

"Oh, Michael! You're great. You know that. Half the

women you meet immediately start crushing on you," she told him.

He grinned ruefully, then shrugged. "The problem is," he said huskily, "it's the half of the female population I *want* that couldn't care less about me."

Lorena felt awkward then, not sure what to say. But feeling awkward was much better than feeling terrified.

"Michael..."

"Never mind. It's true. Women prefer brawn to brain."

She arched a brow. "Are you insinuating that men with brawn can't have brains? I have the impression that you spend a fair amount of time in the gym."

He sat beside her on the desk, crossing his arms over his chest. He sounded amused as he admitted, "Yeah, I go to the gym. But do I want to be out looking for a giant gator? Not in this lifetime. I like hatchlings. They're little. They might bite fingers, but it's unlikely that I'll become dinner for them."

"Michael...have you ever altered a hatchling?"

"Altered?"

"When you crack the eggs. Have you ever experimented?"

"Yes," he said flatly. His eyes narrowed sharply as he stared at her. "Is that what you're after? Trying to steal my vitamin compounds?"

"Vitamins? No."

"Well, that's about all I've worked with. Vitamins in the egg. You want my password? You want to get into the files you haven't been able to crack?" he asked.

She was uneasy again, thinking that he might have

refrained from harming her only because he hadn't decided what she was really doing, why she had come.

Was this a trap?

"Just what kind of work are you doing?" she inquired.

"What do you think?" he demanded. "The same kind of research as everyone else! Alligator meat is already lean and high in protein. I'm trying to make it even better, so someday it can feed the world."

He sounded like her father. But she wondered if he was driven by the same true passion to help, or if he was seeking renown—or just money.

He shook his head with disgust suddenly and walked around to click on his computer. "What kind of work do I do? Research, and yes, experimentation. But you know what? Nothing I know about can create a giant killer gator. So you go ahead and take a look. I hope you're up on your enzymes, proteins, compounds, vitamins and minerals."

"Look, Michael," she began. "I—"

He was typing something when he suddenly looked up. "I just realized something. Why are you looking into *my* research? For a gator to have gotten as big as this one supposedly is, it would have to have been growing for years and years—while both of us were still kids, practically."

"Not that long," she murmured dryly.

He stared at her, then exhaled slowly. "Is there some kind of research out there that I don't know about? Some kind of discovery. That is…what you're saying is impossible."

"Hey," she murmured, keeping her eyes low. "I'm not a researcher. I'm not even an alligator expert."

"So what are you after?"

"I'm not sure. I'm just curious, I guess," she lied. She still wasn't certain she could trust Michael Preston.

He shook his head, studying the computer screen. "There have been big gators, but the biggest one on record wasn't even caught in this state. I suppose someone could have figured out a way to jump-start gator growth, or hybridize a gator with something else. I mean, we only have beefalo because of somebody's bright idea to breed a cow with a buffalo."

He seemed genuinely absorbed in seeking answers, but Lorena found that she was uncomfortable despite that fact.

"Come. Look," he demanded, staring at her belligerently.

She walked over to see the screen. He stood, urging her into the chair.

He had opened his research files. He had been telling her the truth—at least, as far as this proved. There were notes on the eggs with cracked shells. There was a study on albino alligators, with statistics regarding their life expectancy in the wild. There were side notes reminding him to speak to Harry about habitat changes, notations regarding the fact that he intended to set the temperature to create a male so they could eventually breed it with a number of females and track its genetic influence.

As she read his notes, she could feel him. He was standing directly behind her chair.

"Go on," he snapped, sounding angry again. "Keep reading."

Words began to swim before her eyes. She wondered how much time had passed.

It felt like forever.

She pushed the chair away from the desk, pushing him back, as well. "Michael, I told you, I'm not a researcher, so I don't even understand what I'm reading. I was just curious." She stood. "And I'm tired, really tired."

He shook his head. "You're not leaving here. Not until you tell me what you're up to."

"I'm not up to anything," she lied flatly.

"Then why break into my lab?"

She lowered her head, seeking a plausible explanation. She looked up at him again, knowing she had to be careful. "Michael...you're an attractive man."

"So?"

"I...well, frankly, I was interested in you. As a man. As a scientist. I was curious about you. I wanted to know what made you tick, why you're so fascinated with such strange creatures. But then..."

"Then you met Jesse."

She shrugged, not wanting to commit.

"You're sleeping with him," he accused her.

"Michael, that's really none of your business."

"Ah, I see. You break into my lab because of a crush on me—sorry, interest in my life, what makes me tick—but *your* life is none of my business."

She lifted her hands. "I'm sorry."

"I should report you to Harry."

"Do whatever you feel you have to," she murmured, looking down.

"You're making a mistake, you know."

He was close to her again. Just a foot away.

He reached out a hand. She nearly jumped.

He touched her face. "A big mistake," he told her.

"I'm afraid I've already made more than a few of those in my life," she murmured.

He tilted her chin upward, meeting her eyes earnestly. "No. You're making a big mistake with Jesse. You don't even know him."

"I know something about his past, if that's what you mean," she said.

"He's a loner, Lorena. Do you want to spend your entire life sitting on a mucky pile of saw grass? He belongs here. You don't. His passion is the land and the tribal council. He's decent enough as a human being. But he puts a wall up. He always will. Think about it."

She caught his hand and squeezed it. Like a friend. She was more anxious than ever to get the hell out of his lab.

"Michael, we've got a bigger problem than my love life right now. There's a killer gator out there."

"People have been killed by alligators before," he said flatly.

"Yes, but this is different. And we breed gators here. People are liable to think we have something to do with it."

He laughed a little bitterly. "You think? Who cares? Maybe that gator will make things better here. Think about it. People love to stop and stare at accidents. They love horror movies. People don't mind watching terrible things happen to strangers. I think the fact that there's a man-eater out there will draw even bigger crowds."

"Michael, that's horrible!"

He shrugged. "A lot that's horrible is true."

She hesitated for a moment, feeling another tremendous surge of unease.

"They should be coming back soon," she murmured. "Very soon."

"Are you trying to get away from me?" he asked her.

She straightened determinedly. "I want to see if they're back yet, if they've caught that thing," she said.

She headed for the door.

She felt him following her.

For a minute she was terrified that she wouldn't be able to open the door easily, since it was locked.

She twisted the knob, feeling his heat as he moved up close behind her, almost touching her.

She was certain he was reaching out, about to grab her, but the door opened easily, and as she threw it open, Sally was coming down the hallway.

"Sally!" she exclaimed loudly.

If Michael had been about to touch her, his hand fell away. "Hey, Sally."

"I think they're coming back," Sally was saying excitedly. "Harry was just on the radio with someone. They've got something."

"They caught it?" Michael asked.

"Well, I don't know if they caught 'it,' but they caught something. Come on."

* * *

Jesse felt drained and uneasy when they arrived back at Harry's. Jack Pine had come too damn close to being that alligator's last meal.

But he was apparently the only one who felt uneasy. Everyone else, including the hunters who had come back empty-handed, seemed to be on some kind of a natural high—amazed and excited by the size of the creature.

"It's a record," Harry said as the men made their way to land, a number of them dragging the nearly headless carcass onto the hard ground.

Harry was barking out orders, getting people to take measurements. He, too, seemed pleased and excited.

Jack, who had been given the tape measure, cried out, "Son of a gun, we just beat Louisiana. Twenty-two feet, three inches!"

"I don't care what it costs, we need the best taxidermist in the country. What's left of this sucker is getting stuffed. Hell, who shot the thing so many times? Never mind, never mind, the bullet holes are good. They make him look tougher than a *Tyrannosaurus rex*," Harry said.

"Harry, it's going to a lab. There's going to be an autopsy," Jesse said. He was drenched and covered in muck, and in no mood for the spirit of joviality going around. The thing had been a killer.

"An autopsy? On a gator?" Harry said.

Jesse felt his stomach turn. "We need to know for sure if this was the animal that took down Billy Ray."

Silence fell over the crowd at last as they all realized what Jesse was saying.

The gator would still have been digesting its last meal when it was killed.

"All right, Jesse. Have it taken to the lab." Harry sounded unhappy but resigned. "Do I get it when you're done?"

Jesse didn't answer, just turned away. Lorena was there, standing back in silence.

He felt a flip-flop of emotion.

In the heat of the hunt, he'd forgotten that he'd left her here. Alone.

But she appeared to be fine. More than fine. As ever, she was stunning. A rose in the midst of swamp grass.

"Are you taking the carcass to Doc Thiessen?" Harry asked.

Jesse kept staring at Lorena as he answered. "They'll have better facilities upstate, at the college," he said, turning away from Lorena at last.

Everyone had their cameras out now. They had hoisted the alligator up over one of the steel light poles. The thing was actually bending with the weight. Everyone had gone back to talking excitedly and having their pictures taken with the carcass.

The head…just the head…dear lord. The size of what was left was terrifying.

Lorena stayed apart from the crowd, but he saw that Michael and Sally were posing, Hugh snapping the picture.

"Harry, we'll see about getting the gator to you when we're done, okay?" he said congenially.

"Folks, we got the cafeteria open!" Harry called out, beaming at Jesse's words. "There's just coffee and sandwiches, but you're all welcome!"

Still grinning broadly at Jesse, Harry walked away.

Lorena was still a good twenty feet away, but her eyes were on him.

"Hey," he said softly.

"Hey." She smiled, apparently having forgiven him, and walked toward him slowly.

Damn, but he was in love with just the way she walked. The slow, easy sway of her hips. The slight look of something secretive, something shared, in the small curl of her lips. The way her hair picked up the lights, burning gold.

She reached him and touched his face, apparently heedless as to whether anyone noticed or not.

"You know, Officer Crane, you look good even in muck," she told him.

"I'd be happy to share my muck," he told her.

"Not here," she whispered. He thought she shivered slightly. "Not tonight."

"Are you coming home with me, then?"

Her head lowered; then she looked up, and her smile deepened. "Yeah, yeah, I guess I am."

The feeling of dread and weariness that had taken such a grip on him as they returned seemed to melt away. Strange, how life could be, how human emotions could be changed by something as simple as the sound of someone's voice.

The sway of someone's hips. Her smile.

Chemistry. She had been fascinating but unknown, and now she was known. Everything he knew now made her slightest movement all the more seductive. The thought of touching her again was deep, rich, combustible.

"Should we take my car?" she asked.

He arched a brow with a rueful smile, indicating the state he was in.

"I told you, I like you in muck."

"Down and dirty, eh?" he teased.

"I was thinking of a shower," she murmured.

"Jesse!" someone called excitedly.

He was startled from the absorption that had made him forget that dozens of people surrounded them.

"Jesse!" It was Sally. She came over and gave him a big hug. "Aren't you excited? That's the biggest gator on record, and you're the one who bagged it."

"It was a killer, Sally."

"That makes you one big, bad hunter, then, doesn't it?"

There was innuendo in her voice. Once it had amused him, but now it was an imposition.

She suddenly realized she had her back to Lorena and turned. "Oh, I'm sorry, Lorena. It's just so exciting."

Exciting? Yeah, Sally was excited, Jesse thought. Sally was the kind who found sensual stimulation in danger.

He looked at Lorena, and at that moment he realized that he was falling in love. She was clearly amused by the situation. Her eyes didn't fill with anger, fear or suspicion; there was even a slight smile on her face. She was willing to let him handle it. And she would wait.

"It was an alligator, Sally. Thousands of alligators are killed on hunts. But I guess you're right. There are people who like the hunt. Frankly, I'm not a hunter."

"Jesse! Your people have lived off gators for over a century, hunting them, wrestling them."

For some reason, the way she said "your people"

didn't sit right with him. He realized suddenly that Sally would always be fascinated with someone for what they did, not who they were. He hadn't really given it any thought before, but she'd never been more than someone with whom to enjoy a friendly flirtation. Tonight, he found that he was slightly repelled.

A wry smile came to his lips. That was, of course, because he'd never realized he could actually fall in love with anyone again.

"Isn't the casino the big moneymaker these days?" Lorena asked, her smile growing deeper as she and Jesse met each another's eyes.

"Oh, yeah. Bingo," Jesse agreed. "But we're all glad this guy's been caught. I think he's the one that got Billy Ray, and we'll know for certain soon enough. Good night, Sally."

He didn't actually step around her, just eased into a position that let him slip an arm around Lorena's shoulders.

"Good night, Sally," Lorena said.

The woman stared blankly at the two of them for a moment. Then she seemed to realize that they were leaving. Together.

"Oh! Uh, good night."

They avoided the cafeteria, where people had started massing. As they walked down the hallway, they could hear Jack talking. "I'm telling you, I thought I was a goner. If it hadn't been for Jesse, I'd have been chum."

Outside, Jesse protested again. "Lorena, this is swamp muck. Heavy, smelly dirt. The car—"

"There's a towel in back. You can throw it over the

seat," she said. After rummaging for a moment, she found the towel and put it over the driver's seat.

"Hey, I'm the dirty one," he told her.

"And I don't know where I'm going. You need to drive."

She tossed him the keys. He shrugged. It was true. If you didn't know where to take an almost invisible road off the Trail, you were never going to find his house.

It was no more than a ten-minute drive, and both of them were too preoccupied to talk. And they were barely inside the door before she had slid into his arms, shivering slightly, clinging to him, her arms slipping around his neck, her body pressed to his, her lips seeking his mouth. It seemed an eon of ecstasy that they remained thus, and he felt a renewed sense not just of fervor and hunger, but of that deeper rise of emotion that came from the fact that they had made the subtle adjustment from wanting to needing, from carnal chemistry to a melding of body, heart and soul. She, too, was soon covered in swamp mud, and they made their way to the bathroom, where he managed to turn on the shower spray while disrobing himself and her, barely breaking contact the whole time.

Flesh, naked flesh, soap and suds, and hands. She touched him everywhere. He returned the favor. She had magic hands, taking a slow course of discovery. Light on his shoulders at first, and then with a pressure that both alleviated strain and created the sweetest strain of a very different kind.

Her fingers played down the length of his spine, over his hips. He touched her in return. The darkness of his hands over the pale roundness of her breasts was arousing, his palms rubbing over her nipples before his head ducked and his mouth caressed them. The water sluiced through her hair. He caught it and cast it over her shoulder, turning her against him so that his lips could fall on her nape, below her ear, on her shoulders, her back. He turned her in his arms, continuing his erotic ministrations against her abdomen, her thighs, then between them. She gripped his shoulders, quivered at his touch, moaned slightly, then cried out, sliding down in sudsy sleekness to meet his mouth with the furious hunger of her own once again.

Her hands were delicate, then fierce, stroking against his chest. They knelt together in a steaming spray that seemed almost fantasy, something keener, sharper, than he'd ever known before. She stroked his sex with her hands and tongue, and he wound his arms around her, bringing them both to their feet, bracing her against the tile of the shower, lifting her until she came back down on him and the hard arousal of his sex slid easily into her. He nearly whispered the words to her then, that he was more than physically one with her, that he was falling in love. But he would never have her doubt such words, as she would if they were spoken in the urgent desperation of the desire that drummed through him like a storm tearing the Glades asunder, so he whispered instead that she was beautiful, and the words she returned were ever more arousing. He became aware of the ancient thunder throbbing through his body, his lungs and his heart, and in a matter of moments they climaxed together in the steamy spray. The winds began to ease while they remained entwined.

Later, when they had sudsed again, then slipped into

each other's arms to sleep, but wound up making love again, he held her, spooned against him. He lay awake, stroking her hair, in wonder. He had thought he would never find a woman like his wife again, someone who had loved him fiercely, been brave and funny, sweet and strong, an equal, but able to make him feel his own strengths, that he was very much a man.

And, of course, he hadn't found his wife again. In a place in his heart, he would love and cherish her forever.

He had found someone unique, who was passionate and righteous, confident, her own self. Different, and yet with qualities that resonated in his heart and soul.

He adjusted his position slightly. Pressed his lips to the top of her head. "I think I'm falling in love," he whispered.

She gave no reply. He wondered if he had pushed her too fast, if his great epiphany was not exactly shared.

But neither did she move or deny him.

Then he realized that he had found the words to say what he was feeling too late, at least for that evening.

Her breathing was soft and even, her fingers curled around his.

And she was sound asleep.

He smiled to himself.

It changed what he was feeling, deepened it, to know that she would sleep beside him, that they would wake together in the morning.

That he wanted to sleep this way every night of his life, and wake beside her again and again.

Would she feel the same? he wondered. Enough to really love this place, where predators roamed, the mos-quitoes seemed elephantine and bit like crazy…and the sunsets were the most glorious man would ever see, and the birds that flew overhead came in all the colors of a rainbow.

He rose in the night and padded naked to the back window, looking out on the eternal darkness.

He heard her, felt her, before she came behind him, arms winding around his back as she laid her cheek against him.

Words failed him again.

He simply turned and took her into his arms. Though tenderness reigned, he found himself afraid.

Afraid to break the moment…

Afraid she didn't feel the same.

And later, still awake, he wondered if there was even more that had stopped him.

Fear…?

They had almost certainly killed the man-eater that had gotten Billy Ray.

They had not, however, captured the man who had created it.

Chapter 11

The massive alligator was being taken upstate for examination, but that didn't stop Harry Rogers from trying to use it to improve his tourist trade.

When Lorena arrived bright and early for work, she discovered that Harry knew how to move quickly. Out front, next to the ticket stalls, he had a mounted enlarged photo of the giant crocodilian—his own arm around it.

Lorena hadn't seen what had gone on overnight, so she was amazed to see that a number of the television stations had arrived, along with radio and newspaper reporters.

The monster was, as Harry and Michael had known, good for business.

The day moved rapidly, in a whirl of tours. Lorena took only a few minutes for lunch. Besides helping with the tours, she had to pull out an ammonia capsule to revive an elderly lady who stood in the heat a bit too long, patch up two little boys who scraped their knees, and treat an allergic reaction to a mosquito bite.

Michael was either too harried to bother her about the previous night or he had just gotten bored with the subject and didn't care any longer.

Sam and Hugh were both still a bit on fire, talking about the hunt the night before. Jesse had turned off his phone during the night, so Jack and Hugh, with Harry's blessing, were delighted to keep busy providing the reporters with what they needed.

The place was jumping.

The police waited until closing to make their appearance.

Lorena had just been saying goodbye to a group of tourists near the main entrance when she heard Harry's booming voice, alive with protest.

"A search warrant—for *this* place? What do you guys think that I'm doing here, feeding drug runners to my critters? What the hell are you after at an alligator farm?"

She noted that although a number of cops had arrived in vans with all kinds of equipment, Lars Garcia and Abe were the ones talking to Harry.

Lars sighed. "Harry, look, I'm sorry—"

"This is Jesse's jurisdiction, or so I thought!"

"Tribal law stands, unless the county, state or federal authorities have to step in," Lars said unhappily. He saw Lorena and studied her absently as he spoke. "Look, Harry, Jesse knows that we're here, and he's not feeling that his toes are being stepped upon. Harry, that was a monster they brought down. We have to search all the farms."

"For what?" Harry demanded.

"Evidence that someone's genetically engineering monster gators," Lars explained.

"What?" Harry seemed incredulous. "Look here, that was no creature from a horror movie. It was big, but it was just a gator. Jesse shot it, and it died."

"There has never been an alligator that size in Florida before," Abe said.

"There hasn't been one on record. Doesn't mean there hasn't been one out there."

"It was way beyond the norm, Harry," Lars insisted.

"Harry," Abe interjected, "God knows, you're an opportunist. Let's just hope you're not a crook."

Harry looked at Abe, enraged.

"Harry, please," Lars said, glaring at his partner. "Let us just clear you and your group so we can move on."

"You idiot!" Harry said, still glaring at Abe. "Clear me of what? Hell, am I an idiot? If I could manufacture a creature like that, do you think I'd let it out in the Everglades? Hell, no! I'd be making money on it."

Lars tried once again to explain. "Harry, we all know that a hatchling could get out. Someone could get careless, or someone could steal one, then lose it."

Harry threw up his hands, really angry. "You know what you can do with your search warrant as far as I'm concerned. But you go right ahead. You look into anything that you want to look into. Search yourself silly. I'm calling my lawyer. You know, if you wanted to see something at my place, all you had to do was ask."

Harry walked away muttering. Lars gave a slight smile to Lorena, shrugged and turned away to talk to a distinguished-looking man in a special-unit suit.

She hadn't realized that Michael had come up behind her. "The suspicious cops are your fault, I imagine?" he asked softly.

A shiver shot down her spine as he spoke. She spun around quickly. She didn't have to answer. He shrugged. "Not that I care. But if Harry finds out…mmm. You're in trouble. Big."

"Excuse me, Michael, I'm hungry," she said, and started for the cafeteria.

"I'm hungry, too," he said, trailing after her.

When they entered the cafeteria, Sally was rushing out. She didn't look at all amused. "Hey, sexy, what's up?" Michael demanded, stopping her.

She grated her teeth and cast Lorena what seemed like an evil stare, although she couldn't really be sure.

She might just be paranoid.

"They're inspecting everything, and Harry wants me there to explain the books. I don't get this—I don't get it at all! There was a giant alligator in the swamp—so we get *audited?* Not that there are any problems, I can assure you. My books are always perfect."

"I'm sure they are," Lorena murmured.

The woman might have been in a hurry, but she took time to glare at Lorena. "It's amazing, isn't it?" she murmured. "We were such a quiet place. Then you arrived and all hell broke loose. Did you have a nice time last night?"

"Yes, thank you," Lorena said evenly.

"What did you do last night?" Michael asked with a frown.

"Oh, come on, Dr. Preston! We have a budding romance in our midst, or didn't you know?" Sally asked.

Michael stared at Lorena. "You left with Jesse?"

"We're not required to stay on the premises," Lorena said.

"You're moving in with him?" Michael demanded. Lorena couldn't tell if he was angry or just surprised.

She looked at him incredulously, shaking her head. "That's kind of a leap, isn't it?" she demanded. She kept smiling, but the curve of her lips was forced. "This is my business, okay?"

"We're just trying to watch out for you," Sally assured her, suddenly saccharine. "I mean, well, you work here, so you're one of us. Jesse is…well, Jesse keeps his distance."

"Doesn't seem that he's keeping much of a distance now," Michael murmured.

"Hey!" Lorena protested again.

"Think of us as one big family," Michael told her.

"Okay, *bro.* I'm not moving anywhere. If such a thing ever happens, I'll be sure to inform my *family,*" she said.

"How lovely," Sally murmured. "I'm off to see to my books. You children have a lovely dinner." She waved a hand in the air and left them.

"You know, you are going to have to tell us what's going on," Michael said, a hand at Lorena's back as he directed her toward a table.

She was saved from having to answer at that moment when Jack Pine joined them, sitting down with a weary grimace. "Busy day," he said.

"Oh? At your end, too?" Michael said.

"A bunch of scientist types, or so I'm told, will be in tomorrow. They want to investigate all our stock," Jack explained.

Michael stared at Lorena again. "How come I haven't heard anything about this?"

"Maybe they just haven't gotten to you yet," Jack suggested.

Hugh came over just then, settling down at the table across from Michael. "This is nuts."

"Are we closing tomorrow for all this?" Michael demanded.

"Oh, no. They can work around us. They're taking samples, bringing chemists and vets in, that kind of stuff," Hugh said cheerfully.

"It's absurd," Michael said indignantly. "I mean, my research is…well, it's *mine*. Where are my rights in all this?"

"I suppose the problem has something to do with giant alligators eating people," Jack said with a shrug.

"There are alligators everywhere," Michael protested. "Alligator farms abound in this state. Entrepreneurs run hunts on private property that aren't sanctioned or controlled by the state or federal government."

"Well, Michael, maybe they feel that your research will help them," Jack said. "Who the hell knows? Has anyone ordered dinner yet?"

Looking across the room, Lorena saw that Jesse had arrived. She was both startled and pleased, and jumped to her feet before she realized that despite the fact that their affair was growing obvious, she might have been a little more circumspect.

"Well, well," Hugh murmured.

Lorena ignored him.

Jesse was already walking over to them. He offered her a smile, held out her chair for her, then chose one for himself.

"So you reported Harry's as a hot bed of…what, exactly?" Michael asked.

Jesse frowned. "What?"

Michael leveled a finger at him. "Cops and the people from Fish and Wildlife are going to be crawling all over the place."

"I heard they're checking out a bunch of places," Jesse said with a shrug.

"Why assume that Harry's has anything to do with a giant alligator?" Michael demanded.

"Maybe because Harry sponsors a lot of research—*your* research—into improving gator meat and hides?" Jesse suggested.

"Can we order now?" Jack asked as one of the waiters arrived at the table.

"Sure. We're in the middle of a criminal investigation. Let's eat," Michael snorted.

"I'm hungry," Jack snapped back.

The tension was definitely growing, Lorena thought.

"Michael, they've got to find out what is going on," Jesse said. "There could be more of those creatures out there. And if they don't find the sustenance they need in the wild, that would put people in danger. Come on, Michael. How many attacks on humans do you want to see?"

"There's no reason to think there are more alligators that size out there," Michael insisted. "Maybe our gators are just getting bigger all around, catching up with some of their counterparts in other places. Maybe they should start investigating that before they come out here on Indian land and start poking their noses into things."

"Hey, this may be Indian land, but when it's a county-wide problem—"

"The alligator was caught on Indian land, too," Michael said testily, cutting Jesse off mid-sentence.

Lorena saw Jesse tense, but he wasn't the one who answered. "So what are you suggesting, Michael? That it's all right because only Indians will be eaten?" Jack Pine snapped.

"Don't be ridiculous!" Michael argued indignantly. "I'm trying to be supportive of tribal law."

"Good of you to be concerned," Jesse replied.

"I think we should order dinner," Hugh murmured, nodding to the waiter, who had continued hovering in the background.

Fresh catfish was suggested and accepted all the way around. Most of the tension around the table eased, but a slight chill remained. Jesse seemed distracted, Jack stiff, and Michael annoyed. Only Hugh seemed oblivious to the general air of discomfort.

"So, any clues as to how our gator got to be such a monster?" Hugh asked Jesse.

"It's been sent off to Jacksonville. That's all I know right now," Jesse said.

"Hey, there's Harry," Hugh said. "He looks happy."

Harry, smiling broadly, breezed by the table. "Looking good, looking good," he told them cheerfully.

"What looks good?" Michael asked skeptically.

"This place. The phones have been ringing off the hook. People want to find out all about alligators. It's kind of like Jurassic Park meets the Florida Everglades. Hey, how's that catfish? Can't get any fresher."

"Harry, we don't know. We haven't got it yet," Hugh said, amused.

"Well, it's going to be great. We're on a roll, all of us. Keep up the good work."

Harry left just as their catfish arrived.

Lorena glanced at Jesse. Could Harry possibly be guilty of anything if he was this happy while the authorities were crawling all over his holdings?

Just as Jack remarked that the catfish was indeed excellent, a slender, balding man in a typical tourist T-shirt and khakis walked up to the table. "Dr. Michael Preston?" he inquired.

Michael sat back tensely. "Yes."

The man offered a hand. "Jason Pratt, Wildlife Conservation. Can you give me a few minutes of your time? When you're done eating, of course."

"I guess I'm done," Michael said, throwing his napkin on the table.

"There's no reason for you to rush," Pratt protested. "I just wanted to catch you before you retired for the night."

Since it was still early, it was unlikely that Michael had been about to go to bed. Maybe Pratt was afraid Michael was about to flee?

Michael rose. "No. I'm done. How can I help you?"

He walked away with Pratt. Jesse rose, as well. "Want to take a ride with me?" he asked Lorena.

"Sure," she murmured, rising, too. Jack and Hugh were exchanging glances. She knew that along with the giant alligator, she was definitely a topic of conversation between them.

"See ya," Jesse said, nodding, taking Lorena's hand and heading out.

"Where are we going?" she asked as they got into his squad car.

"To see Theresa Manning."

"Theresa Manning?"

"The woman whose friend was…eaten," Jesse said.

"And what are we going to learn from her?"

"I'm not sure, but I called to see if we could speak with her, and she asked us over for tea and scones."

"Tea and scones?"

He shrugged. "Apparently she likes to bake."

"Jesse…do you think Michael is behind all this? I had the strangest conversation with him last night."

He scowled fiercely, looking at her in the rearview mirror. "You were alone with him?"

She ignored that. "He seriously believes that I'm here to cause him trouble."

"You need to stay away from him."

"But if he's doing anything illegal…he's about to face the music, right?"

Jesse shook his head. "Someone else has to be involved. Someone with money."

"Harry has money, but he seems as happy as a lark."

Jesse's cell phone started ringing. He answered it, then fell silent, frowning. Finally he said, "Call me as soon as you find out anything."

"What happened?" Lorena demanded.

He glanced quickly at her. "The alligator never made it to the university. Somewhere between here and Jacksonville, the truck it was on disappeared."

Michael leaned against his desk, scowling as Pratt and the other investigators—ridiculously casual in jeans and cotton island shirts or T's—went through his research records and his computer.

"What's this?" one of them asked.

Michael came around and looked over his shoulder.

"A record of the temperatures required to create the different sexes," he said patiently.

"And what's this?"

"Maturity level for the most tender meat," Michael said.

"And this…?"

"Breeding for the best skins," Michael said wearily.

The man rose suddenly. Others were still working in the filing cabinets, but most of his records were on the computer.

"I guess that's it for now," Pratt said, smiling cheerfully.

Michael realized that he had broken out in a cold sweat. Now he felt a debilitating rush of relief.

They hadn't found anything. Nothing. Nada. Zilch. Not a damned thing.

"You're done?"

"Yep. Thanks so much for your time and your patience," the man said.

"Hey, uh…sure," Michael said. "Anything to help. Not a problem. Anytime. Come back anytime you think

I might be able to help." He couldn't seem to stop himself from babbling, he felt so relieved.

Pratt thanked him again as he and the others left the office. Michael sank into his chair with a sigh of relief.

"Yeah, any time," he muttered. Then he looked at his computer and quickly logged into his secret files.

"Sugar? Milk? Lemon?" Theresa asked. "And...let me see. Those are blueberry in the middle, plain on the left side, and cinnamon on the right. I do so hope you enjoy them. I love to cook. My husband loved my cakes and pies."

Jesse had bitten into one of the blueberry scones. "It's wonderful," he told Theresa. "And it was so kind of you to make this offer. Delicious. Thank you. And for me, just tea is good."

"A touch of milk," Lorena murmured. "Thanks. And Jesse's right. These are just too good."

Theresa sat, beaming. "Well, I know you didn't come out for the scones. So how can I help you?"

"I know that this is painful for you, Theresa," Jesse said. "But you've heard all the ruckus about the alligator we caught last night."

Lips pursed, Theresa nodded grimly.

"Caught. It was caught," Lorena emphasized gently.

"That one was caught," Theresa said.

"So you think there are more?" Jesse asked.

"I think my friend was attacked by another one of your giant gators," Teresa said with assurance.

"Why?" Jesse asked her.

"They're territorial, aren't they? And yours was caught off the Trail. My friend was killed way out here."

Jesse cast a quick glance in Lorena's direction. "Was there anything strange going on at the time?" he asked Theresa.

"Strange?" Theresa repeated, then sat thinking for a while. "No. Nothing strange. Oh, now and then a few pets disappear, but…well, a small animal is natural prey, right?"

"I'm afraid so," Jesse said. "But you don't think there was anything else going on in the area?"

"Like what?" Theresa asked.

"Lights of any kind," Jesse said.

"Lights?" Theresa appeared confused. Then she gasped. "Why, yes, actually! There were lights in the sky several times right around the time when…" She paused, making a choking sound deep in her throat.

"Did they ever kill the alligator that took your friend?" Jesse asked. "Did animal control or the nuisance-animal division ever find the right gator?"

She shook her head, then returned to his previous question. "We had been joking about aliens arriving," she murmured.

By the time they left, Jesse looked grim. He was silent when they got back in the car, and silent as they drove. At last Lorena asked him, "So…you believe that several of these creatures have grown up in the Everglades, and that big money is behind it. Enough big money so that someone is out in helicopters searching for their missing gators?"

"Yes," he said simply.

"But Harry is probably the one most involved with alligators who also has the most money," she said, lifting her hands in confusion. "And Harry is so happy he's practically singing!"

"We're moving forward," he said tensely. "The noose is tightening, and we will catch whoever we're looking for."

He didn't head back for the alligator farm but wound his way down the road that she would never have found herself, the road that led to his house.

As he parked, he looked at her, arching a brow. "Stay here tonight?"

"I should go back," she murmured.

"No, you shouldn't. Ever."

She sighed. "Jesse—"

"You want to catch a murderer. Well, you've done all the right things. The authorities are involved now. You don't need to go back."

She decided not to argue with him for the moment.

As they got out of the car, she glanced his way with a small smile. "You really are in the wilds out here."

"Pretty much," he agreed, watching her.

"It's been a long, hot day," she said.

"And…?"

"And the last one in is…a fried egg, I suppose!" she said, and dashed toward the door.

She began shedding her clothing once she had reached the patio. And she was definitely the first one in the pool.

The water hit her with a delicious sense of refreshing coolness. She swam from the deep end to the shallow, enjoying the cleansing of her flesh.

To her amazement, he was there, waiting for her, when she surfaced.

As she came up against the length of him, she was elated to feel the strength beneath the sleek flesh. His ink-dark hair was slicked back, and the green of his eyes seemed brilliant. His arms wrapped around her. "Skinny-dipping, Ms. Fortier? How undignified. Is this something you do frequently?"

She smiled and said softly, "Actually, no. This is the first time I've ever been skinny-dipping. In my whole life."

"I'm flattered. And honored."

He smoothed back a length of her hair, his lips brushing hers, hot and warm beneath the faint scent of chlorine. His arms tightened around her, bringing the full length of her body against his. Her breasts were crushed against the powerful muscles of his chest, her hips molded to his, and the perfectly placed thrust of his sex against hers was a titillation that thrilled and warmed her with a heady sense of anticipation.

"Does that mean," he asked huskily, "that the entire concept of sex in a pool is equally new?"

She started to answer, but his lips moved down the length of her neck and the words evaded her. He kicked away from the wall, the force slamming them more tightly together. She was scarcely aware of the slick feel of the tile steps when they landed there. For a breathless moment she met his eyes. Then she felt the full brunt of his body as he lifted her high against him, then thrust himself deeply inside her. She wrapped her limbs around him, and the fire that suddenly seemed to burn between them was an intoxicating contrast to the coolness of the water. She cast her head back, felt again the fury of his lips on her throat, breasts, the hollow of her collarbone.... Her lips met his again as they moved in the water, the night sky high above them, the whisper of the foliage around them, and the thunder of pulse and breath taking over. She buried her head against his shoulder as the power of need, and the agony-ecstasy of longing seemed to seep through her, spiral and grow, seize her and shut away the world. Her arms stroked his back; her fingers dug into his buttocks. She arched and writhed, and wondered that she didn't drown, but he kept them afloat, and in a cauldron of searing carnal mist until it seemed that the world exploded right along with the night stars, and she collapsed against him, still held tight and secure. Then she began to shiver, for the night, without the fire of him, was strangely cool.

"If I'd had any warning, we might have had towels," he said, amused, his lips handsomely curved as he pulled ever so slightly away.

"I was simply seized with overwhelming desire," she told him, and she smiled herself. "Quite frankly, I'm not sure I could have planned skinny-dipping."

"Stay, I'll get the towels," he said.

"But it's just as cold—"

She fell silent. He had already leapt out and, naked and dripping, headed for the house.

She realized that it was colder outside the water than in it, so she waited.

At first she eased her head back and simply smiled. She felt so wonderful that she refused to let herself wonder if she wasn't being a fool, falling in love with someone who made no promises, who was so distant.

But there wasn't a thing she would change, even if she could.

Her eyes opened suddenly, and she wondered why, aware that she was feeling the first twinge of unease.

She glanced around. Lights shone in and around the house, but beyond...

Beyond was the Everglades. Miles and miles of darkness and foliage and swamp, a land that was deep, dark and dangerous. A place where a million sins could be hidden.

She froze, aware then that she was in the light, that any eyes could be looking on from the darkness.

She was suddenly afraid, certain that the night could see.

"Here we are," Jesse murmured.

A towel was wrapped around his waist, and he had one for her in his hands. The sight of him seemed to turn back the darkness.

"Thanks," she murmured, rising, allowing him to wrap her in the soft fabric.

"Thank *you*," he murmured, and kissed her lightly on the lips.

The brilliance of his eyes touched hers, and he repeated the words very softly and tenderly. "Thank you."

He lifted her up, and they headed for the house.

In his arms, she forgot the darkness, and any thought that eyes might have gleamed at her from the black void of the night beyond.

Chapter 12

Jesse was gone in the morning. So was his car.

And she was furious. Despite the night they had spent together, she had no intention of listening to him about not going in to work. She was in no danger at the alligator farm. It was alive with officials—local, state and federal. Nothing was going to happen to her while she was working.

She walked around, fuming, for several long minutes while she brewed coffee.

Just how long would it take to get a taxi out to the middle of nowhere? In fact, was it even *possible* to get a taxi out to the middle of nowhere?

Come to think of it, she didn't know exactly where she was. What did one say? Come out and get me. There's a dirt road off Tamiami Trail, and it looks as if it leads into nothing but saw grass and a canal, but there's really a house out there. Quite a nice house, actually. Swimming pool, state-of-the-art kitchen…

She swore aloud and hesitated, wondering if she should call in to work or just pray that Jesse would show up and drive her to work.

She pulled out her cell phone and stared at it, ready to put through a call to his cell, tell him what she thought of his high-handed tactics and demand that he come back immediately so he could take her to work.

He might, of course, simply refuse. He might even be involved in a situation from which he couldn't extract himself. Too bad. There were others on his day crew. He could send someone for her, and damn it, he *would*.

Just as she was about to punch his number in, her cell rang. Caller ID said the number was the office at Harry's.

"Hello," she said quickly, expecting Harry, though a glance at her watch showed her that she wasn't late yet.

"Hey" came a soft voice. Male.

"Michael?"

"No, it's Jack. We didn't see you at breakfast. We were getting a bit worried."

"We?"

"Hugh, Sally and me."

"That was nice of you, but I'm fine."

"Glad to hear it. Not that you shouldn't be," he said hastily. "Things are just a bit strange around here right now, you know? I mean, who'd ever think *I* would be in any real danger from an alligator? So…we were worried."

"No, I'm fine, just…" She hesitated for only a second. "Jesse seems to have gotten caught up in something. He's not here, and I'm afraid I'm going to be late."

"We'll come get you."

"No, I'm sorry. You don't have to."

"No, no, it's fine. One of us will come. Fifteen minutes."

Jack hung up.

She clicked her phone shut. The hell with Jesse and his high-handedness. She was running her own life. No matter how much she cared for someone, she wasn't going to be ordered about or dissuaded from her course.

Her father had been murdered, and she had never felt so close to capturing the killer. No way was she going to back off now.

Inside, she poured a last cup and turned the coffeepot off. And waited.

George Osceola reported on the missing van. It wasn't much of a report—the van was still missing. It had been on I-95. The driver had spoken to his wife at about ten-thirty in the morning, just after fueling up.

And then...

He and the van had just disappeared. County law enforcement throughout the state had been notified, along with the highway patrol, but so far, the van hadn't been spotted.

A call to Lars provided no further information.

Jesse looked at the phone and thought about calling Lorena. She was going to be really angry. But she hadn't called him to demand that he come back and take her in to work. Maybe she had fumed for a while, then decided on her own that the smart thing to do now would be to stay away from Harry's.

As he stared at his desk phone, it rang. A female voice greeted his ears, but not Lorena's. "Jesse, it's Julie. I was just calling in to see if…well, if anything else had happened."

"We're working on it, Julie, but I've got nothing to tell you."

He could sense her hesitation, then she said, "Jesse, I know it was probably foolish, but I went by the house last night. I mean, I have to go back inside eventually."

"I'd be happier if you'd stay away a little longer," he told her. "Just a few more days."

"A few more days," she echoed. "The police have asked me to wait a few more days, too. Before…before claiming the bodies. They're afraid the medical examiner might have missed something. But about the house… I'm going to need clothes."

"Julie, when you go, I'll go with you. And if you need my help at the funeral home or with the church…"

"It's all done, Jesse, thanks. I knew what they wanted," Julie said. "I didn't call you to cry."

"Sweetheart, you have the right to cry as much as you want," he assured her softly.

"Thanks, Jess, but what I need is to…to bug you and make sure no one stops until my parents' killer is caught. And also, I called because I keep thinking about the lights I saw out at the house."

"Plane lights? Helicopter lights? Men on the ground with flashlights?" Jesse asked. "What do you think?"

"I know they didn't come from anyone on the ground," Julie said. "To tell you the truth… I know why my mother thought aliens were landing. They hovered right above the trees. I didn't hear any noise. Of course, I was in the car, and they were at a distance."

"Thanks for calling, Julie. I'll look into it. Trust me. I want to help you. I loved your parents."

"I know you did, Jesse. And they thought the world of you. So do I. And I'll wait till we go inside together, okay?"

"Perfect."

He hung up after a minute, then called Lars back. "We need to start checking the airfields. More specifically, we need to find out who has been taking helicopters up."

Lars groaned. "Every television and radio station out there has a traffic and weather copter! And when we were out at Hector and Maria's, you said an airboat had been through."

"So?"

"So we've been talking to a lot of people with airboats, Jesse."

"Yes, and that was a move that needed to be made. Now we need to find out about helicopters."

He heard an even louder groan.

"Lars, I keep hearing stories about lights wherever there's been an event with an alligator. You have more resources at your disposal than I do. Can you get on it?"

He heard the deep sigh at the other end, but then Lars agreed. "All right. I'm on it."

Satisfied, Jesse hung up. He drummed his fingers on the desk. Something had been bothering him, and he wasn't quite sure why.

He looked at the phone and thought about calling his house, then decided not to.

He rose suddenly, since he wasn't getting anywhere sitting at his desk.

He grabbed his hat from the hook by the door. "Where are you going?" George asked him.

"To check with Doc Thiessen or Jim Hidalgo. See if anything else has happened over at the vet's. Call me if you hear anything," Jesse said.

Lorena expected either Hugh or Jack to show up at the rear of the property with an airboat. Instead, it was Sally who finally tooted her horn from the front. Lorena clicked the front lock and hurried out.

"Jesse's trying to keep you away from Harry's, huh?" Sally said.

"Why would he do that?" Lorena asked, hoping she wasn't giving anything away.

"Why? Killer gators, feds all over the place, something fishy in the air," Sally said with a laugh. "Actually, you should be happy. If he didn't care about you, he wouldn't be acting so much like an alpha dog. Well, maybe he's just the alpha-dog type. I don't know."

Lorena shrugged. "Thanks for getting me. I don't know what he got involved in, or when he might get back, but I don't like being late."

"Aren't you even a little bit worried about everything that's going on?" Sally asked her.

"Should I be?" Lorena asked.

Sally laughed. "Michael thinks you're a suspicious character."

"Michael is paranoid," Lorena murmured.

"Maybe. He's a scientist. Maybe all scientists get paranoid. They think their research is better than gold."

"Maybe it is. Sometimes."

Sally waved a hand in the air. "I don't think Michael has created a strain of giant killer alligators."

"Oh?"

Sally shook her head. "He always seems frustrated. He's a good-looking guy. I think he had the hots for you. Actually, until Jesse stepped into the picture, it kind of looked like you liked Michael."

"I like everyone at the farm," Lorena murmured.

"Just the slutty type, huh?" Sally queried.

"What?" Lorena snapped.

"Well, you *were* flirting pretty hard with everyone until you settled on Jesse."

Lorena stared out the front window. "Did you come to get me just so you could give me a hard time?" she asked.

Sally looked at her, eyes wide. "No! Of course not." A small smile curved her lips as she shook her head.

Dr. Thorne Thiessen wasn't in when Jesse arrived at the veterinary clinic.

Jim Hidalgo was there, though. "Hey, how are you feeling?" Jesse asked him.

"Fine. Just fine," Jim assured him.

"How come you're here? I thought you had the night shift? And where is the doc, anyway?" Jesse asked.

"This is the day he does calls. He covers a few of the alligator farms, you know. And he does cattle, as well. There are even a couple of folks with real exotics, snakes and things, and for them, he makes house calls. One day one week, two days the next. I guess it works for him."

Jesse chewed a blade of grass and nodded. "You still don't remember anything about what happened that night, huh?"

"Nothing. You still haven't caught the thief, huh?"

Jesse shook his head. "Tell me if I've got it right. You were in the back, then...wham! And then nothing, nothing at all, until Doc was standing over you?"

"Yeah, yeah, then lights, sirens, cops, med techs... You know the rest. You were here."

"Right."

Jesse shrugged. "So when will the doc be back?"

"Tomorrow morning," Jim told Jesse.

"Where is he?"

"Don't know. He works lots of places."

"And you're in charge until then? What about the day guy?"

"He works with Thiessen, travels with him. Weird goose, if you ask me."

"Because he's white?"

Jim laughed, shaking his head. "Because he never talks. Hey, lots of folks live and work out here who aren't part of the tribe. We all get along. His day guy, though. John Smith. Who ever heard such a name for real? He's a big goon. Never talks."

"To each his own," Jesse said. "Thiessen must trust him. Anyway, you feel safe enough out here alone now?"

"I'm not alone."

"Oh?"

Jim gave a whistle. A huge dog came crawling out

from beneath the desk where Jim sat. He was quite a mix. Evidently a little bit shepherd, chow and pit bull. Whatever else, Jesse didn't know, but it made for one big beast of a canine.

"I just got him," Jim said happily. "I call him Bear."

Bear wagged his tail.

"He likes you," Jim continued.

"I'm glad," Jesse said.

"Anyway, he makes me feel safe. He was sniffing and woofing before you got out of your car. When I told him it was all right, he sat right back down. Got him from the animal shelter."

"Great."

"Doc isn't too fond of him," Jim admitted. "But he knows I'm not happy anymore about holding down the fort by myself on the days he's gone and at night, so…" He shrugged happily.

Jesse nodded. "See you. Don't forget—"

"Yeah, I know the drill. If I think of anything, I'll call you."

"Yep. Thanks."

When he reached his patrol car, Jesse put a call through to the office.

The van with the alligator carcass was still missing. And nothing had been found of the samples taken from the vet's office.

There were no known leads on the murders.

He clicked off, hesitated, and at last called his house.

She wasn't answering. He hung up, then called back, and spoke when he heard his own message. "Pick up, Lorena, please. It's Jesse."

But she didn't pick up. She might have been in the pool, in the shower or in another part of the house.

Or she might have called someone to take her in to work.

He tried her cell phone.

She wasn't picking up.

Okay, so she was angry.

He put a call through to the alligator farm. Harry answered. "Hey, Harry. I'm surprised to hear your voice."

"It's still my place, you know. Despite the goons crawling all over it," Harry said. But he sounded cheerful.

"You just don't usually answer the phone."

"This place is doing twice the business we used to. No one here but me to pick up. The feds said I didn't have to close, just as long as they could go through what they wanted. Hell, they can go through anything, as far as I'm concerned."

"I'm glad you're happy, Harry," Jesse said. "I guess it would be tough for you to find someone to search the throng of tourists and find Lorena for me, huh?"

"Yes, it would be. But I can put you through to the infirmary, in case she's there."

"So you've seen her?"

"Not this morning. But I'm sure she's working, no thanks to you."

"What do you mean?"

"You're trying to seduce my help away from here, aren't you, Jesse Crane?"

"Harry—"

"Hang on, I'll put you through. How do you work this ridiculous, pain-in-the-ass thing?" he muttered.

Harry didn't put him through. He hung up on him. Irritated, Jesse snapped his phone closed.

His house was between the vet's and the alligator farm, so he decided to make a quick stop, see if she was there fuming and swearing at his furniture, then head out to the farm.

A sense of genuine unease was beginning to fill him. It was as if puzzle pieces were beginning to fall together, yet they didn't quite seem to fit.

He closed his eyes for a moment. Someone from Harry's was definitely involved. There had to be a money connection. And someone who knew the Everglades well.

There was more than one person involved, for sure. A connection through Harry's, a money man, someone with a knowledge of genetic engineering, and someone else, a hired goon.

Thoughtful, he picked up the phone to make one last call, then hit the gas pedal.

The phone rang, and Sally answered it.

"Hey," she said cheerfully. Then she glanced sideways at Lorena. "Sure... No... Yes, of course."

She clicked off, then offered Lorena a rueful smile. "Jesse," she said.

"Jesse?"

"Yeah, he wants me to make a quick detour."

"Uh-uh. No way. Let's go in to work."

"I think he's found something."

"What?"

"I think he's made a discovery. Something to do with...if I heard him right, your father."

"My father!" Lorena said, startled.

"Yeah. I didn't know Jesse knew your family. Hey, it's your call. He wanted me to bring you out to what they call Little Rat hummock. It's barely a piece of land, but they have names for every little hellhole and cranny out here. From the days when they were running and hiding out here, I guess. Anyway, what should I do? Jesse sounded all excited."

Lorena's heart flipped; her pulse was racing. She was still furious with him. But if he had discovered something and needed her in any way, she had to be there.

"If Jesse were calling me," Sally said, sounding wistful, "I'd sure be going."

"I'm supposed to be working," Lorena murmured.

"Okay, we'll go to work."

Lorena lifted her hands. "No. Little Rat hummock it is."

"Good thing I brought the Jeep," Sally said. "There's no real road out there."

There wasn't. Lorena thought they were going to sink in mire once and, if not, be swallowed in the saw grass.

But Sally knew the terrain. Right when Lorena was gritting her teeth, certain they were about to perish in the swamp, the wheels hit solid ground. Ahead, she saw a cluster of pines.

"You're not scared out here, are you?" Sally asked her. "You don't need to be. Well, maybe you should have worn boots, but don't worry—the snakes won't get you, not if you leave them alone. Besides here, in the pines, all you really have to worry about are the Eastern diamondbacks and the pygmy rattlers. Well, and the coral snakes, but they don't have the jaws to bite you unless they get you just right." She glanced at Lorena, who could feel herself turning pale. "Sorry. I'm out in the Everglades all the time, and I've never been hit by anything more vicious than a mosquito."

Sally brought the Jeep to a halt.

Lorena looked around.

There was nothing. Nothing but a patch of high ground, a bunch of pines and the saw grass beyond.

"I don't see Jesse."

Sally was frowning, staring ahead.

Lorena heard the noise, too, then. A throb of engines.

"Airboat?" she murmured.

"Yeah. What the hell...?" Sally murmured.

"It's probably Jesse," Lorena said, getting out of the car.

Sally got out, as well. She walked around the car, staring ahead, still puzzled.

"It's not Jesse," she murmured after a minute.

The airboat came around the cluster of pines that lay ahead. "It's Jack. Jack Pine," Sally said.

"So it's Jack. Maybe Jesse asked him to come out here, too," Lorena said.

But Sally shook her head. "No...no...something's wrong here."

Jack brought his airboat to a halt and leapt out.

"Oh, man," Sally murmured. She turned again. Lorena realized that they had walked some distance from the Jeep.

"Hey!" Jack called. "Hey, Lorena! Stop!"

Sally shook her head wildly. "Run!" she advised, and immediately took her own advice.

Lorena stared from Jack to Sally, then back again.

There was a large machete hanging from Jack's belt.

"Run!" Sally called back to her.

"Run where?" Lorena cried, chasing after Sally.

"Follow me. I know where I'm going!"

There were tire tracks in front of his house. Jesse hunkered down and studied them.

A Jeep. Harry's had a number of Jeeps. Any of the senior staff had access to them.

He checked the house quickly, but he knew the minute he entered that she wasn't there. He paused in back, though.

There were tire tracks in the front, but the broken foliage in back indicated an airboat had been by, as well.

At that instant, his heart seemed to freeze in his chest. He headed back for the car, already flipping open his cell phone.

"George, I've got Lars checking on a few things, and I've asked him to get men out here. But we know the area better than they do. I want everyone available out here. Something is going down *now.* Cut a swath from the vet's to Harry's, pie-shaped, fanning south."

"Jess, what the hell…?"

"Do it. Just do it."

Lorena stopped because she couldn't run anymore. Sally, ahead of her, had stopped, as well.

She looked back at Jack Pine, who'd been closing in on them.

Jack had stopped, too.

"What are you doing out here, Sally?" Jack demanded.

"Jesse called," Sally said.

Jack shook his head. "No."

"What the hell are you doing out here, Jack?" Sally demanded in return, sounding frightened.

"Following you. I saw the car from the airboat. I was on my way out to pick up Lorena, so I couldn't help but wonder why you were heading out there, too. What's going on, Sally?"

"Jack, you're a liar and a murderer!" Sally cried, her tone hysterical. "I couldn't let you get Lorena. I couldn't let it happen."

Jack shook his head, looking puzzled. "Lorena, get away from her. She must have been listening on the phone. She had to get to you before I did."

Lorena looked from one of them to the other.

Sally wasn't armed.

Jack was carrying one frighteningly big knife.

She had no idea where she was, only that she was far from the car.

"I have an idea," she said. "Let's all head back to the alligator farm and discuss this whole thing."

"Lorena, don't be ridiculous," Sally said.

Lorena realized that Jack was moving steadily closer to her.

"Get away, Jack," she said.

"Don't you get it yet?" Jack said.

"You're going to kill her—and me!" Sally cried. "Lorena, don't you see? He's going to chop us up and feed us to his alligators."

"No!" Jack cried. "You've got it all wrong. You have to listen."

"Come on," Sally cried. "Lorena, move! One swing of that machete…"

"Lorena," Jack pleaded as he took another step toward her.

"This way!" Sally cried to her.

Lorena tried to maneuver around the three pines that separated her from Sally.

"No!" Jack cried. "No!"

He was coming after her.

She turned to run more quickly.

But as she did, she was suddenly running on air. There was no earth.

No hummock, no ground.

She was falling through space.

Falling, falling, into the darkness of a pit.

She hit the ground with a thud, but after a moment of breathless shock, she realized that she hadn't broken any bones. The ground was not hard. It was muck and mire. Of course. They were below sea level. It would be impossible to dig a dry hole.

She let out a sigh of relief, then heard the thud next to her.

Someone else was in the hole.

And then…

She heard the noise. Loud. A grunting sound, like a pig. No, not a pig. A huge, furious boar. Or…

An alligator.

Chapter 13

Jesse chose to take his own airboat, trying to follow the broken foliage across the Everglades, certain that time was of the essence. His heart felt heavy. There was so much ground to cover. The river of saw grass seemed endless. He'd already seen so much evil done out here. You could search forever to find a body.

No, he refused to think in that direction. She had to be alive. He was certain that Lorena had been lured somewhere, but where, he didn't know. Or even why. Except that she was a piece of the puzzle; she'd been the first to know that something very wrong was going on, and that they were talking technology.

Dangerous stolen technology.

They weren't going to find anything at Harry's Alligator Farm and Museum.

Because Harry wasn't guilty.

And if all went as the thieves had planned it, they wouldn't find the van or the alligator carcass, nor the specimens from Doc Thiessen's lab.

He still didn't have all the facts, but he was certain of one person who might be involved. And that person didn't intend for any of this to be discovered, and it wouldn't matter just how many people died. The frightening thing was that no matter how many people died, mysteriously or otherwise, the techno thief clearly believed he couldn't be caught.

Ahead, he saw one of the airboats from Harry's. And there was someone beside it, gesturing madly.

He cut his engine.

Sally.

"Jesse, Jesse! Help! Quickly. It's Lorena…. Help!"

His heart remained in his throat. "Lorena…?"

"Come with me. For the love of God, hurry. And be careful. It's Jack…he'll kill her!"

Jack? Jack Pine?

Sally was running. Jesse ran after her in a flash. She circled around the pines, then shouted to him.

"Hurry!"

He did. And then he plunged into the hole.

He should have seen it. Even concealed as it had been with bracken and brush, he should have seen it. Hell, this was his country. This god-forsaken swamp was his heritage. He knew it like the back of his hand. He should have seen the damned thing, and realized that it wasn't any natural gator hole.

No. This one had been dug intentionally. And it was deep. In the rain, it would flood. But in the dry season…

He landed hard. The hole was deep, and the thatch covering above kept out all but a hint of light.

"Oh, God, Jesse!" Lorena cried, recognizing him in the meager light. In a second she was next to him, warm and vital. He held her, damning himself a thousand times over. She'd come flying into his arms with such trust.

And he had no idea how to get them out of this mess. He pulled out his cell phone. No signal. Damn!

"Jesse?" Jack Pine moaned.

"What the hell?" Jesse said. He eased himself away from Lorena.

It was pitch black, and he wasn't a trigger-happy kid or a rookie, but Jesse pulled his gun, just in case.

"Stay where you are, Jack. I'm armed."

"I'm not your problem," Jack said.

Jesse blinked, trying to accustom his eyes to the eerie lack of light.

"Stay back," he said softly, his mind going a hundred miles an hour as he tried to figure out what the hell was going on.

Lorena backed up until she and Jack were both flat against the wall of earth and muck.

Above them, Jesse suddenly heard laughter.

Sally's laughter.

"What a pity I can't see you all down there. Sorry, Jack. You were really kind, likable. You shouldn't have been so determined to help Lorena. And Jesse...so gallant. See, Lorena? You were the problem. Everything was going just fine until you appeared. But it doesn't matter. They'll rip Harry's apart, but they won't find a thing. They'll just have to accept the fact that we've grown some big gators in the Everglades—and that they ate you all up."

She sounded as if she were happily reading a children's fairy tale.

"I have to go now. I have to get rid of both those airboats. Goodbye. Nice knowing you."

Jack exploded. "Dammit, Jesse. Do something. She's insane. I mean…she's not the brains behind things, I'd swear it, but when I realized she had Lorena, I knew something wasn't right."

It was then that Jesse heard it. The grunt…the grunt followed by the roar.

He'd been listening to alligators since he'd been a kid. He'd learned a lot about the sounds they made.

Those that had to do with mating.

And those that had to do with territoriality…and hunger. Or both.

"Hell," he muttered under his breath. He could barely see the other two. "Stay back," he warned them.

"Jesse," Lorena said softly. "What are you going to do?"

"I'm armed," he reminded her. But he was worried. Bullets at almost immediate range had barely pierced the tough hide of the alligator they had bagged two nights before.

He wanted to rush over to Lorena. He wanted to hold her, to place his body as a barrier between her and the creature in the darkness. He wanted to say a dozen things to her. He wanted to tell her that he loved her.

He stood dead still, listening, waiting.

The animal was moving. He heard it moving slowly at first, but he knew just how fast a gator could be.

Then there was the rush.

He spun, blinded, but going on instinct. He emptied the clip. The sound was deafening.

The animal bellowed and paused, then slammed into him.

In the dark, he heard the jaws slam shut.

Close. So close that he felt the wind the movement created....

He jumped back.

"Jesse!" It was Lorena, shouting his name.

"Jack, we've got to straddle it!" Jesse yelled.

"Are you insane?" Jack shouted back. "These are monsters. They can't be wrestled down like a five-or six-footer."

"Do you want to be eaten?" Jesse demanded.

The animal had apparently been wounded, because it continued bellowing. Its senses were far better than his own, Jesse knew, but it seemed to be disoriented. He tried desperately to get a sense of its whereabouts.

Then he threw himself on the animal.

He aimed accurately, hitting the back just behind the neck. But the creature was powerful and began thrashing. Right when Jesse thought that he was going to be tossed aside like a blown leaf, Jack landed behind him.

"What now?" Jack shouted.

"I've got to get on the jaws."

"I can't hold the weight!"

"You've got to."

"Wait! I'm here!" Lorena cried.

"Lorena, you don't—" Jesse began.

"We've done something sort of like this before," Jack panted. "Kind of."

There was a flurry of motion as the alligator gave a mighty bellow, tossing its head from side to side.

Lorena landed on the animal's back behind Jack.

"Now what?" Jack demanded.

"The jaw," Jesse said.

"You're mad," Jack responded.

"What? We can't ride this damned thing forever," Jesse said.

"But—"

"Big or little, if I can get the jaw clamped, we'll be safe."

"Yeah, yeah…if you don't get eaten first. Go for it."

He did. He had no choice. He tensed, feeling every inch of the creature beneath him, sensing with all his might, trying to ascertain what the creature's next twist would be.

And then he moved. He leapt forward, landing heavily on the open jaw, snapping it shut. The creature was mammoth; the jaws extended well beyond his perch.

He'd snapped the jaws shut, and still the animal was trying to fight him off. Its strength was incredible. It would shake them all off if they weren't careful.

Trying to maintain his seat, he reached into his pocket for a new clip. The animal bucked. He nearly fumbled the clip.

He tried again.

"Hurry," Jack breathed.

The alligator made a wild swing with its tail.

Lorena screamed. Jesse heard the whoosh as she flew through the air, the thud as she slammed against the mud wall of the pit.

The alligator bucked, fighting him wildly, beginning to get its jaws open, despite his weight.

"Jack, hold him!" he cried.

"Damn it, I can't. I can't!"

Then he heard Lorena, rising, breathless but as tenacious as the creature beneath him. "I'm coming."

"Watch it!"

The alligator swerved, knowing exactly where Lorena was, trying for her.

She moved like the wind, flying past him, landing behind Jack once again.

He could barely hold the gun, much less insert the clip. He had to. He had to, and he knew it.

He locked the clip into place.

He felt for the eyes, and he fired.

The ferocity of the bellow that erupted from the creature nearly threw him. The sound of the bullet exploding was terrible, almost deafening.

But he shot again.

And again.

At last the gator ceased to move.

For long, awful moments, none of them moved.

Jesse's ears were ringing when he finally said huskily, "Lorena, try getting up."

She did so, slowly, carefully.

The creature remained dead still.

"Jack."

Jack moved, but Jesse stayed. He groped around and found the base of the skull, then warned them, "I'm shooting again."

He delivered two more bullets into the creature.

Then, at last convinced that the creature had to be dead, he moved, too.

In the darkness, he felt her. But she didn't collapse against him the way a lesser woman might have. She strode over to him, and her arms wound around him as his wound around her.

Only then did she start to shake.

He heard Jack sink to the ground. "I think I'm moving north," Jack muttered. "Somewhere with ice and snow and no alligators."

Jesse allowed himself a moment to revel in simply holding Lorena, in feeling her, breathing her scent above the gunpowder and the muck.

"What the...?" Jack said suddenly. "Hell."

"What?" Jesse demanded sharply.

In the darkness, they could hear Jack swallow.

"What?" Jesse demanded again.

"There, uh, there was someone else down here," Jack said very softly. "There are...body parts."

"Oh, God!" Lorena breathed.

"Hey, we've got to keep it together," Jesse said sharply. "It's not over yet. We've got to get out of here. Quickly. They'll be back."

"They?" Jack said dully. Then he added, "Of course. They."

"Come on, Lorena," Jesse said. "I'll hike you up first."

He lifted her, and with Jack's help, he got her to his shoulders. From there, a shove sent her out of the pit.

"Hey! I found a big branch," Lorena called. "You guys can use it as a ladder."

She nearly hit Jesse in the head with it, but as soon

as they got it in place, Jack reached upward, bracing against it. Jesse gave him a push.

They heard the tree limb cracking, but Jack was nimble for his size, and grasping for both the ground and Lorena's hand, he managed to throw himself to the edge of the pit. He turned then, ready to help Jesse. "Come on!"

Jesse eyed the height of the pit, the broken branch, and the length of Jack's arms. "Back off," he said.

"What?"

"Back off."

He gave himself a few feet, then ran at the tree limb, using it as a stepping-stone and no more.

He just made the rim of the pit, then hung there.

His grip slipped in the muck.

"Jack, where the hell are you?"

Jack didn't answer.

Jesse dangled. Then he got a grip, and at last, straining, he dragged himself over the rim of the pit. He rolled, then lay panting in the bright sunlight.

"Damn you, Jack," he said, turning.

And then he fell silent, knowing what had happened to Jack.

Both Jack and Lorena were still there. Completely covered in black muck and mire.

But the true killer, the thief, the one determined on getting rich at the expense of so many lives, had at last arrived himself.

Jesse made it to his feet, aware of the Smith & Wesson pointed at his face, and the grim features of the man he had once respected.

"Doc," he said. "Doc Thiessen. I've been expecting you."

"Damn, Jesse, why do you have to be so hard to kill?" Thorne Thiessen demanded.

"Hell, I don't know. I just like living, I suppose."

Sally was standing right behind Thiessen. Jesse noticed that she hadn't gotten rid of both airboats. There were two on the little hummock, his own and the one Doc had come in.

"So, Doc... I kind of figured you were involved in this," he said smoothly. He was playing for time now, but Doc didn't know that. Doc didn't know that the troops were already on the way.

"Oh, bull! You didn't have the least idea," Doc Thiessen said.

"Yeah, I did, Doc, but I was awful damn slow putting it all together. At first I thought it was Harry, because Harry has money. But so do you. I admit, I didn't figure out right away who you had working for you, and I sure as hell didn't suspect Sally, but after I talked to Jim Hidalgo a few times, I knew you had to be involved. He gets whacked on the head, and the first one he sees is you. And those samples... You should have had them all prepared and studied and on their way somewhere else. You had to steal your own samples. And I'm willing to bet that by now Lars Garcia has found out that you own a helicopter, though I doubt you were the one flying it around, looking for your gators. That was probably John Smith. I'm willing to bet that the altered gators are marked somehow. They would have found out just exactly how if the one I shot had reached the veterinary school, as it was supposed to. I didn't suspect

Sally at first, but I should have. She was the one who gave Roger a shove, wasn't she?

"So let me see if I've got it worked out. You were the leader, and Sally and John were working for you. Who did all the dirty work for you? The killing, Doc. Who killed Maria and Hector—and Lorena's father?"

"I really don't have time for this," Thiessen said, shaking his white head. The face that had always seemed so kindly was now twisted in a mask of impatience and cold cruelty.

"Come on. You beat me." Jesse tried to assess the situation. Doc was the only one with a gun, and it was now aimed at him. Jack and Lorena were standing to one side, where they'd been forced in the last seconds while he'd been getting himself out of the hole.

But neither Jack nor Lorena looked as if they were about to collapse. As if they had been beaten. They were survivors. Lorena had a steely strength to have gotten this far.

In fact, she looked both defiant and angry. She wasn't going to go down easy.

And he couldn't count Jack out, either.

Thiessen smiled. "Actually, you'll find out who does my dirty work in just a minute or two. But first I've got to decide how to do this. You killed my gator, Jesse. In fact, damn it, you've killed two of them."

"C'mon, Doc, what else could I do?" Jesse said. "But listen, since I'm going to die anyway, do me a favor. Explain it all to me first, will you?"

Doc shrugged. "Easy enough. Sally heard about the research, made the contacts and came to me, since she didn't have the expertise to work with what she'd found.

I've worked my fingers to the bone out here, and you can't imagine the millions to be made off a formula that can create an animal this size. The old man up in his research lab panicked. He didn't have to die. But he found out I'd gotten hold of a few of his specimens. Found out that they were growing, and he didn't keep his mouth shut, the old fool. He had to go and confront me about it. He hadn't figured out Sally's role yet, but I couldn't take the chance he would. She'd worked for him briefly, and if she'd been caught, that would have led back to me. So he had to die. Just the way things go," he said coldly. "Now, as to Lorena being the old man's daughter, well, it took me a while to make the connection, I'll admit."

"You bastard!" Lorena said softly.

For a moment Jesse thought she was going to fly at Doc, but she controlled herself, tense as a whip.

Her eyes touched Jesse's. He realized that she was trusting him to get them out of this.

He couldn't fail her.

Thiessen was on a roll. "You should have accepted that accident, Ms. Fortier. The cops would have gone on believing that Hector and Maria had been involved in drugs. As to old Billy Ray, well, I didn't kill him. The old drunk ran into one my gators, that's all."

"Just how many killer gators are there?" Lorena asked tightly.

Thiessen appeared amused. "There were four. One died on its own—near Hector and Maria's. You killed two, Jesse. There's still one of these beauties out there somewhere, and trust me, I'll find it. I've had Sally eavesdropping all along, and as soon as there's word,

I'll know. None of this was as hard as you're trying to make it look, Jesse."

"And getting away with it won't be as easy as you think, Doc," Jesse said. All he needed was a distraction. He was certain that Doc knew how to shoot, but he was no ace, no trained officer. A distraction, and...

He swallowed hard. Did he dare? He'd be risking Lorena's life. And Jack's.

Lorena was staring at him, waiting. She still seemed to trust in the fact that he intended to do something.

And if he didn't?

Then they could all be dead anyway, unless the cavalry got here pronto.

"Lars Garcia will put all these pieces together, Doc."

"Don't be ridiculous. Other people out here have helicopters, and airboats? They must number in the thousands."

"People who know reptiles as well as you do are harder to find," Jesse commented. "And I've already mentioned your name to Lars. What was it, Thorne? Not enough money in what you were doing, or not enough glory?"

"The world is changing, Jesse. Genetic enhancement is being made on a daily basis. Clones are a dime a dozen now. You're got to be at the front of the flock."

"I'm telling you, Lars is on to you," Jesse said softly. "And you think that Metro-Dade Homicide will let go? You're out of your mind."

Thiessen looked troubled for an instant. "He has no proof."

"He will. I figure you marked those gators, tagged them in some way, and then let them loose on purpose, trying to see how they did in the wild. But you wanted to protect them from discovery at the same time, so you tracked them by helicopter, as well as by airboat. They're territorial creatures, so you probably shouldn't have let that one get so close to a populated area. That was a stupid-as-hell reason for Hector and Maria to die. Whoever killed Hector and Maria came on their property with an airboat. So tell me, Doc. Who did it?"

"I did," Sally offered, stepping around from behind Thiessen. "I did it, you fool. You thought I was nothing more than an attractive piece of ornamentation, a numbers cruncher. Background and nothing more. Well, get this. You underestimated me. You were friendly… you were even warm sometimes. But I could always see it in your eyes. I was nothing to you. But you were wrong. So wrong about me. I know how to be a mover and a shaker."

"And a killer," he said huskily.

She smiled. "And a killer."

She was slightly between him and Thiessen at that point. Jesse cut a quick glance toward Lorena and realized that her eyes were on him.

She was afraid, but not panicking. She would fight until her last breath. He had never felt such a connection to another individual in his life.

A diversion. He needed a diversion.

She was staring at him so intently, he was certain she knew what he needed, how to help.

He prayed.

Then he gave a slight nod.

"Hey!" Lorena cried.

Startled, both Sally and Doc turned slightly.

And he made his move. He threw his body hard against Sally's, slamming her into Thiessen, bringing them all down to the ground.

The gun went off. A scream sounded sharply.

Still smoking, the gun lay on the ground in Thiessen's hand. Nearby was a pool of blood.

Jesse slammed his fist down on the man's wrist, and Thiessen released the gun. Jack Pine stepped forward, kicking it far from the man's grasp.

"Lorena!" Jesse cried, and leapt to his feet. She was standing. Unhurt.

Unbloodied.

She rushed into his arms.

He held her, shaking, feeling as if the world itself had begun to spin madly.

"Get up," Jack Pine was saying harshly to someone.

Jesse pulled away from Lorena long enough to turn and look.

Thiessen was getting up.

Sally lay on the ground, her eyes open but sightless.

A hole in her chest was surrounded by crimson.

"Is it over yet, Jesse?" Jack asked.

Jesse let out a sigh. "Not exactly. I imagine that, in a few minutes, John Smith will be arriving. He'll have been alerted by now to the fact that we're out here. If he does show, he'll be picked up. And I would also say that within minutes half the Miccosukee force will be out here. They'll be followed by the Metro-Dade cops. I can hear the airboats now."

Lorena looked up at him, then down at Sally. She shuddered, but only for a minute. Then she spun on Thiessen.

"Who killed my father?" she demanded.

"Ah, that," Thiessen murmured.

"Who actually killed my father!" Lorena repeated.

"Not me. I didn't kill anyone." He paused, and Jesse could see his mind working, trying to find a way out, to make himself look less guilty. "Sally...the whole thing was her idea. That woman was bloodthirsty. I was beside myself when I learned about the death of your poor father. And Hector and Maria. If she hadn't killed them... But she was certain they knew something and would get Fish and Wildlife in."

"Rather than Metro-Dade Homicide?" Jesse asked dryly.

"She was the one who forced me into everything," Thiessen said.

"Tell it to a jury," Jesse said.

"I intend to."

They heard the whir of an airboat motor coming closer. Jesse spun quickly, ready to dive for the gun if another of Thiessen's accomplices was arriving.

But it was George Osceola at the helm, and a number of tribal officers were with him. In seconds, they were rushing forward, shouting, going for Thiessen.

Seeing that the matter was in hand, George walked over to Jesse. "Everyone all right?"

"Except for Sally. She's dead," Jesse said.

"Sally!"

"Sally killed Hector and Maria," Jesse explained. "Were you able to pick up John Smith?"

"They're still looking for him. But, Jesse, you were right. Lars put out the APB, and Smith was spotted upstate. I'd bet money he abducted the van driver. We'll know more as soon as we get hold of him." George studied Jesse, then went silent. "Meanwhile, we need to get you all out of here."

"Hey!" Lorena cried suddenly. "Stop him! Doc's heading for the water!"

George Osceola swore; so did Jesse. They should have cuffed the man immediately.

Doc Thiessen was fast, and he knew the Everglades. He was tearing across the hummuck, heading for the water.

"Stop or I'll shoot!" George shouted.

Thiessen made a dive into the water. Jesse didn't think the man could make it—not with a trained force on his heels, several of them Miccosukees who had grown up in the area. It was a last desperate attempt at freedom by a desperate man.

They raced toward the canal. Thiessen had plunged deep, apparently hoping to surface at a distance, then disappear into the saw grass.

Jesse streaked toward the water himself, then stopped.

Everyone stopped behind him.

There was a thrashing in the water. Droplets splayed high and hard in every direction.

They were all dead still, watching the awful scene playing out before them.

Alligators were territorial.

And Thorne Thiessen had disturbed a large male in his territory. The dance of death was on.

There was no helping Thiessen.

He'd been caught in the middle of the abdomen, and

now the mighty creature was thrashing insanely, trying to drown his prey.

Thiessen let out one agonized scream.

Then the alligator took him below the surface.

Gentle as dewdrops, the last glistening drops of water fell back on the surface of the canal.

And then all was still.

Jesse heard a soft gasp, but even without it, he had known she was there. He knew her scent. Felt the air tremble around her.

He turned, and her eyes were brilliant and beautiful and filled with tears. She had wanted justice, not vengeance, he realized.

It had been a fitting end to Thiessen, he thought himself. But maybe he needed to learn a bit more about mercy.

He took her into his arms. Felt the vibrance and life in her body.

He drew her tightly to him. And he didn't care about the tragedy they'd just witnessed, the mud that covered them both, or who heard his words.

"I love you," he said softly. "And it's going to be all right."

Epilogue

It was fall. The sun beat down on the water, but the air was gentle. Birds, in all their multihued plumage, flew above the glistening canal. Trees, hanging low, were a lush background for the chirps and cries that occasionally broke the silence.

There had been a picnic. A week had passed since the events at the hummock. They had all spent hours in questioning and doing paperwork for both the tribal police and Metro-Dade.

Michael Preston and Harry Rogers had both been horrified to discover that they had been under suspicion.

Hugh had merely been indignant that he hadn't been in on the finale.

They had all attended the funeral for Hector and Maria. Julie and Lorena were fast becoming friends, just as she was a friend of Jesse's.

Now, with the picnic cleaned up, with the others having talked over everything that had happened and finally gone home, Lorena stared out at the strange and savage beauty of the area and smiled.

Jesse, a cold beer in his hand, came up behind her, then took a seat at her side.

She leaned against him comfortably, taking his hand, holding it to her cheek. "There's one more monster out there," she reminded him.

"Yeah. We haven't heard any reports about it, but we'll arrange more hunts until we get it."

"And when you do...will you capture it or kill it?" she asked.

He smiled at her. "When an animal is altered, it's man's doing, not the creature's," he reminded her. "But these things could mate. Undo the balance in the Everglades. I don't like to make judgments, but if it's up to me... I think the creature is too much of a risk. Too many people have died already. Your father died to protect people from creatures like it, and so..."

"At least they didn't kill the van driver," Lorena said.

"They thought they did, though," Jesse said grimly. "John Smith thought the man was dead when he stole the carcass and drove the van into a canal. It's a miracle that he came to and escaped."

"Every once in a while, we get a miracle," Lorena said.

"So..." Jesse murmured.

"So...?"

"So somehow I doubt that you plan to keep your position at Harry's."

"I was thinking of doing something else."

"You want to leave," he said very softly.

"Actually, no."

"No?" His face seemed exceptionally strong then, handsome and compelling, his eyes that startling green against the bronze of his features.

She sighed. "I know it's soon, but I had been hoping you would ask me to stay here. My real love is the law. And causes. I'm great at causes, Jesse. It occurred to me that the tribal council could probably use a good lawyer now and then. And living here, with you..."

He laughed. "I love you. You know that. I have to admit, I've had my fears."

"You? Afraid?"

"This isn't just where I live. It's part of what I am. And you come from a world that's...glittering. Clean. Neat. Sophisticated. Not that we don't have our own 'Miami chic' down here, but... I'm not knocking anything, it's just that here...well, there are alligators in the canals. Water moccasins, and saw grass hardly stands in for a neatly manicured lawn. And my nearest neighbor is...well, not near."

She laughed softly. "Hmm. Water moccasins."

"I'm afraid so. Though they're not the vicious creatures they're made out to be. They're afraid of people."

"And alligators."

"Normally, they leave you alone if you leave them alone."

"Muck, mud, mosquitoes and saw grass."

"I'm afraid so."

She turned to him, touched his face. "But they all come with you," she said softly.

He caught her hand, eyes narrowing, a smile curving his lips. "Then you really would consider staying? I'd love a roommate, but I'd much rather have a wife."

Her heart seemed to stop. "Are you asking me?"

"I'm begging you."

She threw herself into his arms.

"Is that a yes?"

"A thousand times over."

He gently caught her chin in his hand, thumb sliding over the skin of her cheek. Then his lips touched hers. The breeze was soft and easy. The birds went silent. The night was as breathtaking as his kiss.

The wedding was a month later. They chose the Keys.

The bride wore white. The groom was dashing in his tux.

They were both barefoot, married in the sand at sunset.

They'd taken the whole of one of the mom-and-pop motels, as well as rooms in one of the nearby chains. The attendance was huge, with Seminoles, Miccosukees, whites, Hispanics and, as Hugh, the token Aussie, commented, a bit of everyone in between. Even Roger had made it out of the hospital in time to attend.

The sunset was glorious.

The reception was the South Florida party of the year.

And when the night wound down, they were alone in

their room that looked onto the ocean, feeling the gentle breeze, aware of the salt scent on the air...

And then nothing else, nothing else at all...

Except for each other.

* * * * *

Carla Cassidy is an award-winning, *New York Times* bestselling author who has written over 170 books, including 150 for Harlequin. She has won the Centennial Award from Romance Writers of America. Most recently she won the 2019 Write Touch Readers Award for her Harlequin Intrigue title *Desperate Strangers*. Carla believes the only thing better than curling up with a good book is sitting down at the computer with a good story to write.

Books by Carla Cassidy

Harlequin Romantic Suspense

Cowboys of Holiday Ranch

A Real Cowboy
Cowboy of Interest
Cowboy Under Fire
Cowboy at Arms
Operation Cowboy Daddy
Killer Cowboy
Sheltered by the Cowboy
Guardian Cowboy
Cowboy Defender
Cowboy's Vow to Protect
The Cowboy's Targeted Bride

Colton 911

Colton 911: Target in Jeopardy

The Coltons of Red Ridge

The Colton Cowboy

The Coltons of Shadow Creek

Colton's Secret Son

Visit the Author Profile page
at Harlequin.com for more titles.

A HERO OF HER OWN

Carla Cassidy

Chapter 1

Jewel Mayfair shot up, heart pounding and panic suffocating her with a thick press against her chest. Her bedroom was dark except for the glow from a nightlight plugged into the socket on the wall opposite her bed.

She stared at the light, willing her heartbeat to slow and drawing deep, even breaths to calm down. She'd had the dream again. No, not a dream, it was a nightmare that had plagued her for over two years, ever since the car accident that had taken the life of her fiancé.

Andrew! Her heart cried his name as she remembered the last night they'd had together. Everything had been so perfect. She'd picked him up in her car and they'd gone to their favorite restaurant where he'd surprised her with a proposal, complete with a beautiful ring. And she'd surprised him with some news of her own.

Her hands moved to her flat abdomen. The accident hadn't just taken Andrew from her. It had also taken Andrew's child, who had been growing inside her. Grief pierced her, as rich and raw as it had been when she'd awakened in the hospital after the accident and been told of all that she had lost.

Slowly her breathing returned to normal and she glanced at the clock on her nightstand. Just after midnight. She'd been asleep for less than an hour and she knew from experience that sleep would be a long time coming again.

She slid her long legs over the side of the bed and grabbed the thin robe on the chair nearby. She belted the robe over her short nightgown, then opened the doors that led out of her master bedroom and onto a covered porch.

Despite the hour, the late August heat fell around her like an oppressive veil. Ahead of her was the pool and beyond was the woods that was part of the Hopechest Ranch estate.

In the last six months since coming to Esperanza, Texas, she and the woods had become intimate friends. It was among the tall oaks and thick brush that she spent hours each night when she couldn't sleep. And lately that had been almost every night.

The chlorine scent of the pool hung in the air as she walked around it to the gate in the back. Opening the gate she paused and looked at the house.

It was still hard for her to believe that she was here in Esperanza, running a ranch for troubled children. The Hopechest Ranch was housed in a beautiful Spanish-style structure made of adobe with a tiled roof.

Jewel had her own quarters and there were four additional bedrooms for the children and a married couple, Jeff and Cheryl Cookson, who were part of the staff.

Seeing no lights on and knowing that if any of the children awakened, the Cooksons would take care of things, she walked out of the gate and into the cooler air beneath the trees.

A light breeze ruffled her short, sun-streaked brown hair as she walked down a well-worn path. She tried to erase from her mind the horrifying visions that haunted her sleep far too often. She was exhausted. Her insomnia was getting worse instead of better.

It was ironic that her job as a psychologist at the ranch was to help children heal from trauma and deal with problems, but for the life of her she couldn't figure out how to heal herself.

She stopped walking and leaned with her back against a huge oak trunk. Closing her eyes, she wondered if she'd ever get a full night's sleep again, if the haunting dreams would ever stop. She'd hoped that by moving from Prosperino, California, she'd leave behind the haunting memories of that accident and her loss. But they'd chased her here and if anything had gotten more intrusive over the last five months.

"Jewel."

Her eyes popped open and she froze, every muscle in her body rigid. Had somebody just uttered her name? Or had it been the wind and an overactive imagination? Her heart banged a more rapid beat as she gazed around her.

The warm night turned icy around her as she cocked her head to listen, narrowed her eyes to see. "Hello?" she said, the word no more than a whisper.

The moonlight was full, spilling down enough light to illuminate the path, but not able to pierce the darkness of the thick woods.

"Jewel."

She gasped. Even though she knew it was impossible, that deep male voice sounded like Andrew's.

"Andrew?" she half whispered his name as tears stung her eyes. She sensed more than saw a form just off to her right. "Andrew, is that you?" Her head filled with wild thoughts.

He hadn't really died in the car accident. It had all been a terrible mixup, a case of mistaken identity. Somehow he'd survived and he'd come here to find her.

"Andrew, wait!" she exclaimed as she saw the shadowy form moving deeper into the woods. Her heart was now pounding so hard it made her half-breathless.

Her mind went blank as she waded through brush and stepped around tree trunks. She had to find him. She was certain the voice she'd heard calling her name was Andrew's. She didn't know how that was possible, didn't care. All she wanted to do was to get to him, to feel his arms around her once again.

Goose bumps rose on her skin and she was half-dizzy as she fought the underbrush, felt the prickly bite of it against her bare legs.

She stumbled into a low-hanging branch. The whack of the limb across her forehead jarred her back to reality. And the reality was that she was in the middle of the woods chasing after a ghost.

The figure she'd been chasing was gone…or had never been there, she thought. Fighting back new tears of despair, she turned and screamed as she bumped into a solid male chest.

"Jewel. It's me. Quinn Logan." His big hands grabbed her shoulders. "Are you all right? I heard you scream."

"I bumped into a tree branch." Her voice sounded far away and she mentally shook herself in an effort to get grounded.

"Come on, let's get back on the path," he said. He dropped his hands from her shoulders, but took one of her hands in his and led her back to the path.

As her mental fog lifted, she jerked her hand from his and stared at him, his handsome features visible in the full moonlight.

He had a mane of brown hair, with flecks of gold and auburn that enhanced his lean features. A scar across one of his cheeks did nothing to detract from his appeal. His topaz eyes glowed feline and, as always when Jewel looked at him, a crazy fluttering went off in her tummy.

"What are you doing out here in the middle of the night, Dr. Logan?" she asked warily. Quinn was the local veterinarian. At six foot three, he had broad shoulders and a quiet simmering energy and strength that made people believe he could handle anything a large animal might do.

"Quinn," he said. "Please make it Quinn, and unfortunately sometimes animals don't get sick during normal business hours. I've been over at Clay's place dealing with a colicky horse." Clay Colton was Jewel's cousin and he lived on the large spread next to the Hopechest Ranch.

"Is the horse all right?" she asked, and wrapped her arms around herself, unable to get back the warmth she'd felt before she'd heard that ghostly voice. Had Quinn been the shape she'd seen in the woods? Had he softly called her name?

"The horse is fine. I'm more concerned about you. You said you hit your head?" He placed two warm fingers beneath her chin and raised her face toward the light. Butterflies went off in her stomach at his touch.

"I'm fine," she said stiffly, and backed away from him.

He reached up and shoved a strand of his hair back from his eyes, gazing at her curiously. "What are you doing out here in the middle of the night?"

She hesitated a moment, then decided to be truthful. "I was having some trouble sleeping and thought maybe a walk outside would help."

"How about I walk you back to your place and see you safely inside?"

"No, thanks. That isn't necessary," she protested. She felt off balance, shocked to find him wandering the woods and still confused by thinking she'd heard somebody call her name.

All she wanted to do was get back to the house and into the safety of her own room. At the moment she felt distinctly unsafe, even though Quinn didn't appear threatening in any way.

"I'll just say good night now," she said. She whirled around and hurried back in the direction of the house, grateful when he didn't try to stop her.

She didn't relax until she was settled in her room with the doors locked. She lingered at the door, peering outside, but there was no sign of anyone—ghosts or otherwise.

Moving away from the door, she took off her robe and climbed back into bed. Her heart still thudded with adrenaline and she knew sleep would be far off, if at all.

She'd gone a little crazy out in the woods, thinking that she heard Andrew's voice calling her, believing for a moment that he was someplace out there in the dark woods.

Or was it possible that Quinn had been playing a cruel game with her? She frowned as she thought of the handsome vet. She'd only run into him a half a dozen times since her arrival in town and usually that was out at Clay's place. But, on each of those occasions, she'd been acutely aware of him, had felt more than a little bit of attraction.

There had been a moment when his warm hands had been on her shoulders when she'd wanted to throw herself against him, feel the heat and strength of his arms enfolding her in an embrace.

She closed her eyes and remembered the sensation of his fingers beneath her chin. It had been so long since a man had touched her in any way. Was it any wonder she'd reacted to his simple touches?

She didn't know what worried her more, the fact that she might be losing her mind or that she was attracted to a man who might, for whatever reason, be playing games with her sanity?

Mornings were chaotic at the Hopechest Ranch and the next morning was no different. The sounds of childish laughter awakened Jewel just after seven and she blessed Cheryl and Jeff Cookson who would be in the kitchen preparing breakfast for the seven children who were currently residents.

The children's ages ranged from ten to thirteen, the eldest a girl who had arrived the previous day from Chicago.

Jewel would have a session with the girl, named Kelsey Cameron, this morning. Jewel had official therapy sessions with each child twice a week, but at the Hopechest Ranch therapy never stopped. Every activity, every conversation provided therapy to heal wounds, buoy self-confidence and get the children on the road to happy, healthy lives.

As Jewel showered and dressed for the day, her mind wandered back to those minutes in the woods with Quinn. Even though she was relatively new to the town, she knew Quinn's story. Clay had told her about how several years ago Quinn had diagnosed one of Clay's horses with a disease that had threatened the rest of the stock. Clay had been forced to put down the prized stud. At the time most of the other local ranchers had thought Quinn's diagnosis was wrong.

Ultimately, Quinn had been vindicated, but not before both his reputation and his practice had taken major hits. Clay had stood by his friend and never missed an opportunity to tell Jewel that Quinn was a great guy.

So what was that great guy doing skulking around the woods last night? If he'd gone to Clay's to take care of a sick horse, why hadn't he driven his truck over instead of making the long trek by foot from his place to Clay's?

Once she left her room, there was no more time for thoughts of Quinn. Breakfast was followed by the counseling session with Kelsey Cameron. The young teenager had come to Hopechest Ranch after four years of being shuttled from family member to family member. Her mother, a drug addict, had just awakened one morning and decided she didn't want to be a mother anymore. One of Kelsey's aunts had contacted Jewel. She was worried about the girl, who had become more angry and withdrawn with each passing day.

Jewel got little from Kelsey, but hadn't expected much in the first session. Besides, today was riding-lesson day, something the children all enjoyed. It was a perfect way for Kelsey to start feeling like a member of their "family."

After lunch, when the children all piled into the minibus, Jewel drove next door to Clay Colton's ranch, the Bar None. As she went the short distance, the kids chattered with excitement, talking about the horses they would ride and Burt Walker, their instructor. She glanced in the rearview mirror and saw that Kelsey sat, staring out the van window, looking as if she'd rather be anywhere else.

The three-hundred-acre Bar None ranch was one of the most successful horse ranches in the area. Clay Colton was one of three illegitimate children of Graham Colton and a pretty rodeo rider named Mary Lynn Grady. Clay was a solid, responsible man and since coming to town Jewel had grown to love him like a brother.

She drove past the two-story ranch house and headed toward the stables. Her stomach did a crazy two-step as she recognized Quinn's black pickup parked nearby. She raised a hand to her hair, momentarily wishing she'd taken more time with it that morning. The thought irritated her and she quickly dropped her hand and parked the bus in front of the stables.

As the children piled out of the bus, Burt walked over to greet them. He was a slender man who'd once been a champion barrel racer. He now worked for Clay and conducted the riding lessons.

"The horses have been waiting for you," he exclaimed to the kids. "They told me last night how much they were looking forward to giving you all a good ride today."

Barry Lundon, a ten-year-old with anxiety issues, widened his eyes. "They talk to you?"

Sam Taylor nudged Barry with his shoulder. "Don't be a baby," he said with his twelve-year-old wisdom. "Horses don't talk."

"Of course they do," Burt said. "They just don't use the same kind of language that we do. Come on, let's get inside and get you all saddled up and I'll tell you about horse language." He winked at Jewel, then led the kids to the second stable.

They'd all just disappeared when Clay, Tamara and Quinn walked out of the building directly in front of her. "I thought I heard the chatter of little voices," Clay said with a warm smile.

"We were just headed to the house for some lemonade," Tamara said. Tamara Brown was Clay's ex-wife. They'd divorced five years ago and she'd become a CSI agent in San Antonio. They'd reunited when a body had been found in a ravine on Clay's ranch and Tamara had been part of the investigating team.

"How are you, Jewel?" Quinn's deep voice evoked

memories from the night before when his strong, warm fingers had touched her chin and she'd felt the ridiculous need to jump right into his arms.

"Fine. Just fine," she replied. He looked as attractive this morning as he had the night before in the moonlight. The sun shimmered on his long, thick brown hair finding blond highlights that looked warm and soft. Jewel knew that he was forty-four years old, five years older than she was, but he had an underlying energy that made him seem younger than his years.

"Beautiful day," he said.

"Yes, it's lovely," she replied.

"Before you know it, winter will be here."

Tamara released a tiny sigh of impatience. "You two can stand out here in the heat and talk about the weather until the cows come home. I'm going up to the house for a glass of lemonade." She turned on her heels and headed for the house.

Clay stared after her with the eyes of a man who loved what he saw. *Andrew once looked at me that way,* Jewel thought. She didn't know if she'd ever be ready to pursue a relationship with another man, but she had to admit there were times she missed having somebody look at her that way, as if she were the most important person on the face of the earth.

Clay turned back to face them. "You two coming?"

"I can't," Quinn said as he glanced at his watch. "I've got an appointment in about fifteen minutes. I've got to get going." Once again he turned his gaze to Jewel. "It was nice seeing you again."

She nodded, those crazy butterflies taking wing in her stomach once again. "You, too."

She and Clay watched as he got into his pickup truck. She was grateful Quinn hadn't mentioned their midnight meeting. She didn't really want Clay to know that she often walked the woods between their places because she suffered nightmares. Her job was healing. She didn't want anyone to find out that she couldn't heal herself.

"He's such a nice guy," Clay said as Quinn's pickup headed down the gravel lane. "And such a talented vet."

"Speaking of vets, I heard you had a horse down last night," she said.

He frowned at her. "A horse down last night? I don't know where you heard that, but it's not true. My stock is all healthy."

He'd lied. Quinn had lied to her the night before. The warmth of the sun on her shoulders couldn't quite warm the chill that suddenly gripped her.

What had Quinn been doing in those woods the night before, and why had he lied?

Chapter 2

From the moment Jewel had first stepped inside Clay's white wood-frame, two-story home she'd felt the warm welcome it offered. She followed Clay into the wide entry hall and to the rear of the house where a farm-style kitchen opened into a family room.

The family room held two leather couches that faced each other in front of a massive stone fireplace. Western antiques dotted the room, a wagon-wheel coffee table, two lanterns from the 1800s and a framed torn Texas flag that was reported to have flown at the Alamo. The end result was a feeling of old and new, of warmth and permanence.

They didn't go into the family room but instead stopped in the kitchen, where Tamara had already poured lemonade for them.

"Where's Quinn?" she asked as Clay and Tamara sat at the round oak table.

"He left. He said he had an appointment," Clay explained.

Tamara served their drinks, then joined them at the table. "Did I see a new little face out there this morning?"

Jewel nodded. "Kelsey Cameron. She arrived yesterday from Chicago. Mother a drug addict, father unknown, poor thing has been shuffled from relative to relative for the last four years."

"You'll work your magic, and when she leaves here, she'll have a new sense of self-worth and be wonderfully well-adjusted," Clay said.

Jewel smiled. "You make it sound so easy."

"That's because you make it look easy," Tamara exclaimed. "Your rapport with those kids amazes me."

Jewel waved a hand to dismiss the topic, embarrassed by their praise. "Have you heard that Joe and Meredith are planning a visit?"

Clay leaned back in his chair and nodded. "One of the last stops on the campaign trail."

"I have a feeling the Coltons will be spending Christmases at the White House," Tamara said.

"Uncle President," Clay mused. "Has a nice ring to it."

Jewel laughed. "He's still a few months from winning the presidential election."

"Shouldn't be a problem, especially now that Allan Daniels is out of the running," Clay replied.

Allan Daniels was the current governor of Texas and had been Joe Colton's hottest competition for their party's nomination until his true character had been exposed. Dirty dealing and bribery had effectively neutralized Daniels's threat to Joe's candidacy.

For the next fifteen minutes they talked about the election and how well Joe Colton was doing in the polls. That led to a discussion of politics in general and then the talk turned to more family news.

The Colton family tree was a complicated one. Joe and Meredith had five children of their own and had fostered seven. Jewel's mother, Patsy, who was Meredith's twin sister, had kidnapped Meredith and pretended to be Joe's wife for ten years, giving him three more children. Graham, Joe's brother had two children with his wife, Cynthia, then had indulged in an affair with Mary Lynn Grady and they'd had three children.

Sometimes when Jewel thought about the history of the Colton clan her head hurt, especially when she thought of her own mother, Patsy, who had done horrible things and eventually died in a mental hospital.

Jewel tried not to think of her mother too often. She preferred to think about Charlie and Ruth Baylor, the couple who had adopted her and given her a wonderfully normal Midwestern upbringing. Unfortunately, the couple had since passed away.

"Hello! Anybody home?" The familiar female voice was followed by the sound of boots against the tile entry floor.

"In the kitchen," Tamara yelled.

Clay's younger sister, Georgie, strode into the kitchen, bringing with her the high energy that was as much a part of her as the waist-length red braid that bobbed down her back. Following at her heels was her husband, Nick Sheffield.

"Georgie, Nick." Clay motioned them toward the table. "Have a seat, we're just enjoying some lemonade and local gossip."

"Hi, Jewel. Saw your kids outside in the corral. Got any future champion riders in the bunch?" Georgie asked. Georgie had spent most of her life on the rodeo circuit as a champion barrel racer. Even the birth of Emmie, her daughter, five years ago hadn't stopped her from competing.

"I don't think so." She laughed. "From what I've seen of them, most are just hanging on to the saddle horn for dear life."

Georgie's green eyes seemed to sparkle with more liveliness than usual as she looked back at her brother. "I've got a surprise for you."

"You know I don't like surprises," Clay returned.

Georgie laughed. "You'll like this one." She turned in the direction of the front door. "Come on in," she yelled.

Jewel's eyes widened as Clay's brother, Ryder, appeared. Next to him was Ana Morales, a Mexican woman who had worked for Jewel before her baby was kidnapped in a black-market ring. Ana held the baby girl in her arms and wore the smile of a woman in love as she gazed up at Ryder.

Clay stood, his face reflecting myriad emotions. Jewel knew the history between the two men, that Ryder's bad-boy lifestyle had led to Clay washing his hands of his younger brother. Jewel knew how painful it had been for Clay to shut his brother out, how tormented he'd been by the difficult decision. But Ryder had turned his life around when he'd been sent to a correctional facility and offered a chance to work undercover for the CIA. He'd cracked open a black-market baby-trafficking operation, saving Ana's little girl and falling in love in the process. During this time, Clay had thought his brother was dead, had grieved for his and the family's loss. Now they had a second chance.

"Hi, Clay," Ryder said, his voice husky with emotion.

There was a moment of charged hesitation, then Clay took two steps forward and embraced his brother. Tears filled Jewel's eyes. Tamara's eyes were suspiciously bright, as well.

Jewel jumped up and hugged Ana. "I've missed you so much," she said. She and Ana had formed a friendship while Ana had worked for her. Jewel cooed over the baby, then stepped back.

It seemed that suddenly everyone was talking at once and in the melee Tamara shocked everyone by confessing that she and Clay had eloped and were married.

As a new round of hugging and backslapping began, Jewel slid out of the room and then out of the house, wanting to leave the family alone for their reunion.

She had a feeling that the issues that had torn Clay and Ryder apart were behind them and the brothers were on their way to building a new, close relationship. She was thrilled for them, but as she walked toward the stables a new sense of loneliness weighed her down.

Clay and Tamara were married and it had been obvious by the glow on Ana's face that she and Ryder were probably not far behind. There seemed to be a marriage epidemic breaking out in Esperanza. But Jewel had not caught the bug, and felt immune to anything even remotely romantic.

On more than one occasion Deputy Adam Rawlings had made it clear that he was interested in pursuing a romantic relationship with her. They'd seen each other socially several times but, try as she might, she just didn't feel more than friendship for him. Besides, with the nightmares she'd been suffering on a regular basis, she was probably better off alone. No man would want to spend his nights with her while she was haunted by ghosts from her past.

She dismissed all thoughts of romance from her mind as she entered the stables. The kids were just finishing up brushing down their horses and Burt approached her with a friendly smile.

"They're just about done," he said.

"How did Kelsey do?" she asked, hoping the new girl had opened up a bit.

"Never said a word to anyone, but she's got a natural seat in the saddle. She grow up around horses?"

"No, just the opposite. She's an inner-city kid, probably has never been on a horse in her life," Jewel replied.

Burt looked over to where Kelsey was working on the horse, a look of fierce concentration on her face. "She shows all the signs of being a born rider. I hope she sticks around long enough for me to work with her more extensively."

"She's not going anywhere for a while. We've got lots of work to do with her," Jewel replied.

It took another half an hour to get all the children loaded into the bus and headed back the short distance to the Hopechest Ranch. The noise level was just below that of a jet engine as they all chatted about their horses and the riding experience. The only one who didn't say a word was Kelsey, who stared out the window as if she were lost in a world of her own.

Jewel was determined to break into that world. It wasn't just her job, it was a calling from her very soul.

"Everybody out and you can have free time play in the garage until dinnertime," Jewel said as she parked in front of the house. One section of the three-car garage had been turned into a playroom, complete with toys and games and craft items.

All the kids headed for the garage except Kelsey, who lingered behind. "Is it okay if I just go to my room?" she asked.

Jewel would have preferred she go with the other children and interact, but she also knew it was going to take some time for Kelsey to feel safe here, to feel as if she were part of the group.

She placed a hand on the girl's shoulder. "That's fine. Dinner is at five-thirty so make sure you're in the kitchen by then."

Kelsey nodded and headed inside. Jewel lingered outside, fighting a wave of exhaustion. The restless nights and bad dreams were getting more frequent, and more difficult to handle.

She raised her face to the warmth of the sun and once again thought about romance. Maybe she was incapable of loving anyone. Maybe the love she'd had for Andrew had been all she had and once it had been given she'd been left empty.

Of course, that didn't explain the odd tingle of excitement she felt whenever she was around Quinn. Female hormones reminding her that she was alive—that's all it was, she told herself.

It was impossible for her to fall in love again, especially with her past visiting her every night in the form of nightmares.

Voices in the night. Visions in the woods. Equally as haunting as the dreams was the fear that somehow she was slowly falling into the mental illness that had consumed her mother.

"She should be just fine," Quinn assured Ralph Smith, a local rancher who had called him about a cow who had gotten caught in some barbed wire. "All the wounds are superficial and now that I've cleaned her up and applied antibiotic cream, she shouldn't have any problems."

He slapped the rear of the big animal and with a low moo she headed back toward the pasture. "I'd definitely do something about that barbed wire."

Ralph frowned toward a stand of trees and brush. "I didn't even know it was there, just tangled up in all the weeds, but I'll get it out of here today."

Together the two men walked toward the gate in the fence. Initially, coming out here and meeting up with Ralph had been awkward. Ralph had been one of the loudest, most critical ranchers when Quinn had been forced to put down Clay Colton's prized stud.

It had been the second-darkest time in Quinn's life. The darkest had been when he'd lost his wife, Sarah, to cancer.

Even though Quinn had been proven right in his diagnosis of the disease that had infected Clay's stud, even thought his decision to put the horse down had probably saved the rest of the stock, Quinn had never quite gotten over how quickly some of the locals had turned on him.

The fact that Ralph had called him to come and check out the cow was an olive branch he had extended to Quinn. It had been a long time coming, but Quinn wasn't a man to hold a grudge. Life was too damned short.

"Just let me know if the wounds begin to ooze or look infected and I'll come back out," Quinn said as he reached the door of his pickup truck.

"I appreciate it, Doc." Ralph held out his hand and the two men shook.

Minutes later as Quinn drove away from the Smith ranch and back toward town, he thought about those dark days when many in the town had turned their backs on him, made darker because he was still grieving for his wife. At the time all he had was his work and when that took a hit, he considered packing up and leaving Esperanza.

Instead, with the support of the Coltons, Clay in particular, he'd stayed and held his head high. When his decision to put the stud down had been vindicated, he'd put the whole ordeal behind him and got on with his life.

As he drove down Main Street, he decided to stop for dinner at Miss Sue's Café, where he took many of his evening meals. He told himself it was because he hated to cook, but the truth was he dreaded the evening hours spent alone.

An old-fashioned cowbell heralded his arrival as he entered the quaint café. "You're a bit early today,

Quinn," Becky French, the owner of the establishment, greeted him with a warm smile.

He smiled at the short, plump woman. "It's never too early for a good meal." He walked over to one of the wooden tables by the window and sat in a chair where he could easily see out the window.

"Got some new pictures," Becky said as she poured him a cup of coffee. There was nothing Becky loved more than to show off pictures of her grandchildren. She set the coffeepot down and dug into her apron pocket to withdraw a handful of photos.

Quinn took them from her and studied each of the smiling childish faces. "They're beautiful," he said.

Becky smiled and nodded. "They are." She tucked the photos back in her apron. "I'll just give you a few minutes. The special is smothered steak and mashed potatoes."

"Then I don't need a minute. That sounds good." He returned the menu and leaned back in the chair to sip his coffee. She scurried away, the gray bun on top of her head bobbing with her brisk walk.

Kids. At one time Quinn had hoped to have a house full, but fate and cancer had stolen that dream from him. He and Sarah had never had a chance for children.

Even though it was early, there were already other diners in the café. Quinn had never been in the place when there weren't at least a handful of people. Most mealtimes the place was packed.

He'd just finished his coffee when Georgie Sheffield, her husband, Nick, and her daughter, little Emmie, came through the door.

"I hear we just missed you this morning at Clay's,"

Georgie said to him. "We had a reunion. Ryder and Ana are back in town and we took them to Clay's." Georgie's green eyes sparkled brightly. "It was wonderful."

Emmie sidled up next to Quinn. At five years old, the little girl was the spitting image of her mother. Her red hair was cut pixielike to frame her face and she was dressed just like her mama in jeans, a Western-style shirt and cowboy boots.

Emmie was bright and precocious and had spent most of her young life on the rodeo circuit with her mother. The little girl considered Quinn a special friend because he fixed horses when they got sick and there were few things Emmie loved more than horses and cowboys.

"Excuse me, Mommy, but I want to talk to Mr. Quinn," Emmie said. Georgie smiled with amusement and nodded. "Guess what happens next week?"

"I can't imagine. What?" Quinn replied.

She leaned closer, bringing with her the scent of sunshine and childhood. "School begins."

"Ah." Quinn smiled at her. "And what are you, in the second grade, the third?"

"Maybe I should be because you know I can already read," Emmie exclaimed. She leaned even closer. "But, truly it's going to be my very first day of kindergarten." A fierce look of determination crossed her petite features. "And I'm going to make one new friend, even if he or she isn't a cowboy."

"I think that sounds like a wonderful plan," Quinn said.

Emmie turned to her mother and Nick. "And now I'll go pick us out a table."

As she left the adults behind, Georgie offered Quinn a weak smile. "I can't believe she's starting school. She's so comfortable around adults. Her friends have always been rodeo cowboys. I just hope she fits in okay." Her eyes clouded and sparkled with sudden tears of worry.

"I'm sure she'll be just fine," Quinn said.

"Of course she will," Nick agreed, and placed an arm around Georgie's shoulder. "She's as strong as her mother and almost as pretty."

Georgie laughed and leaned into Nick. He grinned at Quinn. "You just wait, maybe someday you'll have to live through the trauma of the first day of school."

As the two of them joined Emmie, who had chosen a table toward the back of the café, Quinn thought about what Nick had said.

He and Sarah had talked about having children one day, but before that dream had been realized she'd been diagnosed with the malignant aggressive brain tumor that had taken her in six short months. They'd had only nine months of marriage before her diagnosis.

Sarah had been a quiet, thoughtful woman and when she died, she did so as quietly and unassumingly as she had lived. He'd grieved deep and hard for a long time. Now when he thought of Sarah, the sharp despair was gone and he was left with a loneliness and a growing desire to get on with his life.

"Here we are," Becky said as she delivered his meal. "Anything else I can do for you?" she asked as she poured him another cup of coffee.

"No, thanks. I'm good."

"You're not good," Becky replied, her blue eyes sparkling with the liveliness that was her trademark. "You know I'm not happy unless I'm minding everyone's business but my own. You need a woman, Quinn. You spend far too much time at this table all alone—no offense."

He laughed. "None taken. I was just sitting here thinking the same thing."

"We've got a lot of nice single women in this town who'd love to see you socially. You're that strong, silent type. A little bit of that is quite romantic, but too much of it puts off the ladies."

"I'll keep that in mind," Quinn replied. It was impossible to be offended by Becky's advice because he knew how well intentioned it was.

As she left his table, his thoughts turned to the woman he'd met in the woods the night before. Jewel. From the moment he'd first met her, she'd intrigued him.

Certainly he found her amazingly attractive with her short, tousled, streaked golden-brown hair and big brown eyes. Although slender, she had curves in all the right places and legs that seemed to go on forever.

Last night wasn't the first time he'd seen her wandering the woods around the Hopechest Ranch, although it was the first time he'd let her know he was there.

Quinn had a feeling he and Jewel suffered from the same afflictions—insomnia and loneliness. Quinn often spent the nighttime hours at Clay's place where he boarded his horse, Noches.

What he didn't understand was what had made Jewel scream in the woods the night before and why she'd looked positively haunted when he'd encountered her.

Chapter 3

As the purple shadows of twilight began to deepen, a responding tension filled Jewel. It wasn't natural for the coming of night to bring something that tasted very much like suppressed terror into the back of her throat.

Jeff and Cheryl were in the process of getting the kids ready for bed and Jewel sat at the kitchen table making a list of school supplies she needed to purchase before school began next week.

When she finished her list, she would tuck each of the children in for the night. Those minutes just before bedtime, when she connected with each of the children with a good-night kiss and a wish for sweet dreams, was an important part of the routine of love that abounded at the ranch.

A knock sounded on the front door and she looked

at the clock. Although it felt much later, it was only just after seven.

She hurried to the front door and opened it to see Deputy Adam Rawlings. As usual not a strand of his dark brown hair was out of place and he was impeccably dressed in his khaki uniform. "Hi, Adam."

"I was just out making rounds and thought I'd stop by and say hello," he said.

Jewel flipped on the outside light and stepped out on the porch to join him. "Quiet night?" she asked.

"Most of them are quiet," he replied. "Not that I'm complaining. I heard you've got a new boarder. How's that working out?"

She nodded. "A thirteen-year-old girl named Kelsey from Chicago. If you'd asked me yesterday how things were going I would have said not well. She was quiet and withdrawn. But today she appears more open. She loved the riding lessons at Clay's yesterday and wanted to know when we'd be going again." She broke off as she realized she was beginning to ramble.

"How's everything else going?" he asked. His gaze narrowed slightly. "You look tired."

"I am," she admitted. "I was just sitting at the table, thinking about everything I need to buy for the kids to start school next week." She smiled. "Trying to figure out school supplies for seven kids in seven different classes is enough to make anyone tired."

"I'll let you get back to it. I just thought I'd check in and see how you were doing." He shifted his muscular body from one foot to the other. "If you get a minute to yourself and want to get dinner out or maybe see a movie, you know all you have to do is just call me."

She smiled. "Thank you, Adam. I'll keep that in mind."

They said goodbye and then she watched as he left the porch and walked back to his patrol car. He seemed like such a nice man, good-looking and obviously interested in her. Unfortunately, she just didn't feel anything for him except a mild friendship.

As his car pulled away, she went back inside to the kitchen table. She finished making her list and by then it was time to kiss the kids good-night.

She went into the boys' bedroom first. The room held two bunk beds and at the moment all four sleeping places were occupied. Barry and Sam, the two older boys, had the top bunks and eight-year-old Jimmy Nigel and seven-year-old Caleb Torrel had the lower bunks.

"All tucked in?" she asked Barry as she approached him first.

He nodded. "Will you keep the nightlight on?" he asked anxiously. "I'm not scared or anything, but I just don't like the dark."

Jewel smiled at the dark-eyed boy. They had this same conversation every night. "The nightlight will be on until morning. Sleep tight, Barry."

As she moved from Barry to Sam and then to the two younger boys, she couldn't help but think of the baby she'd lost. She'd desperately wanted to be a mother, had been thrilled to discover she was pregnant. The minute the doctor had confirmed what she'd suspected, her heart had filled with a happiness she'd never known before and hadn't known since.

As she moved from the boys' room to the girls', she

shoved away thoughts of the baby she'd lost and dreams of what might have been.

There were three girls in residence at the moment. Kelsey slept on the top bunk of one of the beds and on the lower bunks were Lindy Walker and Carrie Lyndon, both ten years old.

Jewel went to Kelsey first. She didn't touch the girl in any way, wouldn't invade Kelsey's personal space unless she was invited to do so. "Ready to call it a night?"

Kelsey nodded, her green eyes less guarded than they'd been the day before. "I'm not used to going to bed so early."

Jewel smiled. "We believe in the routine of early to bed, early to rise around here. Besides, with school starting next week, it's important that all of you get plenty of sleep."

Jewel moved to the other beds, where the girls demanded good-night kisses and hugs, then she left the room and turned out the light. As in the boys' room, a small nightlight burned in a wall socket.

She met Cheryl in the hallway and smiled tiredly. "Another day done," she said.

Cheryl returned her smile and swept a strand of her long, dark hair behind an ear. "I wanted to run an idea by you. Jeff and I would like to plan a day trip for the kids in the next couple of weeks. There's a Native American museum two hours from here and we thought it would be fun to visit the museum and have a picnic lunch at a nearby park."

"Sounds like something they would enjoy," Jewel replied.

"We haven't finalized a day yet, I just wanted to put a bug in your ear about it."

"Let me know what you and Jeff decide and we'll work out the details."

Cheryl nodded. "Then I'll just say good night."

As Cheryl headed toward the front bedroom where she and Jeff slept, Jewel returned to the kitchen. She tucked into her purse the list of supplies she needed to buy, then once again sat at the table to make notes in the files she kept on each of the children.

Busywork. In the back of her mind she knew that's what she was doing, creating work to keep her mind off the fact that soon it would be time to go to bed.

To sleep.

To dream.

Again the taste of dread mingled with a simmering terror. If only she could have one night of peaceful sleep and happy dreams. If only she could wake up in the morning well-rested and happy.

If only Andrew hadn't died in the car accident.

She sighed and focused back on the files in front of her. These were her children, the ones who came to Hopechest Ranch in need of stability and love. They were all she needed. And maybe a good night's sleep was vastly overrated.

She didn't know how long she'd sat working when she heard a strange scratching sound. She got up from the table and followed the noise to the front door. Definitely sounded like something scratching for attention.

Equally curious and wary, she unlocked the door and cracked it open. The door shoved inward and a chocolate-colored dog jumped up at her. In surprise she stumbled backward and fell on her behind. The dog licked her face as if she were a long-lost friend that he was thrilled to see again.

"Okay, okay," she said with a burst of laughter as the dog continued to lavish her with kisses. She looked up to see Quinn standing in the doorway. Her heart jumped with a quickened beat.

He stepped inside and took the dog by the collar. "Sorry about that," he said as she quickly got to her feet. "He's a Lab and just a puppy so he hasn't learned his manners yet."

"It's okay." Jewel reached up and self-consciously raked her fingers through her hair. As always the sight of Quinn sent an electrical tingle through her. "He's a cutie. Is he yours?"

"Actually, I was hoping he'd be yours," Quinn said.

"Mine?" She looked at him in surprise.

The dog sat on the floor next to him, looking first at Quinn, then at Jewel, as if aware that they were talking about him.

"It might be presumptuous of me, but I thought maybe you could use a companion, especially when you decide to take a walk in the woods late at night." Quinn shoved a strand of his thick, wavy hair away from his eyes, and shifted from foot to foot, as if suddenly extremely uncomfortable. "Maybe it was a stupid idea."

"No, it was a lovely idea," she replied, touched by the thoughtfulness of the gesture. "Actually, we've talked about getting a dog since I first opened the doors here, but we've just never gotten around to it. What's his name?"

"He doesn't have an official name yet." Quinn's eyes

were a warm topaz. "I have to warn you, he's only twelve weeks old. He's not quite housebroken, but he's a big lover and has a terrific personality. Most important, he's great with kids."

"Then how can I possibly turn away such a wonderful gift?" she replied. The children would be positively thrilled with this new addition to the family. "Maybe we'll put him in the garage for tonight. Do you think that's okay?"

He nodded and clipped a leash to the collar. "I'm sure that's fine. Why don't you take him and I'll unload the supplies from the truck."

"Supplies?"

He smiled, a warm, beautiful gesture that detracted from the scar across his cheek and transformed him from slightly dangerous-looking to more than slightly wonderful-looking. "In the truck I've got a doggie bed, food and water bowls, a couple of toys and several bags of kibble."

"Quinn, you didn't have to do all that," she protested as she took the leash from him.

"It wouldn't be fair to give you a gift that cost you a ton of money," he replied. "And along with the gift comes free veterinary services for the life of that guy. Consider it my donation to Hopechest Ranch."

She started to protest once again at the generosity of the gift, but then changed her mind and smiled. "Thank you."

Together they walked out of the door. She headed for one of the three garages as he went out to his truck. The first garage was the playroom for the kids. The second was where she parked her car and the third was currently empty. It was to the empty one that she led the puppy.

As she waited for Quinn she crouched down and stroked the puppy's back. "We'll let the kids give you a name," she said. He gazed at her with big, brown, adoring eyes.

Her heart expanded with warmth. Quinn had brought her a dog to walk in the woods. It was one of the most thoughtful things anyone had ever done for her. He thought she could use a companion.

Had he sensed the deep, abiding loneliness that had been her constant companion for the last couple of years? A loneliness that never went away, no matter how many people surrounded her, no matter how the children filled her days and nights.

She stood as he approached with two big sacks of dog food over his shoulder. Although he was tall and lean, he had broad, strong shoulders that easily managed the heavy bags.

"I can't believe you did this," she said. As he drew closer, a new spark of electricity swept through her.

"I figured maybe if you're grateful enough you might invite me in for a cup of coffee." He set the bags on the garage floor.

"I think maybe we can work something out," she replied. She told herself that the crazy buzz she felt at the very idea of spending some time with him was nothing more than the pleasure of having somebody fill these hours of darkness before she finally called it a night.

It took him only minutes to unload all the items from his truck. She got the pooch settled for the night, then Quinn followed her inside and to the kitchen.

The kitchen was one of the largest rooms in the house, but as Quinn took a seat at the long wooden table, she felt as if the room shrank. He possessed a simmering energy beneath his calm, cool exterior, an energy that seemed to shimmer in the air around him.

"I'm not keeping you up, am I?" he asked as she made the coffee. "I didn't realize how late it had gotten until I got to your front door."

"It's not a problem," she assured him. "I normally don't go to bed too early." It was only when she turned away from him to check on the coffee that she remembered what had happened the night before—their encounter in the woods and the lie he'd told her about what he'd been doing there.

Quinn wasn't sure what happened, but one minute her brown eyes were warm and inviting and the next minute they chilled and held a new wariness.

"You lied to me last night," she said. "You told me that you had been over at Clay's because he had a horse down, but I asked him about it and he said all his stock was healthy."

So that's what had caused the change in her expression. She'd obviously just remembered what he'd told her the night before.

"Yeah, I lied," he admitted. "It was a stupid thing to do. I was embarrassed that I'd bumped into you, embarrassed to tell you the truth."

She remained standing by the counter next to the coffeepot. The coffee was finished brewing but she made no move to get cups. He had a feeling that she was waiting for his explanation and if she didn't like it, then the offer of coffee would be rescinded.

And he didn't want that. It had taken him all evening to work up the nerve to come here. In fact, it had taken him months to work up his nerve to be here. He wanted to have coffee with her. He wanted to know more about her.

"And what, exactly, is the truth?" she asked, the coolness in her voice strong enough to frost his face.

"I don't sleep well, haven't for years. On the nights when I know I won't be able to sleep I go to Clay's and spend time with my horse, Noches. I board him there and right now he's my favorite nighttime companion."

She searched his face, as if on his features she'd discover if he was telling her the truth or not. "Jewel, why else would I be out in the woods in the middle of the night?" he asked.

She turned her back on him to reach for two cups in the overhead cabinet, but not before he saw a flash of emotion in her eyes, an emotion that looked something like fear. "You should have just told me that last night," she replied. She poured the coffee then joined him at the table.

"I haven't been eager for it to get around that the town vet suffers from insomnia. The first time an animal dies for whatever reason everyone will say it's my fault because I don't get enough sleep," he said.

She took a sip of her coffee, her brown eyes gazing at him curiously over the rim of her cup. "It must have been difficult for you," she said as she placed the cup back on the table. "When you had to put down Clay's horse and so many in the town turned against you. Clay told me all about it."

"It was difficult," he agreed, "but it's over and done with, and I try to keep difficult things from my past firmly in the past." As thoughts of Sarah drifted through his mind, he decided a change of topic was in order. "I understand I missed a big reunion over at Clay's place this morning."

"You did." A smile curved her lips and Quinn felt the beauty of the gesture in a starburst of warmth in the pit of his stomach. "It was wonderful to see Clay and Ryder together again. Finally, I think they're going to have the relationship they both want."

Quinn nodded. "I know how badly Ryder's lifestyle hurt Clay, the bad choices his brother made when he was younger, but it sounds like he's turned it all around."

"How did you hear about it—the reunion, I mean?" she asked curiously.

"I ran into Georgie and Nick and Emmie at the café this evening." He smiled. "Emmie told me she's excited to start school next week and she's determined to make one friend who isn't a cowboy."

Jewel laughed and again Quinn's stomach filled with a welcome warmth. She had a nice laugh. "That one is a pip," she said. "I know Georgie has been worried about her fitting in at school. Emmie has spent her whole life on the rodeo circuit with adults as her peers, but I keep telling Georgie that Emmie is going to be just fine. She's so bright, she shouldn't have any problems."

There followed several long moments of uncomfortable silence. Quinn felt like a teenage boy on a first date as he desperately searched for an interesting topic of conversation. He'd been wanting to get to know her better ever since she'd come to town, but it had been years since he'd done the dating dance.

"I'll bet your kids…" he began.

"How did you get…" she said at the same time.

"Go ahead," he said.

"I was just going to ask where you got the dog."

"I helped deliver a litter of four and the owner insisted I get pick of the litter for helping out. I already have a dog and so figured I'd just try to find him a good home. I think this will be a great place for him."

She smiled. "The kids will love him and taking care of him will be therapeutic for them."

He leaned back in his chair, some of his tension beginning to ebb. "You like what you do here."

She nodded, her golden-brown hair sparkling beneath the artificial light. "I love it. I was working for Meredith Colton at the Hopechest Ranch in Prosperino, California, and when she offered me the opportunity to come here and open up a ranch, I jumped at the chance."

"Was it a tough change? Moving here from California?" He took a drink of the coffee.

"Not really. I was ready for a change and, of course, Clay has been very supportive."

"He thinks a lot of you," Quinn said.

"He thinks a lot of you, too."

"He's been a good friend and a great support over the years." Quinn took another sip of his coffee.

"You know, I have the same problem you do with insomnia," she said. She wrapped her slender fingers around her coffee cup and looked more vulnerable than she had moments before. "I start dreading the coming of night just after dinner."

He wasn't surprised by her confession. "Have you seen a doctor? Maybe you could get a prescription for some sleeping medication."

She waved one of her hands. "I don't want to do that. I don't want to medicate myself to sleep. What about you? Have you seen a doctor, Doctor?" she asked lightly.

"No, I'm like you. Eventually after a couple nights of restlessness I manage to get in enough sleep to keep going." He hesitated a moment, then added, "From what Clay has told me, that's not the only thing we have in common."

"What else do we have in common?" One of her eyebrows danced up quizzically.

"We've both lost people we cared deeply about. Clay told me about your fiancé. I'm sorry for your loss."

Her eyes darkened as her complexion paled. "Thank you. It was a tragedy, but it's in the past."

It was obvious by the tightening of her lips, the paleness of her skin, that even though it was in her past, she still felt deeply the grief of the loss. She cleared her throat. "What about you? Who did you lose?"

"My wife, Sarah."

"I'm sorry. I didn't realize you'd been married." Some of the color returned to her cheeks.

"We weren't married long before she was diagnosed with a brain tumor. Six months later she was gone."

To his surprise Jewel reached out and covered his hand with hers. "Oh, Quinn. I'm so sorry."

Her touch sizzled through him and he turned his hand over so that he now grasped her hand. "The only reason I told you this is because I want you to know that I understand grief, that if you need somebody to talk to, I have a good ear and strong shoulders."

She pulled her hand from his as if suddenly uncomfortable by the physical connection. "I appreciate the offer, but I'm doing okay. Tell me about Sarah. What was she like?"

"Quiet and sweet. We met while I was in school. I was getting my degree in veterinary medicine and she wanted to be a nurse. It began as friendship and grew into love. She loved animals almost as much as I did and we talked about having a dozen kids and twice as many dogs and cats. What about your fiancé, Andy… wasn't that his name?"

"Andrew, never Andy," she replied, her eyes going soft. "He owned an accounting firm. He loved numbers and puzzles and he'd asked me to be his wife on the night that he died."

"Clay told me it was a car accident."

She nodded and once again wrapped her fingers around her cup, as if seeking warmth from the coffee it still contained. "We were driving home from the restaurant where we'd eaten dinner. It was misting and the road was dark. A Hummer seemed to come out of nowhere and steered right into the driver side of our car. I was knocked unconscious." One of her hands moved to splay on her stomach. "The driver of the Hummer was never found."

Quinn wanted to reach out to her, to pull her into his arms and hold her until her haunted, vulnerable look went away. "Even though you can't ever prepare yourself for the death of somebody you love, I had six months to prepare myself for saying goodbye to Sarah, but you had no time to prepare yourself for saying goodbye to Andrew."

She shrugged. "It happened. It's over and life moves on." She glanced at the clock on the stove.

"It's getting late," he said, taking it as a hint. "I should get out of here." She didn't argue and he stood and carried his cup to the sink. "Thanks for the coffee," he said as they walked to the front door.

"Thanks for the dog," she replied. "It was a very thoughtful thing for you to do." She opened the front door and leaned against it.

He knew she was waiting for him to walk out, but he was reluctant to leave. "Jewel, I'm sorry if our conversation brought back bad memories." He'd finally gotten an opportunity to talk to her one-on-one and the topic of conversation he'd chosen was their painful pasts.

To his horror her eyes misted with tears. "I'm sorry," she said as the tears spilled onto her cheeks.

He stepped toward her then, unable to stand by while she cried, feeling guilty because he was responsible for her tears. He should have talked about the weather, or about town politics, about anything but loss.

He opened his arms to her and to his surprise she walked into them and laid her head against his chest. He embraced her, the scent of her soft, floral perfume eddying in the air.

The last thing he'd expected when he'd arrived here tonight was to have her in his arms, but when she raised her face to look up at him, he knew he wanted to take it one step further. He desperately wanted to kiss her.

Chapter 4

Jewel knew he was going to kiss her. His intent shone hot in his amazingly gorgeous eyes. In the back of her mind she knew this was crazy, that she didn't know this man well enough to kiss him and she certainly wasn't interested in a relationship of any kind.

Still, that rational part of her brain was no match for the wave of sharp, visceral desire that swept through her as she gazed up at him. She parted her lips as he dipped his head to take her mouth with his.

Crazy. It was pure madness that possessed her, but she gave in to it. His mouth was hot, the kiss sending a shaft of warmth up and down her veins. She welcomed the feeling, welcomed him as she opened her mouth more to him, allowing him to deepen the kiss with his tongue.

She knew she should step back and call a halt to

things, but it had been so long and Quinn's arms were so strong around her and his kiss made her ache for more.

His hands stroked the length of her back as his mouth continued to ply hers with fire. She wrapped her arms around his neck and tangled her fingers in his soft, sexy mane of hair.

She swirled her tongue with his, felt her knees weaken and threaten to buckle. She clung to him more tightly, her heart beating a rhythm of desire.

His mouth finally left hers and moved down the length of her neck, nipping and teasing with slow, deliberate intent. She dropped her head back, allowing him to kiss her throat, and trail his hot mouth along her collarbone.

It didn't matter that she'd only known him on a casual, social level until now. She didn't care that this was probably one of the most foolish things she'd ever done. For right now, in his arms, she wanted to be foolish and abandon herself to being held by Quinn, being kissed by Quinn.

Once again his mouth captured hers and as she pressed more tightly against him she realized that he was aroused. This knowledge only made her desire flame higher.

She wanted to make love with him. She wanted to lose herself in his caresses, in the very mindless sensations of sex.

She'd heard enough about Quinn from Clay to know he wouldn't hurt her, that she was safe with him. She wasn't concerned about consequences. The most she'd have to worry about was perhaps a little embarrassment the morning after. But she didn't care about the morning after—all she cared about was here and now.

"Miss Jewel?"

Jewel and Quinn shot apart like two guilty teenagers at the sound of the young voice drifting down the hallway. Jewel recognized the voice. She drew a deep breath to steady herself, not looking at Quinn. "Lindy, what's wrong?"

"You'd better come quick, Kelsey is packing her suitcase and says she's gonna run away."

"I'll be right there." Jewel finally looked at Quinn as she felt the heat of a blush warm her cheeks. Okay, so her embarrassment hadn't waited until the morning after.

"You need help?" he asked softly.

"No, I'll be fine. Please, just go." Now that the heat of the moment had passed, she was appalled by what had just happened between them...what had almost happened between them.

She was grateful that he didn't argue but simply nodded and left. She closed the front door behind him then hurried down the hallway to the girls' room where Kelsey was throwing her clothes into the battered cloth suitcase she'd arrived with.

"Kelsey, what's going on?" Jewel asked.

The girl didn't stop her activity and kept her eyes downcast. "Nothing. I just don't want to be here anymore."

"Has something happened? Did somebody say something to upset you?" Jewel took a step closer to the young teenager.

"No. I just gotta go, that's all. I've got to leave." She glanced up at Jewel, tears filling her bright green eyes.

Jewel stepped toward her and held out her hand. "Come on, let's go someplace where you and I can have a little private chat."

Kelsey hesitated a moment, then slipped her hand into Jewel's. "Lindy, Carrie, back to bed and lights out," she said as she led Kelsey from the room.

She took the girl into the kitchen and gestured her to the chair where Quinn had sat. "Want a glass of milk? Maybe a cookie?"

Kelsey shook her head, her face radiating abject misery. Jewel sat in the chair next to Kelsey's and took the girl's cold, small hands into hers. "Honey, I can't help you if you don't talk to me," she said softly.

Kelsey caught her lower lip in her teeth, then released it and sighed. "I like it here. That's the whole problem."

"I'm sorry. I don't understand," Jewel replied.

Kelsey frowned. "Every time I get someplace where I like to be, then somebody makes me leave. I figured this time I wouldn't wait around for somebody to kick me out. I'd just go, before I like it so much that it hurts to leave."

A sob escaped her. "What's the point of staying here and being happy when I know sometime I'll have to leave and won't be happy again?" she cried.

Jewel leaned forward and gathered the girl into her arms. "I never turn up my nose at happiness," Jewel replied as she stroked Kelsey's hair. "What you have to do with it is grab it and hold it as close as you can for as long as you can. Then when it's gone you have special memories to help you through the bad times.

Besides, one of the things we want to do while you're here is teach you some skills so that you can learn to be happy wherever you are."

Kelsey raised her head and looked at her through tear-glazed eyes. "I'm afraid to be happy because it hurts so much when it goes away."

Jewel held her close, her heart aching for the girl. "I know, honey. But I'd like you to stay here with us and grab on to all the happiness we can give you. Let's not talk about when you leave. Heavens, you've only been here for one day."

Kelsey laughed as Jewel released her. "I really don't want to leave," she admitted. "I want to ride the horses some more and I like the other kids, too."

"Good, then how about we get you back into bed? There are a bunch of activities on the schedule for tomorrow and you don't want to start the day tired. You can unpack your things in the morning."

Kelsey nodded and together they walked back to the girls' room. "Good night," Kelsey said. Jewel watched as she moved her suitcase off the bed and then climbed into the bunk.

With the crisis handled, Jewel returned to the kitchen where she turned out the lights then headed for her own quarters.

Her head filled with a vision of Quinn, and she couldn't believe what had happened between them before he'd left, couldn't imagine what might have happened if they hadn't been interrupted.

Or maybe the problem was she *could* imagine all too well what might have happened. Her mouth heated as she remembered the kisses they'd shared. In another minute she would have led him to her bedroom, allowed him—no, encouraged him—to make love to her.

God, was she so desperate, so lonely that she'd just fall into bed with anyone? She entered the dressing room and stripped off her jeans and T-shirt and threw them into the hamper, then stood in front of the wall mirror and stared at her reflection.

She raked her fingers through her short sun-streaked brown hair and frowned as she saw the tired lines that radiated outward from her eyes.

No, she wasn't desperate enough to fall into bed with any man who showed an interest in her. If that were the case, she would have slept with Deputy Adam Rawlings by now. He'd certainly made it clear he was interested in a romance with her, but she had never wanted to kiss him. Not like she'd wanted to kiss Quinn.

It was Quinn who stirred her like no man had for a very long time. She turned away from the mirror and reached for her nightgown. From the moment she'd first seen him, something about him had drawn her not only on a physical level, but on an emotional level, as well.

There was a solid gentleness about him that attracted her and nothing he'd done this evening had changed her mind. Still, she was a bit embarrassed by how quickly she'd responded to him.

Clad in her nightgown, she went into her bedroom and pulled down the covers on the bed, surprised to realize she not only felt tired, she felt sleepy.

Maybe the conversation with Quinn had relaxed something inside her, or maybe it had just been his calm, steady presence that had created an unusual sense of peace inside her.

She crawled into bed and glanced at the clock on her nightstand. Almost eleven o'clock. Maybe tonight she could actually sleep. She turned out the light on her nightstand, then closed her eyes.

A vision of Quinn at the table filled her mind, his topaz eyes shining with an inner strength, his mouth curved up into a gentle smile. Almost immediately she felt the heaviness of sleep overtaking her and she gave in to it.

The dream began almost immediately. She and Andrew were seated in the restaurant. It was their favorite place to eat, an Italian café with traditional checkered tablecloths and candles in the center of each table. The food was impeccable and the atmosphere conducive to romance.

They had just finished eating when Andrew smiled at her, his blue eyes holding suppressed excitement. "I've spent the entire day today trying to figure out a wonderfully romantic way to do this, but I'm an accountant at heart and that means I'm not very creative." He reached into his shirt pocket and withdrew a ring box.

It was magic. The man, the ring and the moment. The scene shimmered in a golden haze as it played out in her dream. The engagement ring sparkled as he reached for her hand and slid it onto her finger.

And the magic only grew stronger, brighter when she told Andrew her secret, that she was pregnant with his baby. Andrew had been thrilled and they'd excitedly talked about wedding plans and baby names. They'd laughed as they'd left the restaurant.

"Here, baby, you drive," she'd said, and handed him the keys to her car. She'd picked him up at his office and driven to the restaurant. "That way, I can sit and admire my new ring," she'd said with a laugh.

The scene shifted abruptly, as dreams often do, and they were in her car, Andrew behind the wheel. The golden light that had shimmered was gone and everything was in the sharp colors of harsh reality.

Even in sleep Jewel knew what was coming and she fought to wake up, not wanting to see the images. But the dreamscape held her captive and she saw the Hummer appear out of nowhere, a bright yellow monster with sharp silver gnashing teeth.

"No!" she cried, but the monster didn't listen. She watched in horror as those scissor-sharp teeth slammed into their car, then snatched Andrew and shook him like a rag doll.

As the monster tossed Andrew aside, it came for her, biting into her stomach, killing her baby, killing her dreams.

Her screams woke her. She shot straight up in the bed, her heart stuttering so fast in her chest she thought she was going to die. Deep sobs wrenched through her, making it difficult to breathe.

She grabbed her stomach, as if to protect, to save, but she knew it was a futile gesture. The monster had won. He'd managed to take everything away from her, leaving her empty inside.

She remained in the center of her bed, shivering and silently weeping as the nightmare lingered in her head. Why hadn't the driver of the Hummer stopped? Why hadn't he tried to help?

If medical help had been summoned immediately,

would Andrew have been saved? Would her baby have lived? These were haunting questions with no answers.

Finally, tears spent, she reached over and turned on her nightlight, knowing that it would be a very long time before she fell asleep again.

She rolled to the side of the bed to get up, and frowned as she heard the crinkle of paper. Puzzled, she slid over and spied what looked like a page from a newspaper.

She picked it up and stared at the headline: Tragic Accident Kills Accounting Executive. She dropped it as if it burned her fingers. It was the original article that had appeared in the paper years ago when the accident had happened.

Her heartbeat, which had finally slowed to a normal pace, now crashed and banged so painfully she couldn't catch her breath. How had the article gotten in her room, in her bed?

Somebody had been in her room. Had someone crept in while she was sleeping? Earlier in the night while she and Quinn had been in the kitchen?

Was he still here now?

She jumped off the bed and grabbed the baseball bat that leaned against the wall in the corner of the room. She didn't want to alarm anyone else in the house, but she needed to make certain that nobody was here who didn't belong here.

Heart pounding so loudly she could hear it in her head, she went back into her quarters, flipping on the lights in the dressing room, the bathroom, then her bedroom. She checked closets and behind doorways. When she'd cleared her quarters, she went through the rest of the house. She checked all the doors and windows, but found nothing out of place and nobody there who didn't belong. The doors and windows were locked tight and showed no breach of any kind.

She finally crept back to her bed. It was just after one. There would be no more sleep for tonight. She sat with the baseball bat clutched in her hands, and waited for morning to come.

"Rover," Barry exclaimed. "That's a good name for a dog."

"That's a dumb name," Sam replied. "We should call him Champion or Bruno. Those are good dog names."

They were all in the kitchen, where the dog was running from child to child, his tail wagging with happiness. He lavished kisses on everyone he met and Jewel wasn't sure who was happier—the dog or the children.

"He looks like a cup of hot cocoa," Kelsey said.

"That a good name—Cocoa." Carrie clapped her hands. "Here, Cocoa." The dog ran to her and nearly knocked her down.

"I think Cocoa is a wonderful name," Jewel said. Her eyes felt gritty from her lack of sleep and the fear that had gripped her when she'd seen the newspaper article on the bed still simmered just beneath the surface of her consciousness.

"And now what we need to do is divide up the responsibility of taking care of Cocoa," she said, trying to stay focused.

As the kids talked about who would be responsible for feeding and providing fresh water for him, and who would take the dog out for walks, Jewel's thoughts once again returned to the night before.

It had been just before dawn that the idea of something other than a mysterious intruder struck her. On the top shelf in her closet was a cardboard memory box. Inside it were family photos and memorabilia from her past.

She'd had several copies of the newspaper article inside the box. While she had no way of confirming that the copy that had been on her bed had come from her box, she suspected that it might have.

Maybe she'd gotten up in the middle of her nightmare and had taken the article from the box and laid it on the bed. She wasn't sure what frightened her more—the idea of an intruder whose motive apparently was to torment her, or the possibility that she was unconsciously haunting herself.

Was this the way it had begun with her mother? Was this how true madness began? She remembered reading an article in a psychology magazine once about a woman who believed she was being stalked. She received threatening notes in the mail, her car tires were slashed. One incident after another plagued her and the truth was only discovered after her family hired a private investigator. The truth was that she was doing it all to herself with no conscious knowledge of her actions.

"Can we walk him now?" Barry's voice intruded into her disturbing thoughts.

"There's a leash for his collar out in the garage. Sam, why don't you run out and get it, then you can all take turns walking him in the front yard," Jewel said.

As Sam went off to retrieve the leash, Jewel looked

at Cheryl. "I've got some things to do in town today. It's possible I'll be gone most of the day."

"Not a problem. Jeff and I can keep things running smoothly here on the home front," she replied.

"Don't forget that at two today Mark Potter is coming to give an art lesson." Jewel had hired a local artist to come twice a week to give the kids art lessons. She believed in the therapeutic quality of art.

Sam returned with the leash and within minutes all the kids were out in the yard with Cocoa and under the supervision of Jeff.

Jewel went to her bedroom and grabbed her purse, then left the house and got into her car. She waved as she drove down the driveway and smiled as she saw Cocoa, with an exuberant leap, knock Carrie on her behind. Carrie laughed and wrapped her arms around the dog.

The dog had been a great gift from Quinn. Quinn. As she headed toward town, the handsome vet filled her thoughts.

She knew what his mouth tasted like, had felt the silky softness of his amazing hair and his strong shoulders beneath her fingertips. But she didn't know where he came from, what kind of family he had or even what kind of food he liked.

The whole kiss thing had been crazy and as she thought of seeing him again she wasn't sure if the thrum of nerves that tingled inside her was dread or anticipation.

She dismissed him from her mind as she pulled into a parking space in front of the town library. At some point in the early morning hours, with sleep deprivation weighing heavy, she'd wondered if maybe her unconscious mind was trying to tell her something important, something about the accident that had taken everything she loved away from her.

In those dark predawn hours, she'd realized there was a lot about Andrew and his work she hadn't known. There had always been a small part of her that had believed the accident wasn't an accident at all. The Hummer hadn't attempted to swerve to avoid hitting them. The driver hadn't jammed on the brakes or taken any action to prevent the accident.

Although the authorities had ruled it an accident, due to the mist that had made the country road a bit slick, Jewel had never completely embraced the notion that it had been nothing more than a tragic accident.

She could have done some research on the computer at the ranch, but for some reason she'd felt it was important to keep this separate from her life there. One of the library computers would do just fine for a little research into Andrew's business.

As she entered the library, she was surprised to see sixteen-year-old Sarah Engleleit behind the counter. The teenager had spent some time at the Hopechest Ranch two months ago when she'd run away from home.

"Sarah," she exclaimed. "I didn't know you were working here."

"I just started last week. It's just part-time but I really like it. How are things at the ranch?"

"Busy, as usual." Jewel smiled. "I'm just going to use one of the computers for a while. I'll see you later."

Jewel made her way to one of the computer stations, a new burst of nerves attacking her as she realized she was about to go backward in time, back to where dreams held possibility and the horror of having that possibility stolen away.

For a moment she sat in the chair and fought the impulse to rub her eyes, knowing they were already red enough for somebody to mistake her for a vampire.

She couldn't remember the last time she'd felt so exhausted. It was as if all the nights of insomnia had finally caught up with her this morning, making concentration difficult.

Long and Casey Accounting had been a powerhouse in the business world in California. Andrew had owned the firm and Gray Casey had been a junior partner. When Andrew died, his younger brother stepped into the position Andrew had held and the company had continued to thrive.

The first thing she researched was the accident. There had been several news articles about the tragedy in the days following the wreck.

She tried to maintain an emotional distance as she read over the articles that had been in the local papers, but she learned nothing new from the printed accounts.

By keying in the search words *Long and Casey Accounting* she got over two hundred results. The morning turned to afternoon as she checked each one, unsure what she was looking for, but compelled to continue. She took notes of things she thought might mean something.

It was three o'clock when Sarah came over to where Jewel sat. "I'm leaving and just wanted to say goodbye," she said.

Jewel got up and gave her a hug. "You know you're welcome out at the ranch anytime."

"I know. Maybe one day after school I'll drop by for a visit."

"I'd like that," Jewel replied. As Sarah headed out the front door, Jewel returned to her reading. Her eyes, which had burned earlier, now felt raw.

She was just about to give up the search when she hit an article that caused her to sit up straighter in her chair.

Successful Entrepreneur Indicted for Tax Evasion, the headline read. She scanned the page, wondering why a news report about a James Corrs had been brought up by her typing in Andrew's firm's name. She found her answer on the second page of the article. It had been Andrew who had turned in James Corrs to the Internal Revenue Service.

The date on the newspaper was three weeks before the car accident that had taken Andrew's life. Could this James Corrs have sought revenge against Andrew? Certainly he'd had a lot to lose by battling a tax-evasion charge.

Dear God, was it possible the car accident hadn't been an accident at all, but rather a murder?

As a firm hand fell on her shoulder, a scream of surprise escaped her.

Chapter 5

"I'm sorry, I didn't mean to startle you," Quinn said as he took a step closer to Jewel.

She hurriedly closed the folder in front of her and hit the button to return the computer to the home page. It was as if she didn't want him to see what she'd been doing. "I didn't mean to yell," she replied. "I was just so engrossed that I didn't see you there."

"Engrossed in what?" he asked lightly. She looked both beautiful and terrible. She wore a pair of jeans and a sleeveless blue blouse, but it wasn't her clothes that captured his attention. It was her eyes. They were so red they looked as though, if she opened them wide enough, they'd start to bleed. That, coupled with her drawn, exhausted look, had him worried about her.

"Just a dry psychology article," she replied. Her gaze

didn't quite meet his. "What about you? What are you doing here?"

He held up two books and tried not to think about the searing kiss they'd shared the night before. "I ordered a couple of books from the library in San Antonio and they came in this morning."

"Must be interesting material for you to order it all the way from San Antonio," she replied. She looked nervous, on edge as she clutched the file folder to her chest.

He smiled. "Yeah, *Animal Husbandry* and *New Medicine for Old Health Problems in Animals.* If I try to read them before I go to bed, they just might solve my insomnia problem."

She laughed, but even that sounded stressed and tired. "I've tried reading before bedtime to get sleepy, but it doesn't work for me." She released a small sigh as she set the folder down on the desk. "Lately, nothing seems to be working for me."

"Ah, but I'll bet you haven't read *Animal Husbandry.* You want to go get a drink?" The invitation sprang from his lips almost before his brain had formed the intention.

She looked so miserable and he was reluctant to just say goodbye, turn and walk away from her.

To his surprise, she hesitated only a moment then nodded. "Actually, a drink sounds great." She got up from the computer station and grabbed her folder from the table. "Where do you want to go?"

"There's a new Mexican place down a block on Main. It's got a nice little bar inside. It's called Joe's Cantina."

She frowned, the gesture emphasizing the tired lines across her forehead. "I haven't heard of it before."

"It's only been open about two weeks. I checked it

out last week. The margaritas were great and the food was terrific."

"Okay, sounds good to me," she agreed.

"If you want, we could walk from here."

A moment later they walked out into the late-afternoon sunshine. Quinn dropped off his books in his truck and she put her folder in her car, then together they headed down the sidewalk toward the restaurant.

"Did everything go okay after I left last night?" he asked. "The girl who was going to run away? Did you get her settled down?"

"She didn't really want to run away," she replied. "Poor thing was just scared because she likes the ranch and she didn't want to get attached and have to leave. She's afraid to be happy because she knows what it feels like to have happiness vanish."

"That's a tough thing to know so young."

Jewel nodded, the sunshine catching and sparking on the gold highlights in her hair. "It's tragic. That's the problem with most of the kids who come to the ranch. They've already experienced things that no child should have to go through. Oh, by the way, the dog now has a name. Cocoa."

"Nice," he replied. "So the kids were happy with him?"

She smiled. "Happy is an understatement. They were overjoyed."

"I'm glad. I know Cocoa will be happy there."

As they reached the door to the restaurant the scent of salsa, tortillas and spicy meat filled the air. Quinn opened the door for her, then followed her into the establishment.

On the right side was the seating area for diners and on the left was an intimate bar with small round tables and low lighting. They settled at one of the bar tables and both ordered margaritas.

"I usually don't drink before dinner," she said, as if it were important that he understand that. "And until last night I've never kissed a man who brought me a dog." Her cheeks flamed pink.

Quinn's blood heated as he thought of that kiss. It had taken him a long time and an icy shower after he'd left her ranch to cool down and given the opportunity to kiss her again, he wouldn't hesitate. Even now the thought of kissing her again created a ball of tension in the pit of his stomach.

"Jewel, if you're worried that somehow I think you're a fast woman because of what happened last night, put that worry out of your head. Neither of us planned for it to happen. It just happened, but I'd be less than honest if I didn't tell you that I wouldn't mind if it happened again."

She was saved from having to respond by the waitress, who delivered their drinks and a basket of chips with a bowl of salsa.

"You mentioned last night that you knew a lot about me from Clay, but I don't know much about you," she said once the waitress had left. "Where are you from? Do you have other family?"

"My family lives in Oregon and it's a big one. I have three brothers and two sisters."

"Wow, that *is* big. Are you close?"

Quinn reached for a chip. "We're very close. A day doesn't go by that I don't get a phone call from a brother or sister or one of my parents. All my siblings are married with families of their own and they hate the idea that for the last five years I've been alone." He dipped the chip into the salsa, then popped it into his mouth.

"So how did you end up in Esperanza?"

"I went to school in San Antonio and fell in love with Texas. When I graduated, I started looking around the area for a small town that needed a veterinarian. Esperanza fit the bill. The vet at the time, Dr. Eliot Patterson, was about to retire and he invited me out here for a visit. I fell in love with the town and the people. What about you? Are your parents still alive?"

"The story of my parents is a twisted, sordid tale." She paused to take a sip of her drink, her eyes darkening. "My father was a used-car salesman named Ellis Mayfair who came through town twice a month to see my mother. At that time my mother was living in Sacramento. The short story is she got pregnant and Ellis wasn't happy about it. I was delivered by Ellis in a motel room. When my mother fell asleep Ellis gave me to a doctor who adopted me out in an illegal adoption. When my mother woke up and found out what he'd done, she stabbed him. He died and she went to prison."

"My God, Jewel." As he thought of his own family closeness, he wanted to grab her to him and hold her until he figured out a way to somehow change her history. As if losing her fiancé weren't enough, this bit of information made him realize just what kind of a survivor Jewel Mayfair really was.

"It's all right," she said hurriedly. "The story has a happy ending. Charlie and Ruth Baylor adopted me and raised me in a small town in Ohio. They couldn't have kids of their own and were loving, wonderful parents."

Although her smile was genuine as she spoke of her adoptive parents, the darkness that had deepened her eyes when she'd first spoken of her real mother and father didn't lift.

Quinn had a feeling there was more to the story than the thumbnail sketch she'd given him, but he was reluctant to pry too deep too fast. Still, he couldn't stop himself from probing a little more.

"Did you ever get a chance to know your real mother? Is she still in prison?"

Her fingers tightened around the stem of her glass. "No, she eventually got out of prison, and we managed to meet, but she passed away soon after that."

"I'm sorry." Once again he wanted to wrap his arms around her and hold her until the haunted darkness in her eyes receded. Instead, he decided a change of topic might be more appropriate. "So, how did you get involved with the Hopechest Ranch?"

Some of the tension left her face as she took another sip of her drink, then relaxed into the back of the chair. "Originally, I had my own small practice. Then when the accident happened, I pretty much fell apart. I gave up the practice and sort of drifted in a deep depression. It was my Aunt Meredith who suggested I spend a couple hours a week at the Hopechest Ranch in Prosperino, and when she decided to open the ranch here, she offered me this position and I jumped at the opportunity."

"It must be amazingly rewarding working with the children."

"It is, but I'm sure you feel the same way about your work with animals."

He nodded. "It's very rewarding and at times heart-breaking."

She smiled. "That defines my work at the ranch perfectly."

For a moment they were silent, but it was a comfortable silence. It lasted only a short time, then they began to speculate on Joe Colton's run to become president and talked about how excited Jewel was about Joe and Meredith's upcoming visit to Texas and the Hopechest Ranch. At some point during their conversation he noticed the stress that had lined her face easing and the shadows in her eyes backing away.

Quinn glanced at his watch, then back at her. "Look, it's almost six. I don't know about you, but smelling all the food cooking suddenly has me starving. How about we move to the other side and get some dinner."

"I'd like that," she said. Her immediate acquiescence both surprised and pleased him. He wanted to know more about her. He wanted to know everything about her and it had been a long time since he'd felt that way about a woman.

For the last five years Quinn had grieved deeply for the wife he'd lost, but now he was more than ready to share his life with a special woman. From the moment he'd seen Jewel, he'd had a feeling she might just be that woman and everything he'd learned about her and in the kiss they'd shared only made him more certain.

But there was no question that Jewel had secrets. He saw them in the dark places in her eyes and her quick movements to hide whatever it was she'd been doing in the library only emphasized that.

Quinn was a patient man and he was determined to unlock all the secrets that Jewel Mayfair possessed.

It's just dinner, that's what Jewel told herself. They were simply two adults enjoying the pleasure of each other's company over a meal.

Still, she couldn't deny that being in Quinn's company relaxed her, that the quiet steadiness of his nature drew her and calmed the chaotic noise inside her head.

Even with the rich scent of the Mexican food in the air, she could smell the scent of his cologne, a masculine woodsy scent that she found wonderfully appealing.

It was impossible for her not to think about the kiss they'd shared the night before. Just looking at his mouth made hers heat with the memory.

"Another margarita?" he asked as the waitress arrived to take their orders.

"No, thanks. One is definitely my limit." Instead they both ordered soft drinks to go along with their meals.

"I haven't had enchiladas for a long time." She placed her napkin in her lap.

"Mexican food is one of my favorites," he replied. "Along with Italian and Chinese and good old-fashioned American cuisine."

She laughed. "You sound like a man who just likes to eat."

"Guilty as charged." He reached up and pushed back a strand of his magnificent hair.

She smiled. "I've been thinking about getting some

animals for the ranch, petting-zoo kinds of animals. Caring for them would be terrific therapy," she said.

"That's a wonderful idea," he agreed. "Unconditional love is what you get with animals. They don't care where you've been or what you've done. When you decide to do that, let me know and I'd be glad to go with you to purchase the animals you want."

"I'd appreciate it. I was thinking maybe some baby lambs and goats to start." No question, she was physically attracted to Quinn. There was a simmering sexuality about him that was even more appealing because he seemed so oblivious to it.

By the time the waitress arrived with their meals, he was entertaining her with stories about the various animals he'd encountered over the years.

She couldn't remember the last time she'd laughed as much and she'd forgotten how wonderful it was to share laughter with a good-looking man.

"Cocoa is the first animal I've ever owned," she confessed.

He looked at her in mock horror. "No dog when you were growing up? No pet rabbit or kitty or turtle?"

She shook her head. "Nothing. Ruth was allergic to pets and when I finally got out on my own, it just didn't seem that important."

"I've had a dog all my life. Right now I have a schnauzer. Sabra has been the only woman in my life for the last four years, but I'm hoping that's going to change."

There it was, that whisper of heat flashing in his eyes, a heat that said he liked what he saw when he looked at her. A responding warmth swept through her.

Was she ready for a new relationship? The possibility shot a little thrill through her.

"Is Sabra the jealous type?" she asked in an attempt to keep things light.

"Not that I know of, although I've never had another woman in my house."

His words surprised her. "I would think all the single women in Esperanza would be banging down your door."

He grinned. "I have to admit, I have had a few questionable casseroles brought to my doorstep by some of the local women, but I just wasn't interested until lately in pursuing anything."

She had the distinct impression he was courting her.

He leaned forward. "I know I'm not the most exciting man on the block. I'm forty-four years old. I know my limits when it comes to drinking. I take my friendships very seriously and, except for last night, I usually don't kiss on the first date."

He was definitely courting her, and it was working. He didn't seem to have a clue that the picture he painted of himself was far more appealing than a wild bad boy. Solid and dependable—that's what Jewel wanted in a man.

As the waitress came to remove their plates and ask them about dessert, she declined, but Quinn insisted she needed some coffee and sopaipillas to complete the meal.

Laughing, she settled back to enjoy dessert with him. Her research into Andrew's death had long ago left her mind and being in Quinn's company made her feel as if somehow everything in her life was going to be all right.

They took turns dipping the puffed pastry into a bowl of honey and split the vanilla-bean ice cream that Quinn had added to the dessert order.

The conversation remained light and easy. They talked about their favorite foods, movies they liked and didn't like and mutual acquaintances they knew.

It was after eight when they finally left the restaurant and walked back to where their vehicles were parked at the library.

He walked her to her car and she leaned against the side and smiled up at him. "Thank you for dinner, Quinn. It was an unexpected pleasure."

He stepped closer to her, invading her personal space, but she didn't mind. Remembering how she'd felt the night before when his big strong arms had surrounded her, when his mouth had plied hers with heat, she definitely didn't mind at all that she sensed he wanted to kiss her again.

"I'd like to do it again," he said.

For a moment she thought he was talking about kissing her, then she realized he was talking about having dinner together.

"I'd like that," she replied. She found something almost hypnotically peaceful about being in his company, but it was a peacefulness coupled with a huge dose of an emotion that felt strongly like desire. And it had been so long since a man had moved her on any level.

"There's something else I'd like to do again." He took another step closer to her and this time there was no mistaking what he was talking about.

Her heart two-stepped as he reached out his hand

and with his index finger traced the outline of her lips. "Do you mind?" he murmured.

"No." The single word whispered out of her with a sigh of anticipation.

He leaned forward and took her mouth with his. He tasted of honey and coffee and a passion that was contagious.

Before things could spiral out of control, she ended the kiss. "Dr. Logan. I think you could be a dangerous man."

He stepped back from her and smiled. "If we were someplace more private, I'd like to be a lot more dangerous." His smile fell away and he gazed at her intently. "I like you, Jewel. You're the first woman since my wife whom I've wanted to spend time with and get to know better." He shifted from one foot to the other, as if uncomfortable as he waited for her to reply.

"And I'd like to get to know you better, too," she replied. "I'll tell you what. Sunday I'm planning on taking the kids on a trail ride at Clay's. With school starting Monday, I thought it would be a nice way to end the summer vacation. Why don't you plan on joining us?"

There was no better way to judge a man's true character than to see him interacting with children, she thought.

"I'd love to share a trail ride with you and the kids," he said without hesitation. "In fact, why don't you let me bring a picnic lunch for everyone?"

She laughed. "Are you out of your mind? I mean, I do have seven kids in residence at the moment."

"Then it's lunch for nine. Just tell me what time and I'll take care of the rest of the details."

"Okay," she said, helpless to turn down what appeared to be a heartfelt offer. "Why don't we plan on meeting at Clay's at eleven? We can ride for two hours then have lunch around one." As he nodded his agreement she opened her car door and slid in behind the wheel. "Good night, Quinn."

As she pulled out of the library parking lot and onto Main she couldn't stop herself from taking a quick glance in her rearview mirror to get one last look at him.

He stood by his truck watching her drive away and once again her heart fluttered with a sense of anticipation, of sweet possibility.

She turned on her headlights against the approaching darkness of night and wondered if it was possible that she was finally ready to look ahead instead of dwelling on a past she couldn't change.

Had her grief over Andrew and the baby ebbed to where she could entertain the idea of a new man in her life? She tightened her hands on the steering wheel. Maybe, she thought. Maybe it was the right time.

She liked Quinn and the more time she spent with him the more she liked him. He stirred up a desire inside her that half stole her breath away.

She glanced at her watch as she turned into the lane that led to the ranch. Good, she'd be just in time to tell the children good-night.

Funny, how the exhaustion that had weighed so heavily on her as she'd gone through the morning, the same exhaustion that had burned her eyes and ached in her shoulders at the library had disappeared while she'd been in Quinn's company.

He excited her and energized her while at the same

time bringing to her a kind of inner peace she hadn't felt for a very long time. It was a heady combination.

Cheryl was in the kitchen when she got home. Jewel made the nighttime rounds to say good-night to the children, then she sat at the table and listened as Cheryl filled her in on the day.

"Mark had the kids do some acrylic oil painting today. He brought birdhouses for each of them to paint. The kids loved it and we now have seven interesting-looking birdhouses to hang in the trees," Cheryl said.

"We'll have to see about getting them up this weekend. Maybe we can hang them in the trees out there so they can be admired while we have our meals." She pointed to the kitchen window.

"That would be nice," Cheryl agreed. "Barry had a bit of a meltdown this afternoon. His mother called and started talking about all the things that would be different when he got home. He got anxious, had a panic attack, then got angry. Jeff took him for a walk so he could cool down."

Jewel made a mental note to have a session with Barry first thing in the morning. She and Cheryl talked for a few more minutes, then they said their good-nights and parted ways.

Jewel went first into her sitting room, which served as her office and took a few minutes to make notes in Barry's file. Calls from his mother always upset him. Barry's father had died a year ago and within a month his mother had remarried. Almost immediately Barry had started having panic attacks with bursts of extreme rage. His mother seemed to be clueless that she hadn't given her son time to grieve the loss of his father.

She closed the file and yawned, her thoughts immediately shifting back to Quinn. She wondered how he had gotten the scar on his cheek. It actually enhanced his attractiveness, giving his face interesting character.

She was curious to see how he'd be with the kids. It was easy to enjoy the company of children who were well-behaved, but the children at the Hopechest Ranch were here because their behavior wasn't perfect.

Yawning again, she went into her master bath and got ready for bed. Maybe she'd read for a while. It was just after nine and she was in the middle of a new book by a famous psychologist detailing her work with borderline personality disorder.

Minutes later, snuggled in her bed with the bedside lamp on and her book in her arms, she tried to focus on the words, but her mind kept drifting back to the time she'd spent with Quinn.

There had been a time following Andrew's death and the loss of her baby that Jewel hadn't wanted to live, when the depression had been too huge for her to stand. The incapacitating grief had passed, but it wasn't until Quinn had gazed at her with his simmering topaz eyes that she felt as if she were truly alive again.

Even now, just thinking about him, her heart quickened and a smile curved her lips. She closed her book and placed it on the nightstand. Maybe if she went to sleep right away Quinn would fill her dreams. That would be so nice.

She shut off the light and burrowed back down beneath the crisp sheets. "No bad dreams tonight," she whispered in the dark. "Please, no bad dreams."

She closed her eyes and listened to the ordinary

sounds of the house at rest, the soft hum of the air conditioner, the faint tinkle of the wind chimes that hung outside on the back patio. Familiar sounds, comforting noise that lulled her into that twilight state between consciousness and unconsciousness.

That's when she heard it—the sound of a baby crying—and even though she knew it was impossible, she knew it was *her* baby crying. She felt the mournful cries in the depth of her womb, in the center of her soul.

No, not again. Not tonight. The cries seemed to come from all around her and pierced through her with the sharpness of a needle.

"It's not real," she said aloud. But it sounded so real she wanted to leap out of bed and go searching for the baby she'd lost, the baby who cried for her from the beyond.

This had happened before. She'd heard this sound before and had jumped out of bed and tried to find the source. She'd wandered the woods in search of the baby who needed her, who cried for her, and had found nothing.

She refused to leave her bed tonight. Instead, she clapped her hands over her ears as deep, wrenching sobs escaped her.

She knew the cries weren't real and yet they echoed through her with an authenticity that was heart-wrenching.

"Go away," she whispered. "Please, stop crying."

It seemed to last forever, but as suddenly as it had begun, it stopped.

Tears ripped from the very depths of her and she realized they weren't just tears for the baby she'd lost, but also because she realized now that she could never have anything with Quinn Logan. She could never have a relationship with any man.

There could only be one explanation for the baby's cries that haunted her, for the sound of Andrew's voice calling to her from the woods.

She was losing her mind.

Her mother had died in a mental institution, the lines between reality and madness so blurred and undefined that in the end she hadn't even known her own name.

As sobs racked through Jewel, she feared that was her future, that eventually the lines would blur for her and she'd wind up like her mother, alone with only her mental illness and locked away from the world.

Chapter 6

Jewel had just finished the early morning watering of the flowers when an unfamiliar truck pulled up to the front of the house. The truck might be unfamiliar, but the man who climbed out of the driver's seat wasn't.

"Ryder!" She greeted him with a surprised smile.

"Hi, Jewel." His long legs carried him to where she stood. "Hope it's not too early for a visit."

"Of course not. Mornings start early here at the ranch. You want to come in for a cup of coffee? Some of Cheryl's blueberry muffins are probably left over from breakfast."

"No, thanks, I just finished breakfast." He raked a hand through his shiny black hair. "Actually, I'd like to talk to you about a job. You probably heard that Ana is going to be teaching at the bilingual school. She starts in two weeks."

"No, I hadn't heard, but good for her. I know that's what she's always wanted to do. She'll make a wonderful teacher."

He nodded. "And I've decided to go back to school." His ebony eyes glittered with a newfound pride. "I want to be the best husband for Ana, the best father for Maria that I can be, and I've decided an education is the first step."

Jewel placed a hand on his forearm. "Good for you, Ryder. I'm sure Clay is proud of your decision."

"He is, but more important, I am. I'm committed to turning things around for myself. I'm here for a couple of reasons. I was wondering if you could use some part-time help and if there's a possibility that while I'm in school you'd be available to add Maria to your group of kids. To be honest, Ana and I wouldn't trust her in anyone else's care."

Jewel thought of the sweet baby girl and her heart expanded. "I think we could definitely work something out," she replied. "I've been thinking of having a pen built for some goats and lambs and small animals. Think you could handle that?"

He grinned. "Not a problem. I won't be starting school until the spring semester so until then I was hoping you could use me twenty to twenty-five hours a week."

She nodded and for the next few minutes they worked out the details of his employment and baby Maria's care. She showed him the area on the side of the house where she wanted the pen and assured him that Jeff would be available to help.

As he got back into his truck to leave she waved,

wondering if it had been a simple case of maturity or finding the love of a good woman that had turned the bad boy into a good man.

After he left, Jewel went back inside to grab her car keys and the list of school supplies that needed to be bought. "I'm off," she told Cheryl who was in the kitchen. "Thank goodness I can get this shopping done today and not have to be in town tomorrow. I hate shopping on Saturdays."

"Jeff and I have a whole day of shopping planned for tomorrow. I told him I want to drive into San Antonio and get me a good pair of shoes. All you can find around here are cowboy boots and sneakers."

Jewel smiled. "Make him take you out to lunch at one of those fancy restaurants on the river walk."

"I plan to," Cheryl replied.

Minutes later Jewel was in her car, headed toward Main Street. Since the moment she'd gotten out of bed that morning, she'd thought about calling Quinn to cancel the plans for Sunday.

After the horrible trauma of the night before, she didn't feel it was fair to give him false hope, to allow him to think that they could ever have a real relationship.

He'd made it more than clear that he was interested in her and, under different circumstances, she would have reciprocated. She liked the solidness of him, the gentle nature that she sensed he possessed. And if she were truthful with herself, she'd admit that she also loved the width of his shoulders, the simmer of sensuality that lit his eyes.

But how could she, in good conscience, follow her

heart when she suffered visions of a dead man, heard the sounds of her baby crying out from the grave?

It would be best to call him and cancel, to stop whatever might happen between them now before one of them got hurt. The problem was she wasn't sure how to gracefully withdraw the invitation she'd extended. She could cancel the trail ride altogether, but that wasn't fair to the kids.

She sighed as she pulled into a parking space in front of the local discount store. It took her over an hour to get everything for the kids to start school Monday morning.

She was juggling her bags to the car when she saw Quinn walking toward her. Despite her desire to the contrary, her heartbeat raced a little faster at the sight of him.

"Let me help you with those," he said as he took two of the bags from her.

"School supplies," she said. "It's amazing what's required by the teachers these days."

He opened the back car door and put the bags he'd carried inside, then took the other two from her and stowed them, as well. When he turned to look at her, his eyes glowed with a warm light. "I just came from Miss Sue's café where I arranged for lunch for nine to be ready for Sunday. She's working on a real picnic menu—fried chicken and coleslaw and buttermilk biscuits."

"You shouldn't have done that," she protested in dismay. There was no way she could uninvite him knowing the trouble he'd already gone to.

"I don't mind. In fact, I'm really looking forward to it and you know I've never met a kid who didn't like fried chicken." He checked his watch. "Unfortunately, I've got to run. I've got an appointment with a horse. I'm looking forward to Sunday, Jewel." He said her name as if it were a caress.

She nodded and watched as he hurried off. Okay, so much for canceling Sunday's plans. Deciding to stop into Miss Sue's for a cup of coffee and a cinnamon bun, Jewel headed down the street toward the café.

As she walked, she realized that a part of her hadn't wanted to cancel, but instead yearned to spend another day in Quinn's company.

The kids would be with them, there would be no opportunity for him to kiss her again, to touch her in any way. She'd give herself that time with him and after Sunday she'd make sure they had no time alone together again.

A sadness swept through her as she realized that she was making the choice to be alone, but what other choice did she have? She would embrace her work, spend her life helping and loving other people's children. It would be enough because it had to be enough, but that didn't mean it didn't hurt.

Quinn Logan had suffered tremendously in burying a wife. She wouldn't want to add to his heartache by getting close to him, allowing him to care for her and in the end having to tell her goodbye as mental illness overwhelmed her.

What she hoped was that the auditory hallucinations were just a manifestation of her grief. Right now they only seemed to affect her at night, just before she fell asleep. She hoped that eventually they would stop, but feared what the future might bring.

The cowbell tingled as she walked through the door of the café. Immediately she saw Olivia Halprin and Sheriff Jericho Yates at one of the tables. They waved her over and insisted that she join them.

Olivia had appeared in town a couple of months ago, suffering from amnesia, and it was Jericho who had taken in the injured young woman. Jericho had taken her to his log cabin in the woods and there love had blossomed.

It was discovered that Olivia had worked for Governor Allan Daniels, the man running against Joe Colton for the party nomination. Olivia had uncovered a trail of crooked deals and bribery, and when her memory had finally returned, Allan Daniels had tried to silence her…permanently. Jericho had managed to save her life and the two had been inseparable ever since.

"How are things at the ranch?" Jericho asked as Jewel sat at their table.

"Fine. And how about your place? I heard through the grapevine that Olivia had been doing some decorating at the log cabin."

Jericho gave a mock frown. "She's put in some fu-fu things that have destroyed the rustic character of the cabin."

Olivia laughed and gave him a playful punch in the arm. "Don't let him fool you. He loves the changes I've made."

Jericho reached out and covered her hand with his. "Actually, that's true. She's made it a home."

"So do you know yet if it's a girl or a boy?" Jewel gestured toward Olivia's tummy.

"The doctor thinks it's a girl," Olivia replied. She

smiled at Jericho and then looked back at Jewel. "And if it is, the sheriff has already told me we'll get right to work on a boy."

"That's nice. I'm so happy for you both. And is there a wedding in the future?"

"Absolutely," Jericho replied. "In the very near future."

As Jewel ate her cinnamon bun and drank a cup of coffee, she visited with the couple. There was no question that the two were deeply in love, and while Jewel was happy that they'd found each other, she felt the bittersweet pang of her own loneliness.

It was just after noon when she pulled back into the ranch and reminded herself that she needed to have a session with Barry that afternoon. She smiled as she saw all the kids out in the yard with Cocoa.

Jeff sat on the porch, watching as the kids chased the dog and the dog chased the kids. Jeff approached as Jewel got out of the car.

"We figured a little exercise would be good for Cocoa," he said as he grabbed two of the bags from the backseat.

"I'm not sure who's getting more, the kids or the dog," Jewel replied with a laugh.

"I'll tell you one thing, that dog is smart, but I don't think he's going to make it as any kind of a watchdog. He likes everyone too much. Deputy Rawlings stopped by earlier and I thought Cocoa was going to lick him to death."

Jewel laughed. "That's okay. He's not meant to be a watchdog. Did Adam say why he stopped by?"

"I got the feeling it was just a social visit. I'll take

these bags inside for you." He grabbed all the bags while Jewel walked out in the yard to join the kids and Cocoa.

As she played with the dog and the children's laughter filled the air, she reminded herself that this was what was important. She told herself that she didn't need what Jericho and Olivia had found together, she didn't need anything but this ragtag family of troubled kids and the love of her family to sustain her. Maybe if she repeated that mantra enough times, she would actually believe it.

Quinn arrived at Clay's place early on Sunday. It should have worried him, how anxious he'd been for this day to arrive. But instead he embraced his anticipation, for the first time in years feeling ready to move on with his life, ready to fall in love and fulfill the dreams he hadn't been able to fulfill with Sarah.

And he wanted to do it with Jewel. She both excited and intrigued him. When he was around her, he felt the expectation of something special about to happen, saw a glimpse into a future he desperately wanted to grab.

The food he'd picked up from Miss Sue's was packed in two large coolers and he arranged with Carlos, one of Clay's hands, to have it delivered to a specific place in the pasture around one o'clock.

He was in the stables, saddling up Noches, his black stallion, when Clay walked in. "I heard through the grapevine that you and Jewel were seen looking quite cozy at a certain Mexican restaurant the other day."

Quinn grinned. "Normally I'd tell you that you know better than to listen to the grapevine, but in this particular case, it's true."

"You'll never find a better woman than Jewel," Clay

said. "She's had some tough breaks in her life. She deserves some happiness." There was an edge to Clay's voice, as if he was warning Quinn not to toy with Jewel.

Quinn clapped his friend on the back. "Down boy, you know me better than to think I'd ever intentionally do anything to hurt her."

"I know. I just worry about her." Clay stepped back and leaned against the stable door. "But it sounds like you have a fun day planned for today."

"It should be fun." Quinn finished cinching the saddle and gave Noches a pat on his rump.

"And you talked to Carlos about the lunch details?"

"Yeah, thanks for letting him help out." Their conversation was interrupted by the sound of the minibus from the Hopechest Ranch pulling up.

Quinn stepped out of the stable and got a blood rush as he saw Jewel. She looked beautiful with her tousled golden-brown hair shining in the sun. Her brown eyes sparkled and her features were relaxed in a way he hadn't seen before. Worn, tight jeans fit her long legs to perfection and her pink T-shirt deepened the chocolate hue of her eyes.

In the first fifteen minutes Quinn tried to put faces with names as she introduced him to all the kids. Then it took another half an hour to get everyone on his or her horse and out of the stables.

They followed a well-worn horse trail across the pasture. The kids were in the lead and Quinn and Jewel brought up the rear, their horses side by side.

"You look great today," he said.

"Thanks, I feel pretty great. I've been looking forward to today, kind of a final celebration with the kids before school starts tomorrow."

He hoped she'd also been looking forward to spending more time with him, but he didn't ask, was afraid of sounding too forward. He had a feeling he needed to take things slowly with her, that she was like a wounded animal that needed to be gentled. And that was one of Quinn's specialties.

It was impossible to have a real conversation with her during the ride. The kids yelled back and forth to one another and the horses whinnied and nickered as the sound of their hooves on the hard earth filled the air.

Still, Quinn always enjoyed riding Noches, who had just enough spirit to be challenging yet not enough to be unmanageable. And there was the additional benefit of being able to look sideways and see Jewel on the horse next to him.

She was a good rider and looked at ease in the saddle. She flashed him a bright smile and urged her horse into a trot, quickly moving to the front of the pack.

Quinn nudged Noches faster to catch up with her. Noches tossed his head, wanting to run like the wind, but Quinn held tight to the reins, refusing to give the stallion his head.

The trails led through the woods, across a small dry creek bed and then into open pasture. It was only then that Quinn allowed Noches to run. He flew ahead of the group with the wind in his face. The horse responded to his most subtle command. Quinn pulled in as he reached the far edge of the pasture and waited for the group to catch up with him.

"Pretty fancy riding, Dr. Logan," Jewel said.

"Maybe I'm showing off in an attempt to impress you," he replied.

She laughed. "Consider me impressed."

"Me, too," Carrie said as she rode up next to them. "Someday I want to ride that fast, but this dumb old horse won't do anything but walk."

Jewel smiled. "When you've had a little more experience on a horse, maybe we'll find you one that runs."

The ride continued until they came to a stand of trees where Carlos sat on a tractor with a small cart behind it containing the lunch coolers. Carlos unfastened the cart and with the promise to return for it later, he drove away.

They let the horses go to graze and Quinn pulled several large tablecloths from the first cooler and spread them on the ground.

Lunch was chaos and laughter. The kids talked almost as much as they ate and it was obvious they all adored Jewel. Jewel remained relaxed. She laughed often and the sound was music to Quinn's ears.

After lunch Quinn pulled several Frisbees from the cooler and led the kids in a game of catch. Jewel remained on the tablecloth and played cheerleader.

As the kids continued to toss the Frisbees back and forth, Quinn walked over and collapsed next to Jewel. "You're the cutest Frisbee cheerleader I've seen in a long time," he said.

"Have you seen a lot of Frisbee cheerleaders in your life?" she asked teasingly.

"Hundreds. Maybe thousands," he replied. "I travel the countryside seeking Frisbee cheerleaders."

"We both know you're full of beans, as the kids would say."

He laughed and looked over where the kids were playing catch. "They're a nice bunch," he observed.

She smiled. "They know you are responsible for giving us Cocoa so they're on their best behavior with you. Trust me, they aren't always this easy to get along with."

"Kelsey doesn't seem to be having as much fun as the others."

Jewel frowned as her gaze went to the dark-haired girl who stood slightly separated from the others, hands shoved in her pockets.

"Kelsey has spent the last couple of years being shuttled from relative to relative. She's terrified to embrace any kind of happiness because she's afraid it will be taken away from her."

"That's the way I felt right after Sarah died."

Jewel turned to look at him, her gaze curious. "You're so much more open than I thought you'd be. Clay had told me you were the strong, silent type."

He smiled. "Normally I *am* pretty quiet, but I've been working on changing that." He looked back at the kids and frowned thoughtfully. "After Sarah died I realized there were so many things I hadn't said to her, so many thoughts I hadn't shared. I decided I'd never let that be a regret again."

Their discussion was interrupted as Lindy joined them on the blanket, her face flushed from her exertions. "I've gotta rest," she exclaimed. "I'm pooped, but I think maybe another piece of chicken would give me my energy back."

Quinn grinned at her. "There's only one thing better than a piece of fried chicken." He reached into the cooler and pulled out a container of chocolate cupcakes.

Lindy's eyes lit up and she turned to where the other kids were still playing with the Frisbees. "Hey, guys, we got cupcakes," she yelled, sparking a stampede as they all ran for dessert.

It was almost five by the time they made their way back to the stables. "They'll all sleep well tonight," Jewel said as she brushed down her horse.

"Nothing like fresh air and sunshine to bring on a good night's sleep," Quinn replied. He didn't want the day to end. While he'd enjoyed his interaction with the kids, he didn't feel as if he'd had enough time with Jewel.

He led Noches into his stall, then returned to where Jewel was finishing up with her horse. "I have an idea. Why don't you take the kids home and get them settled in then meet me back here for a sunset ride."

She looked up at him and in her eyes he saw indecision. "Come on, Jewel," he urged. "There's nothing more beautiful that a horseback ride at sunset. Meet me back here about seven-thirty." He smiled at her. "I promise you it will be a painless experience."

She smiled then and nodded. "Okay, you talked me into it."

"Great, then I'll meet you back here."

A few minutes later Jewel went with the kids and Quinn left to go home to check on the animals either boarding with him or recovering from illnesses.

Quinn lived in a three-bedroom ranch house. It was simple and efficient but he spent most of his time in the front building, which was the heart of his veterinary practice. The building was divided into four areas—a small office, an area for boarding animals, an examination room and an operating room.

He checked on the boarders, made sure they had food and water, then decided to shower the day's dirt off before the ride with Jewel.

As he redressed in a clean pair of jeans and a navy T-shirt, he tried not to think about what he'd really like to do with Jewel. He'd love to take her on their sunset ride, then dismount and make love to her beneath a starry sky.

She'd confused him today. There had been a distance in her eyes. She'd been more closed off than before, as if afraid to share too much of herself with him.

He didn't want to screw up by pushing her too fast and yet a part of him thought she needed a nudge back into life. He was so ready to embrace her, to embrace love again but, more than anything, he wanted to discover the source of the darkness he sometimes saw in her eyes, a darkness that worried and confused him.

Chapter 7

Jewel hadn't intended to agree to the sunset ride. She knew Quinn liked her, but it wasn't fair to make him think that there was any chance for a romance between them.

But she felt such deep loneliness and so enjoyed his company. It was difficult to deny herself the pleasure of spending more time with him. Maybe they could become good friends.

She stood beneath a hot stream of water in her shower and tried to imagine just being friends with Quinn. It would never work. Friends didn't want to kiss friends and now that she knew what Quinn tasted like, how she felt in his arms, she would never be satisfied with just a simple friendship. And she had a feeling he wouldn't be, either.

"You're overthinking," she said aloud as she stepped

out of the shower. That was the problem with being a psychologist, sometimes she analyzed way too much.

She put on a clean pair of jeans and a short-sleeved cotton blouse. Even when the sun went down, it was still warm, despite being the beginning of September.

She was just ready to walk out the door when Adam Rawlings pulled up. As usual, not one of his dark brown hairs was out of place as he got out of his car and ambled toward the porch.

She stepped outside to greet him. "Evening, Adam."

"Jewel." His brown eyes gazed at her intently. "Haven't seen you around lately."

"I've been busy, you know with school starting tomorrow and all."

"You need to take some time off." He smiled, his brown eyes warm and inviting. "Maybe see a movie with me or go out for a nice meal."

"I appreciate the thought, Adam, but now just isn't a good time for me. Maybe when things calm down around here." This wasn't the first time he'd asked her out and he never seemed offended that she never agreed to go out with him.

Perhaps she should. He'd certainly be a safe date for her because she felt absolutely no sparks with him. Unlike Quinn, who by merely looking at her could set her very skin on fire.

"You need to focus on yourself, Jewel," he said, concern radiating from his eyes. "It's a great thing what you do here for these kids, but you should remember that you're a young woman who should have a life of her own."

"Thanks, Adam. Actually, I was just on my way out."

She couldn't very well tell him she was on her way to meet another man, so she offered no other explanation.

"Then at least let me walk you to your car," he replied.

She nodded and stepped off the porch. "Everyone has been talking about the Coltons coming to town," he said as they walked to the garage. "It's not every day we get the man who's probably going to be president, and his wife in Esperanza."

"I can't wait," she exclaimed. The thought of seeing Meredith and Joe again filled her with warmth. "I'm planning a good old-fashioned Texas barbecue here during their visit."

"Sounds like a good time. I'm sure you'll want Jericho and all of us deputies here for additional security."

"I want you here as guests, as well," she replied. She punched the button on her remote to raise her garage door. "It will be a wonderful day filled with family and friends."

"Those are the best kind of days," he agreed. "I'll just say good night now and let you get on your way."

"Thanks, Adam."

He cocked an eyebrow upward. "For what?"

"For always checking in with me…for caring."

He smiled and there was a fierce intensity in his gaze. "I do care." He nodded a goodbye, then turned on his heels and went back to his car.

Jewel got into her car and backed out of the garage as Adam disappeared into his. He was a nice man. He had a great body for a man who was forty years old. Funny, she'd never heard him talk about any family. She assumed he was no stranger to loneliness, either.

The minute she pulled out of her driveway, thoughts of Adam disappeared as Quinn filled her mind. The sun hung low in the sky. Another thirty minutes and it would be sunset.

When she pulled up in front of Clay's stable, Quinn was already there, both his horse and the one she'd ridden that afternoon saddled and ready to go.

She couldn't help the way her heart leapt at the sight of him, so tall, so strong-looking and with that smile that made her feel as if she were the most important person in his world.

As she got out of the car and approached him, she couldn't help the lightness that filled her heart, the emotion that felt remarkably like joy.

"Hi," he said.

"Hi, yourself. Looks like you've got us all ready to go."

"I've even got a bottle of wine and a couple of glasses tucked into my saddlebag for a sunset toast."

"Wine and a sunset—sounds like the perfect ending to a day," she said. And of course, there was also the handsome hunk to add to the heady combination.

She was glad she'd come. As they mounted the horses, she told herself not to think, not to analyze, but rather just to enjoy the beauty of the night and Quinn's company.

At a leisurely pace, they followed the same trails that they'd ridden earlier in the day. For a few minutes, neither of them spoke. It was a peaceful silence, one that didn't demand to be broken.

Birds flitted from tree to tree, emitting their last

melodic songs of the day and a faint breeze provided a pleasurable relief from the afternoon's heat.

"I enjoyed the kids this afternoon," he said, finally breaking the silence.

"They think you're awesome," Jewel replied. She'd been impressed watching him interact with the kids. He'd treated each of them with respect and kindness. He'd listened patiently to all of them and she'd known instinctively that it hadn't been just an act for her benefit.

"Kelsey seemed a bit standoffish."

Jewel nodded. "She's afraid to be happy. I'm trying to teach her that happiness isn't a constant state of being and you need to grasp it when it comes and hold tight."

He frowned. "It's a shame a child that young has to have that kind of fear."

"You like kids." It was a comment rather than a question.

He nodded. "I do. I always wanted a big family of my own. Unfortunately, it just wasn't in the cards for me."

"You still have time," she protested. "It's not as if you're over the hill."

He grinned and reached up to sweep his hair away from his eyes. "No, but sometimes I feel like I'm halfway up that hill."

She laughed. "If you're halfway up the hill, then I'm right behind you."

For the next few minutes they kept a slow pace and talked about the afternoon and each of the children. "Carrie told me she loved Cocoa but she really, really loved kittens," he said. "And Barry told me he'd love to have a lizard." He flashed her a grin. "I think I may have started something."

Jewel laughed again. "Maybe I can satisfy them with the goats and sheep I intend to get once I have a nice pen ready. I hired Ryder to work on building the pen."

"What's the story on Ryder and Clay's father? I've always gotten the feeling that things weren't great between them all."

"Ryder, Clay and Georgie are Uncle Graham's children from an affair he had while he was unhappily married to Cynthia, who was an extremely wealthy woman. Although everyone said he truly loved their mother, Mary Lynn Grady, he loved money more and so refused to leave his wife."

"It's a foolish man who would choose money over love."

"Uncle Graham has been on the outs with the family for a long time," she continued. "I think Uncle Joe tried to be close to him and gave him one opportunity after another to do right, but Uncle Graham continued to make bad choices and I think it hurts Uncle Joe that the two don't have any kind of a relationship now." She smiled ruefully. "Aren't you sorry you asked?"

"Not at all. To be honest, I find the Colton family history fascinating. It makes me realize how truly boring my family is."

"I'm sure the Coltons would have gladly taken a little more boring over the years," she replied.

They rode to the spot where they'd had lunch earlier in the day, then dismounted. Quinn pulled a blanket from his saddlebag, along with the wine and two glasses.

They sat side by side as the sun dipped lower in the sky, spreading out the last gasp of daylight in vivid pinks and oranges.

"To a beautiful sunset and a beautiful woman," Quinn said as he raised his wineglass to hers.

The toast might have sounded cheesy coming from any other man, but the light in his eyes told her the words came from his heart.

She stretched out on her side on the blanket and propped herself up on an elbow. "You should find a nice woman, Quinn."

He laid down facing her and crooked an eyebrow upward. "I have," he replied.

She shook her head. "You need somebody without baggage. Unfortunately, I have a ton."

"I don't know if you've noticed or not, but I have big, strong shoulders."

"Trust me, I've noticed," she replied dryly.

"Then why don't you trust me?" His eyes held her gaze intently.

She broke the eye contact and instead took a sip of her wine and stared at the sunset slowly fading into a night sky. "It's not that easy," she replied softly.

He reached out and covered one of her hands with his. "You can trust me, Jewel. You can tell me whatever is on your mind, anything, anytime."

She pulled her hand out from beneath his, finding his touch far too pleasurable. "You don't know anything about me. You have no idea where I come from."

"Then tell me. But hear me, Jewel. I can't imagine anything you'd tell me that would change my mind about you." His deep voice held a certainty that sent a rush of warmth through her.

"Did you know that my mother and Meredith Colton were twins?" she asked.

"No. I hadn't heard that," he replied. He showed no surprise at her seemingly abrupt change of topic.

"After my mother got out of prison for killing my father, she attacked Meredith. Meredith had amnesia and my mother switched identities with her. My mother impersonated Meredith for almost ten years while Meredith suffered amnesia and in those ten years my mother wreaked havoc on Joe's life."

"And what does this have to do with you, Jewel?" His tone was as gentle as the night breeze that caressed her skin. He moved closer to her, so close she could smell the scent of his cologne, feel the heat from his body radiating over her.

"Your mother was obviously a troubled woman, but I've seen you with your kids, I know the kind of heart you have, and if you thought by telling me about your mother I'd back off, then you were wrong." He set his wineglass aside.

This man was killing her with his heated eyes and his open heart. She wanted to tell him that she heard voices in the night, that phantom baby cries ripped at her guts. She wanted to warn him that she might be as unstable as her mother had been, but at that moment he reached out and touched her lips with his index finger.

"I want you, Jewel, and the only thing that will make me back off is if you tell me that you don't want me." With a slow deliberation, he took her wineglass from her and set it just off the blanket.

She knew he intended to kiss her and even though she told herself she shouldn't let it happen, she shouldn't want it, want him so badly, she did.

He gathered her into his arms and kissed her. Soft and gentle, his lips whispered against hers and her heart fluttered in response.

Was it wrong of her to want him even knowing that she wouldn't, couldn't have a long-term relationship with him? If it was wrong at this moment, she didn't care. All she wanted was for him to hold her forever, for him to keep kissing her until she lost the capacity to think.

She opened her mouth, urging him to deepen the kiss. His tongue touched her bottom lip, then delved deeper to swirl with her own.

His hands moved up and down her back, caressing lightly as she tightened her arms around his neck. She leaned into him, wanting full contact with his lean, hard body.

Night shadows deepened and still they kissed, the only noise the sound of the horses shuffling their hooves nearby and Jewel and Quinn's quickened breathing.

She wanted more. The yearning that filled her was so intense that she could think of nothing but Quinn and her need to have him make love to her.

Her fingers found a button on his shirt and she unfastened it, wanting to run her hands over his bare chest. He released a small gasp as she unfastened another button, but his mouth didn't move from hers.

She used both hands, eager to get the shirt unbuttoned, and when she did, she slid her hands over his sculpted, hard chest. His skin was fevered heat and she loved the feel of his muscles, his bare flesh, beneath her fingertips.

He slid his hands up beneath her blouse, his palms warming her from the outside in, firing a desire in her to have more from him. His mouth lifted from hers but only to move to her cheek, then to the sensitive spot just behind her ear.

She was lost…lost in his touch, lost in the sensations that he evoked inside her. She wanted to stay in this pasture with him forever, with his mouth on hers, with his hands warming all the cold places in her heart and the night air surrounding them. But without warning he dropped his arms from around her and sat up.

He raked a hand through his thick mane of hair and released a deep sigh. "Not like this, Jewel," he said. "I want you so badly it hurts, but not like this. Not in a pasture. I want you in a soft bed with sheets to cuddle beneath and the entire night stretching out before us."

"Then take me home, to my bed and stay the night with me," she replied. She was shocked by her own words, but that didn't mean she wanted to take them back.

Just one night. She wanted just one night with him, with no sense of reason interfering, no common sense at play. She wanted one night of not thinking, of keeping the ghosts at bay.

He placed his palm on her cheek, the heat in his gaze igniting a faster burn inside her. "Are you sure that's what you want?"

"I've never been more sure of anything in my life," she replied.

In one fluid motion he stood and held out a hand to

her. She reached for his hand and he pulled her to her feet and back into his arms. "I think I've wanted you since the very first time I laid eyes on you."

She looked up at him. "I feel the same way."

He released her and without saying another word he grabbed the wine bottle and glasses, then the blanket and stowed them back in his saddlebag.

As they rode back to the stable, she waited for a whisper of caution to flit through her head, a protest against what she was about to do, but all she felt was a calm peacefulness sweeping through her as she thought of spending the night in Quinn's arms.

Stars had begun to twinkle overhead, along with a half-sliced pie moon. The horses moved quickly toward home, as if they sensed their riders' eagerness.

When Jewel and Quinn reached the stables, it took only minutes for them to unsaddle the horses and get them into the appropriate stalls. Jewel then got into her car and headed for home with Quinn following in his truck.

She wouldn't be able to write this off as a crazy, impulsive move made in the heat of the moment. At any time during the ride back from the stables she could have changed her mind, but she didn't.

She wasn't giving him forever; she wasn't promising a thing. Consenting adults slept together all the time—it didn't have to mean anything except a single night of pleasure.

When she reached the ranch, she pulled into the garage, then stood by the door while Quinn parked and got out of his car.

He walked toward her and she felt the thrum of sexual excitement singing through her veins. She didn't remember feeling this intense hunger for Andrew. Making love with Andrew had been warm and fuzzy, not hot and edgy and that's exactly how Quinn made her feel.

When he reached where she stood by the front door, she felt his hesitation. "I'm only going to ask you this one last time," he said. "Are you sure about this? I've got to warn you, I'm not the kind of man who wants to make love to you then sneak out like a thief in the night."

She answered him by opening the front door and pulling him inside. The house was quiet and she led him through the entry and into her private quarters.

When she'd left the room hours earlier she'd had no idea that Quinn would be here with her, in her private, intimate space.

Although the room was quite large, he filled it with his presence. He held her gaze as he unbuttoned his shirt once again and shrugged it off his shoulders. His muscled chest gleamed in the light on her nightstand. He sat on the edge of the bed and took off his boots and socks, then stood once again.

Her throat went dry and her knees threatened to buckle as his hands moved to the button on his jeans. A rush of heat went through her, watching him step out of his jeans, leaving him only in a pair of low-riding navy briefs.

He came toward her with slow, deliberate movements, then unfastened the buttons on her blouse. When he was finished, he shoved the material off her shoulders and it fell to the floor behind her. His lips claimed hers once again and he cupped her breasts through the thin lace of her bra.

She unhooked her jeans, wanting nothing more than to be naked with him, to feel his hot, firm flesh against her own. He broke the kiss as she peeled off her jeans, then she walked over to the bed and slid in beneath the covers.

He grabbed his wallet from his jeans, set it on the nightstand, then joined her in the bed and wrapped her up in his arms as their lips met in a fiery kiss of desire.

The kiss continued while he unfastened her bra, swept the garment away as if it offended him, then captured her breasts in his hands. She hissed with pleasure as his thumbs raked over her taut nipples.

"You are so beautiful," he murmured, his mouth laving hers. He raised up just enough to stare down at her face. "You have no idea how much I want you."

"It can't be anymore than how much I want you," she replied.

He dipped his head and captured one of her nipples with his mouth. Sweet sensations of both pleasure and want crashed through her as she tangled her fingers in his thick, soft hair.

It didn't take long for them to rid themselves of the last of their underwear and their caresses grew even more intimate. She loved the smooth skin on his chest, broken only by a smattering of hair in the center. She loved the smell of him, a scent of the outdoors coupled with woodsy cologne and clean male.

He seemed to be in no hurry as he nibbled on her ear, slid his hot, hungry mouth down her throat, explored her inner thigh with his hands and moved her closer and closer to explosive peaks.

Refusing to be a passive partner, Jewel discovered

that he moaned with pleasure when she ran her hand across his lower abdomen, close but not touching where she knew he wanted her to. He gasped as she licked his flat male nipples.

They caressed and tasted each other like two people who had been sensory-deprived for an eternity. His fingers finally found the very center of her, sliding against her moist heat, and she arched to meet him, need clawing at her, taking her up to new heights.

As she felt the approaching climax, she clung to him. Every muscle in her body stiffened and tremors of pleasure rocked through her, leaving her gasping and spent, yet wanting more.

She reached down and encircled the hard length of him, reveling in his moan of pleasure as she stroked him. He only allowed her touch for a moment, then he rolled her over on her back and reached for his wallet on the nightstand.

It took him only seconds to put on a condom, then move on top of her and between her thighs. For just a moment he remained poised above her, his eyes glowing like those of a wild animal.

In that moment, she felt more loved, more cherished than she ever had in her life. It was in the tenderness, in the hunger of his golden-brown eyes.

As he eased into her she closed her eyes, giving herself to the magic of his lovemaking. And it *was* magic. He entered her and paused to kiss her with a gentleness that stole her breath away.

He began to move against her, back and forth with slow, even strokes intended to produce the most pleasure. She raised her legs and locked them around his back, urging him deeper and faster as she felt the build once again begin.

Crying his name over and over again, she was lost in the act, in him. They moved faster, frenzied, and their pants and gasps filled the room.

She was there again, crashing down with earth-shattering tremors. He cried out her name as his own release washed over him. He shuddered once…twice, then remained still, his weight supported on his elbows as he sought to catch his breath.

He placed his hands on either side of her face and kissed her. "I'll be right back. Don't go away." He rolled out of the bed and padded into the adjoining bathroom.

Jewel felt weak with sated pleasure. She felt as if she had melted into the mattress and only an atomic bomb could force her to get up.

Quinn returned to the bedroom, and she turned off the bedside lamp. She was glad he wasn't dressing to leave but instead slid back into the bed and pulled her into his arms.

She lay with her upper body across his chest and she reached out a finger and touched the scar on his cheek. "How did you get that?"

He smiled. "Her name was Molly and she was the meanest mare I've ever met. I was working on her shoulder, where she had a sore, and she reared up and knocked me in the face then stomped on me."

She looked at him, horrified. "I had no idea being a veterinarian was so dangerous."

"I was young and careless and wasn't as wary as I should have been. It was as much my fault as it was hers."

"I'm glad you didn't jump back into your clothes and backpedal out of here." Jewel released a soft sigh and placed her head on his chest where the sound of his heartbeat was strong.

He stroked her hair with his big, strong hand. "As far as I'm concerned, the cuddle time afterward is almost as important as making love."

She sighed again, surprised to find her eyelids heavy with sleep. Her body fit perfectly against his and each caress of her hair brought sleep closer and closer.

"Quinn? Sometimes I have nightmares," she said, feeling as if she needed to warn him in case she had a bad night.

He slid his hand from her hair down her back, his palm like a miniature heating pad against her skin. "You won't tonight, Jewel."

He said the words with such confident assurance that she believed him. They shifted positions. She turned on her side and he spooned around her back, an arm flung over her as if in protection. Feeling more safe than she had in years, Jewel slept.

Chapter 8

Jewel awakened to early morning sunlight filtering in through the curtains at her window. Her first thought was that there had been no dreams, no ghostly cries from the beyond. She had slept deeper and longer than she had since the death of Andrew and their unborn child.

Her second thought was of Quinn. She turned over in the bed and found herself alone. He must have crept out earlier and she was almost grateful. She would not have to explain to Jeff or Cheryl and the children why the handsome vet was in the house before breakfast.

Rolling over on her back to stare up at the ceiling fan, her head filled with visions of the night she'd shared with him. Just the memory caused her to tingle from head to toe.

He'd been a wonderful lover, both gentle and commanding and it frightened her more than a little how much she would love to repeat the experience.

But she couldn't. She'd already been unfair to him by allowing last night to happen. She knew Quinn wasn't the kind of man to take his relationships lightly and that would make everything more difficult.

She couldn't date Quinn knowing that she would never, could never fully commit to him. It wouldn't be fair to him and ultimately her.

Time to distance herself, she thought as she got out of bed and padded into the bathroom, then got into the shower. Even though she had slept dreamlessly last night in his arms, that didn't mean that she would no longer be haunted by Andrew and the baby she had lost.

It wouldn't bother her so much if she only heard Andrew softly calling her name and the baby crying in her dreams, but there had been far too many nights when she'd been wide awake and had heard them.

And that's when the true haunting began, when she remembered her last visit with her mother in the mental ward. Patsy had been lost to the world, muttering incoherently and laughing inappropriately, hearing voices that weren't there, answering questions that nobody had asked.

As Jewel dressed she heard the sound of the children in the kitchen getting ready for breakfast. They were louder this morning, their voices filled with first day of school jitters.

Initially, Jewel had considered having her kids homeschooled, but ultimately she'd decided that interacting with the kids in town would be far healthier for them than isolation and the feeling that they were different.

Besides, she wanted the town residents, who had harbored reservations about a ranch for troubled kids, to see that these kids weren't a threat.

An hour later she stood by the road that ran in front of the Hopechest Ranch, waiting for the school bus to appear. The sun overhead was brutal even at this time of the morning. The morning weather report had indicated that for the next week or two the temperatures were supposed to be well above normal.

"And the bus will bring us right back here after school, right?" Barry asked for the fourth time.

"The bus driver will drop all of you off at this very same spot," Jewel assured him.

"I hope my teacher likes me," Lindy exclaimed.

"Don't worry," Kelsey said, and placed a hand on Lindy's shoulder. "What's not to like?"

Jewel's heart warmed as she saw the older girl reassuring Lindy. It was the first sign she'd seen from Kelsey that she was reaching out, forming bonds, and that was important.

The bus lumbered into sight, spewing up a cloud of dust. It was only eight in the morning and already Jewel felt as if she could use another shower.

She saw the kids off, waving until the bus roared out of sight, then she turned and walked back to the house. She'd just reached the porch when Ryder arrived.

Maria wasn't with him and he explained that Ana was home today with the baby. Her school wasn't to start until the following week.

"Gonna be a hot one today," she said.

"Supposed to be vicious for the next couple of

weeks," he replied. "I've got the supplies coming for the pen this morning."

"Great, but make sure you stay hydrated while you're working out here," she cautioned. "Come inside and cool off whenever you need to."

He flashed her a grin. "Don't worry, I won't let the heat defeat me."

"I don't want to push you, but I'd love for the pen to be up and functioning by the time Meredith and Joe come to town."

"That's what, two weeks from now? I'm hoping Jeff and I will be able to have it knocked out by next weekend. That will give you a week to get the animals you want for the kids."

"Sounds perfect," Jewel replied.

With a wave he headed toward the area where the pen would be constructed. Jewel went back into the house.

"If it's okay with you, Jeff and I would like to take the kids on that field trip we talked about next Saturday or the Saturday after that," Cheryl said as the two women sat at the table and sipped a cup of coffee.

"The week after would work out perfect for me," Jewel replied thoughtfully. "While you're all gone, there are some things I want to do around here to prepare for the barbecue I'm planning for Joe and Meredith."

"Great! I'll tell Jeff we're on," Cheryl replied. The phone rang and she jumped up to answer it. She held out the phone to Jewel. "It's Quinn Logan for you." She covered the mouthpiece as Jewel hesitated.

"Tell him I'll call him back," she finally said. Her heart ached as Cheryl delivered the message. She'd love to hear his voice this morning, to tell him that she'd slept better in his arms last night than on any night since she'd arrived in Esperanza. But what was the point when she intended nothing more between them?

"Everything all right?" Cheryl asked, hanging up the phone.

"Fine, I just didn't feel like any social chitchat this morning. I'm going to go back to my office and catch up on some paperwork," she said, feeling the need to escape Cheryl's skeptical gaze.

Once she was at her desk, she leaned her head back against the chair and forced herself to think of anything but Quinn.

That day in the library—when she'd been researching the accident that had forever changed her life—seemed like months ago. She realized that she hadn't followed up on any of the information she'd learned that day.

What ever happened to James Corrs after Andrew had turned him in for tax evasion? She hadn't gotten that far before Quinn had interrupted her.

With the kids at school and no fear of interruption she logged onto the Internet and searched for news articles related to James Corrs. It didn't take her long to find what she was searching for. James Corrs had gone to prison for federal tax evasion. He'd been sentenced to fifteen years. That was a long time to spend behind bars.

Before going to prison had he paid Andrew back by ramming into her car? What she wanted to do was call the authorities in California and have them reopen the case, investigate fully James Corrs as a suspect in the fatal hit-and-run.

But she knew what they would say. The accident had been ruled just that, they had other crimes to investigate and couldn't spend the time or manpower on a hit-and-run that had happened almost three years ago.

Wrapping her arms around her shoulders, plagued by a chill despite the warmth of the room, she thought about that moment when she'd awakened from one of her nightmares and had found the news clipping lying next to her.

It was crazy to think that somebody had snuck into the house and placed the clipping on her bed for her to find. But it was no more crazy than the logical explanation that she'd gotten up in her sleep and had dug the clipping out of a box of keepsakes.

Quinn had kept the ghosts at bay last night. It had been the first time in a very long time that she hadn't suffered any nightmares or heard voices or crying in the night.

Once again she found herself fighting the impulse to pick up the phone and return his call. Instead, she got up from her desk and decided to head over to Tamara and Clay's. They'd pulled a fast one eloping. Jewel wanted to hear all the details from Tamara and hadn't had an opportunity to talk to Tamara since learning the news.

Maybe part of the reason she wanted to talk to Tamara was because she knew her friend had never really warmed up to Quinn. By talking to her, Jewel could get the man out of her brain and would be able to forget the crazy yearning she had to fall back into his arms.

She drove the short distance to Clay's and parked in front of his house. She stepped out of the coolness of the car and the midmorning heat slapped her in the face.

Tamara answered her knock, her pretty face lighting with a smile. "Jewel, what a pleasure. Come on in."

"Thanks, I just thought I'd pop in for a quick visit. Is this a bad time?"

Tamara linked arms with her and walked her toward the kitchen. "Actually, it's a perfect time. I was just getting ready to have a glass of iced tea."

"Sounds wonderful. I can't believe how hot it is."

Tamara unlinked her arm with Jewel's and pointed her to the table. "And according to the weather reports it's only supposed to get worse. So I guess you're at loose ends today with the start of school."

Jewel smiled. "It's going to be strange having the kids gone during the weekdays."

"And I hear you have a new houseguest." Tamara set a glass of tea in front of Jewel then poured herself one and joined her at the table.

Jewel frowned. "A new houseguest?"

"Woof woof," Tamara replied.

Jewel laughed. "Ah, you mean, Cocoa. Yes, it was Quinn's idea." It was a perfect segue into the topic she most wanted to discuss. "I always got the impression you didn't much like Quinn."

Tamara smiled. "I have to confess that when he had to make the decision to put down Clay's stud, I hated the man. It was purely an emotional response. I saw how that decision hurt Clay and I guess it was kind of like killing the messenger. But since I've been back here I've changed my mind. Clay is constantly telling me what a stand-up guy Quinn is and I have to confess, I agree."

She raised an eyebrow. "Do I sense some interest there? Is it possible Adam Rawlings has some competition for your affections? Adam certainly hasn't hidden the fact that he has the hots for you."

"Unfortunately, the feeling isn't mutual and no, there's no interest with Quinn." The lie left a bad taste in her mouth. "I think I'm one of those women who are best alone."

"Human beings are not meant to be alone," Tamara countered. "We're built to thrive when loved and when loving. Trust me, Jewel, I tried it alone and it's not all it's cracked up to be. If you have an interest in the handsome vet, I say go for it."

For the next three days Jewel thought of Tamara's words. Quinn called several times each day and if Cheryl didn't answer and take a message, Jewel let the machine pick up.

She knew it was only a matter of time before she had to face him. What worried her was that she knew she was weak as far as he was concerned and for both of their sakes she had to stay strong. She had to stay away from him.

It had been four days since Quinn had heard from Jewel and he didn't intend to let another day pass without speaking with her.

It was obvious that she was avoiding his phone calls, so this morning he refused to give her a chance to escape him. At eight o'clock he parked his truck at the end of her driveway, where he assumed the school bus would pick up the kids.

He got out of the truck and walked around to the back, where he sat on the edge of the bed and waited.

He wasn't sure what was up with her. When he'd left her bed in the predawn hours after making love with her, he'd believed that they were on their way to building something meaningful, something magic.

He couldn't accept that he'd simply imagined the way she'd responded to him, not only in bed but also on their sunset ride when they'd shared pieces of themselves with each other.

Something had spooked her and he was determined to get to the bottom of it. She was the first woman who had captured his interest since his wife's death, and he wanted her to be the last.

The sun beat down on his shoulders as he watched the house. Maybe he'd rushed things with her. They'd gotten intimate so fast. Maybe he should have spent more time courting her. But there was no question that he felt an enormous passion for her, a passion that was hard to deny.

He sat up straighter as he saw the front door open and the kids began to spill out. Jewel followed them with Cocoa on a leash and he saw the exact moment she spied him. Her shoulders went rigid and she slowed her pace as if dreading what lay ahead. He was shocked by the quick stab of pain that coursed through him at her reaction.

Cocoa, on the other hand, jumped and leapt with eagerness as soon as the dog saw him. "Dr. Quinn." Lindy greeted him with a wide smile. "Did you come to see us get on the bus?"

Sam tapped her on the back. "Duh, he's here to see Miss Jewel."

"I got here extra early so I could see all of you," Quinn replied.

"See, he wanted to see us get on the bus," Lindy exclaimed in triumph.

Quinn smiled at Jewel. "You've been a difficult lady to get in touch with the last couple of days." *Keep it light,* he told himself. He took a step toward her and petted Cocoa.

"Things have been crazy around here this week," she replied, her gaze not quite reaching his.

"Too crazy for a quick phone call?" A note of censure crept into his voice.

Before she could reply, the bus appeared. It wasn't until the kids were loaded and the bus pulled away that he spoke again. "Did I move too fast?"

She finally looked at him. "No, it's nothing you did wrong. It's me. I've just realized I'm not ready for any kind of a relationship."

"You seemed more than ready for one before we fell into bed with each other," he replied.

Her cheeks turned pink and she looked away from him, staring back at the house as if longing to run inside and escape him. "It was that night that I realized I just wasn't ready for this…for you."

"And when will you be ready? Because I'll wait. Ask around town, Jewel. People will tell you I'm a very patient man, especially when it comes to something… someone I think is important."

She looked up at him again and in the depths of her chocolate eyes he saw a yearning and he knew for certain that they were worth fighting for. All he had to figure out was exactly what he was fighting against.

"If we moved too fast, we can slow things down," he continued. "I'll take you out to dinner. We can see a movie and I won't touch you, won't kiss you again unless you give me express permission."

A half laugh, half sob escaped her. "Oh, Quinn, you're making things so difficult. That's why I didn't want to talk to you—because I knew you wouldn't just accept what I said without question."

"I accept things when they make sense, but so far you haven't told me anything that makes sense." He placed a hand on her shoulder. "The other night was amazing and confirmed for me that you're the woman I've been waiting for all this time. I thought I could be the man you were waiting for, too."

She stepped away from his touch, as if finding it painful and that only confirmed his feeling that she cared about him and was running away from him for another reason.

"Talk to me, Jewel. Tell me what's really going on." He'd thought he'd never find love again when Sarah died. He'd believed all chance of happiness had died with his wife.

But after spending time with Jewel, after making love to her, he knew she was his second chance for happiness and he wasn't about to let her walk away without an explanation that made sense.

She straightened her shoulders but her gaze didn't quite meet his. "You're a nice man, Quinn. And I got caught up in the moment with you, but I'm just not ready for any relationship with a man. I'm sorry if I led you on, but there's nothing else to say."

She didn't wait for his response, but rather turned

and headed toward the house with Cocoa running at her side.

Quinn watched her go, his heart a leaden weight in the pit of his stomach.

Quinn had never been an egotistical man, but he didn't believe her. He didn't believe that she'd gotten caught up in the moment and now realized she didn't care about him. When he'd touched her, he'd seen a flare of desire in her eyes. She wanted him still.

Jewel Mayfair had secrets. He'd sensed that since the moment he'd met her and he was determined to get to the bottom of things, to discover the secrets that kept her from a life of happiness with him.

Chapter 9

The night wrapped around Jewel like a lover with a fever, the heat of the day maintaining its grip long after night had fallen.

She'd spent the last two hours tossing and turning in bed, unable to find sleep no matter how hard she tried. She'd finally given up and decided to take a walk in the woods.

This time it wasn't ghostly voices or baby cries that had kept her from falling asleep. Rather, it had been thoughts of Quinn.

Seeing him that morning had been far more difficult than she'd thought it would be. Telling him she didn't want a relationship with him had been sheer torture. All she'd really wanted to do was rush into his arms, hear his deep, reassuring voice telling her that they were going to have a wonderful future together.

But as long as she questioned her own sanity, she would never allow herself to be with any man who would have to go through with her what she'd lived through in the final months of her mother's life.

It had taken her years to connect with Patsy and even though the Baylors had raised her with love, she'd needed something from her mother that they hadn't been able to give her. Unfortunately, she'd never gotten it. Patsy had been incapable of giving love to the daughter she rarely recognized and could no longer remember giving birth to.

It had to be like what family members of Alzheimer's patients went through and Jewel wouldn't consciously choose to put somebody she loved through that.

The brush rustled to her left and she caught her breath in surprise. Slowly she breathed again as she realized she must have disturbed some poor creature's slumber. Nice that somebody could get some sleep tonight, she thought ruefully.

Even though she was dressed only in her nightgown and a lightweight short robe, the heat was oppressive, pressing in on her from all sides. There had been a number of power outages over the last couple of days due to the heat and the overload on the electrical grid. And there was no break in sight.

She heard a rustling from someplace behind her. She froze again. It hadn't sounded like a little night creature. It had sounded big. The sound came again, this time a little closer, a loud crashing as if something or someone was running toward her.

She thought of all those times she'd felt as if somebody was watching her and a lump of apprehension jumped into her throat. A burst of adrenaline shot through her and then came the taste of fear.

As the noise grew closer, she ran blindly down the narrow path, her heart pounding. She threw a glance over her shoulders and although she saw nothing on the path behind her, she saw movement in the tangled woods and brush just off the path.

There was no question in her mind. Somebody was after her and the fact that he hadn't said a word, was rushing at her out of the dark, terrified her.

She was afraid to run full tilt on the dark path. If she banged into a tree or tripped over an exposed root, then whoever was behind her would catch her. If she ran fast enough and far enough, she'd eventually reach Clay's place and safety, but the crashing noise let her know that whoever was chasing her was getting closer.

Tears filled her eyes, making vision even more difficult. She tripped and painfully smashed a knee to the ground. She scrambled back to her feet and kept moving, a sob escaping her lips.

"Jewel?" The deep voice boomed from just ahead of her.

She sobbed in relief as Quinn appeared on the path in front of her. His tall, lean silhouette in the near-darkness appeared like an island in a sea of shark-infested waters. She didn't hesitate but ran directly into his arms. "S-somebody chasing me." Her teeth chattered despite the warmth of the night.

He tightened his arms around her. "It's okay. You're safe now."

She hid her face in the front of his clean-smelling shirt and after a moment had passed she didn't hear any noise except the beating of her own heart, and the beating of his. Here was safety, in his big, strong arms.

Looking up at him, she saw his gaze taking in the woods around them, felt the slight tension that filled his body, the tension of a man ready to fight whatever might crawl out of the darkness. It only made her feel even safer.

"I don't see or hear anything," he finally said. "Whatever it was or whoever it was is gone. Come on, I'll walk you back to your house," he said as she finally stepped away from him.

He took her by the arm, as if to keep her close to him as they began to walk back to the ranch. She welcomed his touch, the reassuring feel of his warm hand on her arm. "Why don't you have Cocoa with you?" he asked.

"I was afraid he'd bark at everything that moved and disturb the kids," she replied. With each step she took with Quinn at her side, her heartbeat slowed to a more normal pace.

"Quinn, I didn't imagine it. There was somebody chasing me," she said as they left the path and entered the gate that led into the pool area.

In the moonlight his gaze held surprise as he looked at her. "It never entered my mind that you imagined it," he said. He motioned her toward one of the pool chairs. "Let's sit for a minute, let you calm down before you go inside."

The idea of sitting and talking to him was much more appealing that her going back to her bedroom alone with only her thoughts as company. She sat in a chair and Quinn next to her, close enough that she could smell his familiar scent.

"Better?" he asked after a minute of silence.

"I was better the minute you appeared on that path," she confessed.

He leaned forward and took one of her hands in his. "I get the feeling that there are things you aren't telling me and I wish I could make you realize that it's okay to trust me. I don't want to give up on you, Jewel. Nothing you said to me makes me believe we can't have a future together."

She felt as if her heart were being ripped in half. "Did you know I lost a baby?" The words tumbled from her lips before they had fully formed in her head.

He drew in an audible breath and his hand tightened on hers. "No, I didn't know that."

"It was in the accident that killed Andrew. I was four months' pregnant when I left the restaurant with Andrew that night. Then the accident happened and I was knocked unconscious. When I regained consciousness the next morning, both Andrew and my baby were gone."

"I'm sorry, Jewel. I'm so damned sorry for you."

The grief in his voice oddly enough eased some of her own. *Tell him about the cries,* a little voice whispered inside her. *Tell him that you hear Andrew calling your name during the night.*

But she didn't. She couldn't. What if he told somebody else and word got out that Jewel Mayfair was unbalanced, that she heard and saw ghosts in the night. She would lose her position here at the ranch, and that, along with the children here, were all that kept her from utter despair.

"Jewel, I know that what you went through was horrible and there will always be a place in your heart for all you lost, but isn't there a place for me, as well?"

Again a new pain ripped through her as she gazed into his beautiful eyes, felt the warmth and caring radiating from his hand holding hers.

"You're too young a woman to allow grief to forever rule your heart. There can be other babies. You can have a life filled with love." He leaned back a bit. "Maybe what you're suffering is a bit of Kelsey-itis," he continued.

She frowned. "What do you mean?"

"You're desperately afraid to grab on to happiness again because you know that it can be stolen away. You told me that you've told her that you need to grab on to it when it comes and hold tight so that you at least have memories of happiness if it goes away. Maybe you need to take your own advice. You need to let go of Andrew to make room for new happiness."

Was it possible that the voice and the cries of a baby were nothing more than her trying to keep Andrew and that distant happiness alive? Was it possible that in embracing what Quinn offered, in allowing him into her heart, the cries from the grave would finally be silenced forever?

For the first time since arriving in Esperanza, her heart filled with a fragile hope. She wanted to reach out to Quinn. She wanted him in her life.

"We can take it slow, Jewel," he said. "We can take it as slow as you want. I know you have a lot of things on your mind right now with Joe and Meredith coming to town next weekend and I realize your job here takes up a lot of your time. I'll take whatever you can give me. Just don't cut me out."

"I don't want to cut you out," she said softly, and this time it was she who tightened her grip on his hand. "Maybe I *have* been afraid to let go of the past," she admitted slowly.

"Trust me, I understand. After Sarah died, I grieved for a long time. I was afraid that if I let go of the grief I'd have nothing, be nothing. It defined me for a long time. Then one morning I woke up and the sun was shining and the birds were singing and I decided I wouldn't let my grief define me for another moment. It was time to start living again."

"Have you ever thought about being a psychologist?" she asked teasingly.

He laughed, that low, deep sound that wrapped around her heart and warmed her from the inside out. "I have enough problems figuring out the psychological problems of animals. I wouldn't attempt to try to analyze people. I'll leave that to you." He released her hand. "Now why don't you try to get some sleep?"

She nodded and stood. As always she found Quinn a rock of steadiness, a source of calm that she welcomed. He walked with her to her back door then he took her in his arms and she stepped into the embrace.

"If I call you tomorrow, will you take my call or at least return it if you're out?" he asked.

"Absolutely," she replied. What he'd said about her being a lot like Kelsey had made sense. She was willing, at least for now, to reach out for happiness, reach out to him and see where the path led.

"And if I invited you to have lunch one day this week?"

"I think we could arrange something like that," she replied.

"Good." His eyes gleamed and he pressed a kiss to her forehead. "Then I'll just say good night."

"Good night, Quinn," she replied. She watched as he went back to the gate and then disappeared into the darkness of the night.

She went inside and hoped she wasn't making a mistake. Maybe the haunting she'd been experiencing since arriving here was simply her mind refusing to let go of the past. Perhaps now that she'd made a decision to go forward, leaving her past behind, the haunting would stop.

It wasn't until she was back in bed that she realized that one question hadn't been answered. Who had been chasing her through the woods?

"It's looking good," Jewel said to Ryder the next morning. The pen was almost complete and the kids had spent most of breakfast discussing what kind of animals they'd like to have.

Barry had wanted a hippo and Lindy had her heart set on a baby elephant. It had taken some fast talking to bring them back to reality.

Ryder wiped a handkerchief across his sweaty brow. "We should have it finished in the next day or two."

"Terrific. I'm heading into town. Is there anything you need?" she asked.

"No, I'm good." He picked up his hammer. "I think the kids have the right idea today."

Jeff and Cheryl had the kids out by the pool. The sounds of splashing and laughter rode on the hot, steamy air. "Feel free to join them," Jewel said. "I think they plan on being out there all afternoon. In the meantime, I'm off. I'm meeting Ellie to talk about the plans for next Sunday."

"Have fun," he replied.

Minutes later, as Jewel drove into town, her mind whirled with all the things she needed to check out with Ellie. Weeks ago, when she'd first found out that Joe and Meredith intended to stop here on the final leg of their campaign trail, she'd spoken with Ellie about a tent rental, chairs and tables and all the functional things that were needed to accommodate a big crowd. Today she wanted to discuss the menu.

As she thought of seeing Joe and Meredith again, her heart filled with joy. When Jewel had learned about her real mother and had found Patsy in the mental ward, Patsy had told her of her other two children, Joe and Teddy. Patsy had said she never knew the identity of her first son's father and had hinted that Teddy's father was a member of Joe's family.

Jewel hadn't known what to believe or whether she would be welcome into the Colton family after all that her mother had done. But Joe and Meredith had opened their loving arms to her and embraced her as one of their own. With Patsy gone and her adoptive parents also deceased, Joe and Meredith had become like parents to her.

It was Meredith's loving support that had gotten Jewel through those dark days after the accident, and it was Meredith who had given her a new start here in Esperanza.

Jewel couldn't wait to see them both again and she wanted everything perfect for their visit. She wanted to prove to her aunt Meredith that trusting Jewel with the Hopechest Ranch had been the right thing to do.

Ellie's shop was on Main Street, a tiny storefront with artificial flower arrangements, wooden trellises and a champagne fountain for rent in the windows.

"Ellie?" Jewel cried out as she entered the shop.

"I'm back here." Ellie's voice drifted out from the back room. "I'll be right out."

Jewel sat in the chair in front of the desk and waited for Ellie. The store was a fantasyland of party supplies and Jewel never tired of looking around.

Ellie appeared, her brown frizzy hair looking wilder than usual and her cheeks flushed a bright pink. "Sorry, I was getting things together for a wedding that's taking place tomorrow. I swear, something's in the air around here lately. I've never been so busy." She flopped down at her desk and blew a strand of her hair out of her eyes. She grinned. "Now, let's talk about your big deal next Sunday."

For the next hour they went over the menu and checked and rechecked the lists of things that Ellie and her crew would be providing for the day.

"Your guests are arriving around five, right?" Ellie asked. Jewel nodded and Ellie continued. "My crew will be at your place no later than ten in the morning to start setting things up."

It was after two when Jewel left Ellie's. The heat slammed her in the face as she walked out of the cool store and she was eager to get back to the house and maybe join the kids in the pool. With this heat, no other place sounded the least bit attractive.

As she walked to her car she got that feeling again, the prickly sensation of somebody watching her, of something not quite right. She glanced around, seeking the source of the odd feeling.

Although there were other people on the sidewalks, nobody was paying any attention to her. They were hurrying toward stores, going about their lives.

She dismissed the feeling and got into her car, relieved as she drove away to see nobody following her.

An hour later Jewel was in her modest one-piece bathing suit and playing a game of water volleyball with the kids. Jeff and Cheryl sat in the shade of one of the umbrella tables, Cheryl calling out encouragement.

It was right before dinner that Jewel thought about Jeff Cookson. He was a quiet man, good with the kids, but he always appeared vaguely uncomfortable when interacting with Jewel.

Was it possible that it had been Jeff who had chased her through the woods the night before? Before hiring the couple, who were originally from San Antonio, where they had worked at a juvenile facility, Jewel had checked and double-checked their references and found them impeccable.

She dismissed the idea of Jeff skulking around after her in the dead of night, but that left her with the question that had plagued her since she'd awakened that morning. Who had been in the woods with her?

After dinner Jewel and the children had a group therapy session in the playroom. She talked to the kids about good and bad emotions and the appropriate way to express them. They followed up the session with a movie and then it was bedtime.

With the house quiet and at rest, Jewel curled up in bed with a book. She'd only been reading a few minutes when the phone rang.

"Good day?" Quinn's deep voice washed over her and she smiled with the simple pleasure of hearing it.

"Great day," she replied. "I finalized things with Ellie for the barbecue on Sunday and spent the rest of the day in the pool and doing therapy with the kids. What about you?"

"I operated on a dog with kidney stones, checked out a horse that had rubbed a sore spot on her flank and spent the rest of the day reading the books I got from the library the other day. It was just a normal day in the life of a small-town vet, a normal day made better now that I've heard your voice."

She smiled into the phone. "I feel the same way about hearing your voice. It's a perfect way to end the day."

"Are you ready for bed?" he asked.

"Actually, I'm in bed. I was just doing a little reading. The house is quiet and after all the fun in the sun this afternoon I actually feel like I'm going to be able to sleep."

"Good. Then I'll let you go. I just didn't want the day to pass without talking to you. Can you work me in for lunch one day this week?"

"Maybe Thursday would be good, but I'll have to let you know the first of the week." She had no idea what the week might bring with all the preparations for Joe and Meredith.

"Okay, I'll check in with you tomorrow or Monday. Good night, Jewel, and sweet dreams."

As she hung up, a pleasurable warmth remained. If she let herself she could easily fall in love with Quinn Logan. She was already more than halfway there. She just wasn't sure if she should allow herself to take the full leap.

Yawning with sleepiness, she turned out her lamp and got settled for the night. As she fell asleep she filled her head with thoughts of Quinn, of how it felt to be held in his arms, how endearing it was when he shoved that mane of beautiful hair away from his eyes.

There was something so solid about him, a quiet confidence that made her believe he could handle anything life might throw his way. He'd gotten through both the death of his wife and the damage to his professional reputation with dignity and grace. She fell asleep remembering the feel of his warm lips against hers.

She jerked awake abruptly and sat up, unsure what had pulled her from a dreamless sleep. A glance at the clock told her it was just after two.

Her heart pounded unnaturally fast and she wasn't sure why. Had it been a dream that had awoken her? A nightmare she now couldn't remember?

Maybe a glass of water would calm her racing heart. She slid her legs over the side of the mattress and reached for her robe at the end of her bed. She didn't need her bedside lamp to make her way to the kitchen. The path was lit with nightlights in case one of the kids got up and wandered in the night.

She'd just reached the doorway into the living room

when she heard it—the sound of several heavy footsteps coming from the family room/kitchen area.

Her heart leapt into her throat. Those footsteps didn't belong to one of the children, nor would Jeff or Cheryl be wandering the house in a heavy pair of shoes at this hour of the night.

She slid back into her bedroom and grabbed the bat she kept near her bed. With this being a ranch for children she refused to have a gun, but at this moment she wished she were holding something more lethal than a baseball bat.

If there was an intruder in the house, her sole concern was for the safety of her charges. Gripping the wooden weapon tightly in both hands, she advanced through the living room. She stifled a small gasp as she passed the front door and saw it cracked open.

Somebody was in the house!

Somebody who didn't belong.

Her mind whirled a thousand miles a minute as she crept forward, searching the shadows of the room for potential danger.

When they'd first opened the ranch, there had been some people who weren't thrilled at the idea of a place for troubled kids here. Had somebody who had a problem decided to act on it?

From the living room she walked to the doorway that led to the family room and kitchen area. Her heart hammered so hard in her chest that she felt as if she might pass out. She kept the bat on her shoulders, ready to hit a home run if it became necessary. Her eyes had adjusted to the near-darkness of the house.

She saw nobody in the family room and was beginning to think that maybe whoever had been inside was now gone. She had no idea what they might have been looking for or what they'd been doing, but a tiny edge of relief whispered through her. She relaxed her grip on the bat handle.

Turning, she looked into the darkened kitchen and froze, every nerve and muscle screaming inside her as she saw the tall, dark form of a man. She must have made a noise for he turned to face her, his features covered by the dark material of a ski mask.

"Who are you? What do you want?" The words barely escaped her lips before he rushed toward her.

Chapter 10

Everything seemed to move in slow motion. His heavy footsteps rang on the floor as he came toward her. She gripped the bat tightly and swung.

Strike.

She missed him and stumbled backward. *Three strikes and you're out,* she thought as she fought back a wild, hysterical burst of terrified giggles. But the giggles died a quick death as he once again advanced toward her and tried to grab her by the throat.

She ducked and evaded his grasp, her heart hammering with flight-or-fight adrenaline. She tried to discern his features beneath the ski mask, desperately looking for something familiar, a clue to his identity, but she couldn't even tell the color of his eyes in the narrow slits.

She didn't have to know his identity to recognize that

he was dangerous. She could sense an evil intent wafting from his big body. A scream rose to her lips but she fought it back, bit it away. The last thing she wanted was to scream and have one of the children stumble sleepily into the room.

He growled, like a wild animal let loose after months of captivity. The ominous sound raised the hairs on the nape of her neck, washed through her a terror she'd never known.

As he rushed toward her again, she swung the bat wildly and felt the whomph of it connecting with some part of his body. He grunted in obvious pain then pushed her to the side so hard she crashed to the floor. He ran past her and out the front door.

Jewel scrambled to her feet, ignoring the pain in her hip from the fall. Once again with the bat held ready to hit a home run, she advanced toward the open front door.

Her heart hammered.

Was he there?

Just outside? Waiting for her to run after him? Heart pounding so hard she could hear it banging in her brain, she moved closer. When she reached the door, she slammed it closed and locked it, then leaned weakly against it as a sob choked out of her.

Who was he? What had he wanted? She needed to call somebody. Sheriff Yates. She had to report this. She shoved away from the door and immediately turned on all the lights in the family room. Deep tremors possessed her as she stumbled toward the telephone on the end table.

It took her shaking fingers two tries to finally punch

in the right numbers and connect with the dispatcher for the sheriff's office. She told him she needed somebody out here, that there'd been an intruder in the house. "And no lights or sirens," she exclaimed. The dispatcher told her somebody would be out as soon as possible.

She hung up the receiver and leaned back, the bat still clutched tightly in one hand. What would have happened if she hadn't had the bat? She didn't even want to think about it.

Was the man who had been inside the house tonight the same one who had chased her through the woods? Was he the one she'd sensed watching her?

There had been such rage in that growl he'd released. He'd been like a marauding bear, who wanted nothing more than to rip her limb from limb.

She shivered and rose on shaky legs to go to the front window and watch for Jericho Yates or Adam. Was the intruder still out there? Hiding in the night? Waiting for another opportunity? She checked the lock on the front door, making sure it was engaged.

How had he gotten in? Was it possible the front door had been left unlocked when they'd all gone to bed? She frowned and tried to remember if she'd locked it or not. She just couldn't be sure.

She was vaguely surprised that nobody had heard anything, but then she realized that the assault had all been relatively silent. Other than those initial few words that she'd spoken aloud when she'd first seen him and that horrible low growl, there had been little noise.

She breathed a small prayer of thanks that none of the children had awakened. Not only could they have been physically harmed, but it was vital to their mental well-being for them to believe that they were safe and secure here in their temporary home.

It seemed like an eternity before she saw a car coming down the road. When the vehicle turned into the driveway she saw that it was from the sheriff's office.

The car parked in front and as the door opened she recognized Adam. As he got out of the car she unlocked the front door and opened it to meet him.

"Are you all right?" he asked as he reached her, concern darkening his eyes.

She nodded, for a moment too overwhelmed to speak. Hot tears burned at her eyes, rose up in the back of her throat. Now that she knew she was safe she realized that she was precariously close to breaking down.

Adam gripped her arm tightly. "Is somebody still inside?"

"No." She finally found her voice. "No, he ran out the front door."

"Go back inside. Lock the door. I'm going to do a sweep of the area and I'll be back in a few minutes to talk to you."

She nodded, closed the door and relocked it. Her heartbeat was slowing to a more normal pace and some of the trembling that had possessed her body had finally stilled.

Standing by the window, she saw Adam's flashlight as he searched the front yard. He disappeared from sight around the side of the house and she drew a deep breath to steady her racing emotions.

Although it soothed her to know that Adam was out looking, she didn't expect him to stumble upon the intruder. He was probably long gone…and hopefully with a cracked rib or a broken leg to boot.

What she'd like to do was pick up the phone and call Quinn. She knew the sound of his deep, calm voice would anchor her, soothe her. But she wouldn't wake him in the middle of the night, hated herself for her weakness in needing him, wanting him.

"Jewel?"

She gasped and whirled around to see Cheryl standing behind her, her robe clutched closed, brown hair in sleep disarray and her eyes wide in alarm. "You scared me to death," Jewel exclaimed.

"Sorry. What's going on?" She eyed the bat that Jewel had refused to release.

"Somebody was in the house. A man. He tried to attack me but I hit him with the bat and he ran out the door. Deputy Rawlings is here now, checking out the area."

"Oh my God." Cheryl moved closer to Jewel. "Are you sure you're okay?" Jewel nodded. "Do you know who it was? What he wanted?"

"I don't have a clue," Jewel replied.

"How did he get in?"

"By the front door." Jewel frowned. "I can't remember if I locked it before I went to bed or not."

At that moment a soft knock sounded at the door. Jewel opened it to allow Adam inside. "Unfortunately, I didn't find anything," he said.

"Let's go into the kitchen," Jewel suggested. She finally let go of the bat, leaning it against the family-room wall. "I'd rather not wake the children."

With Jewel leading the way, they filed into the

kitchen area. "This is where I first saw him," Jewel said. "I'm not sure what woke me up, but I thought I heard the sound of footsteps and I grabbed the bat and I saw him."

Cheryl placed a comforting arm around Jewel's shoulders. "You should have called to us. You should have called for Jeff."

"Where is Jeff?" Adam asked.

Cheryl gave them a sheepish expression. "He's still asleep. But if you would have screamed, he would have woken up."

"I didn't want to scream," Jewel replied. "The last thing I wanted was one of the kids waking up and coming into the room."

"Did you recognize him? Did he say anything to you?" Adam asked.

"No, nothing. He had on a ski mask. I didn't recognize him and he didn't say anything to me."

"What about height and weight?" Adam pulled out a small notepad from his shirt pocket.

For the next few minutes Jewel described her assailant, although there was precious little she could tell him. Adam made a sweep of the house, then there was nothing more he could do. "It sounds to me like you probably interrupted a robbery," Adam said.

Jewel nodded. "I think you're right. He probably wouldn't have tried to attack me if I hadn't confronted him." She wanted to believe this. It was the only thing that made sense.

It was after three when she walked with Adam out on the porch. "I'd like to tell you that I'm certain we'll catch this guy, but with the sketchy information you gave me, I don't have a good feeling about it," Adam said. "I'll check with the local doctors to see if anyone shows up with broken ribs or unusual bruising, but the man would be a fool to do that unless you seriously hurt him."

Jewel sighed and tied the belt of her robe more tightly around her. "I hope I busted his spleen," she exclaimed as she wrapped her arms around herself to ward off an inner chill.

"Jewel, I could stay the night if it would make you feel better," he said. He moved to stand next to her and put his hand on her forearm. "You should know by now that there's nothing I'd like more than to have a permanent place here at the ranch with you and the kids."

She realized it was time to be truthful with the handsome deputy. From the moment he'd arrived in town he'd made it clear to her that he wanted a relationship with her. It was time he knew the truth.

"Adam, you're a wonderful man and I'm sure someday you'll make somebody a great husband, but that somebody won't be me. I like you. I like you a lot and I hope we can remain friends, but I just don't feel that way about you. I'm sorry."

He dropped his hand from her arm and stepped back from her, a look of disappointment crossing his features. "No need to apologize. If it's not there, it's not there. I can't say I'm not disappointed, but I also can't say I'm surprised." He offered her a smile. "If we'd both been on the same page, we would have been dating for the last couple of months."

He jammed his hands into his pockets. "I'll let you know what I find out in the next day or two about what went on here tonight. Take care of yourself, Jewel, and if you ever change your mind you know where to find me."

She watched from the door as he walked to his car and got in. She had a feeling there would be fewer impromptu check-ins by him in the future now that he knew there was no hope for them.

When she returned to the kitchen, Cheryl had made a pot of hot tea and sat at the table. "Come on, have a cup of tea. I know well enough that you probably won't sleep for the rest of the night." Cheryl got up and fixed her a cup of tea, then put it on the table.

Jewel sat down wearily. Now that the excitement was over and Adam was gone, she was aware of the throb of her hip and a headache pounding at her temples. "Thanks," she said and cupped her hands around the warmth of the cup.

"Are you sure you're okay?" Cheryl asked as she gazed at Jewel with concern.

"I'm fine. I just have a headache." She took a sip of the tea, hoping the hot liquid would ease some of the pain in her head. "I just wish I knew why that man was inside, what he wanted here."

"Maybe it was a local kid who thought you had psychiatric drugs," Cheryl offered.

"Maybe, but if it was a kid, he was definitely a big kid. I just don't want anything to happen to mess up the big barbecue next Sunday," Jewel said worriedly.

"Don't worry, everything will be fine for Joe and Meredith's visit," Cheryl assured her.

"I hope so." Jewel took another sip of the tea, welcoming the warmth that helped banish the chill that had been with her since the moment she'd opened her eyes and realized something wasn't right in the house.

"Is there anything else I can do for you?" Cheryl asked.

"Yes, go back to bed," Jewel replied with a tired smile.

"Are you sure? I don't mind sitting with you if you want me to."

"No, I'm fine. I'm just going to finish this cup of tea then I'm going back to bed myself. Wait, I changed my mind, there *is* something you can do for me. Would you wait by the front door while I go get Cocoa? I think it's time our furry friend moved from the garage into the house." Jewel got up from her chair and carried her teacup to the sink.

"Sounds like a good idea," Cheryl agreed. "I doubt that dog would bite anyone, but if somebody comes in who doesn't belong he could sure raise a ruckus by barking."

Jewel stopped in the family room to grab her bat, then Cheryl followed her to the front door, where Jewel grabbed the leash hanging on a hook by the door and flipped on the outside light. As she stepped onto the porch, her heart began to bang with apprehension.

Was the man who'd been inside out here lingering in the night? Had he watched from some safe place while Adam searched for him, then left? It suddenly seemed like a long trip between the house and the garages.

"If you see anything or anyone, scream like hell," she said to Cheryl.

"Don't worry. And trust me, I can scream loud enough they'll hear me in town."

Jewel nodded. With the bat gripped in one hand and the leash in the other, she began the long walk toward the garage.

The night was silent and she listened for any sound that might forewarn her of anything amiss, but she arrived at the garage door without incident.

It took only moments to fasten Cocoa's leash then hurry back to the house where Cheryl waited at the front door. Cocoa danced with excitement, obviously thrilled to have his sleep interrupted by human interaction. He had lavished her with kisses as she connected the leash, then pranced next to her as they went back to the house.

"Thanks, Cheryl," she said once they were back inside with the door locked securely behind them. "I'll see you in the morning."

Jewel was thankful that Cocoa didn't bark as she led him to her quarters and closed the door behind them. She took the leash off him and he ran around the room, sniffing every corner and huffing with excitement.

Jewel set the bat against the wall next to her bed, then took off her robe. She was certain she wouldn't get any more sleep, but her aching body yearned for the softness of her mattress.

As she got into bed, Cocoa jumped up next to her and curled up as if he'd spent every night of his life sleeping in the bed with her.

"Don't get used to that," she said to him. "Tomorrow we'll bring in your bed."

He hunkered down and released what could only be described as a deliriously happy sigh. Jewel reached out a hand and stroked his soft fur. The feel reminded her of Quinn's hair, soft and silky to the touch.

As she continued to stroke the dog, she felt her heart-beat slowing and her tension ebbing. It had to have been a botched robbery attempt.

Although the attack had felt personal when he'd emitted that growl and had reached to grab her around the neck, surely it hadn't been personal at all. She'd trapped him and, like a wild animal, he'd sprung to get free.

She'd made no enemies that she knew of since coming to Esperanza. Some of the townspeople hadn't initially been thrilled with the idea of a ranch for troubled kids in their midst, but the last couple of months of the ranch's smooth running had quieted even the most vocal of critics.

Even though she had no intention of falling asleep, she must have, for she awakened to Cocoa licking her arm. A glance at her clock let her know it was a few minutes before seven, time to get up and face a new day.

"Okay, just a minute," she said to Cocoa, who jumped off the bed and began to run in circles near her closed bedroom door. "I'm hurrying." She got out of bed and pulled on her robe, afraid that Cocoa's obvious need to go outside wouldn't wait until she showered and dressed for the day.

She fastened the leash on his collar, then opened her bedroom door. The scent of freshly brewed coffee and frying bacon greeted her. Cocoa stopped in his tracks and sniffed the air, momentarily distracted from his run to the front door by the delicious scent.

"Come on, boy. First things first," she said as she tugged him toward the door. Once she was at the door, she released his leash and let him run while she stood in the yard and watched. He disappeared around the side of the garage and was gone for a minute or two, then came running back to her.

"Good boy," she said. "Cocoa is a good boy." She patted his neck, then reattached the leash and led him to the garage.

She had quickly discovered that having him in the house while the kids got ready for school was too much of a distraction. He chased the children and barked for them to play with him while they were trying to get dressed.

Once the kids were on the bus, she'd let him back into the house. After last night, she was determined to acclimate him quickly to being inside rather than in the confines of the garage.

Returning to her quarters, she showered and dressed for the day and by the time she got to the kitchen the kids were up and the house was filled with the usual chaos of morning.

Once the kids had left for the day, Jewel returned to the kitchen for another cup of coffee. Jeff sat at the table with her while Cheryl bustled around, clearing the last of the breakfast dishes.

"Cheryl told me about what I slept through last night," Jeff said, his hazel eyes narrowed in concern. "I can't believe you tried to take on an intruder by yourself."

"In the light of day I can't believe it myself," Jewel admitted, a coldness seeping through her as she thought of those terrifying moments the night before. "The only good thing is that I managed to hit him hard enough to hurt."

"Still, what good is it to have a man in the house if you don't holler for him when you need him?" Jeff replied gruffly.

Cheryl turned from the sink and grinned at Jewel. "He's having a hero meltdown this morning. He wanted to be the hero and instead you took care of the situation yourself."

"Trust me, if something like that ever happens again, I'll scream," Jewel said. "Thank goodness it was a case of all's well that ends well."

"Maybe Deputy Rawlings will be able to figure out who it was," Cheryl said.

"Probably some kid looking for drugs," Jeff replied.

"That's what I think," Jewel agreed. "He probably thought he could find some good psychiatric drugs in the house."

"On another topic, we're still on to take the kids Saturday for that field trip, right?" Jeff asked.

"Absolutely. That will work perfectly with me. While y'all are gone I'm going to clean this place from top to bottom to have it ready for the barbecue on Sunday." Jewel finished her coffee and stood. "And now I'm going to go get Cocoa and let him back in here. I also want to move his bed from the garage to my bedroom. From now on he'll be in the house at night."

"Need any help?" Jeff asked.

"No, thanks. I can take care of it," she replied.

"Then I'm going to do a little yard work before it gets too hot to breathe outside." Jeff pushed his chair away from the table and stood. "And if my wife loves me, she'll bring me out something cold to drink in the next hour or so."

Cheryl smiled at him and for a moment Jewel felt like a third wheel as she sensed the love radiating between the two.

As she walked outside to the garage, a deep yearning slid through her and her head filled with thoughts of Quinn. She felt as if she were being selfish in pursuing a relationship with him and not telling him about the voices she heard at night, the haunting cry of a baby that made her doubt her own sanity.

But the idea of not grasping on to the happiness he brought into her life was devastating. All her words of wisdom to Kelsey would mean nothing if she didn't embrace the philosophy of reaching out for happiness herself.

She opened the side garage door and stepped inside Cocoa's temporary quarters, expecting to be met as usual with a tail wag and a tongue lavishing, but Cocoa didn't greet her at the door.

He lay on the floor in a pool of vomit. As he saw her he struggled to stand, but his legs buckled and he collapsed back to the floor.

"Oh my God," she cried, and whirled to the door. "Jeff! Come quick. Something is wrong with Cocoa." Her heart leapt into her throat as she crouched down beside the dog. Tears washed from her eyes. "It's okay, baby. You're going to be all right. We just need to get you to Quinn's."

She stood as Jeff entered. "He was fine this morning," she said.

"Definitely not fine now," Jeff said with grim expression.

"Let's get him loaded in the car and take him to Quinn's."

They used a worn blanket and wrapped Cocoa up in it, then placed him in the backseat of Jewel's car. "Want me to come with you?" Jeff asked as she started the engine.

"No. Stay here. I'll let you know what's going on." She didn't take time to say anything more, but quickly tore down the driveway and onto the road to Quinn's.

She kept up a steady stream of chatter as she drove, unsure if she were trying to calm herself or the dog. "Quinn will take care of you. It's going to be okay." It was shocking to her how quickly the dog had crawled into her heart and she knew how deeply he'd already ingrained himself into the hearts of the children.

He had to be okay. He just had to be! She roared down the highway and breathed a sigh of relief as she turned into Quinn's place.

Quinn's house sat back from the road, an attractive ranch-style house with hunter-green shutters. But she pulled in front of the building closest to the road and parked. That one-story building was where Quinn's veterinary practice was housed.

Hank Webster, a local rancher, was just leaving as she got out of her car. "Please, could you help me? I've got a very sick dog and I need help getting him inside."

With Hank's help they managed to get Cocoa inside where Quinn's receptionist, Brenda Lopez, quickly gestured them into an examining room.

With Cocoa on the table, Jewel thanked Hank, who then left. She stroked Cocoa's head and frowned as she smelled the strong scent of garlic emanating from the dog's breath.

"It's okay, boy," she said as tears misted her vision.

He whined, a pathetic little noise that broke her heart. What was wrong with him? What had happened? He'd been fine two hours ago.

She turned as the door to the room opened. Quinn walked in, one leg dragging in an unmistakable limp. He flashed her a quick smile. "What happened?" he asked as he went directly to Cocoa.

"I… I don't know." A chill swept through her, one that had nothing to do with worry for Cocoa. "What happened to your leg?" Her voice felt as if it came from someplace very far away.

"Molly the horse not only managed to tear up my face, she also got me in the knee. It sometimes acts up." He leaned closer to Cocoa's face. "Smell that garlicky scent. That's arsenic poisoning. I need to get him treated. Why don't you wait out in the waiting room?" He ushered her out then called for his vet tech to come into the room to help him.

On wooden legs she moved to one of the chairs and sank down, her worry for Cocoa momentarily banished from her mind.

She felt blindsided. Last night she'd struck somebody in the lower body with a bat and today Quinn had a pronounced limp. There was no way to escape the icy chill that swept through her as she wondered if it had been Quinn in her house the night before.

She desperately wanted to believe that it was nothing more than a coincidence, but all she wanted to do was

run and escape from him and from the terrible possibility that it had been his knee she'd hit the night before, that it had been his hands reaching for her throat.

Chapter 11

Jewel felt as if she might throw up. An hour later as she drove home, her head whirled and nausea rolled in her stomach.

Cocoa had been poisoned with arsenic and Quinn had a mysterious limp. Any trust she'd felt toward the handsome vet had been shattered, leaving her feeling sick and making her realize just how much she cared about him.

She'd been more than half in love with him and given just a little more time she would have allowed herself to fall completely, head-over-heels. But the thought that she'd been the one who'd given him that injury with her bat filled her with coldness.

He'd managed to get Cocoa stabilized, but had told her the dog needed to stay for a couple of days to make sure there were no residual effects from the poison.

They decided he would keep the dog until after the barbecue on Sunday.

She deserved an Oscar for her performance with him. Even when the emergency was over and he'd asked her when they were going to be able to have lunch together, she'd managed to keep her cool and not betray that anything was wrong. She'd told him that until the barbecue was over, they could not get together. She simply had too much to do.

Thankfully he'd had an appointment with a sick cat and with a squeeze of her hand he'd told her they'd talk later. She hadn't been able to escape fast enough.

Tightening her grip on the steering wheel, she thought about that moment when she'd seen the intruder standing in her kitchen. Had he been as tall as Quinn? Were Quinn's shoulders as broad as that man's had been? It could have been Quinn beneath that ski mask.

By the time she reached her place, none of the questions had been answered and the sickness that had gripped her had only grown more intense.

Jeff greeted her as she parked the car. "I found part of a steak in Cocoa's part of the garage," he said when she got out of the car. "I think maybe your intruder left it for the dog."

She nodded. "Quinn said he thinks it was arsenic poisoning, so I guess that makes as much sense as anything right now."

"How's the dog?"

"Serious, but stable," she replied. "If you'll excuse me, I'm going to my room to clean up a bit."

Her intention was to shower again and change her clothes, which smelled like dog vomit. She had no intention of crying. But as she stripped and got beneath a hot spray of water, the tears began.

At first she thought she was crying for Cocoa, but as the tears increased she realized that she was weeping for what might have been with Quinn.

There was no going back. She would always wonder if he had been the man who had broken into the ranch, the man who had growled at her with such hatred, the one who had reached out to grab her around her throat.

Would Quinn, a man devoted to the health and well-being of animals, poison a dog? Why would he break into her house? What possible motive could he have? No matter how she twisted and turned the questions, she couldn't come up with any logical answers.

But she couldn't get that limp out of her mind. That physical injury of his had effectively killed any chance the two of them had for a future.

She refused to love a man she didn't trust. She leaned weakly against the shower stall and wept a lifetime of tears. She cried for the happiness she'd lost when Andrew and her baby had died. She sobbed for the happiness she might have found with Quinn. Finally, she cried because she didn't understand the twists and turns that life had thrown at her, beginning the day of her birth, when she'd been stolen away from her mother and sold in an illegal adoption.

The week passed in a haze for Jewel. She took care of the children, conducted therapy sessions and once again met with Ellie for the final preparations for Sunday's festivities.

Quinn called daily to update her on Cocoa's condition. They'd got the poison in time and Cocoa was doing just fine. She kept the conversation brief and light, although her heart had disengaged. She couldn't allow him back into her heart. She couldn't love him now, with all trust broken and a sliver of fear of him finding purchase in her heart.

It was just after nine on Saturday morning when Jeff and Cheryl rounded up the kids for their day trip away from the ranch.

"Make sure you all behave for Cheryl and Jeff," Jewel told each of the kids as they got into the minibus. "I want perfect behavior reports on each of you when you get home this evening."

"We'll be good," Barry promised, and they all echoed his words.

Although it was still early morning, the sun sizzled in a cloudless sky, promising no relief from the intense heat that had gripped the region for the past three days.

"Make sure they all get plenty to drink," Jewel said to Cheryl once they were all loaded and ready to pull away.

"Don't worry, Mother Hen. We'll bring your chicks home safe and sound," she assured Jewel.

Jewel forced a smile. "And call me if there are any problems," she said. She waved as they drove off and continued to wave and smile until the bus disappeared from sight.

Instantly her smile fell away. She was grateful that at least for the remainder of the day she wouldn't have to force a fake cheerfulness. She wouldn't have to pretend that everything was right in her world.

Sooner or later she was going to have to tell Quinn that there was no hope for them. The only reason she hadn't done so yet was because he would be attending the barbecue and she didn't want any unnecessary tension between them.

Once the barbecue was over and Joe and Meredith had left town, she'd tell Quinn that she wasn't available, that he needed to look elsewhere for a life partner.

The one thing she hadn't done was tell anyone about her suspicions. She'd considered calling Adam and telling him that Quinn was sporting a suspicious limp. The only thing that had stopped her was the possibility that Quinn might have been telling the truth about how his knee got injured.

Quinn had already lived through much of the town turning against him. He'd already faced false accusations that had nearly destroyed his life. She didn't want to be responsible for doing it all over again. She had no real proof, just a coincidental limp.

Just an awful limp that had destroyed everything.

As she stood there alone in the yard with the top of her head boiling beneath the hot sun, a sudden prickly feeling lifted the hair on the nape of her neck, raised goose bumps on her arms.

It was the crazy, inexplicable feeling a person got when she thought she was being watched. Jewel whirled around, eyeing the house behind her, then looked toward the nearby woods.

Nothing.

"Silly goose," she murmured to herself, but that didn't make the feeling go away. If she stood out here long enough, she would totally freak herself out.

She had a million and one things she wanted to accomplish today while the kids were out of the house.

Standing in the front yard giving herself the heebie-jeebies wasn't on her to-do list. She headed inside and carefully locked the door behind her.

Although the children were responsible for cleaning their own rooms, Jewel wanted to give each room a thorough once-over. She knew there would be people with Joe and Meredith who had never been to the ranch before and would be looking closely at Meredith's pet project. Jewel wanted to make certain everything was perfect.

The morning passed quickly as she vacuumed and dusted each of the bedrooms, then tackled the bathrooms that the kids used.

The busywork kept her mind blank and for that she was grateful. Her brain felt fried from all the analyzing and thinking it had done over the past five days. She didn't want to think about anything but Joe and Meredith's visit the next day.

Not only would the day convene family and friends, it would also be an early celebration of Joe's political success. The polls and pundits were all forecasting a Colton presidency.

At noon Jewel stopped her work and sat at the table to enjoy a sandwich of the chicken salad Cheryl had fixed early that morning.

It was only as she sat eating that she realized just how quiet the house was with everyone gone. The silence pressed in on her from all sides. It wasn't a comfortable silence but rather an oppressive one.

And, as always when she had a moment of peace and her head was relatively empty, it filled with thoughts of Quinn. More than once she'd felt as if she were being watched. Was it possible Quinn had been stalking her long before they'd gotten close?

Had he merely stumbled on her that first night in the woods or had he been there all along, watching her? He'd known she often walked at night, had guessed that she suffered from insomnia.

She stifled a laugh of irony. She hadn't wanted to involve herself with him because she'd feared she was losing her mind. What if he was the one who was mentally deranged? An obsessed stalker, who had her in his sights?

Was it possible he had poisoned Cocoa with the intention of saving the dog and being a hero? The very idea sickened her.

She'd just finished eating and had put her dishes in the dishwasher when the doorbell rang. Grateful for a break in the silence and her racing thoughts, she hurried to answer.

She opened the door to Georgie and was ridiculously pleased to see the woman. "What a nice surprise!" she said as she opened the door to let her in.

"Nick and Emmie are having a bonding day. He took her to lunch and then was going to buy her a couple of pairs of new jeans for school. I was at loose ends so I thought I'd drop in and see if there's anything you need for tomorrow's big party."

"Come on in and have a glass of iced tea with me," Jewel said. "I think I have things under control for tomorrow. Ellie and her crew are going to arrive at ten in the morning to set up tents and chairs and everything we need to make the day a success."

As Georgie sat at the table, Jewel poured them each

a glass of iced tea. "How does Emmie like school?" she asked as she joined Georgie.

"She loves it." Georgie's expression was a blend of happiness and wistfulness.

Jewel smiled. "Spoken with the bittersweet expression of a mother."

Georgie grinned. "She's already made friends with a bunch of kids and has assured me there isn't a cowboy in the bunch. She loves her teacher and she gets up every morning eager to go."

"And even though you want her to have friends and love school, it breaks your heart that she's expanding her horizons and doesn't need you quite as much as she did."

Georgie leaned back in her chair and sighed. "Exactly."

Jewel laughed. "Don't worry. You're still the most important thing in her world and will continue to be until she gets to be a teenager. Then she'll think you're the dumbest person on earth and wonder how you ever survived without her wisdom and knowledge."

Georgie laughed and shoved her long red braid over her shoulder. "God, I needed to hear that."

"How's Nick?"

"Bored. He's put in an application with the sheriff's office for a position as deputy, but so far there are no openings in the department. You can take the man out of the Secret Service, but you can't quite take the protect and serve out of a former Secret Service man."

"I think it's so romantic that he gave up his position with the Secret Service to come here for you," Jewel replied.

"Speaking of romance. I hear through the grapevine that you and Quinn have been seen around town, looking pretty cozy together."

It was impossible not to feel a stab of pain at his name. "Just friends," Jewel replied.

"Too bad. You two would have made a great couple."

Jewel took a sip of her tea then said, "I'm really not interested in being part of a couple right now."

"I highly recommend it," Georgie replied.

Jewel forced a laugh. "Why is it that every woman who has recently fallen in love thinks that every other woman on earth should be in the same state?"

"Because loving somebody makes you be more than what you were before you loved." Georgie paused to sip her tea, then continued. "Because loving is what we're made for, why we're on this earth." She gave Jewel a wide grin. "Loving somebody and riding horses, that's my idea of heaven."

This time Jewel's laughter was genuine. For the next few minutes the two talked about the Colton clan and everyone who would be at the barbecue the next day.

"Is Uncle Graham going to show up?" Jewel asked.

Georgia shrugged. "Who knows what Dad is going to do. He's really trying to turn his life around, but sometimes I wonder if it's a case of too little, too late. It would be nice if he and Uncle Joe could somehow put the past behind them and build a new relationship, kind of like what Ryder and Clay have done, but I'm not holding my breath for any miracles."

The two women visited for another half an hour, then Georgie stood. "I'd better get home, if you're sure there's nothing I can do to help with tomorrow."

"Pray for a break in this heat," Jewel said as she walked with Georgie to the front door.

"Isn't it terrible? I heard that a bunch of people were without electricity last night because of an overload of the system. Thankfully, the electric company got things back up and running in a couple of hours."

"I wouldn't even want to be a couple of hours without the air conditioner on days like these." Jewel opened the door. "Thanks for stopping by, Georgie. I really appreciate it."

"We all appreciate what you're doing tomorrow. It will be terrific to have so many of us in the same place at the same time. I'm really looking forward to it."

A few minutes later Jewel stood on the porch and watched as Georgie pulled away. She'd welcomed the distraction, but now it was time to get back to work.

The afternoon passed quickly and about five she started looking for the kids to return. She knew they'd be eager to share their day with her and hopefully they'd be exhausted enough to go to bed early. Tomorrow was going to be a big day for them all.

By six she decided to go ahead and eat something instead of waiting for everyone to return. Jeff and Cheryl had probably treated the kids to dinner in a roadside café.

As she ate leftover meat loaf with green beans and a salad, she thought of the conversation she'd shared with Georgie.

There had been a moment when she'd felt love for Quinn, when he'd filled her heart and soul and she'd never wanted to leave his arms. There had been an aching moment when she'd been brimming with the possibility of him…of them together, but with the possibility gone, she was left empty.

Once again the silence that surrounded her was suffocating. She couldn't wait for everyone to get back where they belonged, for the house to be overflowing with lively chatter and laughter.

It's better this way, she thought, once again thinking of Quinn. Even if he hadn't been the one who had broken into the ranch, even if his limp really was from an old injury, she wasn't in a place to tie her life to somebody else's.

As long as she suffered from those haunting memories after midnight each night, as long as Andrew and the baby she'd lost cried out to her from the grave, called her from the woods, there was no place for another man in her life.

But if she were going to pick the man she'd want to spend her life with, it would be the Quinn Logan who had laughed with the kids in the pasture on the day of the picnic. It would be the Quinn who had made love to her with a gentleness and a passion that had her believing in happy-ever-afters.

And tomorrow she'd have to see him and socialize with him and wonder if he was some sort of psycho stalker or the man she should never have let slip through her fingers.

By seven, all thoughts of Quinn had disappeared as she stood at the front window and stared worriedly out at the road. They should have been home by now. She'd tried to call Cheryl's cell phone twice but each call had gone directly to voice mail.

She opened the front door and stepped out on the

covered porch. The heat was like a sickening slap in her face. With the sun beginning to set, it should have cooled off, but the heat was as fierce now as it had been at noon. Not a breath of air stirred around her. It was even too hot for the insects to have begun their nightly hum and whirr.

Where were Jeff and Cheryl with the kids? The plan had been for them to be home for dinner. What could have happened and why wasn't Cheryl answering her phone?

It wasn't long before she felt it again…that disquieting sensation of being watched. She backed closer to the door and wrapped her arms around her shoulders, chilled despite the heat of the night.

Was there somebody out there?

Watching her?

Somebody who knew she was all alone?

Stop it, she mentally commanded. Those kinds of thoughts would only freak her out.

The sound of the ringing phone pulled her back inside and she raced to grab the receiver in the living room. It was Jeff.

"We've got a busted alternator and a dead cell phone," he said. "Don't worry. We're checked into a motel for the night and the local mechanic has promised me he'll have us back on the road by ten tomorrow morning."

Jewel breathed a sigh of relief. "What happened to the cell phone? Did you just forget to take the charger?"

"Actually, it kind of got crushed. We were stuck on the side of the road for a while. It was hot and Barry got nervous. He had a little meltdown and stepped on the phone. He's fine now," Jeff said hurriedly. "I've got insurance on the phone and everything is okay."

"I was getting so worried."

"I'm sorry. We just didn't have a way of calling until now."

"And you're sure the kids are okay?"

Jeff laughed. "They're calling it the big adventure and we're all in one room with roll-away beds wall to wall. We'll feed them a good breakfast in the morning and we should be there in plenty of time to get them cleaned up for the party."

"Keep all the receipts for everything and you'll be reimbursed," Jewel said.

"I'm not worried about it. We'll see you tomorrow and don't you worry. We have everything under control."

Jewel breathed a sigh of relief as she hung up the phone. Even though she'd known that Jeff and Cheryl would have things under control, she was grateful that everything was fine, that the bus would be fixed and they'd be home in the morning.

Now all she had to do was get through the night alone. Normally, she didn't mind time alone, but she'd been on edge all day and would have much preferred her "family" home with her where they belonged.

Exhausted from her day of work, she took a shower and got into her nightgown and robe. She carried a book into the family room and curled up on the sofa. She turned on a lamp as the darkness of nightfall encroached, stealing the light in the room.

She started to read, but the silence bothered her. She punched on the television and found an old movie that she'd seen several times before. She wasn't interested in watching it again, but welcomed the noise as she returned her attention to her book.

The lights and the television went off as the power failed. The abruptness of the power failure made her heart double-jump in her chest. For a long moment she remained unmoving in the darkness of the room.

Dark energy charged the air, as it often did before a terrible storm, but there were no storms forecasted, even though the area desperately needed some rain.

The heat, she thought as she got up from the sofa. Georgie had just mentioned that the power company was having problems because of the intense heat. There must be an overload of the system somewhere.

She turned off the television, not wanting the electricity to come back on in the middle of the night and wake her suddenly. She grabbed her book and went into her quarters.

The first thing she did was make her way through the darkness to her bathroom, where she had a stock of emergency candles on a shelf. She took out several, lit them and set them on the nightstand next to her bed, then with the candlelight creating flickering shadows on the walls, she got into bed and opened her book.

Abe Lincoln might have been able to read by candlelight, but Jewel found her mind wandering away from her book and back to the past.

The loneliness etched into her heart had existed long before the loss of Andrew and her baby, although that particular devastation had certainly deepened the wounds.

The loneliness had begun at a time when she'd been

desperate to connect to her mother. When she'd been old enough to learn the truth about Patsy, all she'd wanted was to help the woman who had given her life, to find that bond of love that surely had to exist.

The need to help her mother was part of what had driven Jewel into psychology. The fact that she'd been too late to help Patsy had begun the hole of loneliness that gnawed inside her.

Quinn had filled that hole. Quinn had taken away her loneliness for a little while, until she'd seen that limp, until the trust she'd started to give to him had been destroyed.

She closed her eyes and tried to conjure up a picture of Andrew, for a moment surprised when the only man whose vision filled her head was Quinn.

Quinn with his beautiful topaz eyes.

Quinn with that wonderful mane of hair and the endearing habit of brushing it out of his eyes.

She squeezed her eyes more tightly closed. She didn't want to think about him. There was no point in regretting what would never be.

She'd rather think of that moment of sheer happiness in the restaurant with Andrew, when he'd placed the ring on her finger and she'd rubbed her hand across the place where his baby grew inside her.

Tears stung her eyes. God, she'd wanted to be a mother. She'd wanted the scent of baby powder and formula, the sound of baby coos and the joy of kissing a sweet belly as she changed diapers. She'd wanted that more than anything in her life.

Although she loved the children who were under her care at the ranch, she never lost sight that her job was to heal them and then send them back to their real lives and to their own mothers and fathers.

She opened her eyes and blew out the candles, knowing she wouldn't read anymore tonight. Hopefully, in the next couple of hours, the power would come back on, for already she felt the coolness of the air-conditioning vanishing beneath the weight of the heat outdoors.

Maybe she should crack a window open. It wouldn't take long before the house would be stifling. She crept from the bed and opened the window and that's when she heard it—the mournful cry of a newborn baby.

Chapter 12

Something had changed.

Quinn saddled up Noches and while he sweet-talked the black stallion, his mind was filled with thoughts of Jewel.

Something had changed with her in the last week and he couldn't quite put his finger on it.

He knew she was busy with the preparations for Joe and Meredith's visit and the barbecue she'd planned, but what he sensed in her tone wasn't preoccupation with everything that was going on; rather, it was as if she were emotionally distancing herself from him.

She'd been pleasant enough, but there was an edge in her voice that cut through his heart, that definitely concerned him.

He'd thought about stopping in at her place when he'd driven by it a little earlier to go to Clay's, but as he'd passed he'd seen that all her lights were out and assumed everyone was already in bed. The last thing he wanted to do was disturb her if she was getting some much-needed sleep.

The moon overhead was nearly full, spilling down enough light that a nighttime ride had sounded appealing. Besides, concern about Jewel had kept sleep at bay the last couple of nights and he didn't think tonight would be any different.

Noches left the stable with a spirited shake of his head, as if eager to run despite the heat of the night. Quinn held the reins loosely, allowing the horse to lead the way across the moonlit landscape at a quick pace.

The night air made Quinn feel as if he wore a blanket around him even though he was clad only in jeans and a short-sleeved navy T-shirt. Noches didn't seem to mind the heat as he pranced energetically along the path that led to open pasture.

These night rides were Quinn's contemplation and relaxing time. After his wife's death and during those dark days when he'd felt as if the town had turned against him, riding in the evening had kept him sane.

All the aches of the day faded, all the disappointments that life had heaped on him melted away as he just enjoyed the simple pleasure of the motion of the horse beneath him.

But tonight was different. Thoughts of Jewel kept him from finding the peace and relaxation he normally found on nights like this.

He thought he'd finally broken through to her, had gotten past the defenses she'd erected around her heart after Andrew's death and the tragic accident that had taken the baby she carried. Quinn had believed he finally had Jewel trusting him, believing that they had a future together, but now he wasn't so sure.

What she didn't know was that he was a man who didn't give up. He needed her in his life. He wanted her there. And he would do whatever it took to convince her that it was where she belonged.

"No."

The word fell as a whisper from Jewel's lips as the baby's cries seemed to grow louder and heartbreakingly plaintive.

She clapped her hands over her ears. The sound made her dizzy and sick with fear. It pierced her very soul and made her want to both scream and hide in a closet where the sound couldn't find her.

Only a shaft of moonlight that danced in the window broke the profound darkness of the room. But in that moonlight she could see her bed with its rumpled sheets. She could see the book she had been reading flat down on the nightstand.

She was awake.

She wasn't dreaming the sound.

She was either crazy or the sound was real. She lowered her hands from her ears and cocked her head to one side, for the first time really focusing on the noise as unemotionally as possible.

So many nights she'd suffered through this, so many nights she'd curled up in her bed and consciously willed the sound away. She'd always assumed it was the cries of her dead baby haunting her from the beyond.

But what if it wasn't?

What if it was real?

Her mind whirled as she thought of the black-market baby ring Ryder had infiltrated a month before. Was it possible the baby she heard crying was real and not a figment of her imagination?

She stood at the window and stared out into the night, her muscles tensed and her heart pounding wildly. Always before, the sound had stopped as abruptly as it had started. She remained frozen, waiting, praying for it to end, but the sound continued…and continued.

She had to know the truth. She had to find the source. For the first time she recognized the possibility that it might not be in her mind, that she just might not be crazy. She acknowledged that the baby might be real.

Whirling away from the window, she stepped into her bedroom slippers and grabbed her bat, then opened the door that led outside.

She walked around the edge of the pool and to the back gate where she paused and cocked her head to listen. Nothing.

She couldn't hear the baby anymore. The heat wrapped around her, suffocating her, and the night offered an ominous silence, as if every insect and night creature held their breath in anticipation, but anticipation of what?

The hairs on her nape rose and a chill slivered up her spine. Her body tensed in alarm. She sensed something…somebody nearby.

"Jewel." The voice rode a breeze like a hot whisper.

She gasped and gripped the bat more tightly in her sweaty hand. Andrew. It had sounded like Andrew. Her mind felt sharper, clearer than it had in months.

It couldn't be Andrew. He was dead. But the voice was real. She felt it in her very bones. The voice was real and it wasn't Andrew's.

Somebody was stalking her, somebody was making her think it was her dead fiancé calling to her in the night. She couldn't imagine why anyone would do such a thing, couldn't imagine who might be responsible, but she was determined to find out.

"Jewel, come to me." The voice came again, low and hypnotic, but this time she steeled herself against it. She couldn't be sure where exactly it came from. The trees and brush played tricks with the sound, making it appear to come from all around her.

The moonlight momentarily disappeared as a cloud chased across the sky. She unfastened the gate and walked through it and onto the path that led to the Bar None. "Where are you?" She kept her voice soft and low as she walked deeper into the woods.

She sensed that she was not alone. Every tensed muscle in her body, every taut nerve she possessed told her that somebody else was in the woods, something who wanted her to believe that she was haunted by the dead.

She hadn't walked far on the path when she saw a figure ahead of her. She jumped off the path and hid behind a tree, her heart banging against her ribs.

Leaning around the tree, she looked at the figure and as the moonlight once again appeared, she recognized the tall man with the mane of hair.

Quinn.

She wanted to fall to her knees and weep. Only now did she realize a part of her had held out some hope that he truly was the man she'd wanted to believe he was, that he wasn't the person who had broken into the ranch and tried to hurt her. The pain that ripped through her as she stared at him on the shadowy path nearly destroyed her.

A hand fell on her shoulder and she screamed, but the scream was cut short as the same hand slid up and over her mouth. She half turned to see Adam. He indicated for her to keep quiet and removed his hand from her mouth.

"Follow me," he whispered. He grabbed her bat and tossed it aside. "You're safe now," he said, and took her by the hand.

She wanted to ask him what he was doing out here, but she didn't speak until they had gone some distance and she knew Quinn wouldn't be able to hear their voices.

"What are you doing out here, Adam?" she whispered.

He dropped her hand but continued to walk. "Since the night of the break-in I've been watching your place. I saw Logan skulking around and then I heard him call your name. I knew he was up to no good. Now, I need to show you something."

"What?" she asked, struggling to keep the tears at bay as she thought of Quinn.

He shook his head, his expression grim. "You have to see it to believe it."

Heart thudding in a combination of pain and apprehension, Jewel continued to follow Adam, wondering where on earth he was taking her. She could tell that they were on Bar None land, but they were headed to an area of the property where she'd never been before.

They finally broke out into a clearing where an old barn with gray weathered boards stood, listing precariously to one side. "You've got to see what's inside," Adam said.

The door opened with a creak of rusty hinges. A small work light hung from the rafter, creating a small pool of light inside.

The first thing Jewel saw was a tall pole embedded in the ground in the center of the barn. Around the bottom of the pole, brush and dry wood had been gathered.

"Oh my God, what is this place?" she asked.

She turned to look at Adam, his features taut and almost frightening in the dimness of the light and the play of shadows.

He drew his gun and smiled, his eyes gleaming with an ominous light. "This is the place where you'll pay for the sins of your mother."

Quinn had decided to go to Jewel's place and see if he could talk to her. The distance he'd felt from her over the past week gnawed at him and he wanted to talk to her before the barbecue the next day. He needed to make sure that things were okay between them.

He'd gotten halfway to her place when he'd hesitated. What if she were sleeping soundly, peacefully? Knowing that sleep was an issue for her, did he really want to wake her up, knowing that she had a full day ahead of her tomorrow?

He'd stopped on the path and that's when he heard it,

a sharp, quick scream that sounded as if it had been cut short. He froze, all his senses on alert. There was only one woman he knew who often walked these woods at night and that was Jewel.

He raced down the path, his heart pounding as he looked left and right, afraid of what he might see, afraid of what he might not see.

Reaching the gate that led to the pool area of the Hopechest Ranch, he saw that it was open and beyond that the door that led into Jewel's private quarters was open, as well.

As he ran around the pool and to the door, he knew instinctively that she wouldn't be inside sleeping peacefully in her bed, not with the door open.

Still, he didn't slow his pace until he stood in the door leading into her bedroom and saw the empty bed. "Jewel?" he called softly, not wanting to awaken anyone else in the house. "Jewel, are you in here?"

He could smell her, that fresh floral scent that went right to his head. He flipped on the light switch next to the door, but nothing happened.

What the hell? He tried another light with the same result. He knew Clay's place wasn't without power and guessed that his place and this one would be on the same circuits, so why wasn't Jewel's electricity working?

This, coupled with the sound of that half scream had alarm bells shrieking inside his head. "Jewel," he called one last time although he knew in his gut she wasn't here. He ran back to the door and peered outside. She was out there someplace and what scared him more than anything was that something…or someone had made her scream.

* * *

"Adam, what are you talking about?" Jewel stared at him, then at the gun he held on her. She grappled to make sense of what was happening.

My God, was this somehow because she hadn't gone out with him? "I'm sorry if I've somehow hurt your feelings by not going on a date with you." This was Adam... Deputy Adam Rawlings. He was supposed to protect her. What was he doing holding a gun on her?

He laughed and the malevolence in the tone shot a shiver of icy terror through her. "Don't be stupid, Jewel. Do you really think this is because you wouldn't see a movie with me or share a meal?" The laughter faded and his features formed an expression of tense determination. "Turn around." He pulled a length of rope from his pocket.

"Adam, please, tell me why you're doing this. You said something about my mother? How do you know my mother?"

He motioned for her to turn around and, afraid of what he might do if she didn't comply, she did. He quickly tied her hands behind her back, then whirled her around to face him. His eyes were filled with the dark demons of rage.

"Why am I doing this? Because the Coltons have destroyed everything in my life." He grabbed hold of her bound hands and pulled her toward the upright pole. "Heard any babies crying in the night, Jewel? Has Andrew been calling to you from his grave?" He laughed and a new terror soared through Jewel.

"What do you know about Andrew? What do you know about my baby?" Oh God, this couldn't be happening. Her heart beat a rhythm of dread as she stared at him.

He smiled. "I know exactly what his face looked like right before I rammed into your car that night on the road. I saw his surprise, then his horror." His smile disappeared. "But it was supposed to be you behind the wheel. You were the one who was supposed to die that night."

Bile rose up in the back of her throat as she realized that this was the man who was responsible for Andrew's death, for the death of the baby who had never had a chance.

She struggled against the bonds that held her, wanting to get loose, wanting to kill him for what he'd done to her, to Andrew and to their baby.

But he held tight to her and roughly yanked her toward the pole with the dried brush and wood around the bottom, like a pyre for a witch.

He was going to burn her at the stake. The sudden knowledge shot a new wave of terror through her.

"Adam, please, don't do this. For God's sake, I don't understand. Tell me why you're doing this!" Tears blinded her as he forced her through the dry tinder and tied her to the upright pole. When he was finished tying her hands, he leaned down and tried to capture her legs.

She kicked her legs, trying to smash him in the face, at the same time screams ripped from her throat. He ignored her legs, and grabbed a handkerchief from his pocket and shoved it into her mouth. "Shut up," he screamed, the cords in his neck bulging out. "Just shut up."

Once again he reached down to grab her legs. She

twisted and kicked, but to no avail as he managed to grab them and tie them to the pole. After trussing her, he leaned back on his haunches. "I haven't properly introduced myself. My name isn't Adam Rawlings. It's Adam Mayfair. Ellis Mayfair was my father. It's nice to officially meet you, sis, and let me tell you, I've got one hell of a reunion planned for all of you."

Chapter 13

Quinn raced back down the path to where he'd tied up Noches, thankful for the bright moon overhead. The scream he'd thought he'd heard coupled with Jewel's open back door moved him quickly down the path.

When he reached his horse, he dug into his saddlebag and pulled out his cell phone. He had no idea what had happened to Jewel, no real evidence that anything bad had occurred except his gut instinct, and his gut instinct was screaming with alarm.

As he'd run back to his horse he'd searched the path where Jewel usually walked on the nights she couldn't sleep and she was nowhere to be found. He'd called her name out over and over again, but had gotten no reply. If she were out here, she would have answered. If she'd just been out walking, she would have made her presence known...unless she couldn't.

He couldn't get that half scream out of his mind. If it hadn't been Jewel, then who would it have been? And where in hell was Jewel?

He punched in the number for Jericho Yates at the sheriff's office, knowing he might be raising an alarm for nothing, but he'd rather be made to look like an anxious fool than do nothing at all.

Yates answered on the second ring.

"Jericho, it's Quinn Logan. Look, I might be over-reacting here but I just walked by Jewel's place. Her back door was open and the gate leading to the woods was open, as well, but she's no place to be found. The house is dark and I think the electricity isn't working and I thought I heard a scream coming from the woods a few minutes ago."

"Whoa, slow down," Jericho exclaimed. Quinn drew a breath and started again, this time more slowly even though each and every second that passed filled him with agony.

"I'll head out now and see if I can figure out what's going on," Jericho said. "In the meantime if you find her and everything is all right, call me back on the cell." He gave Quinn the number, who quickly memorized it.

As he ended the call, Quinn remounted Noches. He intended to search the property until he found her. She needed him.

And he needed her. It had taken him five long years to find a woman he wanted to spend the rest of his life with, and he knew without question that woman was Jewel.

But she was in trouble. He felt it in his heart, in his very soul. She was in danger and unless he found her, for the second time in his life he'd lose the woman that he loved.

Quinn knew there were three hundred acres of Bar None ranch land and he wouldn't rest until he and Noches had covered every square mile in an effort to find Jewel.

Quinn. His name roared through Jewel's head. She'd thought it was him who had tormented her, who had broken into the ranch. She hadn't trusted him, had been afraid to trust him. But he'd been the one man she should have trusted, the one man she should have believed in.

Adam told her that it had been him who had broken into her house, him who had gaslighted her with a recording of a baby crying and by whispering her name on the nights she went out walking.

And all Jewel could think about was that she'd never get the opportunity to love Quinn the way she wanted to, she'd never be able to accept the love he had for her. She'd been such a fool. She'd refused to listen to her heart and what it had been trying to tell her.

He'd been right. She'd been trapped by the same emotions Kelsey suffered, afraid to reach out for happiness, afraid that it might be snatched away. That fear had kept her from seeing the truth, that Quinn was exactly the man she wanted in her life.

And now it was too late.

"Your mother stole my father from me," Adam railed, once again the cords in his neck standing out with his rage. "And if that wasn't enough Joe Colton has managed to destroy everything that was ever important to me."

Jewel stared at him, unsure what he was talking about. Adam saw the puzzled look on her face and it only seemed to increase his anger.

"I had a cushy life in Reno. I worked as a security guard and one night I saved the life of the owner. Lola Justice was so grateful, she took me in, set me up in high style, then Joe Colton's newspaper the *Register* broke a story about her embezzling from the casino and ruined it all."

He paced back and forth in front of her as she desperately worked to try to loosen the rope that tied her to the pole. "Then I met Rebecca. She was nothing but a barmaid, but she loved me. You remember the story, don't you? I set her up in Georgie's house while Georgie was out of town. We took everything Georgie had and used a computer to start a hate campaign against Joe Colton. But Colton sent Nick Sheffield to check it out and Rebecca ended up dead. Everything... Joe Colton and your mother have destroyed everything in my life."

Tears raced down Jewel's cheeks and she tried to stop the sobs that wanted, that needed to be released, afraid that if she allowed them out, she'd choke to death on his handkerchief.

Half of what he said she didn't understand and certainly wasn't responsible for, but his hatred had obviously festered for years, an irrational, all-consuming hatred of her and the entire Colton family.

Her eyes widened in horror as he pulled a book of matches from his pocket.

No! She screamed the word over and over again in

her head. *No! No!* She didn't want to burn to death. The very idea of dying by fire horrified her.

He pulled off one of the matches and lit it, then laughed as she struggled against the ropes, choking as she attempted to scream around her gag.

He blew out the match, then pulled off another, obviously enjoying tormenting her. "Tonight you'll pay for the sins of your mother and tomorrow I have a little surprise ready for Joe Colton. He won't be making it to the White House. Hell, he won't even see next Monday morning. It was nice meeting you, baby sister." He threw her a mock kiss.

Once again he lit the match, only this time he tossed it at the dry brush at her feet. For a moment nothing happened, then smoke began to swirl up in the air.

"Nice knowing you, sis," Adam said, and then he disappeared out the barn door.

A thousand thoughts shot through Jewel's head. She hadn't been losing her mind. Adam had been behind the voice that called to her in the night, the baby cries that had ripped at her soul. She wasn't crazy like her mother. Adam had been playing with her head.

As she thought of those nights when she'd been haunted by what she'd thought was Andrew's voice, when she'd been certain it was the baby she'd never had who cried out to her, she wanted to weep. All the doubts, all the worries that she was losing her mind—they had all been the responsibility of one hate-filled man.

The smoke drifting up from her feet grew blacker. The barn door that Adam had left open allowed in a faint night breeze and with a crackle some of the brush on the outer edges of the pile burst into flames.

A horror she'd never known suffused her. She was going to die here. The heat from the flames began to toast her feet and the smoke burned her eyes. Choking, she was racked by coughs and managed to dislodge the gag he'd shoved in her mouth.

Her screams were a combination of coughs and sobs as the flames at her feet grew hotter and bigger.

It wasn't enough that she would die here. Adam intended to kill Joe. Somehow he'd make sure that Joe never left Esperanza alive and there was nothing she could do to stop this vicious, malicious man.

Quinn. He would be her final regret. He'd told her she could trust him, but she hadn't believed him and now she was going to die because she'd trusted the wrong man.

I'm sorry, Quinn. I'm so sorry. She would die with her regret, with the knowledge that she might have found her happy-ever-after with him.

A new spasm of coughing gripped her, leaving her lightheaded. Her chest ached and her throat burned as she continued to struggle to get free, but Adam had done a good job in making sure she couldn't escape.

She closed her eyes, hoping the smoke killed her long before she felt the burn of the flames. A weary resignation consumed her as the smoke filled the barn and the flames at her feet edged closer to the pole where she was tied.

Her eyes flew open as she heard the sound of a horse whinny. Quinn rode into the garage on Noches, who reared up, nostrils flared and eyes wide in fear at the sight of the fire.

As the stallion landed on all four legs once again,

Quinn jumped off his back and Noches turned and ran out of the burning barn.

Jewel sobbed at the sight of Quinn. He raced to her and, stomping out the flames behind her, he managed to untie her feet, then her hands. He scooped her up in his arms and ran outside, into the hot night air, air that smelled amazingly sweet after the smoky interior of the barn.

When they were far enough from the barn not to be in danger, he placed her on the ground and cupped her face with his hands. "Are you all right?" He reached down and touched her slippers, as if to assure himself that her feet hadn't been burned.

"I'm okay," she replied, and coughed. "It was Adam… Adam Rawlings, but his real name is Adam Mayfair. He's my brother, Quinn, and he tried to kill me. He's going to kill Joe. Tomorrow when they arrive in town." She was babbling and coughing at the same time. "We have to stop him. We can't let him hurt Joe."

"I know." Quinn pulled her against his chest and held her tight. "It's all right. He won't hurt anyone ever again."

She looked up at him and he continued. "I saw him sneaking away from the barn. He didn't belong here and I had a bad feeling about it, so I took him down. He's now handcuffed and tied to a tree."

They both turned to look as a whoosh went through the air and one side of the barn caught on fire. "We'd better call somebody," Jewel said.

"Jericho should be here any minute and I already asked him to call the fire department. Hopefully, they'll be here soon."

He helped her to her feet and once again pulled her into an embrace. "Oh God, Jewel, I thought I'd lost you forever."

"Quinn, I've been such a fool." She told him about the break-in at the ranch and believing that it had been him when he'd limped into the examining room. She also told him about thinking she was losing her mind, about how Adam had been gaslighting her.

She told him about the kids being gone and that it had been the sound of a baby crying that had pulled her from the empty house where Adam had been waiting for her. By the time she'd finished, Jericho had arrived along with a fire truck.

The rest of the night flew by as Jericho took statements and the firefighters kept the flames contained to the old structure that eventually collapsed in on itself.

Clay showed up and jokingly told Jewel that Adam had saved him the time and trouble of having the old barn taken down and carted away.

Adam Mayfair was led away by Jericho. He didn't say a word to anyone, but his eyes burned with his hatred for them all. He'd be jailed and would be facing enough charges to keep him away for a very long time.

Dawn was just beginning to peek over the horizon as Jewel and Quinn left the area and began the long walk back to the Hopechest Ranch. They didn't speak as they walked, although Quinn held her hand firmly.

It was enough, his hand holding hers. She didn't need his words to know what was in his heart. She'd seen it in his eyes every time he'd looked at her through the long night. She'd felt it as she'd leaned against him, absorbing his strength and calm.

He loved her.

His love filled her up, warmed her in a way the hot night never could.

And she didn't have to look too deeply into her own heart to know that she was in love with him, as well. When they reached the Hopechest Ranch, they went in through the gate and to the back door where she turned and faced him.

"It's going to be a big day for you," he said.

She nodded. "The first thing I need to do is call an electrician. Adam must have cut some wires or done something last night to make sure the electricity stopped working and I'd be in the dark."

He reached out a hand and placed his palm on her cheek. "I can't believe how close I came to losing you."

She covered his hand with her own. "I'm sorry, Quinn. I should have known that I could trust you. My heart told me I could, but I refused to listen. The worst part of all was thinking that I was going crazy, that I'd end up like my mother, locked away in a mental ward. I didn't want that to be your future with me."

He dropped his hand and instead pulled her tight against him, so close she could feel the strong, steady beat of his heart against hers.

"Even knowing that might be someplace in the future, I'd take the time with you now," he said. "I'd grab on to the happiness we could find together and hold tight to it, build memories of it and those would sustain me when things got rough. That's what I want, Jewel." His eyes flamed with emotion. "You're the woman I've been waiting for, the one I want to spend my life with. I love you, Jewel."

She'd told herself she didn't need the words, but they soared through her, bringing with them a joy that filled her up. "I love you, too, Quinn."

He leaned down and took her mouth with his in a kiss that emphasized the words he'd just said, a kiss that held all the emotion in his heart. And she kissed him back with that same emotion, with all the love and passion she felt for him.

She'd been searching a long time for the place where she truly belonged and she realized now that the place was in Quinn's arms.

When the kiss ended, he reluctantly let her go. "Is there anything I can do to help you with today?"

"No, it's all under control," she replied.

"Then I guess I should go and let you get some sleep or whatever."

She didn't want him to go. She felt as if she'd waited an eternity for her life to really begin and now with her love for him burning bright in her heart, she didn't want to put off starting to build memories.

"You know, Jeff and Cheryl and the kids won't be home until around ten," she said. "You could come in and help me with...whatever."

He grinned, a slow, sexy smile that shot straight through to her heart. "Why, Miss Jewel, I thought you would never ask."

Epilogue

Meredith Colton sat on one of the lawn chairs next to the house beneath the huge tent that had been erected for the day's activities. The tent was packed with people and for a moment she was grateful that everyone seemed to have forgotten her, giving her a chance to just breathe and to sit and observe.

In the months since Joe had thrown his hat into the ring for the presidency, there had been little time for herself, but she'd supported him every step of the way. He had a vision of hope, of prosperity that the country desperately needed.

She gazed into the crowd, seeking her husband. She spied him in a group of men, his handsome face animated as he talked. Her heart swelled. Even after all these years the mere sight of him could make her pulse beat faster.

He would be the next president. There was no doubt in her mind, nor were there any doubts in the minds of Washington's most popular pundits. Short of a personal catastrophe, come January he would be sworn in as the new president of the United States.

A shiver raced up her spine as she thought of the catastrophe that had nearly occurred. Jewel had filled them in on everything that had happened the night before. Adam Mayfair had intended to somehow find a way to kill Joe during the barbecue today.

Meredith's thoughts drifted to her sister, Patsy. Patsy had spent much of her life trying to hurt Meredith and it appeared that her legacy of hatred had lived on after her death in the form of her son. But Adam was in jail now and hopefully that was the end of Patsy's reign of terror.

As always, when Meredith thought of her sister, conflicting emotions roared through her. She felt bad that no matter how many times she'd reached out a hand to her twin sister, instead of gripping it and holding tight, Patsy had bitten it.

A hand touched her shoulder and she turned her head to see Georgie. "You need anything? Want some food, something to drink?"

Meredith smiled and shoved away her sad memories of the sister she'd never really known. "No, thanks. I'm fine."

"I'm better than fine," Georgie exclaimed, her eyes shining brightly. "Nick just had a talk with Jericho. With Adam's arrest, Jericho has a deputy vacancy to fill. It looks like Nick is going to get his wish and be part of law enforcement here in Esperanza."

"That's wonderful. I'm so happy for you both," Meredith exclaimed.

"Uh-oh, I see Emmie bending the ear of one of the servers. I'd better go rescue him."

Meredith laughed as Georgie hurried away. Little Emmie had been charming the crowd all evening as she enthusiastically shared stories of school and new friends.

She wasn't the only little person charming the crowd. Jewel's children had been well-behaved and equally charming as they mingled and tried to help out where they could.

A new warmth filled Meredith, the warmth of happiness for her family. Clay had found his happiness with Tamara and Ryder had become the man they all knew he could be in loving Ana.

All of their children had come to the party and the tent was filled to the brim with Coltons and their families.

Jewel approached Meredith with a smile and a glass of iced tea. "I thought maybe you could use this," she said as she handed Meredith the cold drink.

"Thank you, dear." Meredith patted the empty chair next to her. "Sit for just a minute."

Jewel sat and Meredith reached for one of her hands. "I can't help but notice that the attractive veterinarian hasn't been able to take his eyes off you."

Jewel's cheeks flushed pink and her eyes shone so brightly Meredith felt the sparkle in her own heart. Oh, she knew that look, it was the one she saw in her own mirror when she thought of her Joe.

"He's wonderful, isn't he?" Jewel exclaimed.

"He makes you happy." It was a statement rather than

a question. If it had been a question, the answer was on Jewel's face. Meredith squeezed her hand. "I'm so happy for you, honey."

She'd worried about Jewel, who had suffered such a tragedy when she'd lost Andrew and her baby. When she'd sent her here to Esperanza, it was with the hope that she would heal, and it seemed that she had. The shadows that had darkened Jewel's eyes the last time Meredith had seen her were gone, replaced with the shining light of a woman in love.

They visited for a few more minutes, then Jewel left her to tend to some of the other guests. Meredith smiled as she saw Quinn reach Jewel's side and give her a quick kiss on the forehead.

The two of them were going to be just fine, and Meredith was grateful that Jewel had finally found what she'd been searching for, the love and support of a good man.

Once again Meredith glanced around and spied Graham standing just inside the tent opening. He stood alone, backed against the tent as if unsure of his welcome. His blond hair had gone almost completely gray and he looked sad.

Meredith knew her husband's brother lived in a big house in Prosperino and she suspected that the empty house rang with the hollowness of his life.

Graham had made decisions that had long ago driven his brother from his life, and after that, his children. Meredith had heard that he'd been reaching out to Ryder, Clay and Georgie, attempting to make amends for his poor choices and his absence during their formative years.

Meredith glanced over to where her husband stood and she saw the precise moment he spied Graham. Joe's back stiffened and for a long moment the two men stared at each other from across the room.

Go to him, Joe. She consciously willed her husband to move across the room, to go to the brother she knew he loved, a brother who looked hungry to belong.

Go to him. The past was gone and couldn't be fixed. All they had was the future. She didn't realize she was holding her breath until Joe began to walk to where Graham stood. It was only then that she released a sigh.

She watched as the two men talked and when Joe held out a hand to Graham and Graham grasped it with a smile, Meredith felt a wave of peace sweep through her. It might just be a handshake, but it was a beginning.

Meredith knew that she and Joe were about to embark on the biggest adventure of their lives. Joe would be the next president of the United States and she would be the first lady.

It would be a time of dreams realized, not just for herself and Joe, but hopefully for the nation. There would be successes and failures, laughter and tears, but she wasn't worried about it. The Coltons were survivors and whatever the future held, they'd see it through.

Tonight was about family and friends. It was about embracing this shining moment of happiness that filled her heart and soul. She and Joe would survive and grow with their love for each other and the love of their family to sustain them.

* * * * *

"Get down," he shouted. "It's a drone."

Eva had seen enough movies to know what drones could do. Jumping aside, she dropped to the floor and crawled toward the door, glad of her dark room. If the thing was armed, she wanted to make herself the smallest target possible. Luckily, her window was closed. She figured if it crashed into the glass, the drone would come apart.

By the time she reached her closed bedroom door, the thing hovered right outside her window, its bright light illuminating most of her room. She dived for the door just as the drone tapped against the glass, lightly and precisely enough to tell her whoever controlled it was very good at the job.

She'd just turned the knob when the drone exploded, blowing out her window and sending shards of glass like deadly weapons into her room.

"Eva!" Jesse's voice, yelling out her name. She focused on that, despite the stabbing pain in her leg. Somehow, she managed to pull the door open and half fell into the hallway, one hand against her leg.

Heart pounding, she scrambled away from her doorway, dimly registering the trail of blood she left in her wake.

"Are you all right?" Reaching her, Jesse scooped her up in his muscular arms and hauled her farther down the hall. Outside, she could hear men yelling. One of the voices sounded like her father's.

"Is everyone else okay?" she asked, concerned.

"As far as I know," Jesse answered. "Though I haven't been outside yet to assess the situation. What happened?"

"It was a drone rigged with explosives." Briefly she closed her eyes. When she reopened them, she found his face mere inches from hers. "Someone aimed it right at my window."

Fury warred with concern in his dark eyes. He focused intently on her. "There's a lot of blood. Where are you hurt?"

Hurt. Odd how being with him made everything else fade into insignificance. In his arms, she finally felt safe.

Don't miss
The Widow's Bodyguard
by Karen Whiddon, available January 2021
wherever Harlequin Romantic Suspense books
and ebooks are sold.

Harlequin.com

HRSEXP1220

HARLEQUIN

Save $1.00

on the purchase of ANY Harlequin book
from the imprints below.

*Heartfelt or thrilling, passionate or
uplifting—our romances have it all.*

PRESENTS INTRIGUE

DESIRE ROMANTIC SUSPENSE SPECIAL EDITION

LOVE INSPIRED

Save $1.00

on the purchase of ANY Harlequin Presents, Intrigue, Desire,
Romantic Suspense, Special Edition or Love Inspired book.

Valid from December 1, 2020 to November 30, 2021.

52617010

5 65373 00076 2 (8100)0 12493

Love Harlequin romance?

DISCOVER.

Be the first to find out about promotions, news and exclusive content!

Facebook.com/HarlequinBooks

Twitter.com/HarlequinBooks

Instagram.com/HarlequinBooks

Pinterest.com/HarlequinBooks

YouTube.com/HarlequinBooks

ReaderService.com

EXPLORE.

Sign up for the Harlequin e-newsletter and download a free book from any series at **TryHarlequin.com**

CONNECT.

Join our Harlequin community to share your thoughts and connect with other romance readers! **Facebook.com/groups/HarlequinConnection**

HSOCIAL2021